peculiar, inc

COMPLETE THE CHARISMATIC CHRONICLES

Peculiar, INC

Purgatory's Children

The Greater Greats

peculiar, inc

c.s.r. calloway

Scripture taken from the Authorized King James Version.

This is a work of fiction. All names, characters, businesses, places, events, and incidents portrayed in this novel are either fictitious or used fictitiously.

Peculiar, INC

Published by CSRC Storytelling
Los Angeles, CA 90006

ISBN: 978-1-955382-22-9 (Paperback)
ISBN: 978-1-955382-23-6 (Ebook)

Book cover designed by Sleepy Fox Studios.

First Edition: March 2013

to the OGs
Emily, Jasmine, Jason, Katrina, Katori, Rocky, Tanner, and Tony

Contents

Dramatis Personæ

the Wilbanks Academy graduates
Kimberly Dyna Hamilton
Lakota "Coda" Crenshaw
Shen Long Ezekiel Yang
Enrique "Rico" Gutierrez
Justus Alexander

other graduates
Maya Sierra Mercado, Kim's best friend
Terrance Darry Bozzo, Coda's best friend
Shannon Reese Crescitelli
Benny Commons
Wayne Emerson
Eden Enamorado-Hall
Brandon Evans
Gene Hightower
Bethany Kelly
Rebecca Joy Nathaniel
Christopher Nyberg
Perpetua "Peppi" Ortiz
Hanley Powell
Sheena Thompson
Sam Wesberger

the fam
THE HAMILTONS
Delia Louise Hamilton, Kim's mother
Dr. Lester Hamilton, Kim's father
Rev. Azari "Curly" Templeton, Kim's older half-brother

THE GUTIERREZES
    Mr. Gutierrez, Rico's father
    Mrs. Gutierrez, Rico's mother
    Renata Clelia Gutierrez, Rico's younger sister
THE CRENSHAWS
    Cheyenne Crenshaw, Coda's older sister

the adult associates
Dr. Patricia Preacher
Dr. "Lemming"
Colton, The Vice President of the United States
Madame Endora

the collegiate crew
Miguel, Eden's boyfriend
ALABAMA STATE
    Dishon Cleveland, Kim's boyfriend
    Franklin Griffin
    Nicholas
    Stasia
GEORGIA TECH
    Phil Grayson
    Jordan Vang
MERCER UNIVERSITY
    Maggie St. John
    Professor Sanford
    Professor Charles Henderson
OAKWOOD COMMUNITY COLLEGE
    Duane
UNITED STATES NAVAL ACADEMY
    Commander Scott Gregory

the Sentries
    The Silver Sentry
    The Ebony Sentry
    The Emerald Sentry
    The Violet Sentry

the spirits
Kamiskas / Ambriel, the fallen
Uriel
Tzadqiel
Baraqiel

But ye are a chosen generation,
a royal priesthood,
an holy nation,
a **peculiar people**;
that ye should shew forth the praises of Him who hath called you out
of darkness into His marvellous light;
which in time past were not a people,
but are now the people of God:
which had not obtained mercy,
but now have obtained mercy.

– 1 Peter 2: 9-10

excerpt from The Days of Awakening (Second Edition) *by Dr. Jimmie Stone*

[...] this is the God who opened doors for you where previously there were only walls. The Creator who made your lashes light enough for the blinking of your lids. He wants us to run and we've been too busy sinking in the water.

He's calling us out of our spiritual slumber. He's calling you, yes YOU, to wake up. To get up. A new day has begun and you're already behind. Wake up, I urge you!

The Son is up.

Prologue

It wasn't a night for miracles; they weren't necessary anymore. The Pentecostal days were passed and it seemed there would never be such a generation again, least of all in Glynn County. Miracles suggested a caring, active God, rather than the One that was found in Glynn.

A single star peeked through the clouded night sky, growing brighter as the darkness increased. The humid heat of early summer storms filled the space beneath the star, encumbering the Georgia earth while a cool, moist wind danced in defiance to the temperature. It swirled in the upper branches of the southeastern oaks and found delight along the expansive island beach that nudged the marshes and surrounding ocean.

The doctor appeared patient, which was her intent if not her truth. Patience was never her virtue, and the Vice President was late according to the agreed schedule. The Secret Service had been crawling the grounds for close to three hours, and her pumps, giving up before she had, were now sinking into the sand. Eventually her wait was rewarded as armored helicopters brought her esteemed guest to the oceanfront.

"Welcome to the laboratory, Mr. Vice President," she greeted him, and they shook hands. "I know your message stated that you wouldn't have time for a tour, but I do have people standing by in case—"

"I'm sure you do, Doctor."

Her eyes narrowed, but she continued. "It wasn't clear to me exactly what—"

"Perhaps you should have asked, Doctor."

"Respectfully, sir, I asked several times if you—"

"It would have been pleasant to have received an invitation from you before this visit became necessary," he said casually, eyes raking over the beach's foliage. The laboratory was well concealed, but he seemed to be making a point of avoiding eye contact. Not because he was guilty of something, but because she was.

"Any…invitation that I could offer has stood since we first opened our doors. When you first came into office—"

"You've been here since those doors opened, haven't you, Doctor? All fourteen years?"

"Longer, sir. I've been with the Human Genome Laboratory since it was conceived."

"Mmm."

She stood there, patience being tried considerably more than it had been moments before.

He spoke again, locking eyes with her. His were as silver as his hair. "How are the subjects, Doctor?"

"Growing, sir! They—"

He wasn't letting her finish many thoughts. "Of course they're growing, Patricia. Plants grow—oaks and weeds alike. These creatures are hopefully far more advanced than dandelions. How are they *developing*?"

He didn't take many breaths. She followed suit. "Thirty of them were healthy enough post-preliminary trials to move forward with further testing and—"

"Of the thirty tested?"

She hesitated. She wished she hadn't. "Five have lived, sir."

"And the results?"

Another hesitation. "Grotesque. Yet each is more promising than the last."

"You're an expert at 'promising.' What's needed is delivery."

"We have a subject that we're beginning trials on this very night. Based on the knowledge that we now have—"

"To be frank, Patricia, knowledge is something that *I* indeed have. You, on the other hand, may want to rethink your parlance."

"I thought we could be cordial, Colton."

"You keep thinking instead of delivering and you'll find this operation shut down." His eyes were off in the distance, bored with her yet again.

"Colton, it's no secret that you haven't supported the HGL—"

"None of that would matter, Patricia, if you had anything of substance to offer in this particular time of your increasingly desperate need."

She sighed. "Why have you come, Mr. Vice President? We could've had this swatting of flies on a video chat."

"I've come at the request of the President. You've been crawling along for fourteen years and all you have to offer are tours and promises and nothing even remotely worthy of even that video chat you speak of."

"When the President arrives—"

"The President isn't coming here. You've ensured that. The G8 Summit will occupy ninety percent of his time here, and sleep the other ten percent. If there had been something…*revolutionary* to show him after these fourteen years, that would've been ideal. Instead it's my task to flip the hourglass."

Patricia caught her breath, but not her tongue. "Funny, I didn't realize wicked witches had traded broomsticks for helicopters these days."

"Ah, and now the Patricia I remember squeaks up. I was hopeful that she had curled up and died inside of that shell of what was once a compelling figure on the forefront of hell-bound science. The beast yet fights for breath."

"The lab is a FFRDC—"

"That's the thing about being a special access program working out of a black site. I can't find the Human Genome Laboratory on any official listing, existing register, or long-forgotten physical directory."

Her eyes grew wide. "Are you threatening me with expunction?"

"You have a year to the date." He signaled the Service.

Fury welled up inside of her. "You can't deep-six this program! The strides we've made in tissue engineering and gene-splicing alone—"

"A year to the date, Doctor." He turned back to the helicopters, as the rotors began to turn. "I'm confident I've stated this expectation in a manner that your brain can easily process."

"What would satisfy—"

"Mark your calendar, Doctor," she heard over the aircraft. "I've already marked mine."

The hot sand whipped her face and her body shook with enough rage to sink her further into the sand. In an era without miracles, the doctor suddenly found herself in critical need of one.

He was right in some ways, she reflected as she headed across the vacant shore. Just because her laboratory was a recognized Federally Funded Research and Development Center, by no means had it ever been publicly acknowledged. Only thirty-nine of them were public, and Patricia had heard that the actual amount lingered in the fifties. They had the benefit of avoiding the public's ignorant inquiries, and the drawback of being at the mercy of the private and suddenly bared judgements of government officials.

The dunes adjusted around her, sand rising and sinking. A metal ceiling imbued with lights motored shut above her, as continued vibrations moved the sand into ditch-like formations alongside the room. Leaving the beach above her, Patricia continued with her issue, thoughts morphing like her surroundings. Her team had mastered many scientific breakthroughs, none of them revealed to the government as of yet, as each one was a part of the greater discovery. That had been her decision, and now she was paying for it. If only he had agreed to the tour...

The room continued to shift, and the doctor stepped across the sand towards an opening door.

Key members of the staff awaited, but they had seen on surveillance that the Vice President had declined to join them beneath the beach. That didn't prevent the questions from starting immediately. She ignored them and the questions became updates.

"We finalized our in-lab tests on the RiD," one of the nurses said.

Patricia stopped, her team stumbling to a halt around her. Of the nurses who were heading up the RiD evaluations, two stood there, one holding a few sealed vials.

"Try it on me here," she said. "Here and now." Her eyes cut between them. "I've got cameras. I trust them even if I don't trust you."

Ignoring their crisis, she removed her lab jacket and rolled up her sleeves. She signaled to another doctor to bring her a syringe.

The nurse spoke up again. "We can't verify—"

Patricia rolled her eyes. "Save it. I'm overseeing this entire laboratory. What am I gonna do—sue myself?" She gestured to the surveillance camera. "There's a recording and a request. Your bases are covered."

The same mouthy nurse spoke again. "We've only tested it on a few of the—"

"Hand me a vial."

Her unrepentant eyes didn't leave them until she had what she wanted. They shrank further back into the crowd. Why had they picked now, this moment, to have a conscience?

More briefs and announcements were being delivered and she fielded them as was necessary, but the majority of her staff was quieting down. She was doing this unconfined, with either confidence or desperation. Only she knew which and why.

She prepared the needle, observing the clear liquid in the tubes. The Vice President had no idea how far her research team had gone and how big their footprint would be. She smiled as she injected herself.

A few doctors caught her as she slumped. She hadn't lost consciousness, just a portion of nerve capacity. Her eyes were still open, but unfocused. Her muscles were lax.

"Sit her over there," one said, guiding them towards a near chair.

Moments after they got her positioned, her eyes regained their focus.

"Try it on me," Patricia repeated. Observing their faces, she said, "I've got cameras."

Mouthy Nurse spoke up. "You've already done it, Dr. Pat. Check the video."

Patricia stared at her arm, where the needle had made its mark. She glanced past the group crowded around her to the spot in the hallway where they all had just been, then back to her increasingly excited team.

"Then it's successful," she smiled, and team members made spurts of exclamations.

"How many minutes have I lost to memory?" she asked the nurse.

"We clocked you at six minutes and twenty-three seconds."

Patricia stood, rolling her sleeves back down.

"Bottle it up, kids. We've just created our time machine. Now let's find our future. God forbid we leave it to anyone else."

One of her doctors hurried along beside her. "Should we test the RiD serum on tonight's guest?"

Patricia paused, considering.

"No," she decided. "Tonight's guest is our present. Let's make it count."

1.

Commencement (Black and Gold)

Kimberly Hamilton's mom was known to use humor as a coping mechanism, but when she caught an uncontrollable bout of the giggles at Aunt Pamela's funeral, that was a brand new low. The sight of her mother Delia snorting and gasping as laugh-induced tears smeared mascara across her face caused family and guests alike to stare on in horror. Delia was characteristically self-composed and when she finally gave in to the emotions of losing a sister, Kim was among the masses that so wrongly assumed there would be a period of silent and graceful tears. Instead there were snorts and mascara smears.

Kim knew that that was a small nick in Delia's resilient armor. She saw that side of her mother, that side without control, only on a few occasions during church when Delia was touched by the Holy Spirit and would wave her hands as dignified tears dropped from her eyes. When attending Kim's baby pageants, her mother was known to squeal her appreciation in teeny bursts of ghetto—maybe clap her hands a little bit—but never anything as damaging as Aunt Pamela's funeral.

Delia, however, was just one parent. Lester Hamilton managed to do an exact imitation of a yowling kitten at his oldest daughter's wedding. Kim recalled the vexed expression on her half-sister Shirley's face, not sharing Shirley's disapproval at the time. Yet the moment Delia let loose one last chuckle as her sister was lowered into her grave, Kim felt every inch of her own sister's humiliation.

"Ladies and gentleman, our very own Miss Kenneth D. Wilbanks Academy, Kimberly Hamilton."

Kim blinked, snatched back into the present. As the principal and audience acknowledged her, she stood and stepped towards the microphone, her black robe brushing against her shins.

God give me strength, she prayed, and God heard her.

Her family was out there somewhere—Dad, Mom, Shirley, and her mother's curly-haired son Azari who was probably going crazy with excitement. She had aunts, cousins, grandparents, so many from their blended family were there to watch the Hamilton princess graduate.

Kim placed the speech manuscript on the podium and laid her thin fingers atop the paper. This was the first year in decades that the class president hadn't been designated to deliver the peer inspirational address—senior-class president Bethany Kelly had a very unpleasant expression on her face at that very moment, perhaps due to that decision—and expectations were high for this oration due to her emotional speech at the Miss Wilbanks pageant, which had brought the metaphorical house down. That competition was wrapped up once Kim finished speaking on family values; every contestant that followed paled in comparison.

Standing atop a beautiful float in the city's rinky-dink Easter parade while wearing her glittering crown had been only one of the title's perks. Amazingly, she found herself proud to be the virtual mascot and mouthpiece of this particular group of students. And this convocation was Kim's opportunity to speak to them and for them one final time.

"Dr. Paul," Kim addressed their principal and he nodded in return, "additional members of the faculty and staff, esteemed guests, and you, my fellow graduates in the Class of Conviction."

There were already scattered exaltations. Each grade level at KWA had their own title. Now that Kim's class was moving on, the incoming freshmen would take the mantle of the "Class of Conviction."

"A great woman once said, 'Don't try, just do it.' You may ask if this woman was Harriet Tubman, Sojourner Truth, Eleanor Roosevelt, or Vice-Principal Peachtree."

She had judged well; the crowd rewarded the humor with chuckles. Ignoring the polite reaction, she continued. "It was my mother, Delia Louise Hamilton.

"We the seniors have been told through the years that education was the fuel that our lives would run on. We were told to pass the tests, do the homework, ask all the right questions, and know all the correct answers. 'Know what year Hannibal and his army crossed the Alps on the backs of elephants for the test on Tuesday.' 'Know the difference between an allusion and an illusion for Friday's quiz.' 'Know the absolute value of such-and-such equation on the graduation test.' 'Translate this passage into English for the final exam.' 'Get out of the lunchroom right now'— even if the bell isn't going to ring for fifteen more minutes."

There were vigorous nods of agreement from her classmates, for the Wilbanks Academy lunch ladies were laborers to a belligerent fault.

"We were very rarely told to try; most often, we were told to do.

"When my mother told me 'Don't try, just do it,' she was not telling me that I couldn't attempt; after all, in order to finish, one must begin, and in order to *do*, one must *attempt* to do. My mother was telling me *to* do, to *finish*, to *accomplish* what I had begun. For most, to attempt is good enough. For the excellent, accomplishment is the only goal."

Kim hadn't glanced at her papers once. She maintained eye contact with the grads, reciting her speech word for word as her voice soared into the microphone and pealed across the auditorium out of the speakers.

"It was never good enough to merely study in order to make an A," she said, raising her eyebrows and shaking her head. "You had to understand the questions and how they connected to what you had studied. It was never good enough to simply write the essay. You had to turn it in."

They all laughed and she caught her mother's eye. Delia was beaming with pride.

"It was never good enough to just attend the dances. You had to be *dressed.*" More vigorous nods and Kim found herself nodding as well. "You could not merely try; you had to accomplish.

"My fellow graduates and all that hear my voice: there is only one true God and that is the One Who gave us Jesus Christ His Son."

Shocked silence.

"Maybe the microphone is turned down," Kim said seriously, refusing to back down. She raised her voice and refused to look away from the crowd. "There is only *one true God*; the One Who gave His Son, *Jesus Christ.*"

Smattered applause finally grew into a more acceptable ovation. Even though this was one of the southernmost towns in Georgia—they had five different Christian clubs at school and taught creationism alongside evolution in biology courses and, heck, the graduates were even singing a *hymn* in a few minutes—this was far more immediate and blatant than much that had occurred at an official function since the eighties.

"It is through faith, confidence, conviction, belief in Jesus Christ as the risen Son of God that you will have the strength and the courage to achieve—to accomplish your goals."

More slow applause. She soldiered on.

"In Deuteronomy the thirty-first chapter," she continued, her throaty, deep voice ringing across the room, "Moses tells the people of Israel to 'be strong and of a good courage, fear not, nor be afraid of them: for the Lord thy God, He it is that doth go with thee; He will not fail thee, nor forsake thee.' He tells Joshua, 'Have not I commanded thee? Be strong and of a good courage; be not afraid, neither be thou dismayed: for the Lord thy God is with thee whithersoever thou goest.'

"Class of Conviction, Cheetahs of Excellence: always...*be strong.*"

The applause was heavy. They figured she was done.

"Accomplishment involves many things. How do you feel about the final product? Is it just a'ight?"

Laughter. Prepared and polite.

"Is it good? Is it awe-inspiring? What are you content settling on? Will you let it rise past your ambitions, or will you let it slump to someone else's? We sit here today on the brink of forever. The edge of eternity is here—it's not coming later; it is here. It's not simply good enough to say what you will achieve before you draw your last breath. Accomplish it! 'Don't try, just do.' Reach the goal! Don't just climb a few steps on the ladder."

Polite claps, yet again, as well as a few encouraging yells of appreciation. Time to rile them all up. The stupid black and gold tassel kept waving in front of her eye.

"Whether your choice is to be a happy stay-at-home mom, the engineer of the first hotel on the moon, or a Goodwill Ambassador, don't just say it. Try with the conviction and the excellence of a Kenneth Wilbanks Academy Cheetah and *accomplish it.*"

There it went. The graduates were appreciative.

"Once a KWA Cheetah sets its sights on a goal, it's going to go after it, it's going to grab it and it's going to claim it!"

They were roaring now. Cheering, stomping, releasing the last buckets of their school spirit before their allegiance moved on to higher plateaus.

"Once you try with that conviction and excellence, you will accomplish *anything* that you set your mind to."

Okay, people, she thought. *Shut up and let me wrap this up.*

"What can I say about conviction? It is confidence, it is strength, and it is faith. Remember: no matter what comes your way in the future, you can achieve whatever it is that you set your mind to, because if you have the power of God inside of you, you can do anything. 'I can do all things through Christ Who strengthens me.'

"Class of Conviction, we Wilbanks Academy students have never been ordinary. We've never been *trivial.* Or *unexciting.* Don't try to be the next magnificent graduated class from Kenneth D. Wilbanks Academy. You *are* the next magnificent graduated class from Wilbanks Academy. Be it. Claim it. Live it. *Just do it.*"

And she took her seat to thunderous approving cheers. Delia Hamilton led in the standing ovation.

· · · · ·

From her position sitting on the stage, Kim thought back on the events that had led to this, her final night as a senior. When she was a tiny, dictionary-reading freshman, everyone thought that she had skipped a grade or two and was one of those child genius types. She wished.

She was known to be the best actress that the Wilbanks Drama Club had produced in years, but that wasn't enough to keep Kim busy. Once she had made the cheerleading squad, she went to a couple of debate club meetings, participated in the annual Black history programs, and by senior year she had made Homecoming Court and nabbed more scholarships than anyone else at the high school. In hindsight it all seemed so perfect, yet, as she sat on the stage at her own graduation, she couldn't help but get excited by the prospect that the next year…wouldn't be *quite* so perfect.

The three Wilbanks valedictorians were sitting next to Kim on the stage, draped in the white shawls and red ropes that distinguished their stellar academic achievements. They were seated alphabetically—Justus Alexander first, then Karol Roach, with handsome Ezekiel Yang at the end of the lineup. All three were speaking on the subject of "Attributes of the Black and Gold," the Wilbanks Academy colors. Kim wore those colors the night she won Miss KWA. The same colors were on Gene Hightower's jersey the night he scored his hundredth high school touchdown. They were the colors of unwritten law, the colors of local legend.

Karol used her quavering, soft soprano to speak about the significance and characteristics of the color black, which the girls were wearing. Ezekiel spoke about the gold which the boys wore and Justus brought it all home by commenting on the union of the separate gold and black characteristics and all that could be achieved by said union. Justus even conveyed some knowledge he had learned from a classmate, Shannon Crescitelli, about how graduation caps and gowns in the U.S. were all gray before the 1950s, when students began to request their school colors. Kim considered the subjects to be real advanced elementary, but they served their purpose. The valedictorians had made their speeches quick, funny and thought provoking.

On that night, May twenty-first, around nine forty-five *post meridiem*, the senior class of Wilbanks Academy would graduate: three hundred and forty of the four hundred and eighty-eight mismatched students that had begun freshman year one far off autumn four years ago. Each march across the stage would be a private victory; each person was the documentation of his or her individual journey.

There was odd and reclusive Karol, who never spoke in class but would laugh so loud when reading any book out of her never-ending collection that Kim would lurch every time. There was sexy, yet stupid Wayne Emerson, who no one thought would make it all the way to graduation…well, she didn't see him sitting next to Brandon Evans, where he had been sitting during the graduation practices, so maybe he hadn't. That morning the boys had all teased and toasted to him with their cell phones, saying that he had been there "five-ever." Kim smiled at the recent memory.

The annual rendition of "The Battle Hymn of the Republic" was the last thing on the list before the distribution of the diplomas, yet it was also the last thing that many of the graduates wanted to do. The majority of the students were not musically inclined in the least and they had already turned the last line of the Alma Mater from "all hail" to "Aww, hell!" But this particular song was slightly different. Everyone was looking forward to the solo that was always given to the most prized chorus student of the senior class.

Mr. Johnny Holland, the chorus teacher, had been so impressed with the vocal abilities of a few of that year's chorus students (as well as pained by the vocal disabilities of that year's senior class as a whole) that he designated the majority of "The Battle Hymn of the Republic" to three of his most esteemed students who were now joined at the mike: Justus (suffering from overachiever-itus), Bethany Kelly (having her moment in the spotlight one way or another) and Coda Crenshaw (sporting a cheetah-spotted tie which surely broke the graduation dress code) who was the youngest KWA senior.

Kim watched Mr. Johnny climb the ladder that would enable him to direct for the graduates and show off for everyone else, though there was not much showing off to do since the graduates were going to sound like crap despite the week previous being dedicated to time-consuming practice under his manic watch. Not even zealous Mr. Johnny could make a class of fast food cheeseburgers satisfy like a home-cooked meal in just one week.

The choirmaster nodded to the band director and she in turn instructed for all of the graduating students to stand. Kim, Karol and Ezekiel stood in their places on the stage, adjusting their robes as the massive group of seniors turned to face Mr. Johnny.

The overexcited graduation band was assembled with juniors, sophomores and freshmen for the special occasion (Classes of Integrity, Perseverance, and Determination respectively) and Kim outwardly grimaced as they fluctuated around the notes of the intro. Justus, Bethany and Coda had a rather amusing assortment of faces amongst themselves as they attempted to rediscover the correct key. Justus had the first verse, so the pressure was on his second tenor more than the voices of the other two.

"Mine eyes have seen the glory of the coming of the Lord,
He is trampling out the vintage where the grapes of wrath are stored,
He hath loosed the fateful lighting of His terrible swift sword,"

And with their voices perfectly blended in a complicated harmony, the three continued.

"His truth is marching on!"

Kim listened patiently as Bethany sang the second verse in her strong, motherly alto, waiting for Coda's turn at the mike. The final verse belonged completely to her young friend; even the band had (mercifully) been instructed not to play a note on the next verse.

Coda's green eyes seemed to flash gold as the music desisted. When he opened his mouth, a rich and earnest baritone voice, lightly edged with gruffness, danced slowly with the lyrics. He didn't sing with the voice of a sixteen-year-old. His voice was something else entirely. Kim smiled proudly. Coda's voice was his gift. Maybe his only fully realized one.

"In the beauty of the lilies Christ was born across the sea
With a glory in His bosom that transfigures you and me
As He died to make men holy, let us die to make men free
While God is marching on!"

Kim blinked back tears as Coda held the final note out, a full octave above where it had been arranged. The assembly rose cheering out of their seats yet again, though the band ruined the perfect moment by progressing into the chorus in a multitude of pitches.

The graduates now joined in with full force, though their addition was in fact just another subtraction.

"Glory, glory, hallelujah!
His truth is marching on!"

Kim watched as Justus, Coda and Bethany shared a hug at the end of the song. She gave Coda a thumbs-up as he walked past to go back to his seat and whispered praises to Justus once he sat down. Then it was time for her to calm her nerves as the principal headed towards the microphone. One last speech—commencement—by some old fogey from the Board of Education and then the marching of the graduates would begin.

At the climax of the ceremony, the cheers began before Dr. Paul could even get the first few words of that all-important announcement out of his mouth. Kim wasn't surprised; this was the most exciting night of her life and she could just imagine how it was affecting everyone else. She looked wildly among her classmates to make eye contact with her friends. Ezekiel looked dumbstruck, while Maya Sierra was grinning as wide as her face would allow.

Kim looked for Coda and screamed in surprise when she saw him. He was standing already, audaciously hollering and motioning for all of the spectators behind him to give his classmates a well-deserved standing ovation.

"Get up!" he was yelling, his arms waving wildly. "Get up!"

Kim didn't know if she was laughing or crying and, for one horrific moment, she felt like her mother on the day of Aunt Pamela's funeral. She would miss the very thing that she was losing, but there was also a level of release. It wasn't easy, but they had done it! All the tests God had thrown their way and all of the temptations the devil had attempted to snare them in…they had withstood it all through His power.

A rain of gold and black hats filled the sparkling air, soaring through a cosmos of tangible emotions.

Above it all, Kim heard her father yowling.

• • • • •

Few people dress for car crashes and Kim wasn't one of them. Had she known about the accident, she would have worn sneakers.

Instead she still had on her black pumps when she drove out of the KWA Auditorium parking lot in her small white car. Her robe was slung across the back of the passenger seat and the wind rippled through the window and across her sleeveless black dress, cooling her arms. With one hand she steered and with the other she waved and adjusted her rearview mirror.

Anita Baker was singing on the radio and Kim let the music relax her mind. She recalled all the mornings when she would sit in that very parking lot, playing the radio in Maya's sports car while chatting with Coda and Maya, all of them waiting for the first bell to ring. Certain mornings they'd blast the music, Kim and Maya strutting like Beyoncé beside the car with Coda just being his normal hyperactive self. Other mornings they'd watch the goings on just a few feet away on campus grounds, wondering how Rico Gutierrez had twisted his ankle or laughing at the upperclassmen selling useless "elevator tickets" to unsuspecting new students. The majority of mornings there'd be some type of argument, such as when Coda realized that Kim and Maya had assumed that he was Kim's date to the Black and Gold Ball since Maya was going with the football quarterback Gene Hightower. "I'm going with Sheena Thompson," he had professed mutinously and Sheena naturally stood him up.

Such memories had often stirred emotions inside of her, but tonight, as she left behind the shining lights of KWA, headed northbound for the openness of the coastal highway, she also left behind those trivial tribulations and prepared herself for the less claustrophobic climate of a collegiate lifestyle.

Kim had figured that it would take a while for the realization to sink in that she was now free of high school, but her brain was happily frolicking in this new reality. There would be no more classes taught by KWA's legendary substitute teachers and no more football and basketball games to cheer at. She smiled. And no more silly high school complications.

When she was born, her father had sensed that quick adaptation she had to the changing environment, or so he claimed. Her mother named her Kimberly, but her father gave her the middle name Dyna, short for Dynamite. He often told the story of how impressed he was by the abundance of power in her spirit at her birth. He said she had seemed crammed full like a cornucopia, overflowing with spiritual strength and intelligence. Kim was just grateful he hadn't named her Copia.

The car came to rest at a stoplight and Teena Marie took over singing duties from Anita. Kim sang along, happily off-key while watching traffic and patting rhythms on the steering wheel. If she could carry a tune, she would have joined ShowChoir with Coda and fought him for that "Battle Hymn" solo.

The deal she had made with her parents warranted that she meet the family back at the house so they could go out to celebrate together. (Italian food was the whisper she heard from her brother...she could only hope.) Once that fun was done, she'd be free to join her classmates at Shawn Montgomery's party on the beach. She didn't mind being late, since the beach party was sure to be an all-nighter and most of her friends were making different stops before parking themselves in Shawn's oceanic backyard.

In the distance, the pollution from the Hercules pulp mill drifted high, stinking up the air. Kim was glad her windows were rolled up.

The eastbound traffic raced by almost as fast as Kim's thoughts. Maybe this previous year was the only thing that could ever have moved more rapidly than her mind. The stress of maintaining that Dyna-mite excellence began catching up with her as autumn fell to winter. Studying for her finals far too late after school—maybe it was when a club meeting ended or before some play performance or game—seated on the laughably gargantuan steps of the Arts Building, her focus faded as some young freshmen decided to break the rules and skateboard on school grounds. Watching them perform tricks right next to the street that ran through campus on the concrete staircase stirred something inside of her and she instinctively asked to try. There she was, shoulders deep in a trigonometry textbook, this tiny Black girl in white sneakers, a jean skirt and a permed-to-the-roots bob. The boys thought she was kidding. She wasn't.

She jumped on one board, tipping over and falling off so often that the boys were afraid she was going to seriously injure herself. When she scraped her knee, it was like blood to a shark's senses. This was something new, something to master, something only for her. It stirred an intuition from her bowels that she was at once a stranger to and yet unable to imagine herself without again. So she bought her own skateboard, hiding it and telling no one. The longer she kept it to herself, the more she *had* to.

In the car, she sang Teena's lyrics about needing love, before her voice stumbled into the back of her teeth and the words flew from her brain.

Standing in the intersection between the two northbound lanes amidst the congestion of cars was...a creature. Its face, its whole body if it wasn't wearing clothes, was a cluster of minuscule, iridescent orbs. Its hair, if that was even what one could call the splintery white crown framing the creature's smiling visage, was giving off a radiance of its own. Maybe radiance was the wrong word...there was a supernatural and self-contained lambency, in that Kim didn't see the light's reflection on the flanks of the cars that were passing the Creature by turning onto the highway—exclusive illumination that was characteristic to some narcissistic star.

The Creature was built formidably, yet seemed made for show. The arm muscles were perfect, the chest was huge and the sculpted calves were balanced impressively with the trunk-like thighs.

Kim was awestruck. Anything that looked that good, she figured as she began intently praying, was trouble. Perhaps she should have assumed anything as beautiful would angelic in nature. A resplendent cherub or seraph at best. But Kim knew cherubim and seraphim had wings and this creature had no wings. And Kim had seen angels before, most people had. She knew—well, she had been taught that they look like everyone else, however it's their mere presence that lets you know they're more than human. This creature hungered for anyone who saw it to know it was separate from the average being.

Perhaps most disturbing was the gaze coming from the Creature's incandescently azure eyes. They were searching constantly—not roaming around, but searching within the very thing they were focused on.

It was staring at Kim like it had been waiting on her.

Cars were honking and Kim saw the light was now green. The road in front of her was empty again, as if the blue creature had never been there. She stepped on the gas, wondering if her heart had begun to beat again.

All the expected reactions began, from confusion—Why did the other drivers not seem disturbed by what had just appeared in front of them?—to the self-doubt and concern as to if the stress of the night was belatedly taking its toll. Yet before any singular thought process could fully develop, she spotted it once more.

She was too scared to scream or talk, barely remembering to drive. If she believed the road in front of her, all seemed sane, though once she looked through her rear windshield, the impossible became tangible once more. The Creature was crouched atop a blue Volkswagen Beetle... as if the Silver Surfer had sprouted pearly blue body acne and a ridiculously shaped skyboard.

It was gone again when she looked in her mirrors and she refused to look behind her anymore, so she did not see the Creature as it dropped through the Beetle's roof and into the backseat. It leaned towards the driver, who did not detect the abnormal presence, and began to whisper eagerness into his ear.

With the evil settling inside of his thoughts, the driver of the Beetle began passing cars at full speed and switching lanes at the last possible moment, on a purposeful trek towards Kim's car.

Kim remained decisively oblivious to this, cranking the dial on the radio to full blast and belting out letters and words with Teena Marie, attempting to force the belief that the sooner she got home and in the company of her family, the sooner her world would be set back on the proper tilt.

The campus of Oakwood Community College was to her right, signaling the home stretch to her destination. The green wooden fence surrounding the campus separated the outside world from everything on the property, including the drainage ditches.

Kim glanced to her left and screamed, seeing the Creature glaring at her from the backseat of the bug. And as she watched in fear, the Creature—a demon, she was now sure of it—passed through the back of the car, twisting and flipping in the air as if performing in a deathly ballet, all handsome and horrid at once.

The Creature landed inside of the Chevy behind the bug and Kim struggled to stay in her lane. Where had all this oblivious traffic come from? With all the other drivers ignorant and unconcerned, she was the only one attempting to escape this assumed threat. There weren't even any exits off of the highway until she could pass the campus.

She was still sure that any moment she would realize that this wasn't really occurring and that there was some rational explanation for it all.

As a small mollification, if any comfort could be found in the situation, the Chevy driver who was playing chauffeur to the demon didn't seem to be interested in Kim at all, falling back and behind until he was between Kim's car and a large pickup truck.

When he was in place behind the truck, the driver of the Chevy then became erratic, breaking at random and swaying across the lane. The pickup truck switched lanes in an attempt to pass the car and the car took this opportunity to increase its speed.

Kim caught some of this through her mirrors and began praying that she would make it home in one piece.

The driver of the pickup decided to drive just as maniacal in fallible retribution.

Once their on-wheels-wrestling match got out of hand, the truck driver lost control. The truck rammed into the side of Kim's car, knocking her completely off the road.

Her car was in pain. She could hear it screaming, just as loud as she was, as internal machinery burst and chafed, past the point of repair. The radio hiccuped and Teena Marie was mute.

Now there was only praying and screaming.

Kim's vehicle rolled across the college's barrier wooden fence, green spikes crashing through the windows.

The white car was molding itself around her very body as it spun across the drainage pipes and into the ditch. With windows shattering on all sides and seats crunching against concrete, tears flung from her eyes and breath was ripped from her body.

Prayers and screams were quickly followed by silence.

2.

Bashing

Rico Gutierrez was trying his damnedest to be horny but he couldn't push his feelings past pissed. Anger eclipsed his joy of being a graduate and was a barrier against the joy surrounding him at Shawn Montgomery's. The party was borderline Brobdingnagian, what with the numerous revelers extending from the patio to all three floors of Shawn's house as well as out past his sandy backyard and over the dune bridge to the beach. Hinting at the festivities that had come before, the stars sparkled above the terrace as if the sky had accessorized for a royal occasion.

He was too damned bitter. His interest in the present was weak, despite the best efforts of the girl dancing cutely in front of him. Her black curls shimmered like the moonlit ocean against the dull-black of her graduation dress and her hips rolled in a way that could generally make Rico ready to rock.

"BJ, let's cool it on the dancing for a bit," he hollered over the thumping 808, attempting to loosen his tie. The black fabric was wet with his sweat, so the knot quickly became insufferable, tightening to no avail a few inches from his neck.

BJ pulled her hair back against the nape of her neck as if to fluff it, sending a cool breeze across her flushed face. "Give it here," she said, digging her nails into the moist cloth and eventually sweeping the tie from around his neck. He didn't deserve such love.

"You want some punch?" he asked her, wrapping his arms around her waist as they headed towards the edge of the patio, which was lined with refreshment-loaded tables. "Ten bucks says it's spiked."

"Can't hear you," his girlfriend replied.

The music pumped loud enough to drown out the crashing waves out on the beach, but Rico found himself looking at them anyway as he poured drinks. The same Atlantic waters that were so near to him touched Virginia Beach, which was *so* much further away...

Lakota Crenshaw was nearby, leaning against Shawn's massive speakers, spitting the rhymes almost as hard as artist on the track.

Rico's eyes twinkled. "I thought you didn't listen to rap, Coda."

"This song is poetry," the youngster said as he moved closer, his own eyes glittering green, "so I make the necessary exception."

"It's all poetry," Rico crowed. His voice lulled in a gentle croak as if it had hit puberty and decided to stay there. He was a thin, tall Mexican youth with chestnut lips often turned up in a Joker's grin, mischievous yet feigning innocence. His nose, despite the deep horizontal groove on its bridge, was pointed and aggressive, at odds with his warm brown eyes.

"You want some punch?" he asked his friend.

"I am *not* going home tipsy," Coda responded.

"Doesn't answer my question," Rico said, causing Coda to smile. There was a reason they called Coda the "Cheshire Cheetah." That boy was always grinning.

"Where's Her Cheetah Majesty?" BJ asked as Rico handed her a cup. "Haven't seen her yet."

"Oh, Kim?" Coda pursed his large lips in thought. "I dunno. I didn't get too many moments with her after the big release from shackles that occurred tonight."

Rico laughed. "You, Kim and Maya were like the circle of unbroken tears for a good five minutes while everyone else was already outside taking pictures."

Coda raised an eyebrow, simply responding, "We've been through a lot together."

Coda wasn't lying when he implied his graduation busyness. As a member of student council—treasurer, if Rico remembered correctly—the ball of energy had spearheaded a movement to get each graduating classmate to slip a custom-made puzzle piece into the principal's unsuspecting hand. Coda had got some senior to sketch the principal in front of one of KWA's various buildings and the council somehow got it onto a gigantic wooden puzzle with exactly three hundred and forty pieces. Before the ceremony, Coda and the council supervisor Mrs. Donahue passed out each and every one of the pieces. (Well, except for Wayne Emerson's, who was a no-show. Something about failing one of his English classes. Again.)

"Cheetah-spotted tie?" BJ asked now, sipping her punch cautiously. "How'd you get away with that?"

Coda cackled theatrically, stroking the silk tie he had only loosened. "I didn't. VP Peachtree told me to take it off immediately. She had a whole collection of boring black ones at her disposal. I just said something southern and gentlemanly like, 'yes, ma'am,' and dipped out of her eyesight."

"Not as bad as Brandon Evans," BJ chuckled, "with his golden grill implanted just for the occasion. Did you see that cartoon glint when he smiled at Dr. Paul? The audience gasped in unison."

"And highlights," Rico said, reaching up to touch one of Coda's golden-brown ringlets. The sixteen-year-old turned every occasion into a red carpet event.

"Just in the front," Coda said almost guiltily, playfully swatting Rico's hand away. "I'm not big on bathing my scalp in chemicals and whatnot, so I figured if anything went wrong I could just chop me up some bangs. I considered doing braids with gold or yellow beads, but..."

"Too much," Rico agreed, surprising Coda with a headlock.

According to the freshmen yearbook, Rico and Coda had known each other then, but they didn't remember it. As sophomores they had both attempted to pass a World History class, but they sat with then-separate groups of friends, so it wasn't until senior year in Mrs. Donahue's AP Lit—and the move of Coda's lunch membership to the round table that housed Rico and his friends once the kid had became sort of popular—that they finally got to know each other and quickly discovered that they had much in common.

Both lived in the amber sunshine of California when they were young and neither of them had picked up the Georgia accent that so many of their classmates wielded like weapons. Both of them were minorities in the familiar sense, with Rico's Hispanic heritage and Coda's pan-ethnic background adding up to about fifty-five percent Black ("Geechee," he would proudly trumpet) and a forty-five percent mishmash of European and Native American. Both of the boys were hopeless romantics, yet Rico held a degree in the Fine Arts of Aphrodisia and Coda was a self-declared prude. They were both unjustifiably handsome, but by senior year only Rico had a girl. They were both skinny; Rico was the slender one, however, and Coda's football-ready shoulders suggested that his body would fill out appropriately in time. Both Rico and Coda loved soccer and were ridiculously talented on the field, yet Rico had served as the captain of the KWA Cheetahs. Lakota didn't even play for the school, far too occupied with ShowChior. Instead, he was the team's mascot.

They were also the only two out of their friends to be nicknamed in connection to their talents, and known almost universally by the monikers over their given names. Lakota had been named for one of his genetic tribes before it was shortened to the music passage in school. The boy born Enrique had been christened by his own ridiculous speed from an early age—ricocheting across the soccer field.

During Rico's tenure as soccer captain, his kindergarten teacher mother was there at every game, cheering him on with an amazing strength in her voice that he had forgotten she had. His young sister Renata would come on most occasions, wielding banners and biting her knuckles and yelling curt insults about the other teams. BJ, who played for the girls' team, would always sit near Renata or Mrs. Gutierrez, silently taking in the proceedings. Coda would be in the Cheetah costume, complete with the gold and black cap and jersey, romping around the edge of the pitch.

On the last game of the season, Rico had seen Coda make it all the way around to the other side of the field to taunt the opposing team's cheerleaders. He was surprised his friend didn't abduct one of them as a souvenir.

That had been the game. That particular game decided whether or not the Wilbanks Cheetahs would go on to the championship, and they all desperately wanted to go to that final match at Virginia Beach. The other team had played dirty the whole game without the referee calling over half of the things they were doing. Rico had gotten fouled up the wazoo, Shannon Crescitelli had gotten kicked in his bad knee and had to be lifted off the field, while Benny Commons was benched for his… physical attitudes.

For the majority of the team, the game became a full out war for respect. On top of it all, it was Rico's senior year and as captain, he was hungry for that winning moment that they deserved. His heart had been set on that championship since he had realized near the end of his junior year the team was good enough to go all the way.

They lost though, blasphemy of blasphemies, and instead of leading the Wilbanks Cheetahs to a championship soccer victory, Rico had to spend the night of his would-be-game watching a couple hundred of his classmates accept their diplomas. Maybe after a few days he wouldn't resent God for it.

One of their classmates threw up the peace sign to Rico, telling Coda, "Dude, you sang like a beast tonight, Cheshire."

Coda grinned from beneath Rico's armpit. "Thanks!"

Rico nodded, releasing Coda. "I meant to tell you myself. You were great. Almost made the whole evening worth it."

"Almost?" Coda and BJ asked in unison and, seemingly before he had finished the word, Coda was mounted like a jetpack on Rico's back, gluing his hands to Rico's buzz cut. "Boy, we're finished! Graduated!" He hollered at the top of his lungs, throwing his hands into the air. "FINI-TO!"

"IN CHEETO!" was the programmed response en masse, followed by whistles and whoops.

Rico laughed, one hand holding Coda's thigh and the other bringing his cup up to his mouth. Yep, spiked. This was gonna be a party after all.

Coda had leaned down to whisper in his ear. "I get it, though. You know I wish tonight coulda ended up kinda different, too. I woulda been right there with you at Virginia Beach, sweating through that evil costume."

"I love you, Coda," Rico said, genuinely feeling better. He gave Coda's thigh a squeeze.

Coda hopped off of Rico's back, tugging on the sleeves of his shirt down past his wrists. While Rico tried to interpret the sudden melancholy in Coda's expression—it was as if they had just swapped moods—Coda went back to rapping along with the music.

"Shawshank, stop pretending you're Black," Shannon Crescitelli said, walking by and causing Coda's eyes to darken.

"I'm Black...enough. It's possible to be more than one thing, Shannon. Like you: you're ugly *and* single."

Rico chuckled against his better judgment. Shannon had recently broken up with one of their classmates.

"Too soon?" Coda asked sweetly.

Shannon scowled, eyes darting between Rico and Coda.

"Kiss my boots, Cali fruits," Shannon said, walking off.

"I don't know how you two put up with him," BJ said, taking another tentative sip from her cup. It was obvious she was aware of the drink's alcoholic properties at this point. "He's an idiot."

Rico shrugged. "He's a good dude."

"Well, you accept things from him that you wouldn't accept from other people," she accused.

Coda correctly sensed the turn the conversation was taking and, after giving a pitying smile to Rico, moved further into the crowd of partying graduates.

"He thinks poking at people's differences forms calluses or something," Rico was saying. "He's not trying to be mean." Her look told him she wasn't buying it. He soldiered on, perhaps vainly. "I think he expects some turnabout. Tell him he's too pale to be Italian. Say he looks Scottish or something."

"You're seriously not getting this, are you?" BJ asked, pulling out her cell. "Ugh, the parents are texting."

"They want you to leave already?" That would definitely put a further dampening on his evening.

"No, it's about Rachel," she said, responding to her text with quick fingers as her mouth began to tighten. Something was up with her sister.

"Is she okay?" he asked. "Is it an emergency?"

"No," BJ said, looking up. "Her teachers are telling her to pray about her lupus. They're telling her to pray that Jesus will heal her. Isn't that a croc?"

Rico grimaced, hands involuntarily fingering the rosary he had peeking out of his unbuttoned collar. BJ's little sister was attending Glynn County's freaky little Catholic private school because it's the best education possible and "my parents are dead set on churning out something better than me" as BJ had quoted often enough. BJ's family, however, were practicing Buddhists. Supposedly the school's staff understood that, but they couldn't help trying their hardest to convert the lone heathen in their ranks. BJ and Rico, an active Catholic, had gotten into enough arguments about it for him to know to stay out of this current controversy.

"Why do Christians always push? Didn't you guys learn anything from the Spanish Inquisition?"

She always made it personal. *You guys.*

"I wasn't there," he replied neutrally. They lived in a small, Southern Georgia town. How was she surprised? Christianity in some form was hemmed into the fabric of their daily existence, whether they were believers or not. The majority of their high school assemblies opened or closed with invocations. Benny Commons's mom had petitioned successfully when the rival high school had a horned-devil mascot. The Carver High Devils quickly became the Carver High Fantastics, which was even more hated than the Devils had ever been. Oppressive Christianity was their reality.

"Yeah, but you were there today, cheering on Kim while she used the grad podium as a pulpit. How would she like it if I got up there saying, 'Christians have been deceived into thinking that this life is all about pleasing a guy who's been dead for a few millennia,' huh? What do you think her reaction would be? Let alone the reaction from each of the local bible-thumpers?"

Rico observed BJ's current hand on hippage stance. They were sparring and he didn't like it.

"I think her reaction, like mine, would be to tell you that you're wrong and, until you figure it out, you're going to hell," he responded unapologetically.

She poked his flat chest with more anger than there should legally be in a finger. "There you go, being a dick."

He shrugged. "You started acting like a bitch first."

Poison leapt from her eyes to the rest of her face, but the ringing of the phone prevented her from injecting the venom into him.

"Hello, Ma?" she said, answering. She stuck her still angry pointer into her exposed ear, moving off with one last glare in Rico's direction.

He couldn't care less. He was fine with the fact that she was opinionated—it made her human. Her combative nature, on the other hand, really made him wish he had picked another Wilbanks diva to romance. Shannon's ex, Eden Enamorado, was rather gorgeous, as one example. And Maya Sierra was dancing nearby, arching her back and allowing her generous cleavage to shimmer beneath the party lights. She caught his eye and winked.

Rico downed his cup and reached to pour himself another. His mood needed further improvement.

"That's spiked, you know."

A freckled boy stood next to him. It was a graduate he recognized but didn't quite know, Travis or Tony or something. He had been a transfer from Carver a few years back.

"I can't taste it," Rico said, guzzling the second cup and pouring another. The boy's name was Terry Bozzo, he remembered. Was in Show-Choir with Coda and the rest.

"All right," Terry said, clearly making a silent judgment. Those theatre kids could never disguise their inner workings. "Hope you're not driving."

"Dude, it's graduation," Rico said, annoyed. He gestured to the party. "Everybody's having fun. Will you let me?"

"Yo, just looking out for you. All you soccer guys have reasons to let loose tonight. Losing out on the championship and whatnot."

Rico shook his head. He didn't want folks thinking he was a sore loser. The conversation BJ was already attracting unwanted attention. Maya and her mountainous boobs were glancing over and Shannon was watching intently from a nearby table. "It's just a game, man. We still rocked it out in the end."

Terry laughed. "Nobody says 'it's just a game' when they win, right? I guess you guys didn't lose, you just ran out of time, huh?"

"Yo, dude, shut up," Rico said, rolling his eyes. "Nobody's thinking about soccer right now."

"Okay, whatever… 'Dude,'" Terry said, picking up a plate and inspecting the chip layout.

Rico was steaming. He felt like the conversation still had him looking like a whiny jock flailing for purpose in this pre-collegiate climate, which couldn't be further from who he was or what this was.

"It's not winning or losing that counts, man," Rico said, clipping words more than he'd like. "If you knew anything about sports instead of singing gay-ass theater tunes, you'd know it's about the team and how they play the game."

Terry seemed to snort, not making eye contact as if he was above all of this. "Spoken like a guy who just led his team to a spectacular loss."

Rico had him jacked up in the air by his collar and tie before Terry could finish the last word. Terry's legs knocked against the table and punch spilled out of the bowl.

"Guys," Maya said, coming over to calm them down, while others moved back to watch from a safe distance. Some were pulling out phones to film.

"No, you jackwad," Rico growled. "Spoken like a captain who wants the best for his team instead of just some meaningless trophy. Spoken like somebody who's now itching to bash your face in."

Coda was there too. "Dude, it's not that serious. It's nothing. Just put him down."

"Yo, Rico, man, chill hut," Terry squeezed out, his face turning as red as his hair, flushing out his freckles. "No bashing necessary."

"You think I'm some basic bitch who's on your microscopic level? You think you can bother me?"

"Obviously I did," Terry smiled.

"Now's *obviously* not the time to be clowning, Terry," Coda said warningly.

"He's the one being an insaniac!" Terry accused.

Shannon was there, hand rubbing Rico's shoulder.

"He just wishes he was us, you know that," Shannon said casually. "Jealousy rears its ugly head again. Let me take care of him, dude. Just go enjoy the party."

Maya's hand was on his other shoulder, tugging gently. "Come on, Rico Suave. Let's dance."

Rico dropped Terry, a little faster than he wanted, but the joker was heavier than thin Rico had expected, so it was probably a good thing that it hadn't come to blows.

"Appreciate your diplomacy," Terry said dryly, adjusting his collar. The edges were browned a bit, as if they had stained. "I shall toast this momentous occasion."

"Listen up, pimple pizza," Shannon said. "Rico Gutierrez is a gentleman who's done far more for this school than you could ever squeeze out the pus to do. A flippin' Cheetah warrior who's never been anything but nice to you and your maggot crew. He's got one tiny blemish on his record compared to the acres of blemishes I see on that crater cookie you call a face. So let me break it down for you: You try to jump bad with him again and I'll put my whole leg in the biggest crater I can find and dribble your ostrich-sized brain against your E.T.-shaped skull."

"Careful," Terry said, still baiting. No man ever laid down his ego as easily as his standards. "Make sure you don't use the one with your bad knee, Crescitelli."

Shannon moved in as if to hit him, causing Terry to flinch. Chortling, the Italian walked off and the crowd slowly dispersed, leaving Coda to mend the boy's feelings.

"Come on, Terry," Coda said, pulling him away. "Unclench your fist. Nobody's fighting tonight."

"Amen," Maya said, adding to Rico, "This party's epic, but we don't need epic in the *Gladiator* sense."

"He was pushing me," Rico said, somewhat resignedly.

"You don't have to defend yourself to me," Maya laughed, throwing her braids back. He could never be sure of how aware she was of her breasts, but it was moments like this that made him pretty sure she knew how aware everyone else was of them. "We just had a little episode. No one will remember it in, like, four parties from now. Hell, there's four more parties tomorrow night, at least."

"Yeah," Rico said, glancing after the departing Terry and Coda. "I could have handled that better, though."

"Sure, but don't stress it," she said to him in Spanish. He forgot she was near fluent. Her dark brown skin disguised her Puerto Rican heritage to all of their classmates who thought Puerto Ricans were all as light as Jennifer Lopez. "Let Daft Punk take you away."

Rico sighed, also speaking in his first language. "I don't know why Coda runs around with that clown."

Maya giggled. "Remember that Homecoming, I think it was junior year, when they marched up in the cafeteria on Decade Day blasting that boombox?"

Rico laughed. "Bozzo looked like a reject member of Run DMC."

"Complete with the Adidas," Maya nodded. They were back to English. He wasn't sure she noticed. "And Coda looked like the Disco King."

Coda had been dressed in striped bellbottom overalls mismatched with a polka-dotted shirt and some dangerous-looking platform shoes. His hair had been teased into its full Afro glory. Terry put on some Bee-Gees for Coda to groove to and afterwards, Coda took command of the ghetto blaster and Terry laid down some cardboard and began to break-dance. They received a standing ovation afterwards.

"Remember Superhero Day this year when Brandon Evans came as Condom Man?" Rico asked.

"And he was handing out condoms at lunch! Can't forget that."

Rico couldn't stop grinning. "He gave seventeen to Wayne Emerson alone."

"Hah! It wasn't a favor, either. It was a message."

Rico laughed until he had tears coming out of his eyes. "Thanks, Maya."

"What'd I do?" she asked innocently.

"For being the first person tonight who actually let me have fun."

"Aww, boo, you were having a rough go?" she asked sweetly. "Well, you're welcome. I have to look after my boys."

Maya and Eden had been co-captains of the cheerleading squad, forming close relationships with every team captain that KWA had. Sometimes it seemed that Maya was romantic with football captain Gene Hightower, especially when they were voted Homecoming King and Queen.

She was right about how they all stood up for each other. You messed with one of the KWA royals, you messed with them all. That's why Shannon was so quick to jump to Rico's aid. Coda, too, even though he was close to Terry, followed the unspoken hierarchy laws. High school was a closed government and it was safe, if unfair. That's the only way they could make it through. There was a comfort level in having a place and knowing that place.

"What was your favorite memory from high school?" Maya was asking him now.

He did his best to wrinkle his forehead. "Probably the night of graduation when you and I gave our virginities to each other."

Maya arched an eyebrow, only slightly phased. "Mmm, that's not a memory, boo. That's a dream."

Rico grinned. "Maybe I'm just cocky. You know what cocky means, don't you, Maya?"

"I'm too through with you," Maya laughed. "Aren't you dating BJ?"

Rico feigned confusion. "Who said that?"

"Everyone at school," Maya said pointedly.

"But never BJ or I," Rico said, avoiding any personal implications. Maya wasn't a gossipmonger, but many of her fellow cheerleaders undoubtedly were.

Maya laughed. "Fair enough. Everyone says Gene and I are a couple, which couldn't be further from the truth."

"What is it that you don't like about him?" Rico asked about the quarterback. "It bothers BJ that he always wears long sleeve shirts with shorts."

Maya snorted. "Year-round! Yep, that's definitely one. And he's so *loud!* 'Hey, Maya,'" she imitated, "'you have something hanging out of your nose! I don't think it's a booger, though. Maybe a hair.'"

Rico found himself laughing again. "That's nasty. You just made this conversation nasty."

"Not as nasty as you, mister," she said accusingly.

"Yeah, but mine was the good nasty and yours was pox."

She laughed with him. "Then I apologize."

"Where's your mini-me?" he asked.

"Kim?" Maya creased her forehead. "She said she'd be running late. Who knows? After her speech tonight, I'm sure she's on cloud nine."

• • • • •

"I'm gonna buy you a giant spoon if you insist on stirring up mess, Terry."

"You hang out with pricks," Coda's redheaded friend responded, retying his necktie around his hair as a headband.

"I hang out with you," Coda said pointedly, undoing the laces on his Stacy Adams.

"And I'm the most spunktastic one there is," Terry smiled, kicking off his loafers.

Coda rolled his eyes. "See, you would fit in with them."

"I do fit in. Where I get in, that is." He gave Coda a side eye. "*You* don't."

Coda looked behind them towards Shawn Montgomery's massive house. Terry had led them further down the beach once the outside graduation festivities grew closer to where they had sat near the water's edge. The male graduates had used their ties for the purpose of high-spirited three-legged races—the type of thing Coda would have initiated had he remained with the revelers. Instead, he was at water's edge with Terry, and he had no idea why. He just followed Terry's lead in moments like this.

"I don't have to fit in, buddy," Coda grinned. "Stardom leads from the front."

"Whatever, Cheshire. You're just lucky that Tweedledee and Tweedle Double-Ds got popular and dragged you to all of their gatherings."

Coda shrugged, kneeling to swirl his fingers in the wet sand. "You're popular."

"Did we just have separate experiences?" Terry paused, in the middle of rolling up his pants. "Shannon Almighty just made it pretty plain that I'm not under the insipid protection of popularity. I am, as I said, cool in my element."

The calls of "Red Rover" traveled down the beach. Terry followed Coda's gaze and groaned. "That is *so* not my element."

"What are you doing?" Coda asked as Terry grabbed his elbow and began leading him into the water. "Why did we even roll up our pants?" he asked moments later, and Terry laughed. The water was up to their armpits. If Terry hadn't been dragging him, Coda was sure he would have turned around.

"It gets worse before it gets better."

He was right. After a certain point, the water receded until it was below Coda's ankles. The moon shone full, and Coda realized that Terry had led him atop a sandbar.

"Ok," Coda breathed. "It's better."

Terry squeezed his hand for reassurance and passed his foot over the wet shore and the sandbar was set ablaze in neon color before fading back to the simple reflection of moonlight.

"Whoa," Coda breathed. "What is that?"

"Baby jellyfish," Terry said.

Coda's voice took on an unnaturally tight tone. "Did you say jellyfish?"

Terry nodded. "Isn't it beautiful? They get beached here when the tide goes out." He passed his foot alongside the graveyard again and rainbow-shaded fire burst along the black-tie horizon.

"Yes," Coda breathed. "This is super cool, but I'm going to climb on your back now."

Terry started laughing. "Don't be scared, Cheshire!"

"I'm not scared," Coda replied, gripping Terry's ribs with his legs. "I'm smart."

The redhead laughed, toting his friend back away from the sandbar towards the shore. Once enough distance was placed between the boys and the jellyfish, Coda graciously walked alongside.

Terry resolved to fill the night with words instead of thoughts. "Your silence most offends me, and to be merry best becomes you; for out of the question...'"

He hesitated. Shakespeare's next line stated "you were born in a merry hour." Coda's mother had died in childbirth.

Coda looked over towards the crowd of revelers, initially seeming unfazed. "No, sure, my lord..." He smiled sadly. Fazed. "My mother cried; but then, there was a star danced!" He began to balancé in the surf, splashing Terry with seawater and laughter. "And under that was I born." He attempted a pirouette, losing his balance instead. Terry tried to catch him and they both went under.

They surfaced, gasping and still laughing.

• • • • •

The doctor carefully stirred the fluids in his beaker, waiting for the faint traces of color to dissolve into complete transparency.

"Beakers," he said to the watching nurse. "Quite crude, eh?" He glanced up at her. "Tonight's efforts will change the world, and everything that happens needs to be exact."

"I wasn't judging," she said. "The RiD crew handled Patricia's dosage quite similarly. Of course, none of us knew that it would actually be *Patricia's* dose at the time."

"That's Patricia, for you." The doctor placed his stirring rod down thoughtfully. "Why do they refer to the treatment as 'RiD?' As far as I know, the substances that were compiled don't exactly produce 'R,' 'I,' or 'D.'"

"'RiD' references 'roses in December.' A quote from Sir J.M. Barrie."

The doctor shook his head. "I'm not familiar with it."

"It's a quote about memory," the nurse said. "Dr. Pat loves Barrie."

As the doctor began to fill the vials, the nurse spoke again.

"You head up the tissue engineering department, don't you, Doctor?"

He nodded.

"What are you calling the solution that you're working on?"

"There's not a name for it yet."

"Well, if I may ask, what does it do?"

The doctor secured the cork in each vial before answering, taking the time not to phrase an appropriate answer, but to suppress his own unease.

"There's not a name for that, either."

• • • • •

The heat was rooted as stubbornly as the giant Georgia oaks, unmoving, invasive, and ruining the streets. The party was stomping and rocking enough to give both the heat and the oaks a run for their money.

"I thought you said 'block' party," Terry had cracked as they arrived.

"I did," Coda replied, not getting Terry's joke at first.

Upon arrival to Coda's neighborhood, the two boys had realized that the community was throwing a giant function for all of the high school graduates. Only a select few dark-skinned students got invitations to island soirees due to the circles they moved in. The rest of them seemed to be here. He added that "only in Glynn County would both schools graduate on the same night." Some family members had to pick favorites.

As Ray Charles and Chaka Khan dueled in the speakers, Cheyenne Crenshaw approached and crinkled her nose, extending her arm to keep her brother and his friend at a safe distance.

"What happened to you?" she asked, eyeing them warily.

Coda smiled, struggling to contain a laugh. "Terry and I decided to go for a swim."

Terry shrugged. "The water's great this time of year." He shared a gaze with Coda and they both began to chuckle. They were still damp up to their shoulders, undershirts visible through their button-ups.

"In your clothes?" Cheyenne asked disbelievingly. "That's crusty. I *know* you're gonna change."

Coda's sap colored eyes paused on his sister, irritation brewing. "Hadn't planned on it."

They stood there for a moment, some battle of wills that Terry didn't understand, before Cheyenne decided there was no worth in such proceedings.

"Pops left," she said, looking over as a band began to set up on a stage further down the block. "Brother Wright is in the hospital. This may be it."

Coda pursed his lips. Having a pastor for a father was never a convenient thing. "He's missing the party, though." That had come out whinier than he had wanted. Moments before, he hadn't even known there was going to be a party.

His sister shook her head, feathered earrings bouncing to the fading music. The band was about to take over the speakers, and the crowd around them began to thicken. "He never made it here."

Coda began to realize. "When did he leave?" he asked.

"Right after Kim's speech." She said it without empathy. Almost as if to protect him. Almost. Perhaps it worked.

"Okay." Coda said, looking out over the gathered individuals. His father hadn't even seen him sing.

As Cheyenne occupied herself with other conversations, Terry said to Coda, "We totally came here to change."

It was true. Between the two of them, Terry lived the furthest away from Shawn Montgomery's house, on Blythe Island, so Coda had suggested that they head to his house in the city instead, get into some dry clothes, and continue the evening's proceedings.

Coda just shook his head. "She's always gotta prove how un-awesome I am." One of his neighbors approached him and whispered in his ear.

"And you embrace it," Terry said, deftly avoiding an accusatory tone.

"I defy it, Terry," Coda growled, sensing an indictment anyway. He nodded to his neighbor before turning back to his friend. "I'm nobody's puppet."

Terry seemed to be resisting the temptation to roll his eyes. "Why can't we just put on some different clothes? Who cares what she thinks? If you're nobody's puppet, then make your own future, dude. 'It is not in the stars to hold our destiny, but in ourselves.'"

Coda shook his head. "Bad Shakespeare, Terry. Probably the greatest misquote that's not from *Casablanca*. Cassius says that 'The fault, dear Brutus, is not in our stars, but in ourselves, that we are underlings.'"

Terry shrugged. "You've got the bible, Cheshire; let me have Shakespeare."

"Stop bellyaching! The proper quote actually fits tonight's pessimistic party view of yours. 'The fault is within ourselves, blah, blah.' Open some happiness."

"I was happy until you had us standing here in saltwater fashions," Terry grumbled.

"It works for taffy." Coda wrapped his arms around Terry's shoulders. "Hamlet himself would ask you, 'Doubt thou the stars are fire?'"

Terry nodded, eyes grinning. Hamlet was one of his dream roles. "Intensely. Why else would the night hours be so cool?"

Coda snorted. "You call this cool? 'Doubt that the sun doth move?'"

"Helio-cynic!" He slipped from Coda's grasp. "Didn't Galileo discover that we weren't the center of the universe, like, hundreds of years ago?"

Coda laughed despite himself. "I can *Twelfth Night* the crap out of you, too, Malvolio."

They were being utter theatre geeks, as if the current environment had inspired a contrarian nature. Terry had portrayed Malvolio in a local production of *Twelfth Night*, while Coda had portrayed the singing jester Feste. Coda had frequently joked with his friend that the apex of their careers would be *Moor Rhythm: the Othello Musical that Few Asked For and Even Less Deserve*.

"You know my *Twelfth Night* lines?" Terry asked, knowing the answer.

"I know everybody's lines," Coda replied easily. He placed a gallant hand in the air and extended the other to his friend. "'If this fall into thy hand, revolve.'"

"You're posturing," Terry warned, accepting Coda's hand.

"I'm the singer, you're the actor," Coda replied, leading Terry through the crowd. The band's short warm up was congealing. Chords and instruments were combining into something new. "'In my stars I am above thee; but be not afraid of greatness: some are born great, some achieve greatness, and some have greatness thrust upon them.'"

"Why do I suddenly feel like this is a setup?" Terry asked. One of the band members was speaking into his microphone, inciting the crowd.

"Because it is," Coda said, speaking over the music, "'Thy Fates open their hands; let thy blood and spirit embrace them!'"

They were at the foot of the stairs to the stage.

"Coda," Terry groaned, allowing his friend to lead him onto the stage.

The chords of "Celebrate" were coming from the keyboard and the crowd was growing excited with the familiar melody.

"Will you be the Gang to my Kool?" Coda asked his friend, handing him a microphone.

"I'm saying yes, but later you have to tell me what that means" Terry said, holding the microphone behind his back.

With no further ceremony, Coda was ripping through the first verse of the party anthem, gesturing to Terry whenever it was time for ad-libs or backing vocals.

"*Celll-a-braaa-tion,*" Terry warbled gamely, and the crowd ate it up.

Coda grinned, continuing the song. When it was time for a line of harmony, Cheyenne had joined Terry at his mic, brushing her hair and feathered earrings out of her face.

After the friends changed, Coda warned at the snack table, "These are the unknown brand of cookies. One side is supposedly vanilla, the other is dirt, and the middle creme is comprised of SARS."

Terry laughed, inspecting the unique treat. "Ah, the doodoo delicacies of Glynn County. My mom buys these for each get-together I have. Remember when I invited Eden over for that Monty Python marathon?"

"How did that work out for you?" Coda asked slyly, and Terry declined to respond. Nearly every senior guy had tried their luck with Eden Enamorado at some time over their high school journey. Shannon so far was the only one who had succeeded in any romantic capacity.

"Yo, Coda! Why aren't you on The Island?" asked a booming voice.

A giant approached them. Arguably he wasn't much taller than them, but his muscles indicated a far greater mass than the two friends could hope for.

"We *were* there, Gene," Coda responded, knowing his voice sounded weak in comparison. "It wasn't popping, though. Why aren't you there?"

The quarterback shrugged. "Didn't feel like it."

Terry chimed in. "All you're missing is a beachfront game of Red Rover. Real grown up stuff."

Gene glanced at Coda, silently asking why Terry felt the need to exist before deciding to move on.

"Carve 'em up, Carver High!" Terry called after him. "Faaaaan*tastic!*"

Coda flashed panicked eyes at him and Terry laughed.

"What? This party is a neutral zone!"

Coda shook his head. "You're hopeless."

• • • • •

They stood in white, hoods enabling the shadows on their face while the attached capes were draped around their bodies, leaving only an occasional armored extremity exposed. Outside of their heights, three sentries were nearly identical in white pearlescent fabric accented with varied hues between them. A singular cross decorated each robe in a massive fashion, toned according to their respective colors, the vertical bars stretching down the hood into the shrouded faces. The tallest one was accented in ebony, gripping a staff in its matching glove. One kneeled, exposed leg armored in a green shade as prismatic as their white cloaking. The third stood in violet, hands tucked into folded arms and completely still.

In fact, all three were rigid. Sensing instead of feeling. Knowing instead of thinking. As mildly implied by the staff, the three were warriors more than protectors, but protecting nonetheless. They had no need to rescue the girl who still lay in the wreckage of her truck. Their mission was separate.

There was a fourth sentry. Cloaked in white and silver, it stood above the damage of the accident. A sanctuary quelled the air above it, and it found no need to step outside of the invisible cover.

Right on the other side was the legionnaire.

"What's the point of a shield if the damage is done?" the beautybeast asked, observing the atmospheric sanctuary separating it from the sentry.

"Kamiskas," the Silver Sentry responded, "you may not step here. The area has been hallowed."

"You are speaking to me outside of time," the demon spoke, its blue eyes narrowing. "How much more power has El appointed you and your lackeys?"

"Enough," was the reply. "You and the rest of the legionnaires would do good to know that all kinds of heaven is about to be set loose on earth."

The demon was laughing in its own way, glittery pulsations racing across its shell. "You can't keep them from the girl. They're in Protection."

The Sentry raised silver fingers to its nacreous hood. "There is no protection from This One."

The hood was lifted, and a blinding light filled the area, causing the blue demon to recoil, shrieking.

The Sentries moved concomitantly.

The Ebony Sentry used its staff to propel itself into the air, as the Violet Sentry leapt from the ground as effortlessly as if gravity had released its hold. The Emerald Sentry slammed its hand against the grass, sending out a force of wind along the ground.

Outside the area of apparent sanctuary, the approaching human bodies under the possession of legionnaire demons were tossed off of their feet by the wind.

Now the Sentries took more purposeful action. As the invisible shielding lifted from the area, the Ebony Sentry's staff was already cracking across shoulder blades, while the Violet Sentry had bodies piling at its feet. They had a distinct battle to win, and winning was mandatory.

3.

Kimberly Dyna

Kim completed her fifth year out of the womb twelve years earlier near summer's end. The majority of the birthday party recollections had quickly faded in her memory. She remembered the ugly plastic banquet tables borrowed from the church, but didn't recall what food, if any, was served. She remembered the adults dancing in the yard, yet she could not awaken her remembrance to the music that blasted from the boom boxes that night.

She did remember four-year-old, apricot-skinned Kenji Carter and how he always smelled like honeysuckle and Wonder Bread. How his hair curled down his neck and behind his ear, the color of rain-soaked bark. How he was so bold, so innocently impulsive, and how his lips of coral and the snowy pearls he had cut instead of teeth combined into the shyest smile. He was several months younger; she knew him from church and he was the most beautiful life form she had been blessed to see.

Her uncle had the biggest yard, a front yard, which made it even better, so having the party on his property was the most logical choice. Despite this, his actual house seemed smaller than Kim's bedroom. She figured in her young mind that the shack was dying. Dark paneling buckled on the walls, the fan wobbled and wheezed (it never quite whirled), and the screen door…

It was impossible to forget the screen door. The hideous pea green paint cracking on the heavy wood frame and the hinges that jammed if the door was merely pushed shut, inadvertently leaving it cracked—it was the only door in the world children were allowed to—scratch that—required to slam. This caused numerous problems, like when Shirley got beat for accidentally slamming the door in their grandmother's face.

Earlier that night, Kim herself had done it; she mocked the rules knowing Kenji was watching. Dr. Hamilton had raced inside—his reasons were eroded along with the memories of him returning to the outside—and the screen stood open. Kim placed her finger in the doorframe, the crack that appeared between the hinges, rebelling against laws, daring the universe to teach her a lesson. It was a freeing moment, her first of a short spurt. She was loosed, adrift in the air without having to fly. It was a selfish feeling, and she loved the new sensation.

She wanted to keep it to herself. She wanted to be the only one who got away clean with that transgression, otherwise the magic would be lost to her. She watched, lack of restraint flooding within her, as Kenji stuck his pinkie—the right one; she couldn't make herself forget—in the door hinge. He was curious…and he was ignorant.

Kim herself was alien to this new evil that abducted her. She slammed the screen door, and if more malice could be found in a single sound, Kim never wanted to hear it.

She would wake random nights still feeling the pea green flakes falling from her fingers.

It was the only reason she remembered the adults dancing in the yard, for when Kenji's screams reached their ears, they all raced to his rescue. Kim was sure someone must have picked her up and whisked her away from all the unpleasantness, but she had no memory of it. Perhaps she got lost in the frenzy, the safe children forgotten for the want of the endangered one. Either way, she caught a few brief glimpses of Kenji clutching his hand as his pinkie dangled by the skin…and couldn't bring herself to find his young, unfinished face. She was afraid of what would be visible there where she had become so accustomed to discovering perfection.

They all reminded her that it wasn't her fault and that Kenji shouldn't have stuck his finger there. As if it was completely his fault. As if she was innocent.

She never had the chance to apologize to perfect Kenji. She was on a road trip with the family when Kenji was mysteriously abducted from the hospital. She was in Fayetteville, North Carolina when the missing persons was filed. Washington D.C. when portions of his body were discovered in the marsh. It was a local nightmare that the boy and his family didn't deserve. Kim couldn't shake the thought that she had kickstarted his collision with destiny.

Kenji's one moment of imperfection was brought on by her own insolence, so she served her penance by being the new perfect. She became what everyone else wanted. To the world, she was faultless and if that is how it appeared, then truly faultless Kenji hadn't died in vain.

She hadn't spoken a word of this to her parents, her siblings, or even her pastor.

She had to be perfect.

• • • • •

She was lost in a memory, as if her reality had imploded, causing the present to interfere with the past.

It was the Black and Gold Ball. There she was in her strapless, lacy white-gold ball gown, the giant gold ribbon around her waist, the gold heels laced up her shins, and her hair curled at her chin. She wore the very dress she had ordered for the Miss KWA pageant, since she wasn't going to put her father through the hassle of buying her another expensive dress for the senior dance.

"Have you seen Coda?" Kim asked Brandon Evans, who shook his head, not really caring. He grabbed her hand and guided her towards the snack table.

Maya towered near the table with Gene Hightower, both of them decked out in fancy black attire. The details stood out to Kim as if she was living it all over again. Gene had on a black suit with a shimmering golden turtleneck, sporting golden brown Timberlands and a gold stud in his ear. Maya had on a sleeveless ebony mermaid mini-dress, hemmed just below her knees. Black sandal shoes adorned her feet and her golden weave rested across her left shoulder, showcasing a shimmering black chandelier earring on her right ear. Both Maya and Gene looked like they wanted to be somewhere else.

Yes, Kim recalled every specific, right down to the piece of lint on the back of Justus Alexander's head. She was living the memory as it occurred and there was one detail she couldn't fill in.

"Have you seen Coda?" Kim asked, causing Gene to burst into booming laughter.

Kim placed her hands on her hips, tapping a finger on the dress's lace pattern like she had seen Shelley Long do in *Troop Beverly Hills*. Maya was a tad more physical, shoving Gene's shoulder.

"I'm sorry," Gene said, not meaning it in the least. "It's just—did he really think Sheena Thompson wanted to go with him?"

Brandon was laughing along with Gene.

"She said yes," Kim said, with an involuntary neck roll.

"He deserves it," Maya said. "He should've just taken—" Her eyes drifted to Kim and Brandon and she didn't finish her sentence.

Gene read her wrong. "What, you wanna dance? I mean, we can dance! Coda ain't the only one who can dance. I was just saying I don't *normally* dance."

Kim ignored the teenage titans, told Brandon that she'd be back, and set off across the dance floor. Everyone that she ran into, all of Coda's acquaintances and running buddies, had no knowledge of Coda's where-abouts.

She left the dance room, headed out into the hallways. The Ball was being held in a lovely facility on the beachfront and Kim had every reason to be enjoying herself, but she had that feeling in the pit of her stomach that prevented her from putting Coda and his troubles out of her mind. Most had seen him arrive, some had talked to him, but nobody had seen him recently.

She gathered the clues in her brain. Coda was annoyingly virtuous; he was a preacher's kid—of the well-behaved variety. He was young, at least a year younger than most of his classmates, due to a combo of an early start to school on the west coast and grade skipping further along the elementary years. He managed to become one of the most popular students at KWA despite or even because of his immaturity, but he still struggled to fit in. He didn't care about being liked; he wanted allegiance. He wanted to belong. Kim understood that somehow...in her way.

One of the cross-country guys had seen Coda heading out to the beach.

Kim ran. She picked up the layers of the dress and was out of the building and onto the patio. Off of the patio and down the stairs hoofing through the sand.

She spotted him lying at the shore, not moving.

She ran across the sand, not stopping to remove her heels.

Coda, she thought, *what have you done?*

And she was at his side. His olive-green eyes were open, focused on something she couldn't see, and he was mouthing words.

He appeared to be hugging himself when she reached him, but in fact he was cradling both of his arms. A broken shell, whittled to greater sharpness by sand and wind, lay on the ground near him. As Kim collapsed in the surf next to him and drew him close, she saw the gashes on his naked wrists, deeper than they should have been in order to reach his vessels.

The lacerations did not bleed. Through some horrid and blessed phenomenon, he couldn't take his own life.

"Oh, Lakota," Kim whispered, stroking his bright forehead. If only she had gone to the ball with him instead of Brandon. "You stupid, stupid boy."

And she tried to tell herself that it wasn't somehow her fault, but there was no one there to lie to her or unknowingly mislead her like they had years ago. Tears rose in her eyes, while the sand fell from her hands like flakes of paint.

• • • • •

She was running again, but not on the coastal shore. She wasn't sure of how she got there, nor her exact location. How she was able to run was not something she could register either, but the motion was familiar to her. Forward and back, forward and back, as if her arms were swinging and her feet were pounding. Forward and back, forward and back, so fast that her heart should have been battering her chest and sweat should have been streaming down her back. Instead, she continued with the suppositional motion, forward and back, forward and back.

She was in space. She was *somewhere* and she wasn't afraid.

The space wasn't empty, though. Around her, as common as shrubberies and street signs were interstellar terranes. She passed galaxies of every morphology, from the deep pools of the spiral to the waiting doors of the elliptical. With every few paces Kim outdistanced gigantic planets, beached beside her supernatural running path like powerful amethyst whales and dazzling cerulean shipwrecks. Planets with torrid atmospheres, beautiful rings and unrepeated shapes the likes of which Kim had never seen.

Clouds of purple dust drifted in the distance, containing bursts of orange and green fire. Elsewhere were oceans of white stars, washing upon a beach of crimson infinity. On some discreet subconscious plane, a deteriorating anchor to a remembered reality, she was amazed to the point of disbelief. Yet the greater part of her being, the ruling majority, was temperate, as if she belonged out there…as if this region of the macrocosm had been waiting on her.

"Hello, God," she said without speaking.

Hello, My delightful Dyna.

She continued running, taking in all that she could. Two galaxies were colliding to her left, creating a destruction of yellow and red.

There was music in this part of space. It was music unlike any earthly music, yet to designate it simply as "unearthly" was nothing short of demotion. It was an immaculate sound. It was another timbre of God's voice. It was asked through the notes and harmonies if she loved what she saw.

"It's divine, Dad. It's the most beautiful creation I've ever seen."

All of My creations are beautiful. All of my creations are divine.

"At this moment, my eyes are open to see."

Let your ears be open as well.

Kim listened as the music continued and she witnessed a birth of colors she had never seen straight ahead. It was beyond what she could take and, straightway, her being proceeded no further. Again, she understood the musical language of the Father.

You can keep running, the Music continued, *or you can go back.*

Kim sat, crossing her legs beneath her in the middle of space.

She looked down into a lavender-grey pool of heavenly bodies. The stars swam beneath her, waiting in arresting tranquility. She let her legs dangle into the celestial basin and the stars poked at her toes like curious guppies.

The submerged mind wondered if it were all possible. Kim wanted to be away from that part of her mind, to think clearly for the first time. She realized in those moments, grasping at the totality of her situation, that if she went back, that mindset would be the driving force of all of her decisions, that anchor would again be her entire world...

"You're giving me an option, Lord?"

And the Music spoke to her, telling her of the impending storms, pitfalls and pains that lay down one road, the road she was preferred to take. Along that path were threats that she did not have to face and heartaches that were not yet etched in stone.

Where you would lose your life, I will use your life.

Kim pondered these revelations for what felt like hours, letting the knowledge shower over her. Once she had done so, she turned her thoughts to moments in the past. She studied faces, meditated on plans and brooded over dreams. She thought of the hope in her mother's eyes and the joy in her father's. She thought of her brother's laughter and her sister's tears.

Then she thought of the scars on Coda's wrists and the wounds on Maya's heart and the possibilities that Kenji's eyes would never see and how their legacies were intertwined due to the decisions she had made. She knew what her decision was.

"You give me the strength, Lord," she said, "and I'll do it all for You."

When she stood, the lagoon of stars rose with her, striking her in the heels, soaring into the ligaments of her foot, scrabbling across her toes and racing to her ankles. The stars swirled through her calves, into her knees, exploding along her lower thighs. The luminous glitter raced through her entire body, flooding into her mind, and she knew that God had accepted her decision.

You made your choice today, Dyna, yet you have always been chosen.

The chords that followed produced a less complicated melody.
Wake up.

· · · · ·

Kim found herself at the wheel of her car as a paramedic pulled her from the twisted wreckage into the safety of a dangerous realm. Her pumps fell away from her feet and the world was real again, unsettlingly so. The events of the highway scurried back into her brain.

"How are you doing there?" the medic holding her asked, and she let the flashing lights of the ambulance and police vehicles wash over her vision.

Kim got used to the feel of her feet in the grass. She lost herself in the breeze on her skin, the touch of her clothes, the heaviness of the lids on her eyes. She looked to the medic who had just spoken. His eyes were warm. A welcoming gaze, as if he knew.

"I'm fine," she professed and indeed she was. Nothing hurt. Nothing hurt in the *slightest*. "Promise, INC." She began to walk and the medic guided her with a cautionary arm.

"Take it slow there, ma'am," the medic said, but Kim pulled away from the paramedic's grasp and stared up at the sky.

The return wasn't as triumphant as she'd hoped. The heavens seemed so flat and two dimensional from the ground. She was back to the world.

An officer approached her.

"Ma'am, are you hurt? Was there anyone in the vehicle with you?"

Kim gestured towards the medic, only to find no evidence that he was ever there. She glanced around, dismayed. She could have sworn...

"Do you need to sit down?" The officer beckoned to a different medic. A real one.

"I think so," Kim nodded. She no longer felt fine. She felt certifiably insane.

"Will I be able to call my dad?" she asked after a light medical inspection and a statement to the police that intentionally blurred out any supernatural activity. She glanced at the remains of her car and chuckled in spite of her situation. "I might need a ride."

· · · · ·

"You seem nervous."

"Anxiously excited. I understand if it looks nervous."

"But it matters what it looks like, Doc, because if you're about to stick a four-inch syringe into my triceps, I don't need you looking, seeming or being nervous."

The doctor sighed. His boss was watching this entire interaction on the other side of the glass with the rest of the team. He couldn't look incompetent at the beginning of such an important trial. He avoided glancing at them, continuing to cleanse the subject's arm with swab soaked in alcohol.

One type of alcohol made him think of another. "Are there no more graduation parties tonight?" the doctor asked, hoping to lighten the mood.

"Not for me," the teenager replied detachedly.

"Well, not for the next few days, either. You understand that we'll be keeping you under surveillance for the next 48 hours, don't you?"

"I signed it. So I understand it. And, Doc, I'd rather not rehash it."

The doctor reached for the syringe, trying to breathe evenly. The outcome of all of this would be worth the current stress and impudence.

"I mixed this myself," he said. "And I can tell you this: you're about to change the world with your efforts."

The young volunteer smiled for the first time. "You're brushing past the most important part, Doctor. I'm about to change *me*."

4.
Friends in Places

"Coda? Boy, why ain't you up?"

"Good morning, Dyna-na. What can I do for you today?" was the groggy reply.

"I'm serious, Lakota!" Kim stamped her foot on the marble kitchen tile in her home and placed a hand on her tiny hip. "It's eight o'clock in the morning! You get up at six!"

"*Sometimes* I get up at six," she heard Coda mumble.

"Shannon's pool party is today," Kim said, opening the refrigerator, "and I thought I was supposed to pick you up—Hey, *Papacita*, how it be?"

"Slick like fried chicken grease, you know how it be, eeee*asy!*" Kim's small father replied casually as he entered the kitchen with his briefcase and the day's newspaper. He placed a kiss on his daughter's forehead and turned his attentions to the empty stovetop. "What's the breakfast situation, *chicalita*?"

"Cinnamon Sprinkles," Kim replied, pulling a box of cereal from the refrigerator's roof and handing it to her father. She pulled a half-gone gallon of milk out of the refrigerator.

"But if you're not going, I'll just call Gene—" she said into the phone, turning to see her dad staring at her, a single furry eyebrow raised above his glasses.

"No, no, it's okay," Coda was saying. "I'm up; I'm up. Rise and shine... and all that good stuff."

"What is it, Dr. Hamilton?" Kim asked sweetly. She laughed lightly. "Why you looking at me like that flat-like; how it be, *Papaci*?"

"Wow," she heard Coda breathe into the phone. Coda always seemed enthralled with their backward jive exchanges, especially when nicknames were involved.

Her father calmly set the cereal box down on the counter and gestured for Kim to step out of his path.

"Kimberly," he muttered.

Oh, well. Kim concluded that the light-hearted mood was gone.

"You knew that this was your morning to cook," her father said, grabbing a package of eggs and handing them over to his equally short daughter. He turned around and looked at her. "Don't just stand there: get to scrambling. I'll cook the bacon and the grits and you toast some bread. This breakfast had better be ready by the time your mother gets in here."

Kim sighed. "Coda."

"Hmm?" droned Coda.

"So you went back to sleep," Kim accused. "Wake up!" she hollered, pulling a pan from beneath the counter. Her father was pulling some bacon out of the refrigerator. "Be dressed in your swimwear by ten, you hear me?"

"Sure thing," Coda murmured.

"I'm serious!" Kim squealed. She glanced at her father. "Well, lemme let you go. Be ready."

"I'm up, really. Bye."

"Bye, Coda."

Kim reached into the cabinet and pulled out a small mixing bowl.

"How do you feel?" Dr. Hamilton inquired, concern seeping through his expression.

Kim smiled lightly. "Alive." She reached for the eggs.

"Just checking," Dr. Hamilton murmured.

"Thanks, Dad." Kim knew that no scars were visible, but she could sense something there, left over from the accident...pulsating with unknown energies. Her hospital visit the night of graduation was so brief, the doctors hadn't even taken her temperature, let alone noticed any microscopic weirdness crawling across her skin.

"So where are you and Coda going today?" Kim's father asked, filling an empty pot with water.

Happy to place her mind elsewhere, Kim broke open a few eggs into the mixing bowl. "Shannon Crescitelli's throwing a celebration at his house, *Papacita*. And I've got to pick up Coda, since he still doesn't have his license, you know how it be."

"Why doesn't he have his license, yet?" Dr. Hamilton asked, lifting grits off of the baker's rack and purposely refusing to rejoin the silly repartee.

Kim poured some of the milk into the bowl. "He didn't get his learner's until late last summer, so he's still got a few months before he's eligible."

By the time the lovely Mrs. Hamilton entered the kitchen, Kim had set the small glass dining table with powder blue napkins and dishes. The bacon was freshly fried, the grits were soft and hot, the eggs were fluffy, and all was ready to be devoured.

"Good morning, Kimberly," Delia Hamilton greeted, fastening a small gold hoop to her right ear.

"'Sup, Ma?" Kim asked in a deep voice, rubbing her bare chin as if it was bearded. "You lookin' seeeeexy!"

Her mother gave her the same look she gave her most mornings, which meant that she did not intend to descend into useless banter.

"Lester, did you bring the package out of the room like I asked you to?" she asked.

Dr. Hamilton was in the process of scooping some grits onto his plate when he looked up at his wife. On cue, his stomach rumbled.

"I'll get it," Mrs. Hamilton sighed and she exited through a mahogany door into the miniature hallway that led to the master bedroom. When she reentered the kitchen, it was with a shimmering, snugly wrapped tiny package.

"Oh," Kim exclaimed. "What's that? Who's it for?"

"You," her mom replied.

"Ooo!" Kim squealed, prancing over to her mother, exchanging a hug for the package. She gave her dad a hug as well and plopped down across from him. It was a habit she had formed in middle school; she could keep watch of the digital clock on top of their large television in the living room and watch what was going on in the neighborhood outside. Mrs. Hamilton took a seat next to Kim and began making her plate.

Kim tore off the silver packaging. "What's this for?"

"Just a tiny graduation gift," Dr. Hamilton said, after swallowing a sip of orange juice.

"But you already got me so much—"

Kim held up blue plastic bracelets.

"Oh," she said. "Bracelets." She felt that if she had used 'jewelry' to describe the tawdry wristlets that she held so daintily in her hands, she would have sounded ungrateful. In retrospect, she probably sounded ungrateful anyway.

"These bracelets aren't expensive," Lester said.

"They're not?" Kim asked, amused.

"Neither are your dreams," Mrs. Hamilton hummed, as she sliced into the eggs with her fork. "We wanted to buy you something that represented your dreams."

Kim laughed. "Yeah, but my dreams are priceless and these bracelets probably cost fifty cents!"

"Kimberly," Mrs. Hamilton said with a tiny in-spite-of smile that defied her daughter's jest, as her husband chuckled, "when you wear these bracelets, we want you to wear them proudly. Like your dreams. *Some* people may not see their worth, but the important fact is that you do."

"*Mamacita*, *Papacita*, everyone can see their worth. Fifty cents!" She fell over laughing onto the empty seat.

"You'll understand," Mrs. Hamilton hummed. "You'll understand."

Kim giggled. "Your prom dress: too much money. Your cap and gown: too much money. Other graduation fees: Too much money. The fact that your parents bought you fifty-cent bracelets to commemorate the whole of these events: priceless."

"That's enough, Kim," Mrs. Hamilton said, but the laughing bug had bitten Lester as well, so he couldn't back her up. "I suppose you would have preferred another car."

"Maybe for my birthday," Kim replied. "These days I'm having a blast driving *Papacita's* Gigantor truck. Did you say your grace?" she finished accusingly.

Both of her parents paused to bow their heads, causing Kim to fall over laughing yet again. Once she sat back up, she attempted to admire her gift.

"You understand that this means that I have to change, now?" Kim inquired of her parents, slipping the jewelry over her hand.

Dr. Hamilton blinked, while Mrs. Hamilton poured her glass full with juice.

"You be changing anyway, *chicalita*, it be so," Dr. Hamilton spoke, nodding his head towards his daughter's tank and booty shorts.

"I'm going to a pool party, Dad," Kim giggled. "I won't be wearing much more than this."

"I remember now why I dislike the summertime," Lester Hamilton grumbled and this time it was his wife who caught the giggles.

· · · · ·

The Georgia summer arrived to Brunswick in full effect and it was only May. The hoggish sun attempted to swallow the earth in tasty pieces, starting with everything located within Glynn County. Those smart enough to escape the repast did so in the coolness of the frigid sea or the chill of air-conditioned residences. The tar and rock on the streets would boil and melt by mid-morning and would not cool again until at least ten in the evening.

Outwardly, Brunswick was a beautiful port city, shaped like a spinning top and holding more potential than most of its inhabitants realized. It was charted directly between the polluted river and the self-important islands that rested in the burnished Atlantic slightly off the south Georgia shore. Brunswick and the islands that bordered it (St. Simons, Sea, Jekyll, and Little St. Simons, collectively called "The Golden Isles") rested in the burnished Atlantic slightly off the south Georgia shore.

On the north end of the city, Justus Alexander was doing the chicken dance in the front yard of a large house, his black baseball cap gripped in his hand and his dusk-colored hair staying perfectly in place despite his manic energy.

Raven-haired Eden Enamorado approached him, laughing. She had just arrived herself and was swinging a collection of keys around her well-manicured right index finger.

"What are you doing, Justus?" Eden asked, a soft and mellifluous voice floating out of her fuchsia lips.

"This is how I pre-game, Eden," Justus responded with a wicked grin.

Eden managed to look elegant no matter her surroundings and she looked like a glamorous old-school Hollywood pin-up in her yellow bikini. Her raven-colored hair hung just above her shoulders, framing her cinnamon, upsettingly beautiful face, and her soft fingers pressed lightly into Justus's back as she gave him a sweet hug.

"Wasabi, Justus?" crowed Shannon Crescitelli, hopping down from the steps of his parents' house and squeezing Justus in a friend's embrace. He shared an awkward half-hug with Eden, reminding Justus that they had only been broken up for a few months.

His friend was dressed in short trunks and flip-flops, had a rather huge smile—too generous for his meager mouth—bigger ringlet-filled hair, and an even greater amount charisma. His home was of an equally impressive size. It consisted of two burgundy brick stories encased by a huge front lawn that housed scattered oaks dripping with grey Spanish moss. The grass was a bright and strong green that held an arresting contrast with the deep brown of the oak bark and the whiteness of the circular gravel driveway leading up to the front porch and back out to the street. The lawn was currently occupied by vehicles belonging to the many guests who could be heard over the wooden fence, which stretched out from both sides of the house.

Near Shannon's neighborhood, through the many southern pines that held out short bald branches for several feet above the ground before bursting into green harvest, sat Oakwood Community College, the four-decades-old university that most kids attended with the anticipation of transferring to another college after they felt comfortable enough to leave home, or until their GPAs were raised enough to be accepted to those other colleges. The eleven OCC edifices were set upon one hundred ninety-three acres of land that had previously housed some concrete factory that had been taken back by Mother Nature. Beyond the campus running track was a running dirt trail that led through the tangle of trees and greenery and unseen wildlife.

During cross-country days, Justus, Ezekiel, Coda, and Shannon had all gotten to know that trail well. It journeyed along outdoor circuit training stations, beside the high schools' joint football stadium and on towards the busy highway that sent cars south into the hub of the city, past the college and the rich neighborhoods of the marsh. The path then curled around a large, blackish-blue lake, ridden with mosquitoes and frogs, where swimming and fishing were forbidden.

The cross-country boys came to the conclusion that after the rain, the lakeside portion was dangerous. The mud became muddier, the mosquitoes were worse and everyone came back with bitten, black-streaked calves and muck-soaked socks and shoes. Shannon, as team captain and thus leader of the run-line, had endured hell once they reached the locker room back at the high school and got out of the coach's realm of protection.

In the front yard of Shannon's house, Justus listened to the sounds of splashing liquid coming from the backyard, raising straw and berry brows. "Dude, is this a pool party? I didn't bring my swimsuit!"

Shannon paused, lips twitching. "Don't tell me you didn't know!"

Justus cracked a grin, giving himself away. "Guess I'll just have to swim naked."

"Ooh, promise?" Shannen asked.

"While the two of you invent endless ways to be homoerotic," Eden interrupted, "I'm gonna head to the pool."

"I mean, you can join us," Shannon said, racing after her, and Justus followed.

• • • • •

"Girls are God's greatest gift to man," Rico said, stretching from his position lying across a bench on Shannon's screened-in back porch, his head in BJ's lap.

"Why can't man be the gift to *women*?" she pointedly asked, gliding her hands over Rico's scalp.

"Because we were made first," Rico replied, stroking her elbows with his thin fingers.

"Women and men are the same species, so wouldn't they just be gifts to each other?" Bethany said, dripping wet as she walked by, headed to the table across the porch that was piled high with food.

Shannon had invited hordes of their former classmates to this soiree, from his senior class friends to members of the soccer and football teams no matter the grade. There were people outside in the pool fighting off horseflies, in the grass tossing Frisbees and kicking soccer balls, on the wooden swing set near the back fence, and inside the porch's screens. Behind the screens they were mostly dry—eating, talking, goofily playing ping-pong, and reveling throughout games of table soccer. Kim, Coda, Shannon, and Bethany were among the few preparing plates of food. The parents were inside the house, chatting with Mrs. Crescitelli and her daughters.

"God must have a messed up sense of humor to give humans to humans as a gift," Eden responded from her place playing Justus in table soccer. "I want a receipt."

"Goal!" Justus screamed, sporting the ocean blue swimming trunks that he had been wearing underneath his khaki shorts. "*Oh* yeah!"

"Tell me about it," Kim said while piling chips on her plate with her slender hands.

Coda sat on a cooler across from Rico and BJ. He pushed his drooping Afro out of his face, and bit into his hot dog.

"Shannon, these hot dogs are delicious!" Coda said, covering his mouth as he attempted to swallow. "Are they all beef or something?"

"One hundred percent beef," Justus suggested, body wriggling with each twist and pull he made at the foosball table. "Just like Shannon."

"Thank you," Shannon grinned, flexing his arms playfully. Though he wasn't the most handsome guy that had attended Wilbanks Academy, he was quite muscular, with the body of a gymnast. He had frequently teased Coda's thinness until the day Coda pointed to Shannon's face, retorting, "Muscles come and go, but ugly is forever."

Some other soccer player punched Shannon in the gut, and they began a quick round of tag around the food.

"Watch it, boys," Bethany warned them, stepping out of their warpath.

"Did you say your grace?" Kim asked Coda, primly sitting down next to BJ.

As Coda bowed his head, Rico stared at the wristbands that never seemed to leave his friend's wrists, covering the telling scars. Coda had never mentioned it, and so far Rico had no proof, but most people were convinced the rumors were true and that the Cheshire Cheetah had attempted suicide at the Black and Gold Ball.

Turning his head to Kim, he asked, "Where's Maya?"

"Goal!" laughed Eden, shaking her hair out of her face.

As Rico jerked his attentions to the foosball table, Kim let his comment fade and took a bite out of her hamburger. BJ glanced at her.

"Did you say *your* grace?"

Kim smacked her thigh in annoyance; sparkly blue bracelets jangled around her wrist. "Oh, darn."

"I always forget to say my grace," Rico said, all but purring as BJ stroked his head.

"I try not to," Coda said. "Forget, I mean. When you think of all that Jesus did, the fact that he still takes time out to feed me… It's the least I can do!"

"Sounds like you're giving an appeal for an offering," Bethany said, heading back outside to the pool with a plate barely even garnished with food.

"It's an offering of thanks," Coda said.

"I wonder if Adam thanked God for Eve after the fruit incident," mused BJ. "If he was still appreciative of the 'gift.'"

Eden scored again, saying, "Well, Adam ate, too."

"In fact, isn't that what changed the world?" Kim said, done with her prayer and sipping on her soda. "When she ate, nothing happened. After he ate, they realized that they were naked."

"I still don't see how that was a bad thing," Rico chuckled.

"This conversation is ricockulous," Shannon belched. "Nature is a blessing and a curse. It's balance. Besides, all this God talk is ruining my party."

Rico reached to stroke BJ's hair.

BJ grimaced. "Your hands are really warm."

"Really?" Rico put them to his face.

"Yeah."

Rico grinned. "I'd better go chill out in the pool. I'm too hot for you, huh?"

· · · · ·

"So is this Shannon's graduation party or his birthday party?" Coda asked Justus, drifting next to the deck in the deep end of the Cresitelli's gigantic pool. Justus tread water nearby.

"Graduation," was his answer.

"O.K." Coda was saying, as Justus said, "Maybe birthday."

"I think it's graduation," offered Kim, doing a lazy backstroke.

"Maybe it's both," BJ laughed nearby.

"Did anybody look at the cake?" Kim asked. She looked at BJ, Justus, Coda, and their united blank faces and came to a conclusion. "Guess not."

"Either way, the Italian Stallion knows how to throw a good one," Justus stated.

"Did you notice our swimsuits matched?" Coda asked enthusiastically, as Kim groaned. True, his shorts and her bikini had the same color pattern, but—

"Yeah, but he doesn't have to announce it like we planned it," Kim said, exasperated. She felt that every so often Coda laid himself on too thick.

"Where's Maya?" BJ asked, referring to the third musketeer. Before Kim or Coda could grumble a response, a Frisbee knocked Coda upside the head.

"Rico!" Coda yelled, as he gripped the deck and pulled himself along the side of the pool towards his grinning friend standing half-submerged at the shallow end of the pool. BJ followed, swimming beneath the surface, leaving Justus and Kim looking on.

"Rico and BJ: are they like an official couple?" Kim asked.

Justus smiled. "Intermittently."

Kim sighed and submerged herself under the water. The conversations at this party were only killing her. She wished she had Maya to talk to, but Maya was increasingly busy with her boy-toy Gene, as she had been for the majority of the spring. Kim and Coda were definitely taking the slight personal. This was the summer of friendship, not of ill-fated romance. When would they have this summer back?

She surfaced, floating on her back, face to face with Justus.

"Whoa!" Justus started.

Kim struggled to make sense of the fact that while she did not see Justus's body, which should have been there under the water, she saw just his head and shoulders that were above the water. She didn't even see his blue trunks.

"Justus," she was trying to stay calm, "you—"

Justus looked to where she was pointing and Kim watched in horror as every inch of him morphed into a glassy, transparent fluid, at first holding the shape of his body and then slowly becoming a part of the surrounding pool water.

Kim swam away as fast as she could, turning away from him as he became a melting pillar of water. In her fear, she slammed against the side of the pool, not even realizing that the force of her impact had left a dent in the concrete.

"Kim!" came Justus's nervous and rather disembodied voice.

She couldn't scream in time, as the water beneath her shifted and she dropped into the deep end.

5.

Games People Play

Kim attempted to slow her heart's speed on the patio, arresting her thoughts until her world seemed standard. When several minutes had passed and that still had not worked, she turned her attention to something louder and on the exterior.

The boys were in the front yard playing some type of one-upmanship soccer, the only sport that Coda was even decent at, but out in the front yard with Benny, Shannon and Rico, among others, the young one wasn't having much luck.

Kim on the front porch near Bethany Kelly, who was exchanging clipped words with Hanley Powell from a white wooden rocker.

"Why don't you ask Coda?" Bethany was asking.

Hanley's smile never seemed to go away. Neither did she. "He's in the zone, Bethany," she said in her country, condescending voice. "I'm not going to interrupt his game."

BJ cackled nearby. "What game?"

"Give him a break," Eden laughed, looking up from her Joseph Heller novel. "He's the only one out there who didn't play for the school."

"Thank God," BJ said, and the girls on the porch all cracked up.

Hanley turned her attention to Kim, who was serene with Eden in a swing seat.

"Kim, do you know when Coda is having that party?"

Kim pretended she hadn't been listening to everything that preceded. "Hmm? What party?"

Hanley sighed. "I'll just ask him after the game."

Bethany looked ready to choke her.

After Hanley bounced away, Bethany sneered, "Didn't I tell her to ask him in the first place?"

Kim shrugged.

"I don't know how Coda puts up with her," Eden muttered, adjusting her sarong.

"Haha, 'cause they're both weird," Bethany snorted.

Coda was doing a rebel yell/dance combination after blocking one of Benny's kicks, morphing it into a rainbow move, and scoring a goal. As he lost himself in celebratory booty shaking, his giant, unbraided hair was flopping all across his head.

"That was mean," Kim said softly, in reply to Bethany.

BJ chuckled from her position folded into herself on the steps. "But it's true."

Kim just shrugged and Eden turned a page in her book.

"Look *at* Lakota," Kim commented. Rico had enough of Coda's goofballing, tackling him. They rolled in the grass, all bony limbs and shrieks. "His hair is longer than mine!"

"That's one way for him to dry it out," Bethany laughed, fingering her own wet locks.

"So in his element, the strange child," Eden said, looking up from her book.

After a pause, BJ spoke. "He's gonna hate college."

"Mmm hmm," the four girls said.

• • • • •

"How can anybody get this much pleasure from this one game?" Shannon laughed, slamming another goal.

The left side of Ezekiel's mouth twisted up into a grin, his lips full and pink. When playing against Shannon, one had to resign themselves to the fact that the only thing bigger than the boy's ego was his competitive streak…and maybe his hair. Ezekiel wiped the sweat from his brow and prepared his attack on Shannon once again.

Shen Long Ezekiel Yang, being Hong Kong born, filled the final racial demographic in this peculiarly eclectic group of buddies. He was taller than Kim, but he was shorter than all of the guys there, certainly Coda and Benny. He worked out to stay healthy, not for any narcissistic means, and Kim noticed that it was certainly paying off. His theories, though—proven or not—were questionable in her eyes. Even Justus, for instance, told Kim that he refused to believe that in order to keep one's spine healthy, one should sleep on a bed that was as unyielding as the stony pallet Ezekiel snoozed on.

The group had set Ezekiel on a pedestal and, though Kim had realized this long ago, he himself didn't seem to grasp the fact. The majority of them were in the same advanced courses and had GPAs just as good as his and Justus—and Coda could possibly battle him IQ point for IQ point—, but Ezekiel pulled an advantage due to his quick wit and mischievous brain, which was just another disguise for his adventurous search for knowledge. Kim, from her position on the outer cusp of the lot, liked him.

Kim was perhaps the gang's older sister to Ezekiel's older brother. For some reason—at times she genuinely didn't get why—everyone expected marvelous things from her. She had a knack for getting everyone to root for her, but she didn't know how to intentionally round up support. If she had, she would have had a much easier time enjoying high school. She always felt like she was lacking in many departments, regardless of the fact that she was Miss Wilbanks and had also made Homecoming Court (as if that meant anything in the long run). Maybe it was that the girl who had achieved all of these things was one piece of who she actually was. Maybe she wasn't wholly presented.

"Kiss me on me lips, matey; I'm winning!" Shannon was bellowing now to no one in particular.

Kimberly was glad that Shannon was applying his voracious antagonism to such a middle of the road game as foosball. Just the month before, Ezekiel had gotten into an impromptu wrestling match with their sporty friend that left him with an inch-long scar on his shin. He had shown the fresh wound to Kim, who had promptly vomited.

"Shouldn't you be calling your girlfriend sometime soon?" Shannon taunted, raising his score another point.

"Vanessa?" Ezekiel asked, brown eyes gleaming.

"No, don't call her, yet," the curly-haired jester decided. "I want to beat you fair and square, which will happen in about five more seconds." He smiled as widely as he could.

"Ezekiel!" Justus hollered, entering the porch from outside, still drying off from the pool. The salutation broke Ezekiel's concentration and Kim watched as Shannon used the opportunity to score another goal. She was determined to treat Justus as if nothing atypical had occurred.

"'Sabi, Justus?" Ezekiel asked, slapping hands with the blond.

"Is there a word for a two-time loser?" Shannon was asking in his swollen tenor. "Like a twoser?"

Ezekiel laughed, turning back to the game. "Just shut up and play," he advised his friend with a wink.

"I know, Ezekiel!" Kim agreed. "You're being so ostentatious, Shannon-baby!"

Ezekiel chortled, as Shannon repeated, "Ostentatious?"

Kim saw Justus appraising her, but she chose not to make eye contact.

Ezekiel scored a goal and chortled all the more, while Shannon cheerfully complained that Kim was working with Ezekiel to divert his attention.

Ezekiel looked at Kim and grinned his lopsided grin.

"Sure, okay," he laughed. "Blame it on her."

Suddenly a little ball of black fur shot between Kim's legs, heading straight towards Justus.

Mrs. Crescitelli, squat and podgy, stuck her head out of the hallway's entry.

"Did the puppy come this way, Shannon?" she asked. "He just ran out of the kitchen."

"Close the door!" Shannon ordered to Justus, motioning wildly. "He's going outside!"

"He who?" Justus asked nervously, while backing away from the approaching pup with fear stretching wide in his eyes. Once his mind registered the situation, he quickly ripped into a piercing scream and took off out into the busy backyard.

"Justus's afraid of dogs," Shannon suddenly remembered, smacking his head and taking off after both the dog and Justus.

"That was a dog?" Ezekiel asked, and Shannon motioned to them hurriedly.

"Help me catch the dog," he said. "We just got him, so Ma doesn't like him outside. And we don't need Justus throwing a fit on top of the one my ma will!"

"Too late," Kim remarked, as she followed along with Ezekiel.

When they exited the patio and set foot on the grass, Justus had already rounded the entire yard and the included pool, screaming at the peak of his range and waving his arms as if scaring away invisible monsters.

"It's a puppy, Justus!" Kim was yelling in hopes of calming him down. "It's just a puppy!"

"There's too much screaming going on at this party," BJ commented, while Rico looked on in amazement for a second time that day.

Justus raced back inside and the puppy, having forgotten that he hadn't even been chasing after Justus in the first place, attempted to follow. In the process the pup sideswiped Shannon, galloped between Ezekiel's legs and tripped Kim. He was continuing on his unobstructed path until Coda managed to nab him, virtually appearing from nowhere.

"I've got him!" he announced proudly, cradling the tiny dog against his shoulder.

It was too late, however. Justus had escaped through the interior entryway and its adjoining hallway, retreating into the crowded kitchen with all of the adults where he maintained a silent protest to his own shame by refusing to rejoin the party.

Shannon grabbed the dog from Coda and passed it along to one of his brothers.

"Justus," Coda called through the kitchen door, laughing. "All's clear!"

Shannon leaned into the door. "Justus, the puppy is upstairs! Taylor's locking him in the bathroom!"

"He's not lying, Justus," Kim said, leaning against the doorpost.

The door opened and the three Crescitelli daughters leaned out, giggling. "He says he's not coming out."

"Oh, Justus, there's nothing to be afraid of," Kim said kindly.

Coda was doubled over, gasping for air.

Shannon leaned into the kitchen. "She's right, Justus. The pup's gone. Away."

Justus leaned out of the door, surveying the hallway.

"Really?" he asked.

Coda collapsed onto the wooden floor in hysterics and Shannon gave him a dirty look.

"Really," Kim said to Justus.

"That's not funny," Justus addressed to Coda, who laughed all the harder, tears puddling on the floor. Justus smiled in spite of himself, stepping into the hallway with his hands in his pockets and his eyes carefully monitoring the surroundings for anything that fluttered.

Kim bit back her own laughter, kicking at Coda with her foot.

"Did—did—you hear him—scream?" Coda managed.

Justus exited back out of the hallway into the merriment. A gaggle of mature voices rose once more in the kitchen, now that the excitement had passed.

· · · · ·

The sky was too black to be empty. God was there. Kim felt Him; He must be there. She stood still beside her father's truck, allowing the revelation to pound the surf within her before she ultimately remembered how far away the sky was and turned her attentions back to things she could reach.

As a few stars peeked around the opaque, yet imperceptible nighttime clouds, Kim wrapped her skateboard in layers of towels, burying it behind the seats in the gigantic red truck. It was almost an afterthought now. All the sneaking. Once upon a time, Kim never would have done such a thing. Now it was a necessity. Ensuring the skateboard was hidden, she closed the doors and locked the truck.

She missed her car, which was now probably the size of a basketball at some impounding facility. Her father's truck had rules and she was home now because of them. He liked seeing the truck in the driveway before he went to bed.

The Hamilton home was a nice size. The house was a beautiful colonial-style home, built out in the county in the midst of a secluded neighborhood of similar, yet sold-separately houses. Some of the homes displayed seashell exteriors and some homes were two stories high. Some were boringly symmetrical while others were borderline psychotic when it came to the appearance of equilibrium.

The neighborhood circled a surprisingly blue man-made lake where ducks and geese nested and swam during the day. On certain days, Kim would spot one of her faceless neighbors contentedly sailing out in the midst of the large waters and wish that her parents were into boating. Or wish that at least one more Black family lived in the neighborhood.

On this night, as she stared out over the waters, her eyes were brought up to a lit window in house across the street. The illumination through the window came from flashlights, Kim realized. It was the bedroom of her neighbors' little girls, probably a summer sleepover, with loads of magazines and scary stories to keep them up for a few hours. It was far past the seven year olds' bedtime. The hour was so late that even Kim's eyes were content to close. Kim marveled at such direct disobedience to rules.

Then she thought back on a night, forgotten and buried like her skateboard by years of deliberate oversight, and her stomach gripped into knots. She looked away from the window, gripping her fingers into fists to ignore the sensation.

She wanted ice cream. Strawberry mint.

When she entered the house, she was surprised to see lights on in her intended direction.

"*Hola, Papacita y mi madre,*" she bubbled to her parents as she entered the kitchen.

Her father was sitting at their tiny round glass table, reading from a stack of papers that were probably from the office. Honey-skinned Delia was standing at the counter, peeling and slicing some apples.

"Kimberly." Mrs. Hamilton began peeling a new apple. "I'm glad you're home. I wanted to talk to you."

"Mmm," Kim gurgled.

She glanced up at the clock on the wall. Wow, it was ten-thirty.

She took in the contents overcrowding the kitchen counter.

"So we're making apple pie in the middle of the night, now?" She took an apple slice and sat at the table next to her father. "How did this happen? I must know."

"You know your mother," is all she got from behind the newspaper.

Kim took a bite out of the stolen slice, managing to inhale deeply while she chewed. She was as ready as she could be for whatever it was that her mother had ready for her.

"Mmm, so what do you want to talk to me about, Mrs. Hamilton?"

"I want to talk to you about dancing," her mother said with deceitful tranquility.

Kim waited. "Er, dancing?"

"Yes. The foxtrot, the salsa and the butterfly."

"Mom, what are you talking about?" Kim laughed. "And what do you know about the butterfly?" Kim took another bite.

"I know plenty about the butterfly," Mrs. Hamilton professed. "I was quite the disco diva when I was your age. No parking on the dance floor and all that!" Her head started to swing as she forgot where she was. "Child, I didn't come home until my makeup was on my bra and my wig was in my purse!"

Kim almost choked. "Mom!"

Lester was doing a great job of pretending he wasn't listening. Kim should've been so lucky.

"Girl, you're getting me all off topic," the elder lady Hamilton said, suddenly dignified. "Jesus keep me near the cross."

Kim shook her head. Her mom was ridiculous. She half expected her to start humming the hymn.

Delia continued. "Now, when you go off to college, there are going to be many kids who like to dance. And there are a couple of things I want you to consider before you step onto *those* dance floors."

It began to register with Kim. "So you want to have 'a talk.'" Did her mother really feel like she needed to have this conversation with her soon to be eighteen-year-old daughter? And right now?

Her mother chuckled, slicing away. "Kimberly, the foxtrot is a rather complicated dance. If you dance it at weddings and parties, all is well. When there's a good reason. A function…you know."

Kim groaned internally. "See, you're enjoying this," she accused her mother. "Make it stop!" She turned to her dad with an already-tired smile. "*Papacita*, make it stop!"

"But if you begin to dance the foxtrot just because your friends are and you find yourself dancing more than you'd like—"

"I won't become an alcoholic, Mom," Kim assured the female elder Hamilton.

"It's not just alcoholism," Mrs. Hamilton pressed. "It's drunkenness. That's the sin, and it comes long before dependency."

"I'll bear that in mind," Kim said, minding her tone.

"Mind your tone," her father spoke up.

"Yes, Daddy," Kim murmured.

"Now the salsa," Mrs. Hamilton began.

"Mom!"

"The salsa is a dance that I don't recommend. The dance is easy to learn, but it can exhaust your resources a lot quicker than the foxtrot."

"Drugs, *Mamacita?*"

"You have people out there who sell lessons on how to dance the salsa, that's how popular it is."

"Drugs," she was sure.

"Don't dance the salsa. Your body is God's temple—"

"I won't do drugs. Or try drugs. Or hang out with kids that sell lessons on how to dance the salsa. I won't even buy salsa for my chips; I'll use cheese dip. Or the spinach stuff."

"Mind your tone, Kimberly," her father cautioned.

"Sorry, Dad. Sorry, Mom."

"Now that darned butterfly."

Delivery, INC, she thought, *what can this one be?*

"I'm glad that you've made it this far without doing that dance, considering so many kids your age have already danced it more than once."

"Oh, dear," Kim purred.

"Now, many teenagers your age know the steps to the butterfly. Parents tell you about the steps so that you don't dance it by accident."

Kim's father was snickering.

Mrs. Hamilton steadfastly continued. "Now, when you go off to college, even more people your age will be dancing the butterfly. I don't want my baby girl—"

"I may know all of the steps, Mom, but that doesn't mean that I'll dance."

"Oh, trust me," Mrs. Hamilton corrected. "If you know the steps and you like the music, you'll dance. And for once, I'd like to finish my thought before you try to straighten me out, okay?"

"Mind your tone, dear," Kim's father stated.

Mrs. Hamilton threw an apple slice at him.

"Kim, if you do decide to dance the butterfly," Mrs. Hamilton began.

"Use a butterfly net," Kim and her mother finished in unison.

"Got it," Kim said, picking up the tossed slice from the center of the table and adding it to her expanding collection.

She sauntered over to a cabinet full of porcelain figurines of winged creatures that looked remarkably like Denzel Washington and many popular songstresses. Secretly, she had dubbed it the cherubim cabinet, since she had been taught that cherubim were the creatures of God that had two wings.

Staring at one braided Alicia Keys look-alike, she commented, "I want my hair done when I head off to college. I mean a fresh job. I was thinking about micros." She placed an apple slice to her lips and nibbled thoughtfully. "Like Surly's in her wedding picture."

Kim's moody older sister's family, including three juvenile juvenile delinquents, thankfully all lived in Cincinnati. Far, far away. Like she was going. Far, far away from conversations about the foxtrot and the butterfly and all other abominations.

She sat down at the table adjacent to her father, her eyes drawn to a paperback lying next to his mug. He drank everything out of that mug, whether it was his nightcap of warm milk and honey, as it was currently, or his afternoon glass of tomato juice. He didn't even like coffee or anything caffeinated, and assuredly his affinity for the cup was due entirely to Kim and her siblings, who had presented the gift to him about seven old-man-birthdays ago.

Kim slid the book across the glass tabletop to take a closer look.

"Do you want to go see that new Katori Brown flick?" her father was currently asking her mother. "The reviews are saying it's not half bad. And we haven't caught a movie at the theatre since that last Fresh Prince one."

"Lester, she's co-starring with that singer-girl, Lena Park. Totally slumming."

Kim would have laughed if she had been paying closer attention. Her parents talked like they were her age sometimes, hilariously hip with the times, though Delia had this strange determination to call every female songstress "singer-girl." And her father constantly referred to Will Smith as "Fresh Prince." Kim wasn't sure he knew the man's real name.

"You've got to hit the mainstream to get closer to Oscar," Lester said. "I'm sure it was just a business decision."

"Is this yours?" Kim asked, holding up the book.

Both of her parents looked in her direction.

"That's a book your brother let me borrow, Dyna-*mita*," her father replied. "It's a very interesting read so far. I think it was on a recommended reading list at his seminary."

Kim looked at the cover again. *The Days of Awakening* by James "Jimmie" Stone. "*This* is recommended reading at Bible school? I figured they'd be sticking to just one book, if you know what I mean."

"Anything's better than *Gatsby*, right?" her father asked, and memories of Mr. Georgeson and his "Christ symbolism" lectures rushed right back into her cranium.

She looked up at her mother hopefully. "You don't think college professors believe in 'Christ symbolism,' do ya?"

"It was a different time when I went to college," her mom replied.

"Oh, that's right, they had just invented books, huh?" Kim quipped.

"You're not funny," Delia said, though her husband's laughter disproved the statement.

Kim stared at the drapes covering the window. "I'm gonna miss that lake. This house."

Delia paused with her food preparation, mind traveling further than Kim's had.

"Your brother used to hate this house. He had some difficult times here. We all did." Her eyes glazed over and she went back to the apples. "Then things happen—like what happened to Carolyn Carter and poor Kenji—and life gains perspective again."

Ignoring her mother's bunny trail, Kim made herself busy inspecting the jacket of the paperback in front of her.

We live in a world with a God who seems far less accessible than He was in the days of biblical heroes such as Moses and Elijah. Miracles were commonplace and humans achieved greatness found feasible only in historical mythologies and modern comic books. But are miracles truly so rare these days? Can humans achieve anything beyond what we've been told is plausible and

scientifically possible? And what does the possible onset of a modern era of miracles imply for Christians and our contemporary world?

Dr. Jimmie Stone takes a deep look at the history of believers and opens the controversial discussion on...*The Days of Awakening.*

"Hmm," Kim murmured, remembering the craziness in Shannon's pool. She pushed the book back across the table. "Interesting."

Lester looked up from his stack of papers. "Would you like to borrow it for the evening? I'm not sure I'll get back to it before I get back to my pillow."

Kim rose from the table, glancing towards her mother. "No, that's okay. I've got some 'dance' manuals to brush up on. Gonna take up a lot of my time." Before her mother could chastise her, she quickly followed up with, "Don't stress, Delia Louise. I'm in God's hands."

Delia made a noncommittal noise, placing the apple slices in a bowl. "It's your hands that worry me, Kimberly Dyna."

Kim glanced down at her hands, feeling the invisible energy flowing through her tendons. "Those are fine, too," she said, hoping she wasn't lying.

6.
Twilight Zoning

The summer was in full swing, which was apparent because people were already getting bored. All of the Glynn County kids were tiring with the beaches. Some were sick of getting sunburned and some were sick of vacuuming the sand out of their cars. Some of the boys on St. Simons Island—or 'The Island,' as many referred to it—had driven golf carts around their neighborhoods enough to swerve and crash in their sleep. The girls had already bought all of their school clothes and had the first four weeks prepared and hanging in their closets. The hurricane season was looming and some hoped for some weather action to spruce up day after day of moist heat and monotony.

There was nothing to do during the Glynn County summer. That was the biggest complaint. Once you were a ninth grader you stopped going to the skating rink, though no one truly knew why. Senior year, you journeyed to Rocky's Rollerway maybe four times a year and there had better be a good excuse at least two of those times. The littered parks— full of gnats instead of people—were jokes, the mall closed earlier than necessary, and there were no teen clubs. That caused much of the unrest among Glynn County's underage residents. That's why there were so many parties. And so much drinking. And so many STDs.

Kim spent her days cleaning the house and tinkling her mother's piano keys. Her spirit was unsettled and she didn't know why. It's as if her soul itched for more. And the main reason she was unsettled is because she remembered the choice she had made the night of her graduation… and she speculated if that's what her soul craved: the chance for discipleship. She despairingly wondered if she could be ready when the opportunity came.

She had run into Shannon Crescitelli once at the beach on The Island. She didn't go often; mostly it was the white kids that went religiously to the seaside and it's not like she needed to get darker anyway. She had been invited—surprisingly—to swim with Maya and when she got there, the first person she saw was goofy-grinning Shannon with his delicious mop of curls. He made several comments that were just lustful enough for Kim to be turned off but not vulgar enough for her to be offended and she just shook her head in polite declination. She had sworn off high school relationships and Shannon, aside from being…uh, Shannon, was simply too close to high school for Kim to even consider having a relationship with him. Too bad Wayne Emerson and his dimples were still in high school. And too bad three of his girlfriends were showing.

The summer nights were hot and relatively starless. Rico, Coda and Shannon had gone out together one night and hopped a couple of high-class fences to sit in some secluded hot tubs. They conversed about life and women and told stories until the sun blinked over the ocean. Coda was thoroughly unimpressed with the stories Shannon told about his summer flings, but he endured them because he was pleased with their blooming friendship. Rico tended to talk about BJ a lot and neither Shannon nor Coda stopped to consider that perhaps it was because Rico had nothing else to talk about. Rico didn't want to talk about the silent warfare at his home, so BJ was the next best thing. He didn't want to focus too much on his looming years at school, because he'd have the next four years to think about that. Coda didn't have much to discuss either. He hated his job, he wasn't too excited about going to school, and winter was his favorite season of the year. To avoid being a pessimist, he let Shannon and Rico do most of the talking.

The G8 summit came and went without most people in the county even caring it was there. The mall had been shut down one day so that the First Lady could shop alone. That was fine: everyone was tired of the mall already. The international dignitaries had come and gone without much of a hitch and the Brunswick library now proudly displayed a picture of the summit walking down a Jekyll Island beach.

It was on that very island that Justus was found leaning against the outside wall of Tanner's Eatery inside of the Summer Falls Water Park, slowly draining the tea machines. It was a deceitfully coldish and serene morning on the island's marshy coast and Tanner himself had instructed Justus to clean up the outside area of the restaurant while it was still peaceful and not yet unbearably hot. The later scene would be bratty rugrats taking the wrong sandwiches and older, sweatier and chunkier bodies engaged in conspiratorial tones about the whereabouts of extra ketchup and mayo packets.

Justus yawned and scratched his side, then brushed a strand of fire-tinted blond hair out of his left eye. The previous night had not treated him well, sleep wise. After leaving another party in the long line of graduate parties, he had dreamt an odd dream. Being brought out of his slumber by his nocturnal visions, he found that he couldn't return to the other side of consciousness, so he had called Coda to pass the time, as was customary. Coda had late nights due to his restaurant job. Despite the long conversation that had ensued, Justus decided against mentioning his dream. It was as if a mere mention would breathe life into it and the dream would then become an actual moment in time. In his sleep it was real enough and he was not making plans to grant flesh to the bone.

"Justus," called an alto voice from behind him, snapping him back into the present. He laid his eyes upon a gorgeous beauty in a red bathing suit.

"Lifeguarding again this year, Maya?" Justus asked, with a smile that raised his cheekbones by a few centimeters. He lifted up his black cap to get a better view.

"Yup," nodded the stacked girl, twisting around for a moment to inspect the unwelcome tan lines that came with her guard duty.

Maya had chocolate-brown skin and waist-reaching golden-brown braids that thankfully erased all memory of her naturally nappy locks. She was built with extra humanity in every single area and Justus had to remind himself to look into her eyes. Her arms alone were more muscular than his entire body was and when she gave him a one-armed hug, her brown eyes glinted with delight as he whimpered from the power she had displayed with them.

"Weakling," Maya giggled.

"Yeah," he agreed remorsefully, while striking a mock bodybuilder pose. He felt pale standing next to her. His skin was a pale peach anyway, though he had a tendency to tan pink, so standing next to a collector's piece like Maya made him feel quite white.

"Long time no see," he smiled at her. "Missed you at all of the parties."

"Yeah, well, I'm a working woman," she muttered, looking away across the park.

"A sexy working woman," he joked, bothered by her sudden solemnity. "Well, it's working season again. Here at the park, at least."

"When summer rises, Summer Falls," quipped Maya with a smile, leaning her head to one side, letting her ponytail of braids brush against the slender slope of her shoulders.

Justus brought his eyes back up to her face, agreeing, "Always." He still spoke with a trace of the speech impediment that he had attended speech classes for in elementary school. His s's were rather strong and tended to linger on the ends of his words. When they were sophomores, Ezekiel Yang had brought this up nonchalantly in Latin class and Justus sat in his bathroom for hours that night, revisiting old elocution drills.

"You're draining the tea?" she asked, attempting to make conversation.

"It's an important job," he laughed, feeling defensive.

She laughed, too. "So you must be the chief tea drainer," she grinned.

"Yes," he nodded, astutely. "*The* chief tea drainer. In fact, I should go in and crack some skulls because someone was supposed to empty this yesterday when they closed shop."

Was this conversation actually heading anywhere or was Maya just bored? He humored her. He gestured to the front window of Tanner's. "What'd you get?"

"Um…" She held up her white bag. "A muffin."

"The best Summer Falls breakfast," Justus smiled. The side door of Tanner's opened and Bethany Kelly leaned out.

"Hey, Maya," Bethany smiled toothily, catching sight of the former cheerleader.

"Hi, Bethany," Maya smiled back, just as large and just as fake.

"How are you?"

"I'm good," Maya cheesed, her eyes whispering towards Justus in that universal bond most of the graduates shared when faced with Bethany: disguised dislike.

"And everyone's favorite speech mistress, Kim?"

A look passed across Maya's face, just slow enough for Justus to notice, before the plastic smile was back. "It's been a busy couple of days, I haven't seen her since the party you threw for Shannon."

"Oh, I'm sure she'll be at the Rollerway," Bethany said dismissively. She turned to Justus. "Speaking of which, ummm, Justus, baby, if we're gonna make it to Rico's party, we need to be leaving now. First customer comes through that gate and you'll be locked in for hours, you know that. Nice to see you, Maya." She brightly tossed her auburn hair and disappeared inside the restaurant.

Maya made a face, pulling her muffin out of the bag.

Justus glanced up into Maya's eyes apologetically.

"Go," she motioned. "I just came for my muffin." She bit into it, turning to go. "See you at the Rollerway tonight."

"Oh, you're coming?" he asked.

"I can't miss *all* the parties," she chuckled, heading off into the rainbow field of beach chairs.

"You're still sexy, Muffin-eater," he called after her.

Maya half-turned, grinning.

"That's disgusting."

As Justus attempted to stammer an apology for the unintended offense, she continued.

"You're sexy, too, even if you are a lowly tea-drainer."

"Chief tea-drainer," he amended. "Take it easy."

He thought she said, "I will," but there was no telling. Maybe what she said was, "Mmm, banana nut."

After watching her walk for a few moments while telling himself that that's not what he was doing, he grabbed the bucket that had collected yesterday's tea and headed towards the door Bethany had disappeared through. Shoulders hunched, he let his legs lead the way with a loping stroll.

"Justus!" a voice hollered.

Justus, feeling vaguely popular all of a sudden, glanced up and squinted against the sun. He made out Terrance Bozzo, the most memorable of the Wilbanks Academy redheads.

"What's up, Terry?"

"Whoa!" Terry looked alarmed.

Justus froze, staring at him in wonderment. "What?" he asked.

"Oh, nothing. The way your eyes caught the sun…it freaked me out."

"What do you mean?" Justus asked.

"They looked gold or—" Terry shook his head. "Whatever."

Justus shrugged. His feather-shaped eyes were composed of teal, gold, grey, and deep forest green flecks and the corners crinkled when he smiled. He had never heard of them turning gold when they caught the sun, but with hazel eyes he had learned not to be surprised. Once he had put blue jeans up to his face and his eyes turned orange.

"How are you, man?" Justus asked, giving Terry a hug.

Just how Justus's hair appeared strawberry-blond next to blonds, Terry's vibrant crimson Afro turned Justus into a bleached blond. Terry was very pale, much paler than Justus, with wild hazel eyes that tended to enjoy being blue-grey more than any other color. His face was accosted with an assortment of pimples, a lingering courtesy from his extra-long puberty, and he was standing almost head to head with Justus. He had thin lips and his low-rise green trunks lengthened an already long upper torso that was in pretty good shape. He was displaying about six times the abs than Justus ever could.

"I'm good," Terry grinned. "I got you wet."

Justus looked at his freshly damp yellow polo.

"That's fine," he said, waving it off. "I'm leaving soon anyway."

"Oh, you are?" Terry asked. He glanced down at Justus's clothes again. "Is that why you aren't in uniform?"

Justus took in his own attire: a shirt, khaki's and flip-flops.

"Oh, yeah. Big party at the Rollerway tonight and Bethany and I got permission to attend as long as we set up today.

"Oh, that's cool," Terry nodded. "You guys going together?"

Justus shook his head. "I have to stop over at my other job to pick up my check. Bethany's going straight there."

"Ah," Terry nodded again. "I heard about the party. I doubt Rico wants me anywhere near him after our run in at Shawn Montgomery's."

Justus nodded as well. "Heard about that. It's probably all good." They both knew it wasn't. "So what brings you out here today?"

"Well, you know how it is," Terry grinned. "When summer rises…"

"Summer Falls," they droned in unison.

"So you're off today?" Justus asked.

Terry looked pleased. "Yep. My girlfriend told me that she could get me in here for free."

"Charity's a lifeguard, right?" Justus asked, glancing towards the door —the path to his car, and thus the rest of his day—that was a few steps away.

"Yeah. And I was glad to forget about work today, anyway. We had this *massive* rush the other day at Videoville, man, and I was the *only one* working the floor."

"I know how that is, dude. Straight jacuzzi."

Terry's temple crinkled. "What exactly does 'jacuzzi' mean?"

Justus laughed. "You substitute 'crazy' with 'jacuzzi.'"

Terry processed this. "So it can be negative as well as positive?"

Justus grinned. "Exactly!"

Terry chuckled. "You always had the oddest slang." He pointed to the bucket of tea. "Let me let you go, pardner. Tell everyone at the Rollerway that I say season's greetings!"

"Alright dude," Justus said, extending a hand. "Will do."

"Alright, homeslice," Terry responded, slapping Justus's hand in a handshake. "You be cool."

"Take it easy."

And Terry went about his fun and Justus went about his business, appreciating the quiet breeze.

When he got to his car, though, the trouble began. As he went to insert his keys in the lock, he heard them clatter on the ground.

Strange, he thought. He hadn't felt them slip. He knelt down to pick them up and lost his balance.

Crap! As he fell forward he reached to protect his head from the car's metal frame, though his hand found the interior cloth upholstery instead.

What exactly was going on? Was his door open? As he struggled to pull himself up, he saw that he had landed inside of the car somehow. He was now in his driver's seat, but the door was still closed.

"I fell in?" he asked himself. Great, now he was talking to himself. He reached for the handle. His keys were still outside.

As he watched, his hands turned clear, becoming a liquid replica of his usual flesh and bone appendage, passing around the handle without gripping it.

Customers piling out of their cars as the Summer Falls gates were opened were unable to place the source of the high-pitched wail that filled the parking lots. And Justus Alexander couldn't make his hysterical cries stop.

• • • • •

Once Ezekiel Yang reached the dentistry office, he ended the call with her, resigned to a feeling of secrecy…something he didn't like having with her.

He found a seat in the carpeted waiting room and began flipping through a bike magazine that someone had been thoughtful enough to leave for him. Once, his sister Samantha had bought him a subscription to one of the mountain bike magazines, but when Samantha's money got poured into a never-ending well of schooling, the subscription ended. His parents made amends by buying him a very nice bike and he celebrated by riding it all over the island of St. Simons for a month. That very weekend, he almost ran over two kids who were taking an afternoon stroll. The girl proceeded to call Ezekiel a few rude names before she recognized him.

"Ezekiel?" she had cautiously identified.

He could not place her until history class the next week, but he had recognized the boy from a Latin field trip freshman year. From that God-chanced encounter, somehow Ezekiel forged a relationship with BJ and Rico. Only God could have known that their separate roads of life could intersect in the ways that they had so far, especially with a busybody like Coda Crenshaw trying so extensively to ensure that all of his friends forged their own alliances with each other. Maybe Coda was the vessel God was using to execute His mysterious will.

There was a time not long before when Ezekiel believed that man made his own destiny. Now, he saw differently. Some people believe in fate and some people believe in destiny. Ezekiel believed in the will of God. Some say that everything that happens is what God designated for you from birth, but Ezekiel's opinion was somewhat different. After all, if God had picked everyone's path and set it in stone, why wasn't everybody living perfect Christian lives and going on to heaven when they die? No, Ezekiel believed that God had two wills: a perfect will and a permissive will. God may say that a particular thing is going to occur, but He gives humans enough freedom to decide whether or not they want to be the ones who accomplish what God has commanded to be done. Ezekiel felt that if someone did not do what God wanted them to do, God simply gave the task to someone else.

Ezekiel often took extensive journeys through his thoughts in a short span of time—he wondered of someone had ever measured the speed of thought against the speed of light—and he had been in the waiting room for only a minute or two when his dentist appeared in the door-way.

"Hello, Ezekiel," she greeted him, gesturing for him to move into the hallway.

As Ezekiel stepped into her office, his mind began pounding. It wanted exercise; it needed something to do. And ever since the night Ezekiel had been struck by lightning, that something to do had been beyond anything he had ever assumed he was capable of.

"How are you today?" the dentist asked.

Ezekiel thought of something Hanley Powell said at the lunch table back in high school. "I have now decided that dentists fall into two categories: they either *hate* people, or they *love* to see people suffer." He wondered what went on in his dentist's mind.

"Great," Ezekiel offered back, settling into the dentist's chair. He really wanted to know what went on in the dentist's mind. He wiped the sweat from his hands onto his khaki shorts.

The lady doctor's white office was bare, with a few unsettling posters of teeth that hadn't felt the touch of a toothbrush in apparent decades. To his dismay, the dentist mistook his concentration for butterflies and prompted him to relax.

That was it! All he had to do was relax a little. Ease out of the strain he was putting his brain through. And he was…knowing.

He just *knew*; the information flowed into him as if by osmosis. He knew that the dentist couldn't go to lunch until she finished with him. He knew that she had eaten Fruit 'N Fibre for breakfast. He knew she was worried about a lump she had found on her side that weekend.

Previously, Ezekiel had only been able to pick up emotions, wants, … cares. This new…explicit knowledge was beyond anything he wanted. Was this God's will? What had he sown in order to reap this?

"Open wide!" the dentist enthused. Ezekiel opened his mouth, stricken with a sensation that wasn't quite dismay, but definitely wasn't the satisfaction that he expected.

What's wrong with this guy today? he thought. No, the thought hadn't originated in his own head.

"Mmm, Ezekiel." She clucked disapprovingly. "Have we been flossing correctly?"

Ezekiel squirmed inside, as another part of him swelled with untapped opportunity.

Ezekiel Yang was a mind reader.

• • • • •

"Calm down, Enrique," fourteen-year-old Renata Gutierrez muttered to her brother, leaning against the ice blue walls of Rico's room. She was sitting on his bed, her head propped right next to a larger-than-life caricature of her with her brother. The walls were decorated with pictures of Rico's elementary school class photos, soccer pictures, and his adventures with BJ.

Renata, wearing Rico's socks, wiggled her toes into the grey speckled carpet.

Rico leaned over her, grabbed her around the shoulders and began to playfully shake her. "What do you mean? I am calm!" He ended on a half-growl, then smiled and kissed his spirited sister on her forehead.

"You're hurting me!" Renata gasped.

Rico let her go, shocked. "What?" He didn't think that he could hurt her too bad with his skinny frame, but you could never be too sure when it came to girls, especially little sisters that liked to complain.

"It felt like you were burning my arms, brother!" his sister explained. She inspected herself, but found no proof.

Renata's Hershey's colored hair was pulled back into a long ponytail, one of the benefits having never joined the ROTC—or just being a girl. Both Rico and Renata were thin and cinnamon-skinned, however, Rico was much taller.

BJ appeared in the door with a disconcerted expression gripping her face, but when Rico saw her, he couldn't help but grin. She was wearing a cute black dress accented with white piping and her sable strands were pulled back into a modest bun. She was beautiful to him.

"Can you ask your parents if they've seen it?" BJ asked Rico and he could tell she was trying her hardest not to pout.

He glanced at Renata and then nodded to BJ.

"Ma!" Rico hollered, while Renata hollered, "Papá!"

"Dad!" Rico yelled, while Renata yelled, "Mommy!"

Tall, imposing Mr. Gutierrez appeared in the doorway behind BJ, who shrunk away towards Rico in obvious fear. Swiftly swooping behind her husband was Mrs. Gutierrez, who was drying her hands on a towel.

Rico swept BJ up in his arms and asked, "Have either of you seen Becca Joy's purse?"

"A purse?" Mr. Gutierrez asked. "No."

"Thank you," BJ breathed briskly.

Mr. Gutierrez nodded and exited back to whatever part of he house he had arrived from. Rico felt BJ relax. Renata was watching her with disdain.

"What does it look like, mija?" Mrs. Gutierrez asked.

"It's white—"

She couldn't even finish the sentence before Mrs. Gutierrez had grabbed her hand, setting off in search.

"Come, mija. We will look together."

They faded into the distance with Mrs. Gutierrez speaking about how two heads were better than one.

Rico heard Renata chuckle.

"Why is she afraid of him?" Renata asked.

"She's not afraid," Rico mused. "Just not as much in love."

Renata looked to Rico, her eyes snapping, though her tone did not. "Not Mom, your Joy."

Rico glanced over in shock. He glanced back at the empty doorway and shrugged.

"They'll talk," she said, referring to their parents. "One of these days they'll have to talk."

"What will they say?" Rico asked.

Renata shrugged and Rico enfolded her in a hug.

"Maybe they'll say 'I love you' again," his sister muttered.

They stood there embracing.

"How do you feel, Enrique?" Renata asked.

"About leaving?" Rico asked.

"I guess."

"Okay, I guess. I don't know if I should stay or go."

"Do your own thing, Enrique. You spent eighteen years—specifically thirteen years of classroom hell—earning it."

There she went, being all sensitive and selfless about everything. From Rico's early, mullet-sporting days in southern California to his later, buzz-cut days in Brunswick, his life was family, soccer and girls—especially one girl in particular. As his relationship with BJ bloomed, his parents' relationship was falling on rocky ground. Rico stayed strong, mostly for Renata and sometimes for his parents as well. They had all given him much love whenever he needed them. They watched over him while they ignored their own pain. They were overflowing with love for him then and they were there for him now. If anything, he felt the obligation to Renata to be her pillar of strength.

"Okay, we found it!" BJ emerged into Rico's room with her purse triumphantly in her hands and a relieved smile beaming on her round face.

"Can we go now?" Rico playfully whined, as Renata untangled herself from his long limbs. "I can't be late to a party in Kim's honor."

"Yes, you can," talkative Renata corrected him quickly. "We're Mexican, so technically we can run on colored-people time."

Rico grinned, scooping his sunglasses off his dresser. "Never thought about that!"

BJ shifted, visibly too uncomfortable to join in the minefield-like conversation. Rico didn't blame her. When it comes to race issues, one could never be sure. Only the bold and sometimes foolish ones like Shannon would dare tread on such sensitive territory as that. The most BJ had ever mentioned on the subject was the fact that Rico did not look like your run-of-the-mill Georgian Mexican: the ones with the short, bowl cut hair and a farmer-like appearance; he could have simply been a dark-skinned Spaniard.

"We can go now," she offered.

"Thank God," Rico said, wrapping his arms around her once again. "You know, since we're already running late, maybe before we get there we could—"

"Rico!" BJ grinned. She glanced at Renata, who was pretending not to notice their Antony and Cleopatra indulgences.

"Let's *go*," BJ said, blushing.

"All right, Sis, we're leaving," Rico announced, as they headed towards the door.

"Are you wearing that?" Renata asked, pointing to Rico accusingly.

"What?" Rico asked, looking down at his navy blue shorts and green polo. The laces on his boat shoes were untied, but aside from that, he could see nothing wrong. He looked at BJ.

"Your shoes are untied," BJ offered with a little shrug. They turned to Renata.

"Well, if you two can't see it, then I guess it doesn't matter," Renata said, shrugging. "Go to a party looking like that."

"Then we're off, chica," Rico remarked and he gave his sister one last hug, just because.

•　•　•　•　•

Kim stood in the middle of the Concrete Wave, a skate park inside of a downtown warehouse, skaters hurtling down half-pipes and doing all types of tricks in midair around her head. She felt suspended as if inside of a snow globe, surrounded by loud, gigantic, ugly grey snowflakes.

Kim laughed at her internal silliness, grabbing her skateboard and disconnecting the chinstraps from her helmet, heading towards the exit. She was supposed to meet up with Maya once she changed and together they would head over to Rocky's Rollerway for Rico's goodbye party. Thinking about how she would hide her skateboard from even Maya, Kim reflected on how strange her life had become in the past few months. Graduation and other weird occurrences had placed her in a different state of mind than person she had been in high school. Just that very morning, she had seen her personal bench-pressing record triple. She didn't even bench press on a regular basis and even if she had, Maya and Coda would never believe it: neither the record breaking nor the fact that she bench-pressed. She had begun under the feeling that as a cheerleader, well, now a *former* cheerleader—

Her mind was rambling and she was thirsty. She still had enough time before her proposed meet-up with Maya to stop by Wal-Mart, maybe to visit her optician father and possibly purchase something, a soda, maybe. Deciding against that, she stepped over to the water fountain near the restrooms and sank for a drink, letting her skateboard and helmet down next to the wall.

Kim pressed the button to release a cool stream of water, then froze before she opened her mouth, causing the chilled water to splash up her nostrils and into her face. She sputtered and gasped as she stepped back from the fountain, shaking her head violently in reflex. She lifted her hands to her face, attempting to wipe it dry.

It was as if she had seen lightning strike inside of her eyes, right before she had the opportunity to open her mouth to drink. Her vision, everything, had gone white and—

Before Kim could collect herself fully, she was interrupted again. A strange-sounding scream escaped from the ladies' restroom. Glancing around quickly, yet seeing no one who could aid her in time, she ran into the bathroom alone to help however she could.

The stalls were all on one side of the room, with a sink in the far corner. After a quick inventory, Kim realized that the only other person in the bathroom was what looked like a dreadlocked pasty-skinned white boy, barefoot and wearing a tight brown jumpsuit. His dark eyes were shockingly focused on her, not unlike a blue-eyed creature from her recent past.

Kim was taken aback and, as he advanced slowly, she didn't quite know what her impulses were telling her.

He backhanded her and she jolted into action. She punched him in his stomach and he flew into a stall, blood sputtering from his mouth. There was that incredible strength she had discovered in herself. This time she had needed it.

As she turned to run, he was right there. This time, when he shoved her, the force sent her colliding into the countertop, cracking the sink and bending the countertop where she grabbed it. She had never been hit like that before. It was like he was just as strong as she was.

She didn't know if she should hit him with her hands or with the sink. She knew in her guts that she could just rip it-

The ashen boy's face was flushing. Now that Kim noticed the muscles straining the fabric of his jumpsuit, he looked a little older, on the brink of adulthood, maybe. She kicked him. She kicked him where it mattered and, as he crumpled backwards into the floor holding himself in pain, the lightning struck inside of Kim's eyes again.

Kim stood there, her elbow pads swinging around her wrists. The boy was gone. She turned, anticipating a surprise attack, but he was nowhere. It was as if his disappearance coincided with that flash in her eyes. She smoothed down her hair, as she attempted to calm down.

She inspected her white sneakers. They weren't scuffed too badly. Nothing a few minutes with a toothbrush couldn't fix.

Was this only happening to her? she wondered, removing her elbow pads. *That was more than just an adrenaline rush.*

Her cell phone was ringing.

"Coda?"

"Wasabi, chica? Something wrong?"

Kim caught her breath, straining to stay in the moment. Beginning with her next exhale, each breath was a patch of bricks repairing the wall to protect others from all this new strangeness in her life.

"Nothing's wrong, Coda-da; just twilight zoning. *Habari gani?*"

"Haha—*ujima*, chica. I need a big favor!"

Kim was taken aback with Coda's apparent familiarity with the Kwanzaa holiday terms. The only phrase she could recall was the one she said, and there he went going too deep as usual. She squeaked "What does *ujima* mean?" into her phone, but he didn't seem to hear.

"Please help BJ stall Rico," he was saying. "She's done everything she can, but they're on their way entirely too soon. I told him that you needed a ride and he's headed to your place right now. Can you hold them over for a few at your house?"

"I told Maya—"

"Oh, Maya's already here. I had her bring me some more sodas."

Kim sighed. The pains of a perfectly executed surprise.

"Sure," she said, looking at her reflection in the bathroom mirror. "I can handle Rico. You handle the party."

Coda laughed. "I got that part down, Kim! No worries!"

No worries. Right.

As the call ended, Kim continued to stare into the mirror, stepping closer. What was wrong with her eyes? She moved in, leaning over the sink until her nose was barely an inch away from the glass.

Within the typically brown irises of her eyes, she saw an amazing amount of diminutive golden dots, shimmering contentedly amongst the russet ridges.

Kim chuckled, convinced she was losing her mind.

She had stars in her eyes.

7.

Jolly Good

Delia Hamilton set the last candle in the giant party cake and stepped away from the table to admire her handiwork. The cake was actually several various-sized two-layer cakes frosted together to represent a giant purple paw print—evocative of her daughter's status as the reigning Miss Wilbanks and Rico Gutierrez's role as soccer team captain for the Wilbanks Cheetahs. A little last ditch school spirit.

"Okay, the trap's been set!" Coda announced happily, dancing into the party room at Rocky's Rollerway.

Delia looked up as the bubbly boy bounced closer to take his hundredth look at the celebration cake, with his beaded braids clacking along behind his ears.

"Thanks for helping me do this, Mrs. Hamilton. And this cake really rocks!"

Delia crossed her arms over her chest in satisfaction. "You really think so?"

Coda nodded vigorously, sending the beads into another clanging orchestra. "Absolutely. Completely benefiting the royal family of Wilbanks Academy."

Delia turned to the youngster, content to converse to help pass the time. "Does that include you?"

Coda raised his unkempt eyebrows, lost in the purple icing. "Me? I guess so. I got it all by default anyway. No one ran against me during the student council elections." He turned to Kim's mother conspiratorially. "And the only reason I made Homecoming Court is because Ezekiel Yang had some math conference in Cedar City that weekend. I was actually in eleventh place as far as the guys were concerned. But those details don't matter to the masses, so we keep 'em from them."

He turned back to the cake, with a furrowed brow so practiced, it was obvious he was an actor first and someone who truly lived second. It was inflections such as those that showed Delia exactly how Kimberly and Coda understood each other on that innate, actor-y level.

She loved any opportunity that arose in which she could better understand her daughter's friends, since they were the truest reflection of who Kimberly was away from the house. She appraised Coda in all his asparagus-eyed glory. The freckles on his brown face were akin to stars. The closer she looked, more appeared.

Coda continued, "Maya, however, is Homecoming Queen and co-captain of the cheerleading squad with Eden. Kim is Miss KWA and both of them are two of our five Black cheerleaders and the only ones in our senior class. Rico, Shannon, Benny, *and* Gene were captains of sports teams. Nothing default about that. Not like it really matters, though, right? After all, life beyond high school is where we make the lasting definition of who we are."

Delia nodded in agreement, all the while wondering if the skinny Creole boy even had a life yet that he could call his own.

"What are you doing with your life, Lakota? Now that high school's over."

"Life?" Coda seemed taken aback by the question. "It's just began anew, hasn't it, Mrs. Hamilton?" He laughed loudly. There was no other volume she had ever heard him at. "I'm not sure, yet. I mean, what I used to call my life ended with the graduation ceremony. My life was school and all the accompanying craziness. None of us who went to Wilbanks are obligated to be nice to each other anymore, because we don't have to worry about another thirteen years of heightened social discretion. I don't have to worry about bouncing around to every lunch table each day, hoping everyone still likes me."

Delia didn't remember high school being so particular. She remembered being particular as an individual, but she had no memories of others being as fussy as she.

"I don't have to worry," Coda continued, "about tables full of gorgeous girls explaining to me why they'd rather marry me in twelve years than date me now. I don't have to worry about befriending the new kid just because I know how it feels, or letting it slip that purple is my favorite color and then hoping that doesn't make me sound gay."

A muted exclamation escaped from Delia's throat, causing Coda to reflect upon which Hamilton female he was talking to. His eyes ceased from flying around the room and settled back on the cake.

"Now I just have to worry about dying of starvation in L.A."

Another exclamation from Delia, but this one she didn't attempt to hold in. "I thought your dad didn't want you to go!"

Coda shrugged, picking up a deviled egg from the table. "He wants me to go to college."

"And you should, Lakota," Delia said earnestly. "You should go to Clark Atlanta with Kim! It's right in the hub of the city—"

"Oh, but my heart isn't there, Mrs. Hamilton," Coda said, turning to her slowly as if preparing himself for the emotive onslaught he must have known she was considering letting loose on him—an actor's instinct. Kim had it, too. There was a bitter contour to his voice now. "I want to go home to Cali. And I want to be an entertainer."

As Coda bit into the egg, Delia mused that reasoning with a teenager was the same as debating with a skyscraper. It wouldn't budge and would manage to look down on you, no matter if you stood at its side or at a distance.

"Do college plays," she said simply, busying herself by rearranging the yellow-orange plasticware on the table. "That's what Kim's doing."

Inside of her she understood that his desire to create with his art was much stronger that Kimberly's. It was almost a requirement for his existence, and it was impossible for Delia to empathize.

Content at last with the table, she turned from it and laid a light hand on his shoulder. "Trust in God, Lakota. Not your feelings."

Figuring the conversation was over, she exited the party room in order to greet the arriving guests.

· · · · ·

Coda let Mrs. Hamilton's words hang there in the air, hoping a metaphorical wind would send them away.

What was God's voice saying to him? Wasn't God's voice that little voice inside? Wasn't that voice inside telling him to follow his heart? Coda shook his head, suddenly tired. He finished off his deviled egg quickly and absently rubbed his wrists through his sleeves, hearing the voice again.

Where you would lose your life, I will use your life.

Maya and her golden weave peeped around the corner.

"Coda-da!"

"Maya-ya," he responded automatically. "Wasabi?

She stepped into the room, concerned. "What's the matter, Coda?"

He stepped out of his funk, noticing the cell phone in her hands. "Nothin'; just thinking. Call for me?"

Maya held out her cell. "It's Justus."

Justus couldn't make it. Said he got called in to deliver pizzas for Iovenelli's. "This was supposed to be the perfect night," Coda whined, hanging up the phone.

Maya shook her head. "Coda, this is like the third party you've thrown this year and all the rest of them have been pretty awesome and pretty near perfect. One person missing it isn't the equivalent of a failed party."

Coda sighed, knowing she was right. Beyond her he saw a group of girls revisiting the glory days of Wilbanks Girls' Basketball. He hadn't seen some of them since the night of graduation.

"Is everyone else here?" he asked, wondering why he was so hungry.

Maya turned around, appraising the crowd of post-high school teenagers that milled around the skating rink.

"Just about. Rico's family just got here, so it's not long now."

The excitement rose again inside of Coda and his trademark stretched across his face.

"Why are you smiling all of a sudden?" Maya asked.

"Renata's here?"

Patti LaBelle's "It's Alright With Me" was blaring out of the speakers over the skating rink and Coda knew it was going to be a good night. Maybe he could get in a skate with Renata Gutierrez before the honored guests arrived.

It was a great night to be alive.

• • • • •

Kim climbed out of the backseat of Rico's car, smoothing down her bob with one hand and pulling her purse strap over her shoulder with the other.

"Thanks again for helping me look for my purse," she said, looking to the roller rink entrance. She caught Coda's eye and gave him the signal. She looked over at Rico, who had just been looking in the direction she had been.

"Did you just shoot a bird?" she asked. Rico looked at her, dismayed.

"No," he responded. "That was my ring finger!"

"What were you doing with your ring finger?" she asked, looking at BJ for help.

"Don't ask," BJ said, shaking her head.

They headed towards the door into the Rollerway lobby, and Rico started to chuckle.

"What?" BJ and Kim asked.

"It's just funny how you both lost your purses tonight."

"Oh," Kim responded, looking towards BJ. Had she known BJ had used that trick, she would have picked another. Still, she was sure Rico didn't suspect anything. He seemed pretty at ease waiting on her as she pretended to tear the house apart looking for the purse that was hidden underneath her I Love Lucy pillows.

When they entered the lobby, Kim paused.

"There's no music."

"What?" Rico asked. And he stopped. "You're right."

Kim wanted to roll her eyes. Couldn't Coda ever be subtle with anything?

They stepped through the doors into the skating rink to see a congregation of friends and former classmates, standing beneath a giant banner that read "Happy Birthday, Kim!/We'll Miss You, Rico!"

"SURPRISE!"

Kim and Rico were frozen to the spot, as BJ laughed and everyone cheered.

Coda began singing "For He's A Jolly Good Fellow" while Bethany Kelly—ugh!—began singing "Happy Birthday" in a neat mash-up of sorts, and when it was over, Kool and the Gang pumped through the speakers and the celebration begun. It took a while for Kim to take it all in. The gold balloons bespeckled with black paw prints, the giant purple paw print of a cake with soccer-ball iced toes and the giant table of presents under surveillance in the party room.

Rico and Kim had each been led to believe, and were the only ones who were deceived as such, that the party was a surprise for the other, enabling everyone that they knew—parents, friends—to plan openly around them on the majority of the details. Kim's birthday wasn't for another three weeks and she hadn't been surprised since her third birthday, so Coda had come up with the bright idea to surprise her by throwing it during a completely inappropriate month.

"You look beautiful," he said as he squeezed her in a patented Coda embrace. He never held back on his hugs. They were the direct connection between his soul and his world. Kim had never quite been able to achieve that, aside from when she was speaking, but perhaps even that manifestation of hers was feigned. In fact, she was sure of it.

"You are a dirty dog," she squealed, smacking him on his arm. "This was real good," she professed a few seconds later. "Jolly good, fellow." And she hit him again. He just chuckled and skated away.

Kim enjoyed herself capaciously. She enjoyed the food, the cake, the presents, and the skating. She made sure Rico enjoyed it all as well, though she didn't have to try very hard. This was his last bash before he rode into *the* Naval Academy at Annapolis, Maryland on a full scholarship. He was living it up like he had just won the Hermann Trophy.

• • • • •

Eventually, Kim found herself alone in the party room, taking another break for the benefit of her legs. She hadn't been very smart escaping to the skate park on the same day there was a party at the Rollerway. She was athletic, but she was learning there was a limit.

"Square Biz" was the song that forced her parents out of the party room and onto the skating rink. They had some type of history with the Teena Marie song and Kim always forgot what it was, but thinking of Teena took her right back to the night the singer played on the car radio and she quickly forgot all about the party.

"I never got a chance to tell you that you did a great job on your speech at graduation."

Kim, quite surprised, looked over at Ezekiel. He had entered the room to grab some more chips, even sitting next to her as he munched, and she still had not realized he was there until he spoke.

"Thank you," she said, before remembering that he had made a speech as well and it probably would've been polite to attach a "you, too" to her expression of appreciation.

Ezekiel chuckled before she could correct her oversight. "And throwing in that bit about Jesus…I certainly wouldn't have been able to do it."

"Oh, thanks."

"No," Ezekiel said, correctly supposing he had offended her. "I meant that in a good way. Like, you did something that I'd never be able to do."

Kim stared. "Are you asking for a trial or a temptation?"

He appeared confused. "What?"

She shook her head, laughing inside. "Never mind."

"I meant that you're brave," Ezekiel explained.

She observed the fact that he was rubbing his hands on his pants. He was nervous about something.

"Brave?" she repeated.

He turned to her and she noticed for the first time how his eyes didn't quite look brown. "Do you ever wonder if you made the wrong decision?" The question was certain and hesitant at the same time. An odd combination.

"About mentioning Jesus at our graduation?"

Ezekiel shook his head. "About coming back."

For the second time that night, there seemed to be no music in Rocky's Rollerway. Everything had frozen. In fact, she had forgotten to breathe.

Breathe, girl. Breathe, INC, before you kill your stupid self.

"What do you mean?" she heard herself ask, feeling herself breathe again. The automatic actress had taken over.

Ezekiel laughed. "Come on, Kim, I stepped out on a limb here; the least you could do is join me."

The pretense had failed.

"How do you know?" she whispered. "I haven't told anybody—"

"About the lake of stars?" he asked. "That you talked to God? That you chose to come back, just stronger than before?"

Kim twisted her entire body over the bench towards Ezekiel. "I haven't told my *parents* and you're telling me things only God knows!"

"Look in my eyes, Kim," Ezekiel whispered, glancing over as a group of revelers entered the room.

"Why aren't you skating, Kim?" Maya asked.

"I'll be out there, in a little, Maya-ya," she responded, peering into Ezekiel's eyes. What was it about his eyes that made them a color that wasn't quite brown?

The group exited with some fresh cans of soda and Kim saw it. Golden rivets of a jagged sort, inlayed in the brown of his iris.

"You have a lake of stars in your eyes; I have a lightning storm," he smiled.

At this revelation she struggled not to gasp or scream or do any of those stereotypically girly things. The excitement was there, though, a positive spring that overcame how unnerved Ezekiel had made her.

"How?" she breathed.

He crunched on a chip.

"Do you skateboard?" he asked. "Answer the question first," he said, cutting off her inquisitive inhale.

"Yes," she whispered.

"And you can bench-press more than you're willing to do in a public place."

"Ezekiel," she exhaled, "what is this?"

"You're getting stronger," he said to her, "and I'm getting this extreme version of the gift of knowledge." He looked around the party room, adding, "And knowledge about you has been…loud…in here."

He looked back at her. "I can't completely explain it yet, Kim. But I do know that you could have died in a car accident and I could have died from a lightning strike. Neither of us went to the hospital, but I experienced the white light, you know, the kind they talk about on 60 Minutes and such, and then I spoke with some angels."

"When did you get struck by lightning?" Still whispering. Kim felt as if she had discovered the location of El Dorado.

"Last month. That big midnight storm after the party at—"

"Eden's summer solstice thing," Kim remembered. This was insane. "You spoke with angels?"

"If it wasn't for the fact that you spoke with God Himself, I would feel very weird speaking to you about this."

"He spoke to me as music," she said. "It was a completely different language, but I understood Him."

"What did the Music say?" Ezekiel asked.

"Yo!" Rico Gutierrez interrupted, Coda slung across his back. Rico struggled to maintain his balance on the skates until one of the security officials rolled by and told Coda to get down.

"Sorry," Coda said sheepishly, flipping off Rico's back and managing to stay balanced on his skates as he landed. After one last disapproving glower, the watchman rolled away.

"What are you two doing chilling in here?" Rico asked. "The party's on the rink, muthas! Kim, your parents are grooving!"

"Grooving?" Coda repeated. "Kim's about to get a younger sibling!"

Kim barely heard them. "I'll be out there in one minute, fellas."

"Well hurry it up!" Rico exclaimed, but Kim's attention was back on Ezekiel.

"The music said, 'Where you would lose your life, I will use your life,'" Kim said, responding at last to his question.

Coda whirled around, jaw flapping like a sheet blowing in a hurricane.

"What did you say?" Rico asked with a dangerous look on his brow.

Kim looked up, confused.

"When you sprained your ankle," Ezekiel said to Rico casually, evidently enlightened on details Kim was not.

"Huh?" Rico asked.

"The scars on your wrists," Ezekiel continued, to Coda.

Now it was Coda's turn to look dangerous. "What?"

Kim lifted her arms to them. "Where you would lose your life, I will use your life."

Coda seemed to forget that he was on skates, and when he took a step towards Kim, he landed on his butt instead. Kim leapt off of the table and helped Coda to his feet. Tears were in the boy's eyes.

"Who told you about that voice?" he asked Kim and Ezekiel, wrenching himself out of Kim's grasp.

"What voice?" Rico asked, not looking away from Ezekiel. "And what were you saying about my ankle?"

"He said that he sprained his ankle trying to do a hands free backflip," Kim said.

"The most stupid thing I've ever tried to do," Rico nodded, speaking guardedly. "I was trying to show off to my cousins at Christmas."

"What you didn't tell anybody," Ezekiel stated, "was the truth."

Kim watched Coda, who, like her, was engrossed in this exchange.

"You were checking out your dad's gun and you dropped it. You thought it had discharged and took off."

Rico straddled the bench across from Ezekiel, shaken.

"Your dad's gun?" Coda asked.

"Stupid, I know," Rico stammered. "I would have turned into just another mindless headline about gun control. I was thinking about what it would be like, strapped and wrapped as a Navy Seal. When it dropped, I heard it click. Freaked out and thought I was toast for sure."

"You ran."

"And I fell. It was like I was hallucinating. I mean, everything then gold, then red, then everything was speaking... It couldn't have been real."

But Kim could tell by his reaction that he was trying to convince himself of this fact, as he had probably been doing since his accident.

"You heard it, though," Ezekiel continued. "The Voice saying that there was a calling on you greater than you had been reaching for."

"But you were hurt after!" Kim said to Rico.

"When I ran out of my room I wasn't exactly being light-footed," Rico muttered. "Sprained my ankle. That's actually the reason I fell."

Kim nodded, understanding. The only damage done was self-inflicted.

"I heard it inside of me and outside of me all at the same time when I was lying there. That where I would lose my life if it were in my own hands, quickly through stupidity and even gradually in things that I may think are worth my energy, it—He—would use my life."

As Ezekiel quickly spoke of his own experiences, Kim turned to Coda, remembering the night of the Black and Gold Ball. Now she stared at his golden glazed eyes, realizing…

"That's why you didn't bleed!" she said when Ezekiel had finished.

Coda was far away, fingers tracing the scars that were hidden beneath his sleeves. "That's what the Voice has said ever since that night," he said. "'Where you would lose your life, I will use your life.' I should have died that night."

"No," Kim said quickly, grabbing his arm. "You *could* have died. We all could have died, but for God's reasons He chose to let us live."

"He gave us the choice," Ezekiel corrected, looking at his former classmates. "He chose us to choose."

Rico tapped his head against the stone wall, as if trying to beat the situation into his understanding. "God chose us." He looked over at Coda and Kim could see him recounting all the rumors about Coda's covered wrists.

Kim marveled when she caught sight of Rico's eyes again, noticing for the first time that his brown irises were jumping with golden flame.

• • • • •

"Dr. Pat, a video just came in that I think you should see."

The woman, her hair pulled back into a thick ponytail, removed one of her rubber gloves and used a naked finger to lift her goggles off of her eyes.

"It's worth the interruption?" she queried.

"Yes, Dr. Pat. It's from the skate park on the mainland."

The doctor was removing her other glove. "You mean to tell me it's local?"

Her subordinate nodded vigorously. "And it's fresh. It's a surveillance video."

"Give me the rundown so that I can prejudge appropriately."

The other doctor wasn't sure if she was joking, but he obliged. "Teenage girl, showing signs of extraordinary—"

"Don't paint me a picture, Dr. Lemming."

"Uh, signs of offensive stamina, it seems, and another teenage youth —quite similar to ours, actually."

"Ours?"

"Yes, and appearing just as strong as the girl."

Dr. Pat's brow creased. "They were doing what, exactly?"

"Fighting."

She now raised her eyebrows. "Well that certainly sounds entertaining. How unexpected." She seemed to chew on the thought. "Like our beast, huh?"

"Almost purposefully so."

She was immediately irritated. "Facts only, Lemming. For all we know it could *be* our beast. Let's have a look."

"Yes, ma'am," he responded, following her out of the room. "And you know my name isn't Lemming, don't you, Dr. Pat?"

"Know, or care?" she responded dryly as the doors slid closed.

8.

The Days of Awakening

"*Papacita*, how'd we get lost going to Atlanta? We've only been making this trip since the nineteen hundreds!"

Kim's father just smiled from the front seat. "I guess it's time to stop for directions."

Kim's mother, sitting passenger in her own car, added, "I said that about forty-five minutes ago, Lester."

Earlier they had stopped by Dynasty Dog where Delia suggested they ask for directions. Instead, Kim's father decided order food. Kim had gotten her favorite, a number four. A Double Beefer burger with cheese and a large lemon Twinkle soda and a side of curly fries, which she lovingly placed on top of the beef patties and beneath the layers of condiments. That was her favorite way to eat any type of burger, but especially Double Beefers.

Dr. Hamilton pulled onto an exit ramp in search of a gas station. His wife watched their daughter through the side view mirror, though Kim didn't take notice until her mother broke her meditation.

"What are you thinking about, girl?" her mother asked her.

Kim sighed. "It seems like just when it's time to leave, reasons pop up for you to stay."

"In Brunswick?" her mother chortled. "I doubt seriously that there's any reason for you to stay there, honey. I'm trying to figure out why Lester and I are staying now that you're heading to college."

Kim made brief eye contact with her mother through the mirror, wondering if she should tell her parents. She had moments like that every day and she always decided against it, wondering how she could ever believe that they could understand.

"Have you and Lakota become an item?" her mother suddenly asked.

Kim choked on her own silence.

"No," she sputtered, before laughing. She was still giggling when they parked at the gas station.

While her father was inside getting directions from the lady behind the counter, Kim stood a little off from the car watching the sunset turn the sky purple.

"It's a call to royalty," her mom said, staring at the sky as well.

"Mmm, what are you saying, Momma?"

"God's chosen," Delia said, turning towards her daughter. "Greater is He…"

"Hmm," Kim said. She had no idea what her mother was talking about.

Her mom hummed the tune to some church song. The sake of the call, or something like that…

The shirt Kim wore stated "Daddy's Girl" in pink letters over a black background, with a white cross leaning on the words. It was one of her many birthday presents. She didn't remember who had gotten it for her…some lady from church maybe.

For the sake of the call…can you…something.

It's funny that her mom thought she had begun something with Coda, because in a way she had. Nothing romantic, of course. But something deeper than they had before. That night at the Rollerway, she had pulled him to the side near the party's end.

"You're part of the reason I came back," she said to him.

He welled up instantly.

"Kim!" her father called presently. It was time to hit the road again.

As it turned out, her father had gone a bit too far in the wrong direction and Atlanta was actually due east.

"This is why I hate traveling," Delia said at one point, but both of Kim's parents were in awe once they went over that final hill to see Atlanta displayed in front of them like a galaxy strewn across the earth.

At once, in the midst of the night, Kim didn't like it. All blue lights and gold. Cities always seemed to suck the stars from the sky. In the daylight, however, it would seem fine, she was sure.

She stared at the faraway sky once more.

The sky was black. *All of the stars must be in the city*, she thought.

For the sake of the call, will you give your all… You can…sake of the call… Whatever.

"Daddy, you mind if I turn on the light back here? I wanna read some."

"Go ahead, *chicalita*."

Kim opened to the first chapter of *The Days of Awakening*.

The first chapter was entitled, "Miracles Begin in Us." The first line read, "Why do we act as if God created us to be drama-anchored idiots?"

She was deep into chapter four—"Bless the Hell Outta Me"—long after they began their descent into the glittering city.

• • • • •

"Big trouble's coming this way, Coda," warned Terry, squinting his hazel-blue eyes effectively as he pushed down further on the gas pedal. "You know it any time Bethany calls just to say, 'hello.'"

Coda was sitting on the passenger's side, having hysterics to an ugly extent. It wasn't so much in what Coda's friend was saying about their self-important former classmate, rather the way he was saying it. Terry and Coda had often been paired up in Mr. Johnny's numerous Show-Choir shows, and Terry plainly had the comedic gift.

"Especially when she asks about your mother. Break out the guns, it won't be pretty."

"Stop, Terry, I'm having breathing problems."

Terry waited until Coda had calmed down and then hit him with another pun, sending him into another bout of sniggers and guffaws.

They were riding in Terry's white sedan, on their way to the mall to hang with Terry's girlfriend Charity. Coda didn't really care to see Charity since he didn't know her that well, but he needed something to do that Sunday afternoon and Terry had showed up at his front door, so that was that.

Coda had fallen out with his father over his driving, and began suffocating with determination to get his license with no help at all from the older Crenshaw. Terry offered to give him lessons, but they didn't get much time to hang out, let alone practice, so his driving skills sat dormant as he continued riding his bike back and forth to his college campus.

Coda was one of the few who had stayed behind in Brunswick—most of them were in the Atlanta and Macon areas and amazing Rico of course was in Maryland—and of the left behind, fewer still had gone to college. (Wayne Emerson was still working the drive-thru window at Dynasty Dog and may have to get a second job for himself with the rumored three kids on the way.) Coda found himself attending Brunswick's own Oakwood Community College much to his own frustration, despite the fact that all the costs were being paid for by the Georgia HOPE scholarship. His dad was happy, and so was Peppi Ortiz, a fellow Wilbanks graduate who asked him to tutor him in Literature. (He tried, but he barely understood her questions through the thick paste of her Columbian accent, so he had serious trouble breaking down the assigned excerpts from Mavis Gallant's "The Other Paris.") Other alumni of KWA that attended the college with him were Sam Wesberger and Hanley Powell. Hanley was constantly inviting him to the Baptist Student Union. Coda considered it, though he always seemed to be too busy on the days that they held their meetings.

After Coda had left his father's church that morning he was hit with so many questions that he was trying to get away from, if only for a little while. Exactly what had happened on his "choice night," as Ezekiel had referred to the nights that the "Rollerway four" had been made aware of the death option on their lives? Coda realized at the rink those weeks ago that they had all been going through some changes and Coda's hadn't been quite as impressive as the developments of Kim and Ezekiel. Rico, like Coda at the time, was just discovering what a series of weird coincidences connected to mean. Coda prayed about it, but so far God had decided to let him wait it out. So he waited and then would pray again. He figured he ought to pray "without ceasing" like the Bible commands. Or get as close to unceasing prayer as he could. The last thing he wanted to do was ask his dad.

"Did you hear me, Cheshire?" Terry was asking.

Coda replied with a yes and a comment to send Terry off into another spill, though decidedly less humorous, as Coda was caught up in his thoughts.

Coda just had no idea what he was supposed to know. Period. He didn't understand what was going on, so he simply didn't deal with it. He stayed busy. He went to school, to church, to work—at the lovely upscale restaurant that was trying to kill him—and if he had any spare time, he invested it in catching up with his friends—like Terry, who had just asked him another question.

Coda shot out another reply/hidden question combination that sent Terry on a shorter tangent.

Coda remembered to laugh at certain places, but his mind simply stayed away.

• • • • •

"I have to ride my bike home, now," Coda whined.

"I just wanna stay right here," brawny Sam Wesberger said, letting the hot water pour down his massive back and across buttocks large enough to be their own planet.

"But you have a class to go to, Wes. And poor Duane is late," laughed Coda, as he grabbed his towel.

Stocky Duane was at his locker, folding his white gi, their *shotokan* uniform.

"I'm not going," Duane affirmed, very seriously. "I'm just gonna chill out at the library. Rest myself."

Wes laughed from the shower.

"How could she just forget like that?" he asked Coda and Wes. "An extra hundred kicks should stick in someone's memory."

Coda chuckled, remembering how surprised their professor was at the end of the class when her students notified her that they had done six hundred kicks instead of the five hundred they had prepared for.

"At least it was the stomping kick," Coda accepted. "It still requires the concentration, but not the same amount of physical energy."

"Yes," agreed Wes, "but one-hundred stomping kicks—"

He didn't even have to finish.

"Yeah," Duane laughed, folding his belt. They were all still white belts, and in *shotokan* karate, they would be for a long time. "She owes us big time."

"True, true," agreed Coda, grabbing his deodorant.

Within his *shotokan* class, he had created a family of buddies that made the loss of his family of friends easier to take.

"Dude," Duane directed to Coda, "I don't see how you can do all of that with those beads smacking you in the face."

Coda responded, "If you saw what my grandfather could do with his head, you wouldn't be surprised at what mine can take."

His mother's father, a full-blood Cherokee and a drunk, used to knock people out with a single head-butt. Coda smiled, shaking the black beads into a tiny clatter.

A fighting spirit was all through his family, which was surprising on his dad's Creole side since the French supposedly opposed violence. Coda recalled that when he fought, and as a frequent new kid that was more often than not, he'd always see red (he called them 'red-outs') and his body would just react. He wouldn't be fighting, but his body would. He had a theory about possession by angels. He figured that if demons could do it (possession) to those not under the blood, angels could do it for those under the blood. In his mind, that explained how his body could fight so well without his brain being there with it.

Wes laughed as he headed towards his locker, limping ever so slightly as if to prove he was as sore as the other fellas. He began to towel off and told some unimportant story about his father, then his brother and what not, Coda didn't really care. Their conversations used to be about the girls—women—in their *shotokan* class until they made the realization that if the boys could hear the women's conversations from the female locker room, it was most probable that the women could hear theirs.

Wes was no small man; he was at least 6'3" and had the broad shoulders to enforce the height. The tank he pulled over his head barely concealed the bulging muscles Coda remembered him working on so feverishly during high school and his shorts—the atmosphere over that planet of a butt—were showing off his correspondingly powerful calves.

It was because of his Goliath-like size that Coda didn't understand why the Herculean-he always seemed to be overcompensating during class. He tried so hard to impress that it was unimpressive. Back when they were freshmen, Coda remembered him as the rocker type, gaunt and beautiful and Lestat-like. Now he was a Lou Ferrigno wannabe. If he stepped into a room with Gene Hightower, no one else would have room to breathe.

Buttoning his vibrant colored shirt, one of the few pulsating relics of his recent past lingering in his dreary present, Coda asked, "The Funfair's in town. Are either of you going?"

"Of course," Wes responded.

"Naw," Duane said. "Not tonight at least."

"I've gotta go tonight," Wes professed, spraying himself down with some type of body mist. "Busy for the rest of this month with midterms, and I have to write an essay about one of the works of Kate Chopin."

Coda laughed. "I'm going tonight. I have a French test tomorrow that I need to not-study for." Glancing over his shoulder at Wes, he added, "Have you read 'The Story of an Hour'? That ending made me almost as mad as *After the First Death*."

"Wait a minute, Coda," Wes said, wrinkling his brow. "You're not gonna study for your French test? That doesn't seem like the brightest idea."

"No big, Wes," Coda said dismissively, tensing his calves to ensure that they were still there. "Anybody feel like Willie's Weenie Wagon? I've got a serious craving for their pork chop sandwich."

Wes snorted. "Coda, I understand you're sixteen—"

"Seventeen in a week," Duane spouted before Coda could.

"Somebody remembers!" Coda exclaimed happily.

"—so we make allowances for you," Wes continued, pulling his hair back into a Barbie-like ponytail, "but as a college student, shouldn't you have the maturity to make the correct decision here?"

"*Est-ce que c'est une classe de français?*" Coda asked. "*Non, c'est une classe de* karate. I don't study." He shut his locker and picked his jacket off of the concrete bench. "It throws off my groove."

* * * * *

"Coda?"

Coda glanced up from his jumbo hot dog and his world was better.

"Renata?"

Rico's younger sister was standing a few feet away from him, the calm center of a whirling rainbow hurricane. Funfair patrons bustled about with giant electric-colored stuffed animals and spools of cotton candy, yet all the surrounding hustle was muted as he gazed into her chocolate eyes.

"I almost didn't recognize you," she squealed, pulling him into a hug. "You look all grown up with that beard!"

Coda smacked his face sheepishly. "I haven't been to the barber," he said. "They usually give me my shave."

Renata looked behind him as if expecting to catch a glimpse of another familiar face. Coda, after all, was rarely alone senior year.

"Did you come by yourself?" she asked, speaking with that brisk California speed and the most beautifully placed traces of a Mexican accent. She readjusted the purse hanging on her shoulders.

Coda looked around at the storm of babbling enthusiasts, searching above all the heads for one particular form.

"Actually, I brought this girl named Tasha from my church, but she didn't want to do any of the roller coasters… She ran off with some of her friends from Carver. Faaaaantastic." He sighed.

"She's in high school?" Renata asked.

"Yep. Your school—George Washington." He quickly added, "It's not like a date or anything."

"Don't get so defensive," Renata laughed. "I'm not taking fingerprints."

Coda dug into his pockets and handed her two vouchers. "Here. I won these at the archery stand." He inhaled the last bit of his dog and crumpled the leftover paper wrapper.

Renata glanced up from the coupons. "You lost me when you said archery."

Coda beamed, stuffing the wrapper into the pocket of his jeans. "I am a man of many talents, Miz Gutierrez, and archery just happens to be one of them. Robin Hood was my favorite childhood hero, then Batman. You know, people always think it's the other way around and that bothers me." How did he always seem to end up rambling? *Get it together, Coda.* "Anyway, in the fifth grade they took us to this Renaissance Fair up in Atlanta, and I just had a natural…ability." He gestured to the coupons. "Undefeated ever since."

Renata's eyes took in the print on the stubs Coda had handed her, and she sputtered. "Wow! Coda, these are worth a lot of free tickets! This is like, three more days' worth of Funfair!"

"Do you like rides?" he asked.

"What?" She threw her head back and cackled like the Wicked Witch of the West. It was endearing. "Do I ride? You mean like drop towers? Squirrel Cages, Ferris wheels and funhouses? Honey, I ride everything!"

Realization settled across her face. "You aren't seriously giving these to me!"

"What am I gonna do with them?" he asked, throwing up his hands. "This is the first time I've been to a fair since I was five years old. Roller coasters freak me out, and all those games of skill, chance, and deceit… I'd be kidding myself. With you I know they'll be in good hands."

"What about that girl?"

"What girl?" Coda asked. "Oh, Tasha? It's like I don't even exist to her, sometimes. She'll never know."

"Huh." Renata glanced at the vouchers one last time and her brown hair fell across her bony shoulders. Coda tried not to melt.

"Fine," she said, tucking the vouchers in her purse. "But I owe you."

Coda began preparing a proposal that if she would agree to one go-round on the Ferris wheel, then they could call it even, but as he engineered the sentence her cell phone began ringing and she blanched. "Oh, that's probably Mario, wondering where I am. We're supposed to be taking a romantic trip across the fairgrounds."

Coda looked up at the chairlift roped across the park and all the couples sailing along happily with their stuffed neon teddy, koala and polar bears, cursing its existence silently. His prospective statements had promptly lost their place in the conversation.

"Well," Renata said, since he had made no comment, "I'll see you later. Thanks again, Coda!"

"Okay," he grinned, feeling like an idiot.

She turned and was about her business, answering her phone and dissolving into the fair-storm and leaving Coda to shake off the lingering effects of crush.

Renata, Renata, Renata, Renata.

He would be in trouble if she always reduced him to such a muddled mass of slobber just by appearing. He had done better this time by actually holding a semi-normal conversation.

A wind swept in from off the marshes and his beads clattered behind his head. He missed Justus and Shannon and Ezekiel at times like this, with the tang of the marshes in his nostrils. They had all ran cross-country together senior year, and Ezekiel, specifically, was his unofficial running partner; they would run to a rhythm. Ezekiel would breathe in, Coda would breathe in, Ezekiel would breathe out and breathe in again, and then Coda would breathe out. It was those years of ShowChoir's breathing exercises that helped Coda breathe so calmly when working so hard, and basically gave them their particular uneven rhythm that sounded like a beat box. Ezekiel would speed up his running, and Coda would have to catch up. Then Coda would speed up, and Ezekiel would have to catch up. It worked great, except for the time they went to Orlando for a nationwide run, and the humidity slowed Coda down extremely in the end, while Ezekiel shot of like a rocket in retribution for some obnoxious runner who, already in front of Ezekiel, had passed Coda while making obscene noises. Ezekiel passed four people right there at the finish line. Coda had used himself all up by that point, yet he felt the essence of victory in the fact that Ezekiel had sort of did it for him.

Standing there in the midst of people on their own journeys with their own stories, he felt lonely. It was as if he had been erased from everything except his own memory.

He wanted another hot dog.

• • • • •

"Kim!"

Kim looked up from her textbook.

"Coda, there is no way that you finished all those questions!"

Coda kneeled next to her desk. Half of the class wasn't even focused on the Spanish assignment, preferring instead to gossip about their fellow students or the current celestial celebrities as they waited for the impending bell. Kim had enough after school assignments as it was, and if she could finish this classwork in time to prevent it from becoming homework, that's what she was going to do.

"It's really easy," Coda was saying. "All of the answers are right there in the conversation between Ricky and Lucía. Ella quiere ir al cine y él quiere quedarse en casa."

Kim put a hand up to pause him while she inspected the page again, pencil threaded through her thin fingers. "Okay. I see it now. Don't know how you saw it so quickly." She glanced over at Maya. "La Sierra, are you getting this?"

"I am now," Maya muttered. "I thought this class was supposed to be easy."

"Who lied to you?" Coda laughed. "Eleventh grade is like one of the last trials of Heracles. Senior year classes are cake, though. And aren't the odd numbered years supposed to be more difficult than the even ones?" He left out the fact that with her near fluent speaking capabilities in the language, he didn't see why any assignment, speech or written, would be a struggle for her. An easy grade if there ever was one.

"Spanish 2 is supposed to be easy because we passed Spanish 1," Maya said, in a tone implying that if they were having an argument, she was determined to win.

"I'm not here to talk about that anyway," Coda said, effectively withdrawing before the match began. Smart idea, because Maya rarely won or lost without first drawing blood.

"I figured," Kim said. "Oscar predictions or something?"

"Ha. Whatevs. Homecoming! I've been asking you for the last few weeks and you keep saying you'll get back to me, and the dance is next week."

Kim froze a bit. She noticed Maya glance over at them.

"The dance," she repeated.

"What color is your dress?" Coda asked. "I wanna match somehow, and pretty soon, if not already, all the good stuff will be gone."

"You wanna match?"

Another cheerleader was paying attention as well. God, this was gonna be front page news by the end of the school day.

"You're my date," Coda said, in that "duh" tone that he and Maya were so good at. "Think of it as an audition for next year, where you can be the beautiful girl at my side when I get crowned King."

The eavesdropper decided to jump in. "When we're seniors? You'll be lucky to make the court," she laughed. "No one really knows you outside of your choir folks, and besides… Shannon Crescitelli is getting crowned Homecoming King," she said matter-of-factly.

"A track star?" Maya snorted. "Our quarterback, Gene Hightower, is getting crowned King," she corrected, just as matter-of-factly. "And everyone knows Coda," she added helpfully. "Doesn't mean they like him, though."

"Thank you, cheerleaders," Coda said to them, before turning back to the puce pixie next to him.

"You were serious about that?" Kim was asking.

"Of course," Coda said, still oblivious.

"Hmm, Coda," Kim mewed, suddenly interested in the pleats in her skirt. "I didn't know you were serious," she said softly, trying her hardest to retreat from whatever emotion he was about to be conducted by.

But no orchestrations came. He stared at her blankly, then stood and returned to his seat.

"Kim," Maya exhaled, while the other girl whistled. That almost made Kim angry. Who whistles at such things?

"I didn't know he was serious!"

"You knew he was serious," the eavesdropper said, as if she knew. Kim stared at her disbelievingly

Maya added, "It's Homecoming, Kim," as if Kim didn't know.

"I'm going with Brandon," the tiny girl simmered. "Everyone knew that." Why were they—all of a sudden—caring about his feelings when they had been so indifferent in those preceding moments?

"You told him you would go with him before Brandon Evans even thought to ask you," Maya said, turning back to her textbook.

"I didn't know he was serious," she repeated, watching Coda stare off into space, his expression still unreadable.

• • • • •

For a few more moments Coda was lost in his thoughts, moving slowly out of the major fair foot traffic until he stood near the entrance to a random tent.

"Have you been in there?" a passerby asked him. "That chick's for real!"

Coda looked up at the tent, unsure of what was being referenced. Above the door was a sign that read: "Madame Endora: Palm Reader."

Coda grimaced. A fortune-teller. No thanks. He headed over to another tent, one that looked like more fun and had less to do with the volatile spirit world.

"Care for a visit to the House of Mirrors?" the ticket taker asked him. A towering, brightly striped hat perched atop her head. "It's the most elaborate mirror maze this side of the Mississippi!"

"That's not hard, considering everything this side of the Mississippi sucks," Coda muttered. He observed the dark entrance and asked, "How many?"

"Five tickets," she responded and Coda whistled as she continued, "though you get a full refund if you can make it through in less than sixty seconds."

"How can you verify if I made it through in less than sixty seconds?" Coda asked, and she pointed around behind her.

"The exit is right around the corner," she replied. "I see who goes in and who comes out. One guy, a large one, has been in there for, like, fifteen minutes. So far no one's complained about a corpse or anything lewd, so I'll let him struggle a little while longer." She handed him a pair of plastic gloves, knowing he was going in.

Coda placed five tickets in her outstretched hand, laughing. "I don't know who I'm kidding. I'm not gonna make it out in sixty seconds!"

The ticket lady didn't hear him, because she was on to the next customer. He had already been suckered.

The entrance led to a walkway several feet long with glass on both sides through which Coda could see other babes in the woods that were struggling to find their way. It appeared that some of the mirrors were one-way, while some of them had mirrors on both sides. Either way, several people were almost walking into see-through panes of plastic that protected the glass, thinking the entire time that they had a clear walkway.

This would be more complicated than Coda had assumed.

Soon enough, he was surrounded by triangular-positioned mirrors, walking as fast as he could in an attempt to outpace his brain. By letting his instincts carry him forward and keeping his eyes on the black floor matting, he managed to avoid most of the visual tricks. Once he started thinking about it, he knew he'd be stuck, wandering aimlessly.

In fact, perhaps there were beams on the ceiling, or some telling pattern that could serve as a compass to him. Coda looked up with great expectations, only to be amazed at exactly how pitch-black the ceiling appeared to him. As he turned his mental marker back to the carpet, he ran into a mirrored corner.

Dangit! He had begun thinking and now it had gotten him fenced in. He spun himself in various directions, looking for a way out. He had a reflection on all sides, but now he just had to see which reflection was further away. There was no way he was completely surrounded.

No, he had to look at the carpet. The carpet was the surest thing, and Coda followed the corrugation where the carpet met the mirror until he was facing the opposite direction. When he looked up, however, he was no longer alone.

"Wes!" he yelped, leaping. "Don't scare me like that!"

The gigantic Wes was leaning against a pellucid panel across the aisle, staring directly at Coda. He grinned slowly. It was rather intimidating.

"You weren't scared, were you, Lakota?"

Coda's heart leapt into his throat.

To Coda, Wes had just sounded…well, not human, that's for sure. Wes had sounded…beautiful. Wes's voice was the fields laced with dragonflies and the honeysuckle fences at Coda's last California home.

That didn't sit well with Coda. That wasn't the natural sound for a voice to produce.

"Wh-what?" he managed to croak.

"You always say that nothing can scare you." Wes winked, and then arched his back as he stretched into a big yawn, nipple peeking at Coda between Wes's tank and windbreaker like an evil third eye.

Since when does Wes wink? Coda thought. "Now, when have I ever said that to you?" he asked, impulsively taking a step out of the tricky corridor to avoid being cornered in, but at the same time, praying that Wes would speak again.

"Lakota." That's all Wes said, rolling his head complacently onto his shoulder and letting his dark Barbie-ponytail dip past his shoulder.

Wes's eyes…usually were greener than Coda's. A rich jade, jarring against his tan skin. Currently they were blue—a strong, deep, icy blue, and the fact that they hadn't left Coda's face once, even with the yawn, was definitely unnerving.

"Your voice is so…*rich*," Coda tried not to marvel, spirits of longing and agitation fighting between his ears. "And your eyes…"

"Lakota, if you want to seduce me, you're going about it the wrong way," Wes chuckled.

Coda tried to hear Wes's words through that amazing voice. Wes would have never cracked that type of so-called joke. He also never called him by his full name. Coda was confused.

"Wes…"

Wes dipped his head handsomely, though his smile wasn't stretching to those cold blue eyes. Something had definitely changed.

"Wes, when'd you get blue eyes?" Coda asked, afraid that he was wrong. Perhaps Wes had always seen the world through blue eyes.

"Lakota, you should know that that's not my name."

Coda examined his peripherals, seeing multitudes of his frightened face staring back at him and staring away as if even his reflections were scared of his situation. Not a soul could be seen proceeding through his proximity, and even if he hollered for help, how could he be sure that anybody could reach him in time through such a maze?

"I said," Coda repeated forcefully, realizing how alone he was, "Wes, since when are your eyes blue?"

"Wes's eyes aren't blue," the Creature across the aisle snapped.

It smiled again, and Coda realized what white teeth Wes had. Big teeth. Just like the rest of him. Wes took two steps forward, body rippling with each movement. If it really wanted to, whatever it was that was controlling Wes's massive body could snap him in two pieces.

"Lakota," breathed the Creature in that intoxicating voice.

Whatever it was that was inside of Wes had produced an amazing presence within the redhead. Wes looked better than Coda had ever seen him appear. It was so weird; Coda wasn't attracted to him, but he felt drawn to him, all the while feeling repulsion to whatever other spirits were in the room with them—namely the other spirit that was in Wes.

"Lucifer?" Coda asked, before silently admonishing himself.

Why did you say that? You know that's crazy, he thought. But he knew even if it wasn't the main biblical villain, this creature couldn't be a heavenly one.

The Creature didn't flinch, didn't even acknowledge the mention of Satan's original name. Its smile of pearls did not even waver. Coda was thinking of Kim's run-in with a creature at the skate park. Kim had made no mention of amazing beauty; in fact, she had professed that it was rather ugly. Coda was thinking about how none of them, Ezekiel, Kim, Rico, nor himself, knew what to make of their situation. Coda was thinking about how they all had noticed each other's eyes were…somewhat different.

Coda was thinking of everything except what he should have been thinking of, which was the situation at hand, and when he did, the Creature was close enough to poke him.

Coda flinched and, in a split second, visualized the aisle on the other side of the transparent plastic-coated glass Wes stood in front of. His brain flashed red, and he involuntarily ricocheted off the carpeted floor of the mirror maze, leaping over Wes's head and a mirror wall to land on the other side of the panel.

He tried to quiet his accelerated breathing as he stared through the glass at Wes, his vision coated crimson.

Now the Creature in Wes's body reacted. Wes punched right through the pane, shattering the glass and ripping at the plastic until it came apart and he was able to step through it.

Coda felt the Spirit whisper to him. How could he have gotten so caught up in the moment? He was covered in the blood of Jesus Christ! He took off through the maze in his red-out state, keeping Wes in his sight until he was safe on the see-through side of a one-way mirror.

"Calm, dear," it said through Wes's lips, or maybe "come here." All Coda could focus on was how it sounded so amazing. He briefly wondered why he felt the desperate need to escape from such a dazzling being. Briefly, because he knew.

He was exasperated. He saw the floor behind him and did a back flip, furthering himself out of the Creature's path.

The beautybeast swiped at him. Coda just narrowly missed getting tagged, dodging around the corner. His vision was no longer red. He didn't think he could keep this up for long, but he'd go as long as he had to. Six hundred kicks and now this.

The Creature turned the corner and slanted its cobalt eyes.

"What do you want from me?" Coda screamed, a little more girlishly than he had planned.

The beautybeast paused. He, or it, spoke again, and Coda heard Pacific waves pounding on white sand. "You—tell your friends to stay out of my way. It will go easier for all of you Knock-Knocks if they do."

He examined Coda again with those *eyes*. Coda wondered what was happening to his life.

The Creature read him easily. "Your life is insignificant. Your princess cannot be helped."

My princess? Knock-Knocks?

Coda attempted to keep his inner turmoil from showing on his face. He had this. He had this. It was like improv. Old Testament improv. The comparison was doing little to quell his anxiety.

Help me, Jesus.

"Give it up," the Creature said greasily. "And tell her to give it up, too."

"I'll do no such thing," Coda declared. "I'll tell you what you're about to do, though." And just like that, some solid confidence materialized to back up his faith. "You will leave this place right now! Leave me alone and leave Wes alone! In the name of Jesus Christ which is higher and greater and holier and purer than any other name, I command you to leave!"

In that instant, the strange brilliance went out inside of Wes and his eyes rolled up to the ceiling. As they did, Coda saw that they were once again green. Wes crumpled onto the carpet facing the mirrors.

Coda cautiously knelt beside Wes's back, speaking softly.

"Wes."

He sat back on his heels and leaned forward at the waist, slowly reaching for Wes's bicep. "Come on, buddy. Wes."

His fingers connected with Wes's arm, shaking him. He felt a tear drop down his own cheek.

Wes's shoulders shook.

Coda leaned over to look at his face. "Buddy?"

Wes was weeping. The hand that the Creature had ripped at the plastic with was now bloody and Wes was cradling it with his other.

Coda scooted around to Wes's other side and placed Wes's head in his lap. Biting back his nausea, he reached for both of the boy's hands, grabbing the good one and inspecting the other for the source of all the blood.

"Scratches," Coda said. "That's all. Scratches."

Holding Wes's head in his lap, he was reminded of the night on the beach Kim had cradled him.

"Jesus loves you," Coda said. "All of this doesn't matter as long as you realize that and accept it."

Wes nodded, sniffling.

Coda helped the boy to his feet and led him through the maze.

"I'm gonna pray for you, okay, Wes?" he whispered in the teen's ear as patrons suddenly reappeared, laughing, hurrying, marveling, and sadly oblivious.

Was it wrong to think that God had some explaining to do?

9.

Favor, Perhaps

"I got you something," Becca Joy smiled.

"You didn't have to do that, BJ," Rico said, taking the nicely wrapped silver carton from her and throwing his free arm around her shoulders.

"You got me a webcam, so I got you something in return. Give and take," she grinned.

He had bought the webcam more for his own pleasure than hers, but she didn't have to know that yet. BJ looked for the remote and Rico quietly moved it out of her view before beginning to unwrap the package.

BJ sank further back into the couch in the Gutierrez's living room. "Don't rappers have more than women in bathing suits and ugly cars to exploit in their videos? And why do all of the R&B singers need to take off their shirts?"

"It's urban culture; you wouldn't get it," Rico murmured, staring at his new digital camera.

"I want pictures," BJ said, watching his face. "Of everything," she chuckled.

"Thank you, baby." He smiled, then proceeded to thank her in other ways. He knew *all types* of give and take.

At the sound of the front door, BJ slowly unraveled herself from Rico's grasp.

"What's up, BJ? What's up, Enrique?" waif-like Renata squealed, throwing herself over the back of the couch and landing directly between the two lovebirds. She embraced her brother, then her brother's girlfriend.

"So, how were the last weeks of Plebe Summer?" she inquired, focusing completely on her brother.

"Skippy," Rico replied. "I survived."

Renata nodded. "That's a start!"

"Yeah," Rico grinned. "A great one."

Renata caught sight of the camera.

"Oh, coolness! Is that yours?" she asked BJ.

BJ shook her head. "I got it for Rico."

"That's cool, brother," Renata nodded, heading into the adjoining hallway to deposit her backpack in her room. "Oh yeah," she continued over her shoulder, "you got calls from Coda, Ezekiel and that Kim Hamilton girl; they sure do call a lot lately!"

"Oh yeah," Rico said, "I wanna see Coda today. Don't let me forget." He snapped a picture of BJ, who turned and gave him a dirty look. "Has he got a cell phone yet?"

BJ shook her head, declining to verbally respond since Renata was still going.

"I have a boyfriend, now," the younger Gutierrez was saying, "but you can't tell Papá. Where's Mommy?"

"Wait," Rico began, laughing. "¿Que pasa, chica?"

"You have a boyfriend?" he and BJ asked simultaneously.

"Yeah and his name's Mario Suárez and he's from Ecuador and he's the cutest thing and I'm going to Homecoming with him and Papá knows about Homecoming—" She reappeared in the doorway to the hallway. "—but not about the boyfriend complication etcetera, etcetera, so you can't tell Papá. I ask again, where's Mommy?"

"She's not home," Rico replied, wrinkling his brow. His interest had been peaked. "How old is he?" he asked.

"Chill, big hermano. He's only two years older than me. I have so much to catch you up on and we only have a week, huh? He's a junior—remember his name: Mario—no mencionar esto a Papá. He is the cutest thing to ever step foot inside the grimy halls of George Washington Carver High, and when he asked me to go to Homecoming with him, I couldn't believe my luck! '¡Dios mio!' as Mommy would say."

As Renata gabbed about her new love and other updates on her entire existence, Rico listened intently, only breaking concentration to bend down and tie his shoes before deciding to just kick them off instead. Part of his job as a brother was to listen and to care, not to masquerade when both were required.

Without his parents there, existing just to pretend that the other did not, everything seemed perfect again. Having BJ at his side, who was home on a very short fall break, especially improved his world in that moment. He had met her at a rifle range during ROTC and used a prickly façade to get noticed. After he realized that being a jerk wasn't the route to take to win her affections, he started romancing and here they were. Still not officially together, they were closer than ever, yet in just four more days they'd be further apart physically than they'd ever been. The bitter irony.

• • • • •

Kim inhaled the humid air deeply, swinging the skates over her shoulder by their laces. Feeling eyes on her, she turned and caught Rico staring at her with his lips turned up into a casual smile. He exhaled, and it was more than oxygen.

"You caught me," he said, grinning in full now.

"I didn't know you smoked," she commented, moving closer.

"Only weed," he said, and she caught the scent in the air.

"Rico," she hissed. "Are you crazy! We're right outside of the Rollerway!"

"Only you and I," he said, gesturing to the dimly lit parking lot, filled with only vehicles. Beyond the parking lot was the county highway, linking their Middle of Nowhere to the Anywhere But Heres. "No one's expecting me to be out here when the event in there is for me. For you, too," he added, glancing at her.

"They pulled it off, Rico," Kim said, attempting to deflect. He was looking a little deeper into her than she was comfortable with. "A surprise party…it's only so crazy!"

Rico took another hit. Exhaling, he said, "Why aren't you in there, Kim? You already see one of my reasons."

Kim sighed, ensuring that her socks weren't standing in any parking lot surprises. "I'm on stage in there. Sometimes I just like sitting in the wings. Decompress."

"That's when I smoke," Rico said. "Helps me face the future." He thought back on her words from graduation. "We sit here today on the brink of forever," she had declared. Such truth.

Outside of the Rollerway she asked, "What do you mean? Your future's solid."

"It is," Rico said, agreeing. "But you know how sometimes…you forget that you can?"

"Can what?"

"Can anything. It sounds so epically angst and maizey, but… sometimes you don't feel like you're worth what everyone thinks you're worth. Daily life blocks your view of what's possible."

She was looking at him with something akin to awe on her face. He didn't know her well enough to know why. He took another hit.

"I get it," she said quietly.

"After a few hits, I get it, too." He shrugged. "Sometimes I'm such a whiny bitch."

"Who's not?" Kim replied. "Our generation is pretty self-obsessed. But really, Rico. You are worth what everyone thinks you're worth. You were worth Calvary." Gesturing to the blunt, she added, "I should introduce you to prayer."

He chuckled, tossing the blunt. "My mom says prayer provides," he said, "and stress strengthens."

They stood against the side of Rocky's Rollerway for a few moments in silence, united in the pressure of attempted perfection.

They had skipped class once, together, when they were juniors. Mr. Georgeson's, because, well, there was only so much humanly possible to take from that man. At some point when he took the relatable if intangible teenage angst of The Catcher in the Rye and, as was his specialty, turned it into an exercise in Christ symbolism, something inside of the girl had snapped. The next morning Rico overheard her muttering that she couldn't take it. Wouldn't take it, rather. Mad as hell and not gonna take it anymore type of thing.

"I wanna leave."

Rico was casual. "Let's go."

She looked at him, panicked that he had caught her voice on his ear.

"Where would we go?" she asked, half discarding of the idea, half plea for him to have an actual answer.

He shrugged noncommittally. Who knew how far she was willing to take this idea. "Harry's Hash House? I could go for a nice breakfast."

"Harry's Hash House?" Benny Commons had asked. "Can you bring me back a Hashtag Biscuit?"

Rico ignored her. This was between him and the girl who was willing to dip a toe into the reckless side. "Mr. Georgeson always steps out of the classroom right before the bell to grab his coffee out of the lounge. My car is parked right outside the Science Building. He'll never know we were here."

She had let the thought linger long enough for Rico to know that he had watered the seed properly.

It was a prison break. They awkwardly stood as Mr. Georgeson disappeared through the doorway, and Kim stiffly sauntered to sharpen her pencil, though Rico walked straight out of the classroom with his books. Kim left her pencil and hurried after him, begging Gene Hightower to toss her her backpack. Catching it, then catching Rico, they stiff-legged it down the hallway.

"Which side of the Science Building did you park on?" Kim asked, avoiding the eye-contact of familiar—and now strangely alien—students.

"The only side that has parking," Rico replied, heart pumping a little more intensely than he had expected. The last time he had skipped a class was freshman year when he hadn't done Geometry homework. He was pretty sure he had gotten a beating for it.

"Of course," Kim said mindlessly, as they rounded a corner, footsteps sounding like cannon-blasts on the cheap tile.

Outside, it was as if there were sniper rifles trained on them, as they jumped and slid along the sidewalk until they reached the parking lot and finally Rico's car.

Inside they sat, breathing and thanking God for making it that far.

"We can't sit here," Kim said, her inhales turning into hyperventilation. "Didn't Wayne Emerson get caught out here with that Carver High girl because Dr. Paul was doing first period parking lot checks?"

"Let's go," Rico managed to croak, blood banging through his ears as if being beat by a drum major. He cranked the ignition, reversed, and pealed out.

They didn't ask for a table. They felt—and probably looked—guilty as sin. The Oakwood Omelet, a Hashtag Biscuit and a sweet tea for him, a breakfast burrito with an orange juice for her. To go.

They ate in the Wal-Mart parking lot, making stilted small talk. Neither of them could finish their food, and their taste buds could not enjoy what they did partake in. So it was back to campus. And the only parking spot open was in front of the principal's office, with its giant windows.

Rico swore.

"Oh no," Kim moaned, her hands clenched tightly.

They drove around the campus one more time, and sure enough, the only spot remaining was near the auditorium, at Dr. Paul's front steps.

"You were late and I came to pick you up," Rico said, parlaying the excuse they'd probably need.

"My parents are gonna kill me," she said, almost catatonic.

The bell rang, and they both jumped, shoved into action.

They shot out of the car, walking until they mingled with the other students, heading to their second period classes. Once they were safe, the giggles started.

Rico figured neither of them would have the guts to skip again, though his memory turned their frightened excursion into an epic adventure. It was more badass that way.

. . . . .

"Hi, welcome to Miller's Grill," Kim said brightly. "How many are in your party?"

She mechanically sat a party of five at a table near a window, privately wishing that she could be on the other side of that window where freedom waited. At the nearby shopping plaza, maybe, sitting inside of the dark movie theatre with a large cup of ice-cold soda and a big old tub of salt, butter and popcorn, enjoying any movie that would take her mind off the everyday. Kim didn't find her work as a hostess grueling, but she would certainly say it was monotonous. The same type of people with the same type of requests, questions, and preferences would move in and out while Kim felt like she was running in place.

Kim began passing out the menus, launching into the speech that she had already rattled off at least ninety times that day.

"This entire week is our Fall Madness Special!!! All bar drinks are ten percent off and all deserts come free with a meal purchase of at least twenty dollars during lunch hours which end this hour, so you're just in time!!!"

Right. Always insert an annoying customer joke here. Yes, sir. Wow, that was an original one sir. Are you done, now? Good. I have more exclamation points to abuse.

"Your server will make you aware of today's other specials!!! Enjoy your meal!!!"

As she walked back up towards her post at the front door, she glanced at the clock over the takeout bar. *Aha, thank You, Jesus: saved from the next group of customers!*

"Leeza, your turn to man the door," she announced happily as she removed a pencil from her ponytail of straightened strands. A chunky red-faced girl begrudgingly took Kim's place behind the greeters' podium.

Kim headed into the hot kitchen and hollered through the rising steam and over the sizzling pans and clanking utensils.

"Frankie! Let's go!"

A reedy teen, slightly taller than her, which didn't say much for him, turned the corner around a rack of drying dishes, holding a pot full of steaming spaghetti noodles in his hands.

"Is it four o'clock yet?" he asked.

"Boo, I'm off work!" she said, rolling her neck slightly. "What do you think? I'm blowin' this lemonade stand, with or without you. What'll it be?"

"Alright," Frankie said, laughing. "I won't be too far behind. And it's 'popsicle stand,' grrrl."

"Whatever," she giggled.

A server passed with a steaming tray of chicken and pasta.

"Mmm," Kim purred. "Maybe I'll get some of that to go." But she couldn't afford it, so she let the thought slip out of her mind.

After punching her time card and grabbing her jacket, she stepped out into the cool Atlanta air. Praise God, it was so good to be outside again where not everything smelled like steak, noodles and sauces.

It was...odd to be in a large city feeling normal while very weird things seemed to be happening in microscopic Glynn County. Odd, yet nice to be so far away, lost in the wildness of metro-Lanta while those peculiarities happened further south. Weird things like... like Coda's attack. Kim wondered if God would reveal exactly what was happening to her and her friends. Is that what they were, now? Were they all her friends? Coda was for sure, even if she didn't show him often enough. When was the last time she had talked to him?

Her cell phone rang accusingly.

"Hello, Ma? What's up?...Yeah, I just got off work. Frankie and I are about to head back to campus before we hit the mall tonight...Church tomorrow? Well, I had planned to, but...Tell Azari what?...Sure! ¡No problemo, señora!...I love you, too, Mom...Bye."

Azari, Delia's other child, often teased Kim, saying that her phone voice was deep and proper, similar to her speech-giving voice. She had laughed and told him that it wasn't intentional.

Azari pastored a decent-sized congregation in Cabbagetown, which was a convenient distance from Clark Atlanta. That was one of the factors that put the senior Hamiltons at ease, knowing how close she'd be to her brother while still far from home. But Kim had her life and curly-haired Azari had his, meaning they didn't see each other as often as her parents wished.

She sat on one of the wood and iron benches outside of the restaurant's entrance, absently watching the traffic as the many cars passed, parked or departed. Some torn down car slowed as it went by the curb.

"Oh, no," Kim said softly to herself. "Brotha needs to keep rolling."

The driver of the brown jalopy slowed to a crawl and Kim was blinded by the glinting gold on his teeth.

When he drove off without initiating a conversation, Kim released a sigh. There were so many trifling boys around, and Kim couldn't help but wonder how Maya would respond to the many different ones that Kim had run into since August. Maya was phenomenal with comebacks pulled straight out of thin air. She had told one guy at Homecoming, "Oh, you wanna get laid? Crawl up a chicken's feathery butt and wait till spring."

Ugh. Spring. By spring Kim had set her goal of having picked a major. She still had no idea what she wanted. Nothing was speaking to her. She had promised herself that she wouldn't become a four-year freshman, adrift in seminars and tuition, craving direction.

Frankie came up behind her, checking the messages on his cell. Kim chewed the inside of her lip.

"You ready to go, chile?"

"Yeah," Kim muttered. "Frankie, you ever feel like… like you need an extra push to face the future?"

He looked up from his phone. "What?"

"Like you don't know if you're capable of…*anything*." She glanced at him. "Like daily life blocks your view of…" She sighed. "Never mind. I'm being stupid."

Frankie touched her shoulder, staring seriously into her eyes. "Girl. You is kind. You is smart."

Kim fell out laughing, while he continued.

"You is im*paw*tant."

"*The Help*? Really?"

"You speak in movies," Frankie said.

Kim shook her head. "Yeah." Rico had said it. *Prayer provides and stress strengthens.* And she was stronger than most. She would consider this practice. God never gave more than was bearable.

· · · · ·

"I finally get Halloween!" Kim said, remembering to look both ways before she crossed the deserted Atlanta street. In the neighborhoods that she frequented, the sidewalks and front porches were always more crowded than the streets. "I never got it before, but now I get it!"

Maya chuckled over the line. "And why is that, Kim?"

"The parties!" Kim squealed into the receiver. "Clark Atlanta is going crazy with all these Halloween parties!"

"Halloween isn't for another month, though."

"Yeah, that's how crazy they're getting. I've already heard of three parties and been invited to two. One of them's the weekend before and the other's on the actual day, but I don't know if I'll go to either of them."

Maya chuckled again. "*Three* parties?" Her husky chuckle turned into flat out laughter. "How is that going crazy with *anything*?"

Kim giggled. "I don't know. But I never expected this school to be such a...party central! I mean it's crazy, Maya! There's a party somewhere every weekend, plus all of the clubs and the school sponsored activities—"

She pulled open the door to the brightly lit convenience store.

Maya was putting in her own exhausted two cents. "—and the traditions and the tests and—"

"Wayment. That's what you get for going to a historical liberal arts women's college. That's nobody's fault but your own, Maya-ya."

"No, Kim, I love Wesleyan. And the traditions. Maybe not the tests, but I'm just exhausted."

"Me, too, boo," Kim giggled. She picked up a pack of cookies. "I can't sleep. Someone down the hall keeps blasting Lena Park songs day in and day out. She is hot stuff here. I didn't know she was this popular! Did you know that she has a new album coming out this winter?"

Maya laughed dryly. "No I didn't, and, to be honest, I don't really care."

"Well, her new single is supposed to drop in October. Everyone's anticipating it." Kim inspected a can of Vienna sausages, but placed them back in a hurry.

"You know, I get Halloween," Maya was saying. "I just don't like it."

"Yeah, my mom, too. She says it just functions as a day for everyone to live out their fantasies in public. Be crazy without having to be drunk."

"Exactly," Maya said.

"Hey, Maya, did you know that quackle means choke or suffocate?" she asked, looking at stacks of canned sardines.

Maya sighed. "No, I didn't know."

"Yeah," Kim continued, looking at a battalion of Spam, "and a quacksalver is one who falsely pretends to have any type of medicine knowledge."

"Dyna-na, are you reading the dictionary again?"

"Yup," Kim said, returning to the Vienna sausages, "and 'q' words are the best, because they're harder to remember! Hey, Maya, do you think that Vienna sausages would go good with Ramen noodles?"

Maya coughed deliberately. "*No.* Why, may I ask, are you reading the dictionary?"

Kim picked up three cans of Vienna sausages anyway, then thought better of it and set one of the cans back on the shelf. "Well, I'm still in the process of making friends—and a quaint quantity of qu...qu...students I have to choose from—so aside from homework and that online journal, it's only so boring!"

"Oh, okay," Maya mumbled and Kim could tell she was sidetracked. Even so, true friendship rang through. "You only read the dictionary when you're stressed."

Despite her observation, Maya obviously had gotten her attention pulled from the conversation. Kim knew what move to make. "Have you talked to Genie?" she asked.

Maya was silent for a moment, and Kim took the opportunity to consider her two options as far as the flavors of the noodles were concerned.

"Yeah," Maya finally answered, "and we argued."

"You strung him along all year." The conviction came unflinchingly.

"I know and I didn't mean to. He knew it wasn't going anywhere."

"He did not know, otherwise..."

"I wouldn't have been leading him on, I know." Maya sighed. "I did do a pretty sucky thing. I just wish we could stay friends."

"Sure," Kim mumbled, picking chicken just narrowly over beef. "Chicken," she muttered.

"What?" Maya asked sharply.

"Oh, no, boo," Kim responded, wincing at the slang she was using. "I was talking about my noodles."

Maya started laughing. "Your noodles?"

"Oh, sure, that was real funny," Kim frowned. "It just hasn't been my day. Did you know that the phrase is 'blow this *popsicle* stand?'"

"I've got a popsicle you can blow," Maya said, laughing harder.

"This conversation is hopeless," Kim said tartly. She gazed towards the door and all previous thoughts flew from her brain.

A little boy stood out on the sidewalk, gazing in hungrily. He was emaciated beyond belief, right out of those commercials where some white lady sings "Amazing Grace" and a number flashes across the bottom of the screen. His eyes though—they were beyond anything that could be depicted on the television screen.

Kim's thoughts became so powerful that her intense concentration corresponded with an intense grip on the plastic noodle packages, and it burst. A singular crack, like lightning, and suddenly Ramen proceeded to shower down over the entire store. In her surprise, she dropped everything in her hands, though her cell stayed glued between her shoulder and her ear.

A couple of people sporting elaborate hair styles that they shouldn't have purchased in the first place (be it obvious money issues or common good taste) gave her evil looks and some lashed out with their tongue.

Kim prayed that one of her unique abilities was to disappear.

The cashier leaned her head over the counter

"Girl, I hope you know you payin' for that," she said, with a twist of her neck.

"Yes, ma'am," Kim responded weakly. She bent over to pick up the leftover noodle packages and her sausages.

"Girl, let me call you back, quick like," Kim muttered into her phone.

"No, I'll call you. I'm going to be in a meeting for the girls who are rushing the fraternity," Maya said.

"Okay, Maya. You have fun…with your fraternity?"

"Oh, I will," Maya said, ignoring the speculative tone. "And you will, too, I'm sure." From Maya's laughter, Kim knew that she had heard the ruckus.

"Yeah. Bye."

"Bye."

When Kim stepped outside, the little boy was standing off to the side of the convenience store. He was wasting away before her very eyes.

"Hi," she said brightly. "Are you waiting on your parents?"

The boy shook his head in declination.

"Would you like something to eat?" she asked. The boy nodded.

Kim smiled, feeling tears prick her eyes. Crouching, she pulled one of the sausage cans out of her white plastic bag. She reached for the tab and, very carefully so that no more "accidents" occurred, opened the grey can.

"Here you go," she said, handing him the sausages and sticking the sharp lid into her plastic bag.

The boy smiled—his eyes shone gold for a slight moment—and Kim rose to go.

As she stood, the can's lid ripped through the bag and cut into her knee. Kim grimaced horribly and inspected the injured knee.

It was deep enough for certain, but it wasn't dangerous. She'd live.

She stepped off the pavement, straight into a puddle of something she was actually glad she couldn't identify. Her white sneakers were ruined. She swore, then popped her hands up to her mouth and turned in dismay.

"I'm so sor—"

But the boy had run off. Disappeared. Or something. Kim shook her head and stepped out of the puddle, wishing that she had someone to laugh about it with. Or even cry about it with, since she didn't know which reaction this situation called for. On top of it all, with the destruction of a pair of shoes, that would be the eternal grave for a good portion of her upcoming paycheck.

What a great result to her Samaritan deed, but she really couldn't blame anybody but herself. After all, imperfection is what she had asked for during these initial post-high school times. And lately it seemed she always got what she asked for. God's favor, perhaps. For better or worse.

Keep it together, girl, she thought. *Composure, INC.*

"Ay, gura!"

Kim couldn't believe it. It was a different street and a different week, but here was the same Negro and the same brown jalopy.

"You need a ride?" someone spoke up from the back, and she recognized him. He was a cutie in one of her classes. A very specific cutie. "We got an extra seat."

Kim should have said no. "I'm not going too far," she said instead. "You think you could?"

"It 'pends," said the gold tooth from behind the wheel. "You female impersonayin'?"

Kim swallowed her pride.

"No, not tonight."

The boy in the back opened his door and stepped out. "Hop in."

She should have walked. The car was just as torn up on the inside as it was on the outside. There was a female scrub, a little chunky, who turned around with a dissecting gaze.

"I saw you at the gym this afternoon," the scrubette spoke up. "You're a beast."

The fellow in the back laughed, while inspecting Kim from head to toe. "A beast at the gym?" he asked.

Kim had no response, so he continued looking her over. He saw the blood on her knees.

"Uh-oh," he clucked, "you got a little cut there. Maybe I can help you out with that. Stasia," he said to the girl in the passenger seat, "hand me the stuff from the glove compartment."

Stasia was forced to pause with her own scrutiny of Kim in order to dig through the crammed glove box.

"Do you remember me?" the man in the backseat asked.

"Of course, Dishon," Kim smiled. "We have a class together."

"I gave you my number," Dishon added.

"Mmm, you did," she said neutrally.

Dishon began introductions. "That's Stasia up front; Nicholas is driving. You two, this is Kimi."

"Nice to meet you," she said, as Stasia tossed Dishon a plastic container.

"Would you like some salve?" Dishon asked, screwing the top off of container.

"Thank you," Kim said, taking the receptacle from his hands.

"So where are we taking you back to?" Dishon asked as she applied the salve to her knee, and she realized that underneath that Paul Bunyan beard and those animalistic eyebrows there lay the soft curves of a boy's face.

"The Clark Atlanta campus."

"Of course Clark Atlanta," Dishon chuckled. "We know that's where you go, we just want to know what part of the dorms."

"Oh, I'm going to the library," Kim said. "Studying."

"Studying what?" Dishon asked, an old man twinkle in his eye. He figured he was steering the situation. In a few words he had created a relationship and put on the pants. She fumed.

"My Bible."

He raised his eyebrows, but said nothing more about her study habits. "Yo, Nicholas," he hollered over the music that was suddenly pumping through the speakers. Stasia, having just inserted some CD, was nice enough to turn down the volume, if only a little bit.

"Yeah?" was the eloquent response.

"Isn't the library down the street from rehearsal?"

"Yeah," was the eloquent reply.

"Yeah, so you'll just dock when we dock," Dishon notified her.

She handed him the salve and asked, "What rehearsal?"

"Me and Nicholas are in a band," Dishon explained.

"Oh, really?" Kim asked. "What kind of band?"

Stasia laughed as if Kim was the greatest comedian she had ever heard. Kim didn't appreciate the reaction.

"A rock band," Dishon replied. "What other kind is there?"

So this was an actual multifaceted Black man. She of course had expected him to be some aspiring rapper. "What instrument do you play?"

"What support do I provide," he corrected, steering the conversation once again. "To insinuate that I function in only one capacity within our band would be to diminish the role that I serve. I play bass guitar and supply backing vocals. Nicholas plays the drums. Do you play any instruments, Bible Lady?"

"Piano. Sometimes."

"Everyone does," Dishon nodded.

"Mmm. What's the name of your band, Rock Star?" she asked.

"Fallen," he responded, undaunted.

"Fallen," she repeated, wishing that Stasia girl would look away.

"You should come see us play sometime. That is, if you're not, ah, studying."

Kim clucked her teeth playfully. "I don't know; I need an extra helping of Jesus rice dealing with these Clark Atlanta hoodlums.

"Tell me about it. But Fallen isn't compromised of hoodlums. Though I'm sure you'll find that out for yourself. If you're interested." Dishon grinned, a harvest field of white teeth.

And with that smile, Kim turned into a gooey puddle of head-over-heels. Figuratively, of course. As far as powers were concerned, how does the strength of many men match up against the gorgeous smile of one?

10.
Those Mysterious Ways

Justus

sabi? yeah, it has been a while since we've talked, but
i think that's everyone. oh well, how is everything at
mercer? your roommate sounds cool. my roomate's cool, he
likes anime. here it's been cool. my classes are cool,
and i've signed up for hapkido martial arts. christopher
and i ride our bikes about every other day. i'm learning
some cool tricks, ha ha. hope everything goes good with
you. take care.

Ezekiel

No trees were harmed in the delivery of this message,
however several thousand electrons were terribly incon-
venienced.

• • • • •

"They say Lena Park is the Maya Angelou of our generation!" Jordan
Vang chuckled merrily, gracefully brushing her ebony hair over her
shoulders.

"What?" Ezekiel puffed, sitting back on his legs and keeping his
spine straight. Maya Angelou was the Maya Angelou of their generation. "Who says that?"

Jordan laughed, stretching her arms out in front of her as if preparing
a witch's brew. "Okay, nobody, but I like the sound of it. *Upsetting
regrets,*" she warbled. "*Hard-hearted upsets!*"

"Lines that rhyme aren't always poetry," Ezekiel declared.

Ezekiel and Jordan were preparing for their *hapkido* class in the
Campus Recreation Center at Georgia Tech. They were both kneeling in
a line with their classmates; all were uniformed in black karategi. Both

Ezekiel and Jordan sported white belts, but the class had a range of colored belts, from white through yellow, green, blue, red, black-striped, and on to black.

Ezekiel closed his eyes and began his breathing. He heard Jordan mumbling through her mental notes, "Flag breathing, peace breathing, tension release breathing…"

Silent breathing would be nice, Christopher Nyberg, a hapkido classmate and fellow KWA graduate thought, and it was amplified into Ezekiel's meditation. It was so strange how after a couple of months, Ezekiel had gotten very used to hearing, or maybe feeling (seeing, maybe?) thoughts from other minds as if they were in his own. He was enthralled with the fact and wondered what it all meant. One day he had called Justus Alexander to coolly bring up the subject.

"Justus, what would you do if you could read minds?"

Ezekiel had wished he could know what Justus was thinking after Ezekiel asked the question, but his talent didn't work over the phone. If it did, he'd know that Justus was speculating about an atrocious smell was that was escaping from under his bed at Mercer.

"You mean like in that Mel Gibson movie?" was Justus's response. Ezekiel was awestruck at the connection, recalling similarities in the movie and in his own current situation. The biggest difference was that he wasn't accosted by random brain waves. It was just an unsystematic toss of thought now and then, but he had found that if he probed enough, he could dig up the thoughts. Then there were the times, like with his dentist, that information, not necessarily thoughts or feelings, flooded his brain.

"Yeah," Ezekiel had laughed. "Like, what would you do?"

"Go crazy, dude." Justus made it sound so basic. "Oh, dude, I just found out where this horrible smell in my room was coming from."

"Where?" queried Ezekiel.

"One of my socks," came Justus's amused reply. "Last month, I stepped in a puddle of—oh, my grammy's calling. I'll have to let you go." And Justus quickly proved true to his word.

So the conversation hadn't proved as fruitful as Ezekiel had hoped, but the astounding possibilities of what he could do were never too far from his mind.

Back in the classroom, it was time to stretch. The whole class, about twelve students, stood barefoot on carpeted flooring in order to face a tall mirror that spanned the length of the room. Behind the *hapkido* pupils, a padded wall was prepared for fun exercises Ezekiel had yet to learn. The two adjacent walls were glass; the window on Ezekiel's left held a view of the campus and the beautiful city beyond, while the one on the right looked out across the CRC basketball court that sometimes doubled for indoor volleyball and tennis courts. The court didn't stay as crowded as most people would expect, while far above it a running track circled the entire room. Several gorgeous, scantily clad ladies could be seen working up a heavy sweat on the track, which Ezekiel's antenna could decipher from the distracted thoughts of his classmates.

Ezekiel's self-seemingly disfigured eyes were on the glass mirror, however, double-checking his gi. His hadn't been lightened by untreated or over-treated washings like some of the other kids in his class. It also wasn't wrinkled. It had everything to do with self-respect.

Stretches. Fifty knuckle push-ups. He was hardly breaking a sweat.

• • • • •

"Okay, I'm sweating now," Christopher remarked, wiping the perspiration from his brow as he and Ezekiel rode their bikes along the smooth Atlanta sidewalks.

It was not an easy thing to do, getting body heat up in such cold weather. It also was not a healthy thing to do, so it was probably time for them to head back to Georgia Tech. That's what Christopher's statement inferred.

They had donned helmets, bike gloves and jackets to keep the cold wind off their upper torsos. Christopher wore pants that covered his pencil-shaped legs while Ezekiel wore his khaki shorts, his muscular legs unbothered by the November chill.

Ezekiel said nothing, focusing on the sidewalk and the pedestrians. The two often took exuberant bike rides around the streets of Atlanta. At Tech, the thing for everyone, like it or not, was bike riding. Some used them simply as transportation, others were members of cycling clubs, and some, like Ezekiel and Christopher, rode the paint off their bikes. Between tricks and races and every other possible thing that could be done with a bike, they were becoming furious riders. They would ride and ride until either they couldn't go much further, or until one of them had other appointments to keep.

Ezekiel caught a tossed thought: a woman was in pain. He prodded into her well of thoughts before pulling back. He wasn't willing to take on the weight of the world, so it was often better to avoid thoughts he maybe wasn't meant to know. He shook off her depression as best as he could. At one brief point he had unwisely hoped that his riding helmet would protect his head from other people's thoughts, but it was quickly proven that that was not the case. Christopher, for example, was thinking about Governor's Honors.

Ezekiel had gone to Governor's Honors—the best summer camp in the world for high school upperclassmen—along with Christopher, both of them "majoring" in math. He met Vanessa there. He had been jogging shirtless around the campus in the heat of the afternoon and that's when Vanessa took notice. He introduced her to the enjoyments of binary division and in turn, the nice Cedar City girl introduced him to Jesus during their joint spring break. He smiled at the thought, then found himself veering to avoid a drunk.

Through the drunkard's haze burst many vulgar and violent thoughts that Ezekiel blocked by diving deeper into his own mind. In lieu of all the recent developments in his life, Ezekiel had been encouraged by Kim Hamilton, who had also attended that Governor's Honors camp, incidentally, to draw closer to God. He attempted instead to draw closer to Vanessa by telling her about the mind reading. Vanessa got upset and gave him an ultimatum. No more lies, no matter if he was joking or just crazy. So he followed Kim's advice and drew closer to God, even if *church* wasn't something he felt ready for. He used the Bible as his telephone to God's office. He'd spend long sessions in the Georgia Tech library, just studying.

Christopher had invited Ezekiel to his church before, but Ezekiel never showed up. In his mind, church was full of hypocrites. Jesus didn't come down to earth to establish "Christianity." He came down to establish belief and spread the understanding of His grace. Once humans turned Jesus into religion instead of a lifestyle, eventually turning religion into rules and opinions, they lost the true path. That's the way Ezekiel saw it.

"Let's turn here," he suggested to Christopher, and they did, leaving behind a crowded sidewalk and varying unpleasant scents, bound for the familiar crowds of Tech.

"Excuse me, dude," called a voice, causing Ezekiel to look quickly over his shoulder. He glanced up ahead at Christopher, whistled and swung his bike back in a circle. Christopher took notice and followed.

He pulled to a stop in front of a pimply teenage boy who had an uncomfortable expression on his face. He was shielding himself from the hillside wind in a denim jacket.

"God says, 'Fight,'" the teen said bluntly, thrusting his hands in his pants pockets.

Christopher laughed.

Ezekiel stared at the kid, steadying himself atop the bike on his tip-toes. "What?"

"Don't think I'm weird or anything, but God says, 'Fight.' He told me to tell you. You're Shen Long, right?"

Christopher looked at Ezekiel, disbelievingly.

"*God* told you? Fight what?" Ezekiel asked. How'd this kid know Ezekiel's given name?

"I'm just telling you exactly what He told me," the boy said defensively. "Um, there's a time of war and a time of peace." He shrugged again. "Fight."

"Right," chuckled Christopher.

The boy shot an annoyed look in Christopher's direction. Turning back to Ezekiel, he quoted, "'For My thoughts are not your thoughts, neither are your ways My ways,' saith the Lord. 'For as the heavens are higher than the earth, so are My ways higher than your ways, and My thoughts than your thoughts.'"

Ezekiel let this marinate. "Fight," he repeated.

"Can we go?" Christopher asked, not buying into the exchange.

Ezekiel turned his bike around, prematurely breaking eye contact.

"Thanks," he said, though not sure if he meant it.

He took off down the sidewalk alongside Christopher, racing the falling sun.

• • • • •

"Boo," whispered a familiar voice near Ezekiel's ear.

"'Sabi?" Ezekiel asked, only slightly daunted.

Jordan Vang smiled her familiar smile and scooted into one of the wooden seats across from him, holding a school folder in her hands. Right behind her was their *hapkido* classmate Phil Grayson. Phil was a little taller than Ezekiel, but plump with tiny eyes.

Ezekiel was sitting at a thick wooden table in the Tech library, surrounded by more wooden tables and gigantic bookcases. A few scattered students were studying at the adjoining tables and some at the computers across the room, but the library wouldn't fill up until around seven that night and would stay that way until it shut down early in the morning for a few hours.

"What are you doing?" Jordan asked, as Phil leaned his stuffed backpack against the table on the green swirled carpet.

Ezekiel gestured to the religious books that formed a Stonehenge around him. "Research."

"What kind of project?" Jordan asked, destroying his formation by picking up and inspecting a concordance.

"Not a project," Ezekiel said. "Just research."

"It's not for a class?" Phil asked.

Ezekiel laughed. "No."

"Oh," Phil and Jordan said in unison.

"Weird, huh?" Ezekiel asked. He wondered why they were there.

"Yeah," Jordan giggled. She was always in high spirits—probably because she could kick the butts of any guy on campus. She wasn't the best student in their karate class, but there were advantages to being the only girl.

"Well," she sighed, "we just came to bother. We have to study for the School of Earth and Atmospheric Sciences."

Ezekiel laughed. "Okay," he said, meaning, *whatever*.

Jordan reached to replace the concordance atop a prophecy dictionary and a lexicon. "Get back to your—"

The Stonehenge became a line of dominoes as the pressure Jordan put on the concordance knocked them all over, some of them onto the floor.

"Oh, darn," Jordan said, giggling. She began to pick up the books, aided by the boys.

"What do you need a lexicon for?" Phil asked, holding up the thick manual.

Ezekiel shrugged. "I don't know what I need it for or even *if* I need it. It was just in the section, so I thought it would be better to be safe than sorry."

Jordan stood from where she had been clearing off the floor. She placed a printed editorial on the table.

"'Human Voltage: What Happens When Lightning Strikes Flesh?'" She sat again. Her interest had grown. She asked, "What exactly are you researching, Ezekiel?"

"Umm, lightning," he laughed, growing uncomfortable. Why did she have to knock the books over?

Phil was looking over the article.

"Lightning strikes or just lightning in general?" Phil asked. "I'm asking 'cause this article is just about lighting striking humans."

"Lighting striking humans," Ezekiel nodded.

"And the Bible?" Jordan asked, stacking the books neatly.

Ezekiel sighed. "A good friend of mine was struck by lightning, but came up with practically none of the post-strike symptoms."

Phil's eyes grew wide. "And they're alive?"

"Yeah," Ezekiel said, "and they don't have the permanent burns, any Lichtenberg scars, no internal trauma, the fractures or anything, you know? They didn't have any neurological injuries, either. They did, however, suffer from temporary loss of consciousness and, for a good while after, a slight version of amnesia where they didn't remember what had happened in those moments before they were struck or how they got back in their beds."

"Plural?" Phil asked.

"Uh, no, sorry. Her bed."

"You mean she was struck by lightning and woke up at home?" Phil asked.

"Yeah. Umm—"

"And did she go see a doctor?"

"Well, since then, yeah, but not about *that* because she didn't…know how to say it at first, and, like, when she did, there didn't seem to be any point since she hadn't struggled with any symptoms—"

"And she figured it was nothing too serious," Phil snorted, but nodding as if he understood. His eyes pored over a separate research article, entitled "Adrenaline: The Hysterical Strength."

Jordan held up the concordance again. "So you think that it might be an act of God, Ezekiel?"

Phil smiled, looking up from the column. "That God and those mysterious ways," he said in a sportscaster voice.

…neither are your ways My ways, saith the Lord.

Ezekiel responded to Jordan's query. "Well, my other friend thinks so, so I was just seeing what Biblical mentions there were of lightning, and the ones I found are just saying stuff like 'and there was thunder and lightning and the people were afraid' and 'they were fast as lightning' and stuff like that."

"Do you have a list of those scriptures?" Jordan asked. Ezekiel handed her what he had. She opened up the lexicon and found a cause to giggle. "Oh." She replaced the lexicon and picked up the Bible.

"Are you okay?" Ezekiel asked, oblivious to her mistake.

Jordan just smiled, smothering her embarrassment with giggles and the sound of flipping pages.

"Just to be clear," Phil held the article in his hands and spoke, "this 'friend' wouldn't happen to be you, would it?"

"Phil!" Jordan tsked, as Ezekiel covered his uneasiness with a cool gaze in Phil's direction.

Phil shrugged. "Just figured that would be cliché. Plus you said 'she,' so… But I do have a different question. What if you're just looking up the wrong things?"

Ezekiel pondered this question. "What do you mean?"

"I mean, what's happened to your friend since then? After she was struck by lightning? You mean to tell us that the only side effect was unconsciousness and being supernaturally transplanted to her bed? Is she sure that her parents didn't find her?"

"Where was she?" Jordan asked.

"She was on the highway, next to her car, you know? And when she woke up, well, like I said, she said that at first she didn't even remember the lightning."

"Right," Jordan said, following encouragingly.

"And then she remembered, but, I mean, her car was there at her house and…"

"Were there any other side effects?" Phil asked. "Neurological or otherwise? Because I think you're looking up the wrong stuff."

· · · · ·

She had heard the intruder from the hallway, pulled the gun from behind the china cabinet and entered her study with determined stealth.

"How'd you get in here?" Patricia asked, gripping the weapon in a sure fashion, intent that he see it. She needed him to put the case of vials down. He couldn't possibly know how important the RiD serum was to her, but she didn't want him to register any potential leverage.

"What matters is the fact that I'm here."

His voice was young, anonymous. Some kid trying to live large or impress his friends. She could barely make out the color of his eyes in the darkness, though the rest of his face was obscured by some type of dark mask.

"This isn't just a house, little boy. This is a home." Her words implied the emotion that her tone didn't. "I suggest you leave the same as you arrived. Empty-handed." As soon as he put the serum down, she would kill him.

"I didn't come empty-handed, Patricia."

She caught her breath. He knew her name. This wasn't a random break-in. So what the hell was it?

She gripped the gun a little tighter. "This is a big kids' game."

"Let me show you how it's played," he said.

She didn't even seen him move. Clutching her neck where the needle had been, she realized he had known about the serum. He already had an injection prepared in case someone interrupted him, maybe for her specifically. None of her realizations mattered. He was gone before she hit the floor.

When she found herself again, it took her moments to figure out the gist of what had occurred in her quickly erased past. In less than seven minutes someone had made off with the RiD solution. It had been precise and timed. It had been in her own house.

Whoever it was had been ready for her. And she hadn't been ready for them, but now...

Now she was ready to do damage.

11.
Fallen

Eden's onyx hair swung between her shoulder blades, dancing across her back like two liquid lovers as she swayed to the blasting rhythms of punk rock. Her tight red flamenco dress matched her painted lips and the flower blooming like a young crush over her left ear. Her delicate skin had paled slightly since her Brunswick days, but she was no less beautiful, just as a summer day with a Popsicle is no less blistering. She smiled a big smile at Kim when they spotted each other and they embraced tightly.

"Dang, Kim, it's so nice to see you! What are you doing *here*?" Eden asked, careful not to spill the contents of her blue plastic cup when she gestured to the wild party thumping, grinding, and falling around them.

They were standing in the middle of a Halloween-themed party night at one of the most popular, if least secure clubs for collegians in Atlanta. Music was blasting and people were dancing. Alcohol was being passed around and people were passing out. Kim could have sworn she saw a cloud of smoke—a very specific type of smoke—drifting up the stairs into the abyss of the upper darkness, but Eden had asked her a question, so she clamped her shocked jaw shut and focused her surprised eyes on the Spanish-American.

"Athens isn't that far from Atlanta," Kim responded. "However, I should be asking you—who drives all the way from Rome just to go clubbing in Athens?"

Eden laughed, all perfume and flowers. "It's Bethany's birthday this upcoming Monday, the first day of November. She's having some big celebration this weekend, so here I am!"

Kim shook her head. "The things we do for friends! My buddy's band is trying to get more exposure and they're supposed to be playing here tonight."

Eden's oak colored eyes widened. "Oh, a band? Then they're downstairs in the Mud Shed."

"Where?" Dishon hadn't mentioned stairs or a shed.

"Don't worry, girl, I'll show you." Eden took a sip from the cup. "I was wondering why you didn't dress up!"

Kim looked down at her brown pants and her shirt, swirled with purple, silver and brown, overlaid with a purple leather belt. Considering her outfit in conjunction with her purple earrings, silver bracelets and deep brown complexion, Kim thought she looked pretty close to irresistible, costume or no costume. She had wanted to wear her blue bracelets, but couldn't put together an appropriate ensemble.

"Who did you come as?" she asked in her melodic voice, appraising Eden's outfit with attentiveness on her face but an amused smile in her eyes. "A Romani, I wanna say."

Eden struck a pose.

"Not just any Roma," she said with a flourish of dramatics. "The tragic Carmen." She glanced around the illustration of sophisticated wildlife that surrounded them as if she were looking for someone.

"Miguel is around here somewhere," she informed Kim. "He came dressed as Don Juan."

Kim felt that she had missed something important. "Miguel? Don Juan?"

"My boyfriend, yeah. Don Juan Tenorio."

Kim didn't know Eden had a boyfriend. More importantly, Kim didn't really have anybody to tell, so she lost interest in the subject pretty quickly.

"Can you get me to the Mud Shack?" she asked.

"Shed," Eden corrected. "But yeah, let's go," she said, and soft hand joined soft hand.

Together they maneuvered through the horde of revelers, Eden leading the way. Crunched onto the dance floor, Kim saw a devil and an angel grinding, an Asian Cleopatra dancing solo, and a guy who appeared to be wearing only bubble wrap, doing things that Kim wished she had never seen.

"Eden," a deep voice called hoarsely. A young man appeared through the crowd, stepping up behind Eden and grabbing her hand. He was dressed in some type of Old Spain outfit, like gypsy meets Shakespeare's Romeo.

Eden turned, her hair tossing over her shoulder as she gazed up into the man's brown face. Kim couldn't help but think they'd make a great cover for a romance novel.

"Hey." Eden's eyes hardened, all snakes and jewels, and she involuntary threw an embarrassed glance Kim's way. Her friend reeked of Cuervo.

"I'm going upstairs, you wanna come?" he said, successfully keeping the slur out of his voice.

"No, I've got to show my friend to the Mud Shed," she said calmly, nodding her head in Kim's direction. "Kim, this is Miguel, my boyfriend. Miguel, this is Kim, my homey." She giggled like a meadow of fairies, pristine and mischievous all at the same time. "We went to Kenneth Wilbanks together."

Miguel tried—unsuccessfully—to focus his dark eyes on Kim, shifting his stance a bit, straightening up. She felt like a llama that the lion was evaluating. Was she a pointless assault or worth a little exercise?

"Hi," Miguel slurred. "Who are you supposed to be?"

Eden's eyes narrowed.

"Kimberly the Great," Kim said solemnly.

"I loved that movie," Miguel said.

Kim glanced at Eden, a grin threatening to splash across the llama's face. "Mmm, so did I," is all she said.

"Find me later," Eden instructed, kissing him on the cheek. She then grabbed Kim's hand and they set across the club floor once more. Kim sidestepped many dancing ghouls and princesses as well as a few old school gangsters and some new-school witches. She kept her eyes on the back of Eden's lustrous head until they came to a condensed and equally cacophonic area near the back wall.

Eden dropped Kim's hand and pointed with a bejeweled finger. "There it is."

There was the staircase, descending into a spot even smokier than the club was.

"Right down those stairs, Miss Wilbanks. Mind your head."

"Thanks so much, Eden," Kim said, heading into the deleterious fog, ducking as the beams of the lower ceiling became visible.

It was completely different downstairs. Sure, the Halloween theme had leaked over—the underground pub had temporarily been renamed "Blood Shed"—but upstairs was a shimmering disco of macabre and fairy tales and here it was an earthy, wooden bacchanalia. Best of all, the music was live.

The primary purpose of the Mud Shed was to ensure that everyone was nice and drunk. A solitary waitress, suitably costumed as a naughty French maid, traveled steadily among the patrons, taking their drink orders and their money (she tried to get an order out of Kim, causing her to realize that they really didn't check IDs at all), and the demon-horned bartenders, sans the full devil costumes, were constantly serving drinks and handing out beers. However, a great side effect to the drunkenness was that once the patrons got enough drinks inside of them, they loved the music even more.

Kim didn't need any extra substances in her body to enjoy the music. Fallen was on stage, and she immediately spotted Dishon and his bass guitar, his mini-Afro nodding at certain measures in the song or as a precursor to some key change. He noticed her soon after her arrival and beckoned her closer to the stage.

Nicholas was tearing up the drums, a bald guy with red eyebrows was jamming out on the keyboard, and there was an awesome lead guitarist. The lead singer was wearing a shirt that seemed too small to be paired with his choice of low-rise jeans, and he had black-feathered wings strapped to his back and a bleeding fleur-de-lis tattoo on his shredded upper abdomen. Sweat trickled from his sideburns, the only sign that his body was making an effort to produce the beautiful sounds that soared from his mouth.

Dishon's voice wasn't too shabby, either. He had an earthy baritone, while the keyboardist was the functioning falsetto.

Kim grooved to the music, which was some odd, if delicious crossroad between Blues Traveler and a mid-seventies David Bowie, with a dash of Pearl Jam and jazz-fusion thrown in. As they drifted into different songs, the lead singer would break out bongos or other rhythmic instruments, and at one point the keyboardist broke out his own electric guitar for an awesome guitar duet, while the vocalist soared over it all with his phenomenal voice.

"Kim?"

She turned and was suffocated in a giant bear hug that could only come from one person.

"What are you doing here?" Shannon Crescitelli asked, releasing Kim with as much vigor as he had seized her with. He was unsurprisingly flashy in a toga and the corresponding winged helmet and sandals. "You didn't dress up, ninja," he accused.

"I'm with the band," she managed, before being quickly swallowed in a second hug.

"Let's see if I can guess which one belongs to you," he hollered over the music.

The band was doing an awesome punk rock cover of Lakeside's "It's All the Way Live" as Shannon raked his eyes over them. His face was a little thinner since the last time Kim had seen him. His hair was a little shorter as well, but he seemed like the same old fun-loving partier.

"Hermes?" she asked.

"Nope, just a rash," he responded. Once her stomach—and jaw—dropped, he turned back to her, laughing. "Yeah, the Greek god of mischief, thieves and commerce! Now, my turn…" He turned back to the band. "The guy on bass," he said triumphantly. "That's your boyfriend!"

"Mmm, we're just friends," Kim said.

Shannon laughed and she smelt alcohol on his breath. "That's right. You stay hard to get. He'll be the easy one, no doubt!"

He picked up two beers from a nearby table where he had previously set them down. "You want one?"

Kim declined. "They don't seem to card here, do they?"

Shannon copped his silly grin, stretching as wide as his miniature mouth allowed. "They'd lose half their business if they did!"

Kim nodded, understanding. She looked up and noticed Dishon watching her. She smiled and waved, hoping that put him a little at ease. Shannon was no competition.

"How's school?" she asked, crossing her arms.

"UGA?" The Italian laughed again. "I wouldn't know. I'm usually hung-over during class."

Kim shook her head. "Be careful, boo."

"No," Shannon drunkenly proclaimed. "I will not be careful! I have the rest of my life to be careful! I'm young and in college, I'm grabbing the bull by the horns and grabbing life by the balls!"

He leaned forward to whisper in her ear. "And I'm doing it commando, 'cause I got it like that!"

Kim laughed, pulling her slender fingers to cover her nose and her mouth as her body jerked unnaturally.

Shannon continued. "Whenever you want someone truly instrument savvy, you just come see me, ninja. Stay copasetic, Miss Wil."

He backed away easily, still grinning, with arms outstretched and beers waving goodbye. Kim waved and turned back to the stage. Shannon was a character. She didn't know what to make of him sometimes.

A few songs later (a couple of original tunes and a 10 minute jam session to The Dave Matthews Band's "What Would You Say" where the European-blooded lead singer may have proved he was professionally trained on the tambourine or had at least studied at a few C.O.G.I.C.

services), they were finished. As Third Eye Blind began pumping through the speakers, Kim watched Dishon pack up his guitar, take a swig from a complementary bottle of beer, and step off the stage, eyes trained on her. She struggled to understand how he could synchronously make her unsettled and soothe her.

"Pretty cool place, huh?" he asked, gesturing to the pub surroundings.

"This would be an awesome place to work," Kim said. Inside she wondered how the heck she could figure that the response given was the proper answer to his question.

"I don't know about that," Dishon muttered, glancing across the room.

Kim followed his gaze, and watched as a crowd of collegians poured their bottles of beer into the upturned winged helmet Shannon held in his hands. Once the last drop of alcohol drizzled into the cap, they all began chanting for him to chug, and that's exactly what he did, proudly securing the hat and whatever remaining beer atop his curls as he finished. Roaring with much feverish brouhaha, he grabbed his crotch through the draping cloth and thrust his other fist in the air.

Kim laughed, half amazed and half grieved.

"I went to school with him," she said. "He's…he's peculiar."

Dishon took a swig on the beer. It was obvious that he felt challenged merely by Shannon's presence.

"Did you like the set?" he asked.

Gazing at her beneath those rough eyebrows, he reminded her of some ancient barbaric, philistine warrior. Before she could ask him if anyone had ever tried to make him trim his eyebrows, he kissed her. Just like that, before she could even register an answer to his own question. The roughness of his fingers discovered the smoothness of her cheeks, and his tongue didn't wait for an invitation to meet with hers. Once Kim connected with the situation at hand, she relented. Her hands discovered the blades of his shoulders, and her body discovered the warmth of a closer embrace. She was definitely kissing him back.

Because she deserved it.

· · · · ·

Hanley Powell's hair was akin to a troll's. It was long and thick, and she was probably the only person who knew how to manage it so expertly. She had it pulled back into a giant bushy ponytail, though it was probably thicker and longer than any pony's tail. It seemed to reach through Coda's layered clothing and cause his skin to itch like pox.

Glynn County had rolled into mid-fall and the increasing Brunswick chill kept Coda's thin frame encased in thermal undies. The wind blew and the trees would bend as the freezing air raced through and lowered temperatures further than they had been just seconds before.

Hanley reclined on top of Coda and he did likewise to the front windshield of a four-wheeled rattletrap in the front yard of Hanley's two-story brick stay.

Terry lay next to Coda and Hanley, occasionally poking Coda's ribs whenever she said something nonsensical or awkwardly flirtatious.

As Hanley talked on in her thick Georgia accent about some possibly interesting situation—who could tell?—Coda stared at the dusk sky and wondered at the possibility that his last remaining high school friend had decided to take part in a two-month mission trip to South America, thankfully (however) returning just before Christmas. A selfless decision on Terry's part, though it stirred very selfish emotions in Coda's heart.

"Every once in a while, it's nice to move *with* the world, not just on it, you know?" Terry placed these words into the air with confidence and more meaning than Hanley and Coda grasped. His chest rose and fell; the stars stared with their hidden mysteries.

As the night grew on,—the stars blinking and whispering—the three continued to talk, watching their words appear transiently as spirits in the air.

"I wonder how the stars will look in Peru," Terry mused.

"The stars in Peru?" Hanley asked. She giggled softly. "Probably more beautiful than they look from here."

"Maybe," Terry said, his voice cracking in a way that made Coda think of Rico. Gosh, he was doomed to miss everybody.

When Hanley announced that it was time for dinner, Coda managed to unknot their fingers. After she stood, he was immediately ungrateful, for the dancing chill quickly blew away the body heat she had supplied.

"Time for me to go?" Terry inquired, glancing at the surrounding trees as he hopped off the car.

"Unfortunately," Hanley said.

Hanley had picked Coda up after school so that he could help her with a school project. When Terry called requesting Coda's company, Coda notified him that he'd have to come all the way out to the "boon-dock-marshes" in order to pick him up. The northeast marshes out in the county were where well-to-do families like the Hamiltons and the Crescitellis resided, and then there were the Brunswick marshes…the wilderness, nature unknown, potato guns and bonfires: the *boondock-marshes*.

And because Terry had his heart set on seeing Coda before he left for those two months, he made the journey to Hanley's place in the heart of the wilderness. Hanley had been cool with it, since she vaguely knew Terry from high school, but for Coda, once Terry had shown up, Hanley became a nuisance.

"Are you staying for dinner?" Hanley asked Coda.

Coda inhaled, looking over at Terry, off into the rustling blackness of the disfigured pines, and finally back to Hanley. "I should be going now. Gotta spend time with my boy."

An intense wind ripped across the marshes and into Hanley's yard, and Coda had to struggle to hold his balance.

Terry laughed. "We should head out before it gets any worse. Don't want Coda blowing out of your yard."

Coda wrapped his arms around his body protectively. "I can't help my skinniness."

Terry chuckled. "You know if we didn't bang so much, *cara mia*, you'd probably be able to gain some weight."

Coda cracked up, but not before panting, "*Mon cherie*," and Hanley tried to ignore their guy-weirdness.

"Okay," she said, gripping Coda in a hug. "I'll see you at school Monday."

"Alright, dear," Coda said, squeezing back.

"Nice seeing you again, Terry," she waved. "Save a million souls."

"Come on, Coda," Terry motioned and they climbed into his Sedan.

"Where to?" Terry asked.

"The beach," Coda suggested.

"You asked for it," Terry warned.

Coda cheesed at his Afro-ed buddy. "Actually, you did. Just now."

Terry's foreboding was not for naught, for the winds at Neptune Park on St. Simons were much stronger than the marshwinds in Hanley Powell's front yard.

"Now I find myself fearing for your life," Terry cracked as the freckled pals trekked the waterfront walkway. "If Mother Nature tosses you into the ocean, the currents could grab a hold of you and take you back to Africa."

Coda's jaw dropped. "Terry Bozzo, you red-haired redneck! You are So Wrong for that!"

"How so, Kunta?" Terry asked with a goading grin.

Coda gestured to the seven-foot wall of boulders and concrete chunks, deferring the effects of erosion between the park and the seashore below. "With such a low percentage of body fat, I'd just sink like one of these rocks!"

Terry pushed Coda's head to one side. "Don't forget to incorporate all that brain-impeding hot air into those calculations of yours, Cheshire."

"Don't be mad because you're becoming a chubster, Bozzo the Clown," Coda retorted, tagging Terry in the gut.

Terry doubled over, then glanced up with dramatic deliberateness in his movement. "You bastard!" he exclaimed in an outlandish faux-Spanish accent. "You killed my child!"

"Why should I care, ranga?" Coda said, matching Terry comical accent for comical accent, but pulling his from Australia. "Your child was not my problem."

Terry shook his head. "You were always horrible with accents, dude." He tapped Coda's arm and took off into a sprint. "Come on!" he called.

"Come on *where?*" Coda asked.

"Don't let the light catch you!" Terry hollered into the wind, which carried his words back to Coda.

Coda glanced up and saw the rotational beam of the towering lighthouse sweeping towards them. He darted after Terry.

"Are you crazy? We're gonna race the lighthouse?"

Terry turned around, jogging backwards. "Are you not up to the challenge? Consider this Shakespeare and I'm already the lead to your poorly read cameo."

"You punk," Coda laughed, and he increased his speed.

Initially there wasn't much difficulty outpacing the light and Coda and Terry laughed and dodged a few water fountains and trash receptacles. However, on the other side of the lighthouse and diametric to Neptune Park a large parking lot complicated things.

"Where'd these cars come from?" Coda asked, panicking slightly.

"The bars we can't go in," Terry laughed. "This just got a little more knotty."

Feeling just as excited as he felt silly, Coda looked behind him to see the light following at a close distance. His vision turning red, Coda threw caution to the wind and traipsed across a car so lightly, the hood didn't buckle beneath his weight even once.

"Whoo!" Terry exclaimed, patting him on the back. "You are five types of crazy, did you know that?"

Coda laughed. It was so easy to lose the reality of the moment. The mechanical rotations of the lighthouse had become as powerful and evil as any childhood boogeyman.

Coda tucked himself into a forward roll, leaping out of that into a series of cartwheels until he was out of the parking lot and leaping across the grass, headed back into the playground of Neptune Park. This was far more fun than it had been in the mirror maze with a certain other approaching evil.

Terry, as impossibly athletic as he was, leapt onto the metal frame of the swing set, climbing it easier than most people climbed ladders. He proceeded to perform a series of somersaults across the metal beam, dismounting onto a spring rider.

"The light!" he screamed to Coda, who had pulled up short to marvel at Terry's limberness, forgetting the beam of light that had caused this awe-inspiring display of athletics and immaturity.

Coda leapt onto the monkey bars, clearing them in one swing, throwing himself through the metal beams on the other side, skidding to a landing in the sand before continuing to run until he collapsed beneath an oak, the beam unable to find him through the numerous branches.

His eyesight was no longer stained coral and his breathing told no tales, as if he had simply walked the giant lap around the lighthouse. His muscular calves and his fingertips twitched, on pause and waiting for a return to the jollification.

"Where you at, Terry?" he called over the pounding of the tide. "I think you got caught!"

Terry dropped down from the tree branches dexterously, landing in front of Coda, who scrambled away in shock.

"I think it missed me as well!" Terry announced, beaming brighter than the lighthouse.

Coda stood, softly punching Terry's chest.

"If I'm five types of crazy, then you must be fifteen! Since when can you do that?"

Terry placed his hands on his waist, breathing just as easily as Coda. "Since when can you? You were always too gangly for gymnastics. Back-flips and acting were the two things I always had over you."

Coda shrugged. "That was nothing. And I'm thickening out."

For a brief passing moment, Terry's face became difficult to read, as if he was sure that Coda was holding something back. It couldn't be, though. Neither Terry nor Coda wanted to believe that they had any secrets from each other.

"Sure," he replied, turning from Coda to watch the surf.

"And do you really think you're a better actor than me?" Coda asked. "Because we could take that to the mat."

"Shut up," Terry chuckled. "It wouldn't even be a contest. And you don't even know what 'taking it to the mat' means."

The stars observed from over the ocean, unblinking as if they understood.

12.
Solitaire

You wanna live a dream
  I'm an insomniac
  Rescue me from a dragon and I will lay down
  on the railroad tracks
  You wanna play a scene
  I don't care for any of the parts
  Baby, I play solitaire
  not Hearts

Beautiful courtyards and blooming greenery were scattered all around the Georgia Tech dorms, combining with the red brick of the dormitories to give the atmosphere a romantic ambiance. Brick and concrete walkways maneuvered amongst the many trees, while ornately detailed wooden and iron benches were scattered beneath the shade.

BJ was standing in the doorway of Harrison Residence Hall with a poorly put together pop-rock song blasting free from behind her.

"Have you heard that new Lena Park song, Ezekiel?" she asked, sucking on a lollipop. She was directing her question to the handsome, trim student heading down the walk towards Harrison, where she resided.

"Who is Lena Park?" he asked.

"Here," she smiled, handing him a pack of color pens with her free hand. "I need them back tonight, okay?"

"Sure thing," Ezekiel said, turning and heading back in the direction from whence he came: the Towers Residence Hall.

He had tons of homework, including an essay for Literature and an aerospace engineering project, and wasn't in the mood to focus of the current status of the pop charts. Besides, he had another Lena Park song reverberating in his head.

Upsetting regrets...

Ezekiel had once told the kids at his lunch table; who included Eden, Coda, BJ, and Rico; that he planned on having a career in interstellar lodging by designing the first lunar hotel and they all figured that he would be the one to do it, so much so that Kim had given him a special shout-out during her graduation speech. He had been voted "Most Intelligent Guy" by the Wilbanks senior class and even if he really wasn't, no one could tell.

He pulled out his key to unbolt his dorm room lock. Entering, he dropped his backpack beneath the window on the far side of the room, feeling once again that his room was too small. Fairly often he found himself staring out at the expanses of the green quad just outside of his window. This particular day, however, he kept the window down and made sure the heater was on before removing his jacket and hanging it in the closet. The Atlanta weather was past chilly. Pretty soon it would be December, and that meant a possibility of snow. That also meant vacation and he had to be sure he aced all of his classes.

Ezekiel sat down at his desk beneath his loft bed, hoisted above him on towering legs, in order to get a head start on finishing his projects.

His currently-absent roommate's side of the room was decorated with Japanese anime posters and collectibles, while Ezekiel's side, characterized by the solid blue fabrics and well-thought out arrangements, contained the gadgets. The computer that sat on his desk had a very large screen and a PC tower whose inner workings were viewable through a clear plastic window. A cool effect, he thought.

Atop the PC sat the printer, bringing the eyes up to the wall, on which was mounted a large and laminated, though fragmentary, puzzle containing popular cartoon characters. Vanessa had the other laminated half. He missed her. She was still hours away in Cedar City, but they talked everyday.

Targets hung on the wall, a hypnosis spiral hung from his quad-branched floor lamp, and on top of the computer sat a 3-D optical illusion of a dragon that followed him around the room if he watched it with one eye closed. Or if he was videotaping with his digital camera. Sometimes the dragon looked more like a serpent. A big, vicious one.

He touched the computer's mouse and the screensaver of a Chiyu Designs bike vanished into his computerized plans for a hoverboard. It had been a fleeting fancy of his that had turned into his aerospace engineering project. When he was younger he had thought hoverboarding was all about electromagnetic propulsion (like in magnetic levitation, or maglev trains) and things of that nature, but he had studied a few months back, and found that there was no way to have so many magnetic guideways for all the places people would want to go on their hover-boards, unless they all traveled in packs as if on a maglev highway of sorts. But too much of that was not important anyway. All he had to do was design the hoverboard with the school's expensive software and show his measurements, estimations and calculations. They didn't need to hear all about reversing airflow or any of that and Ezekiel thought he was taking enough of a risk just by designing something that didn't quite exist, yet. He enjoyed beating the system, not breaking it, so for the next projects he figured that he'd focus on airplanes and rockets and the like. But the unexplored held the charm for him.

He minimized the screen, pulling up a web browser to do some additional research for his Lit essay. His eyes glanced over a headline about some government conspiracy about a disgraced cloning scientist. That was all it took for Ezekiel's brain to shoot off into the cosmos. He wondered what the Bible said about cloning. Justus might have an answer if asked and Coda could always consult with his pastor father if they were on good terms that particular day. Pastors. Ezekiel tried to look past all of those fun Bible studies with Vanessa and recall the last time he had actually stepped inside a sanctuary and sat under the tutelage of a preacher of any kind. He could at least find one who had a degree in biblical studies. Someone who would teach instead of solicit. A boy could dream.

Autumn seemed to be flying by fairly uneventfully and since Ezekiel had no misgivings about his current situation, he didn't worry. His studies were going good and there were barely any hitches in his classes.

He was adjusting to college life fairly well. He and his roommate got along, even if he did talk too much like Coda did, and get excited over weird things like Justus did. Christopher lived down the hall, so if Ezekiel ever needed an escape, that's were he'd head to, plus BJ was a quick trip down the sidewalk. He and his roommate didn't pretend that they were friends. They got along because it made life easier, not because they planned on keeping in touch well into their forties.

His parents would call to check up on him and Ezekiel had almost gotten used to the fact that even when he spoke in Mandarin, his roommate understood him word for word. During public school he had adjusted to the fact that none of his friends knew what he was saying when he was on the phone with his parents, aside from the recurring "uh-uh's," "okay's," "no's," and 'maybe's" that littered his speech. Shannon used to get an unnatural kick out of those conversations and mock Ezekiel's Chinese publicly. Shannon used to get on his nerves.

Vanessa would call to check up on him as well. They didn't talk much on the weekdays, with both of them studying, but Ezekiel would frequently spend the sum of his Sundays on the phone with Vanessa. She was so sweet and had such intelligence. Once, when she was preparing for her Regents exam, they had gotten into a spirited debate about whether adding a false story about what she had done the weekend before was an ingenious move or an unwise one. She made such excellent points—he hated winning the debate in the end. He didn't always win. And he enjoyed that. He just wished that she would believe him...

Sometimes Jordan would show up in the library to help him study. With Phil's unique thought that Ezekiel should biblically research the side effects instead of the cause of the side effects, Ezekiel had compiled a surprising amount of information that he could hardly wait to divulge with one of his "choice night" cohorts. Jordan was nice about it. He knew she was extremely curious and wanted to know the whole story, but she never asked for him to say anything that he didn't want to. He felt bad, but he figured the best course of action would not be spreading wild stories around his college about the state of his abilities.

He continued to get surprised. One morning, soaping up in his dormitory's network of showers, he couldn't keep his feet on the ground. It was as if he had entered an anti-gravity terminal, though the water that was shooting out of the shower-head was definitely dropping naturally towards the scummy tile. After a full petrifying minute, God decided to bring an end to the heavenly teasing and roughly set Ezekiel back on the shower floor, though not exactly on his feet. Ezekiel mastered the technique of levitating only a few days later. He assumed that he could fly if he wanted to, but he would rather his feet stay at least one foot near the ground.

• • • • •

Jordan smiled at Ezekiel nervously. "Don't hurt me," she mewed, giggling.

It was open practice for *hapkido* at the CRC, and Ezekiel, Jordan, Christopher, and Phil had agreed to work on some techniques. While Phil and Christopher worked on grips, Jordan and Ezekiel decided to work on the One Armed Shoulder Throw that Master Thomas had taught them the evening before. Ezekiel put on what he privately called his *Hapkido* Face. It was also his My-Cool-Is-Not-Forced Face, his I-Know-You're-Watching Face, his I-Have-To-Go-To-The-Bathroom Face, and his I'm-Discontented-By-You Face (but not his Embarrassed

Face, that was a totally different beast, usually followed by guffaws and movements in a more inoffensive direction).

Ezekiel stood even-footed with Jordan. He seized her right wrist with his left hand, turning to the side and planting his right foot perpendicular to her right foot. His right arm slid under her left, gripping her forearm as he backed into her, lifted her onto his back and sent her over his right side and onto the floor at his feet.

"Okay," she squealed, picking her self up. "Don't do that."

"What?" he asked, unfazed.

"Don't put on that *Hapkido* Face. It's intimidating," she said, dipping her chin in the way that she could.

"My *hapkido* face?" He couldn't help laughing.

Jordan's mirth was infectious. He knew that she was cute, but there wasn't an attraction there. He just thought of Jordan as his buddy. They didn't share a correlation like the one Ezekiel shared with Vanessa.

"Not your *hapkido* face;" she was admonishing him, "your *Hapkido* Face. There is a difference."

Ezekiel just laughed, surprised scrawny Jordan could speak in capitals. It was her turn, and she grabbed his hand, lifting him but barely getting him over her back. She giggled.

"You could stand to loose a few pounds." She was teasing herself more than she was teasing him.

It was Ezekiel's turn again. "No *Hapkido* Face," Jordan reminded him.

"Okay," he said, twisting up one corner of his mouth before his grin captured the other corner. He observed his foot placement in preparation. He loved how his body became more conditioned with each karate class.

Jordan was giggling. "Stop admiring your body and throw me! Throw me now!" Jordan cried.

Christopher paused, holding Phil hostage in his Cutting Wrist Lock, staring at Jordan questioningly with a smile in his eyes. Phil was guffawing.

Jordan laughed, tossing her hair. "Oh, Ezekiel, throw me!" She hammed it up to extinguish her embarrassment. "Yes, throw me now!" Their classmates laughed, and Jordan smiled at Ezekiel. "Sorry," she said softly, attentively.

"It's okay," he said, doing his half-grin.

He was not aware that he had backed up very close to the edge of the carpeted raised floor. The carpet, and thus the karate students as well, rested on a raised level of the floor. There was only a small hardwood walkway along the length of the mirror, and during practices it was usually piled with a collection of backpacks. Currently, only Christopher's book bag was lying there, because he had come straight from some weekend classes.

Where are you? came a loud and raspy, feminine voice, internal to his being. He was stunned, equilibrium destroyed and sending him to the edge of the carpet. He labored to pull his body away from the mirror, holding his hands in front of him, reaching in vain for surety.

As he struggled to maintain his balance he received various snatches of thought from his companions, mostly confusion. Phil was reaching for Jordan, attempting to pull her away from something that he observed was about to occur. It was all going so dreadfully slow for something that was happening so dreadfully fast that he had virtually no control over.

He lost his battle with gravity and as he fell, he remembered the clause in the release form that that all the *hapkido* students signed at the start of class that mentioned the "in case of death" conditions. How bitter were his thoughts and strong were his prayers as he slammed backwards into the glass mirror, sending shards of shattered glass everywhere.

He heard Christopher scream rather like a girl. He must not be unconscious.

That was a good sign, right?

"Somebody should call the ambulance," Phil suggested, but they were frozen.

"How badly is he hurt?" Jordan asked. Ezekiel's eyes were coming into focus. "He's moving," she noticed. "Is that good?"

Ezekiel slowly rose from the glittering pile of glass, ensuring that his body was reacting properly to the signals he sent to it with his brain.

"Ezekiel?" Phil called.

"Yeah?" came Ezekiel's surprised reply. He stood, feeling absolutely no pain, save the ringing in his ears from the clashing shriek of the glass giving way. He inspected himself and found nothing, not a cut, not a bruise, not a splinter...

"Ezekiel?" Jordan was in shock. Ezekiel turned around and saw the damage. The mirror had buckled and gave way under his weight. Christopher's bag and some of the contents therein had been sliced by the large glass shrapnel. The glass had sliced and ripped Ezekiel's uniform, though the trippiest part was how his body was unharmed, as if the glass had simply fallen around him. It had certainly gotten into his clothes. He loosed his belt, releasing large and small pieces of glass that had collected in the shirt of his gi. He shook his head and watched pieces of glass painlessly fall from his head. He wasn't as shocked as many others would have been. He just was trying to figure out what—and if—this had to do with everything that had occurred to his body after the lightning.

He started walking towards the exit. Upon hearing gasps from Jordan, he realized that he was barefoot, walking on broken glass. He smiled at the allusion.

"I'll be fine, I just have to use the bathroom," he said as he exited.

Jordan turned to Phil in the increasing silence. "The bottom of his feet must be ugly if they're calloused enough to walk over that."

That broke Christopher's shock and they began to feel better, with laughter.

"Where's Rod Sterling?" Phil asked.

"Who's that?" Jordan asked.

The boys laughed harder, yet they had all seen something that Ezekiel had yet to see. Slowly expanding across his shoulder blades was a Lichtenberg "lightning flower" scar, the very kind that he hadn't had after he had been struck by lightning.

Jordan and Phil had spent enough hours researching with Ezekiel to know that his own body had just given him away.

• • • • •

The voice belonged to someone who wanted him to hear, that much Ezekiel knew. It was much too loud to be one of the many random thoughts. This thought was yelled. Someone had guaranteed knowledge that someone else would hear.

Ezekiel knew that Christopher, Phil and Jordan would come up with a lie that was good enough to explain what had happened. They figured it was all just a weird fluke, but Ezekiel knew it had something to do with all the changes that had happened to him after that night

Jordan and Phil had left for the night, but Christopher had ran back to his dorm to bring Ezekiel back something that he could wear to his own dorm. Ezekiel was leaning against the counter in the darkness of a bathroom adjacent to the *hapkido* room, since the CRC was clearing out, but it wasn't closed and he was not about to walk all the way down the stairs and onto a campus bus in what he had on. His gi was virtually indecent.

As he stared into the mirror at his lightning-marked eyes, he tried to recall the last time he had gotten a knick. A cut, any type of flesh wound.

And it had been months. And the small Shannon-given scar on his shin had never gone completely away.

There was an unnatural screeching and the bathroom door suddenly flew in-between Ezekiel's nose and the mirror in front of him, knocking a sink from the wall. He turned, quite ill at ease.

He hadn't turned on the bathroom light and now he saw the inconvenience of that decision, for in the dimness of the evening she was difficult to make out: a woman, standing there in an obvious costume. Perhaps some type of uniform. The onyx bodysuit was overlaid with what appeared to be a red ballistic vest. Her hair, perhaps a wig, was just as red, as was the leather on her knee-high boots. Her head was leaning to the right, as if she was trying to make out what Ezekiel looked like in the dim bathroom.

Something akin to a red surgical mask covered the lower part of her face and her eyes were spectral—pure black—all pupil, with a red heart appearing beneath one almost like a mole. Even so, perhaps solely due to the peach skin visible around her eyes, she had a very human look to her. And her body was remarkable. She was a three-dimensional work of art and the doorposts framed her.

"I don't know about you, but this bathroom thing isn't for me," she said, clapping her red-gloved hands to shake loose the assumed filth, taking in the surroundings with a contemptuous expression as well as confirming Ezekiel's suspicions that this had something to do with the boy Kim had dealt with in the skate park bathroom…and perhaps the Creature Coda had faced at the Funfair.

She was making him nervous, taking him in with her evil eyes. She had spoken with traces of that raspy voice she had sent out for him earlier. Like her throat was beyond dry.

She tilted her head further and pulled out a very disturbing knife.

"Steve?" she queried; despite the mask, her voice wasn't muffled in the slightest bit. "How're David, Sammy, and Eli?"

"My name is not Steve," Ezekiel said, probably superfluously. Either what she had just said had something in it that he was supposed to understand, or there was some guy out there named Steve that she was trying to hurt badly. Despite this, he didn't have time to comprehend any of it. She was holding a very disturbing knife.

"Mine's Solitaire." She winked at him. "Not Hearts."

He was trying to place that comment when her next question caught him off-guard. "Weren't you going to tell me your name?"

She was referring to an alias. She had been looking for him, though Ezekiel wondered whether she knew who he truly was without the mask of shadows. She expected him to give her a pseudonym of sorts, like hers. He racked his brain for a quick answer, thinking about the recent accident, the many Bible studies he and Vanessa had conducted together, and then he thought of that dragon on his computer that followed him around the room.

"Leviathan," he said.

She didn't vocally acknowledge that he had said anything. She simply de-tilted her neck, turned and disappeared from the doorway. Ezekiel would have raced after her, yet he was aware of how he would appear to a person unfamiliar with his situation, so he took a piece of the cloth hanging from the leg of his ragged *hapkido* uniform and tied it around his eyes as a makeshift domino mask.

God give me strength, he prayed and then raced after her.

As soon as he stepped in the doorway, she was there, attacking with that monstrous knife, pushing him out into the middle of the deserted basketball court. Her hands were like lightning, though Ezekiel was growing to hate the reference.

He wasn't fast enough to escape the slashes, but she wasn't piercing the skin of her target despite the fact that she was indeed connecting with him. She halted, surprised.

With the opportunity given, he smacked her one with everything in him. He then raised his right leg in a side thrust kick, sending her flying.

Why did I do that? he wondered. He had wanted to keep her close. What could he do, now? He decided to probe her mind. Her hands involuntarily flew to her head.

She lowered her arms across her chest, cleavage—and yes, there was cleavage—heaving. "Leviathan," she demurely sighed, "your eyes get weirder when you try that."

He widened his eyes in bewilderment. She had just blocked him! He had given himself away through his eyes; he didn't know that was possible. Next thing he knew, she had lifted off the floor in flight and was in his face, punching him dead in the nose. He rolled a distance across the freshly waxed flooring and rose into a crouching position.

The blow didn't hurt him; his skin was resilient to all of this abuse. With the second nose-punch, she stepped back, completely thrown off by the fact that he wasn't bruising.

She rose and set herself atop the basketball goal, inspecting him like a supermodel gargoyle.

"The knife came down," she said, almost to herself, "missing him by inches…"

"You didn't miss," he rasped.

"What happened to your outfit, Leviathan?" she asked.

"Solitaire," he said, using her fictitious name while rising in the air to attack her from above, "I can fly, too." He tried to keep the uncertainty of his power out of his face as he exceeded the height limits he had previously set for himself. Between the flight, the mind reading, the thick skin, and the adversary, he was beginning to feel quite like a superhero.

She rose to greet him in the air, sheathing her knife in her vest. As he went to punch her, she blocked him, grabbing his arm between hers, and thrust her hands, and thus his arm, into his face. The force of his own blow was enough to send Ezekiel flipping through the air to crash back into the cross-court basketball goal.

Ezekiel patted the painful area on his face where his fist had damaged him. What had she done? He was trying to think of all that Coda had said. All that Kim had said.

She was upon him again, this time with no mercy. She sent him down onto the waxed floor, then up into the base of the running track. Each time he'd attack her, she'd use it as an attack against him. If he ever had a chance, he lost it somewhere around the third bruise, lying dizzy atop the track.

"I changed my mind," she whispered, breathing harshly. "The bathroom doesn't sound like a terribly sucky place after all."

She grabbed his legs and swung him over the track. He crashed into the stretch of wall above the bathroom and when he disconnected, falling into the entryway, she punt-kicked him and sent him crashing against the bathroom's back wall.

And she was upon him again. He couldn't rest and he couldn't think, so he couldn't fight back well enough to defeat her. He didn't have a fighter's instinct.

Solitaire rose victorious and smiled down at a battered Ezekiel.

"I'm going after Eli, next. I hope he's an actual challenge."

Those eyes… His mind was warbling. Or wandering. Maybe it was warbling, he thought, because that's what it felt like. A cross between warbling and being crushed by a giant semi-truck as it warbled. What did warble mean? What was this Eli/Steve thing? He had to figure it out. He had to get up. She was hoping it would get under his skin like her knife couldn't—no—she was hoping he'd figure it out. She liked the challenge. Why couldn't he get up?

But where had she gone? He had just been looking at her. It was like she was Merlin in *The Once and Future King* and had signaled the air and it responded with a quickness, taking her to some unknown environment. The brown-suited boy, Coda's mysterious creature, and now that red woman with her vanishing trick… Something big was up, he just didn't know what. Eli… Steve… What other names had she mentioned? David and Sammy? Eli? What was he missing?

What was he doing? He needed to get away from the site where all the noise had generated. He had to avoid any further commotion. Bad enough that he wouldn't be able to explain the door, nor the mask that he presently ripped off his face, as an accident in the manufacturing.

Christopher was supposed to meet him here. Christopher couldn't walk in on him. Not into this, not like this.

The water was spurting from the busted drain beneath the broken sink and Ezekiel was cautious as he headed towards the destroyed doorframe where his bag lay. He had to find his cell phone.

"Hey, Christopher?" Ezekiel said breathlessly.

"Yeah, who's this?"

He caught his reflection in the mirror and stifled a groan. "This is Ezekiel."

"Hey! Didn't sound like you for a second. What's up?"

"Don't worry about the clothes, dude. I already have a ride and everything." Ezekiel left his reflection behind and headed to the bathroom's lone window. He lifted up the windowpane, pushing on the screen until it fell down onto the pebble-coated turf below.

God, he was on the second floor! The second floor of the CRC was like the fourth floor of any normal building.

"You sure?" Christopher asked. "'Cause I was just about to walk out the door and head over—"

"I'm sure, dude," Ezekiel said. "Thanks."

"No problem, Ezekiel. Oh, and we told them that the mirror just buckled and busted at random, like from humidity or something. Not sure if that's a thing, but there didn't seem to be any smudges or blood or anything left by you, Phil checked, so they probably won't have any proof that we're big bad liars. I don't think they'll be looking for any proof, anyway. They say they were planning on doing a complete renovation of the room over winter break."

"Okay," Ezekiel said, biting back the panic in his voice as he looked down at the ground. He had never tried this before. "That's cool. Busted by humidity. Thanks, man."

"Yeah, Ezekiel. I would say anytime, but, you know, I hope not. We'll talk later."

"Sure," Ezekiel squeaked, and they ended the connection. *Here goes,* he thought, and jumped out the window.

13.
Gifts of the Spirit

Blessed be the Lord my Strength Which teacheth my hands to war, and my fingers to fight: my Goodness, and my Fortress; my High Tower, and my Deliverer; my Shield, and He in Whom I trust; Who subdueth my people under me.
Lord, what is man, that Thou takest knowledge of him! Or the son of man, that Thou makest account of him!

    – Psalm 144:1-3

September 23rd—

So Ezekiel could fly, Rico mused, sitting in class far north at Maryland's Annapolis Naval Academy. It seemed unfair that Coda could do crazy flips and that Kim could beat up The Rock and Vin Diesel at the same time without breaking a sweat, but now Ezekiel could not only fly, but he could read minds as well and even had an outer shell that rivaled any turtle Rico had ever seen. All Rico could do was heat stuff up with his hands. He had thought that that was cool enough, until he heard about Ezekiel falling into a mirror and hopping up unscathed. Rico had pricked his finger in a rash experiment and the blood that flowed from it had been enough to let him know that the thick skin was a gift given to Ezekiel certainly, and not to him.

Rico had asked his mother what she thought about God giving people extra-human abilities and she said that God didn't. The abilities that the humans have were the ability to call on God and have Him do all of the extra-human things. Rico knew he hadn't called on God when he inadvertently melted a cafeteria tray.

Rico zoned out in class on a regular basis, meaning he'd listen for about forty minutes, allowing his mind to file away the professors' input before churning with his thoughts until he was far away. He might occasionally think about some things that pertained to the class, but for the most part, the class disappeared from his awareness. If the professors began to ask questions, Rico would then give them his full attention, so in classes where the professors questioned at random, the lanky fellow fought hard to stay completely in the moment. He just wasn't the sedentary type of person. He was active. He didn't like saying something, he liked showing. Doing, even.

That's why girls thought he was so horny; he didn't mean to be. After all, what was the point in staying with saying "I love you" year upon year upon year? He just liked to think ahead and keep things fresh. And he liked to involve the senses.

He was a very passionate person. Generally passive in confrontation, perhaps, but not afraid of a challenge—if a person was wrong, Rico would tell them straightforward that they were incorrect in their thinking. He wasn't belligerent. He was straight-up. It came in handy with a girl like BJ in his corner.

BJ sometimes decided to be a conscientious objector, and Rico thought that she did it just to bother him. One day she'd be shooting off rounds into the targets during ROTC practice, then she'd tell Rico that she didn't understand how he could call himself a follower of religion—Christianity or otherwise—and not feel remorse in killing. She called it *akusala*, the Buddhist idea of poisonous foundations.

"Even if someone is staring me down with the barrel of a shotgun, I won't kill them," she had said.

"So why are you learning how to shoot a gun?" he asked and she had shrugged and laughed, before meditatively changing her mind.

"David said that God allowed him to kill Goliath," Rico said, sometimes, "and David's life wasn't directly in danger then. And all through the Old Testament," he said, knowing that she would shrug all of this off, "God would tell different people to kill people."

And BJ would say, "So let's say that fiction is history—it still was way back then. When's the last time God told you to do something? Like, 'Hi, there, boy-o, I'm God!'"

Rico couldn't say much, because aside from the burning arms—which he would *not* mention—God had never spoken to him plainly like that. It was always those, "Something told me to do that!" That was how God spoke to him. And there was no way he was gonna mention the talking flames to BJ.

So many religious terrorists professed that the destruction they caused by ending the many lives that they did was done all as a gift to who they saw God to be. Rico disagreed with the thought of killing others who simply had opposing viewpoints, no matter how radical, no matter how ignorant, no matter how ridiculous he saw those viewpoints to be. If people did not know the correct way of getting to heaven, why would he end their lives before they could correctly accept Christ as their own?

Rico would kill to preserve God's own, however. That, surely, was God's intention when He sent the ancient rulers on spiritual and physical warpaths.

And he wouldn't mind one bit if he had to kill someone who was threatening the safety of his mother, sister, father, or BJ. He wouldn't even have to think.

The professor asked him a question. Great. He had no idea what topic they were on.

· · · · · ·

October 16th—

The tallest building in the Yard at the Naval Academy was definitely Chapel Towers. It was so big, and so green, that it was almost *the* landmark of Annapolis. It was nice to have a religious landmark around, Rico thought. Between the guttural navy vernacular and the trying days when he felt so screwed up as a human being, it was nice to have that tremendous reminder of God.

The inside of the Chapel was impressive. The pews were of a deep coffee color, leading to the front of the sanctuary where there was an altar and a pulpit. The pulpit sat in a beautifully concave portion of the white, ornate sanctuary. Behind the pulpit was a stained glass window, containing a picture of something or somebody, but Rico hadn't quite figured it out.

At mass service he'd keep his ears open for all kinds of signs pertaining to his predicament as far as his hands were concerned. The academy had a massive pan-faith system, where no matter one's religion, there was a chaplain there who represented it, could teach it, and could make it apply.

Several Sundays ago, one of the Catholic chaplains ministered on the subject of developing one's talents, from the twenty-fifth chapter of Matthew.

Most of the Catholic midshipmen who were present for service assumed that the sermon was about post-college decisions and took it for no more than casual military propaganda. Rico himself planned on sticking with the Navy for several years at best, but didn't see the message as referring to career field choices.

It was in the richly decorated building that Rico found the same chaplain who had preached the sermon earlier that day on talents. All of the chaplains, whether they were Catholic, or Muslim, or Jewish, were members of the Navy that were permitted to be based at the academy for spiritual guidance. It was a busy day, all the chaplains were buzzing with the news of some pastor in Baltimore who had been indicted in some government cover-up.

Rico hadn't paid much attention to the news or to the warnings that had come from Kim, Coda and Ezekiel. He abso-freakin-lutely *knew* that there was no possible way that whatever was happening elsewhere could happen at a military school. Classes, lunch, formations. More classes, personal fitness, dinner at five-thirty. Study, call BJ, call home. Then do it all again. Who would attempt anything at a place so rigorously redundant? What would be the point of it? Well, what was the point of any of it, anyway? It made Rico's head hurt.

On that particular Sunday, Rico was dressed in full uniform, as they did for religious services. His white suit was clean without a flaw and his buttons were as polished as the Chapel's magnificent stained glass windows.

"Yes," Father Gregory greeted Rico, a little hurriedly.

"Good evening, sir," Rico politely greeted the chaplain, removing his hat. "I had a question about your sermon."

Father Gregory blinked in surprise. He rarely got visits from Midshipmen with spiritual issues, let alone kids that wanted to discuss his sermons. He was already turning into his father, a war and life veteran who drove around with a bumper sticker that read, "We have enough youth, how about a fountain of SMART?"

"Did you find something wrong with it, Mr. ...?" His light blue eyes squinted at the handsome, yet spindly freshman in front of him.

"Rico Gutierrez, sir."

"Rico, did you have disagreements with the message?"

"No, sir, not even! But I do have a question about the talents God gives…"

And so Rico experienced his first Bible study. Rico enjoyed it immensely, because outside of the official-this-and-that of service, he could be much more personable. Father Gregory, who had dropped whatever it was that had him bustling before, seemed to be feeling the exact same release of formalities.

Rico just nodded and absorbed as much as he could. Every once in a while he'd ask a question, but for the most part, the chaplain was answering the questions before the young Gutierrez could ask them.

"Too many times we're so focused on what we can do," Father Gregory explained. "We can do this; we can do that. It's not us, Rico! It's God in us! Sitting on our talents is sitting on God and what He can do in our lives. We've gotta start giving credit where credit is due. Moses didn't take Israel out of bondage. God did, with Moses as His vessel. Psalm eight and four states, 'Who is man, that God is mindful of him?' Rico, more explicitly, what can we do without God?"

Indeed, Rico thought. *Indeed.*

Once the day had darkened to dusk, as if to prove that no rose was without its thorns, he stumbled upon two of them while coming out of the Chapel Towers.

Rico froze, at a loss, not quite believing that he was experiencing it for himself. Sure enough, there was that girl dressed in red and standing guard while a pale boy that looked like he needed a wardrobe more befitting of the season was busying himself with one of the cornerstones of the building.

The girl in red caught sight of him, spinning towards him with a blank demonic stare. Her companion stood slowly, expression unreadable.

A flicker of flame involuntarily escaped Rico's left index finger, as seemingly natural as a drop of sweat.

In the next moment, the two were gone. But he knew they'd be back.

That was too easy.

• • • • •

"Dr. Pat?"

"What *is* it?"

"Ma'am, we have activity up north."

"Is this connected to the previous data we've collected?"

"No, uh, ma'am. Uh, not quite. At least it doesn't seem so."

"Stop all the hemming and hawing, this isn't a blasted stable."

"Yes, ma'am."

"How far north are we talking, Dr. Lemming?"

"Uh, my name—"

"*How far north?*"

"Annapolis, ma'am."

"My god, near the Naval Academy?"

"No ma'am, *on* the Naval Academy. This one got called in."

"Ours? Or better yet—that girl?"

"Not ours. But they definitely want us to find out whose."

"Holy Captain America. They're giving this one to us?"

"The official word says that they will allow us access. Once they secure—"

"Out of my office, Dr. Lemming. I have some calls to make. You should pack a bag and brush up on your military etiquette. You were military once, right?"

"Air National—"

"Oh, that doesn't count."

She waved him off, picking up the phone.

"Anchors away, my boys," she sang softly. "Anchors away." Her fingers began dialing a number on her cell. "Farewell to college joys, we sail at break of day, day, day, day..."

· · · · ·

November 22nd—

Rico was in town for a full week in celebration of Thanksgiving and, having visited Coda several times during the first weekend of his return, enjoyed Coda's company for a few nights before the holiday. They filled their days doing yard work for Mr. Gutierrez, while some evenings encouraged late-night mall runs costumed in sweatshirts, jeans and stony expressions, convincing everyone that they were thuggish boys. There was a good portion of thug inside of both of them. On lazy days when they didn't feel like raking the yard or trimming foliage or battling like the superheroes they were coming to realize they were, Rico would in turn show him his growing collection of Navy paraphernalia and all of the pictures that he had stored on his digital camera. He had a good eye for photography and it seemed to improve with each picture.

The first night of the week, Rico had lost the ability to sleep...closing his eyes and lying still with a strange sort of intensity, he found himself listening to the radio DJs play "Upsetting Regrets" over and over and over. Discontent, he hopped onto his computer to surf, and was able to put the world out of his mind for a few minutes until his computer decided to freeze. He turned off his computer and his radio, stepped over Coda who was snoring lightly and walked from bedroom to hallway.

Light escaped from under his sister's door, leading Rico to knock lightly. Without a response, he opened the door slightly to see his sister sprawled across her bed with her Bible lying next to her. She had fallen asleep reading. She was near impossible to outclass, he mused. He flipped off the light and closed her door.

He ambled into the living room, greeted by his father's snores. Rico just stood there, watching his father sleep peacefully on the couch. Rico's mother was probably sleeping just as soundly in the bed that his parents used to share. Rico wondered how long the marriage would last. They had fought on for dear life for the benefit of Rico and Renata, but it seemed as if the Gutierrezes were about to join a larger demographic: broken families. He knew that Renata had taken their wedding picture, which showed Mrs. Gutierrez in a beautiful white gown and her hair up in a bun and Mr. Gutierrez in a purple velvet suit and a nice-sized Afro, and placed it on her dresser, right next to her alarm clock.

He wandered into the kitchen and looked at the dishes his mother had set out on the counter for Thursday's Thanksgiving dinner. He opened the refrigerator to stare at some food he didn't feel like eating, then closed it back.

"I do have a question about the talents God gives…"

Rico heard his own voice as if he was standing next to himself. Was he gifted? What about the others who had been selected and set aside? They might as well be called "talented" though not in the way Coda was accustomed to take the word. "Chosen," even.

He walked back into his room and pulled his glasses out of a drawer, since there was no point of putting his contacts in, especially if he fell asleep. He picked up his Bible. Gifts, gifts, gifts… there might be a scripture somewhere about gifts…

The back of his Bible had a list of trivia questions. One day after Mass, he and Renata had quizzed each other to see who knew the most. Renata had won. *So* impossible to outclass.

Aha! Spiritual gifts. "Charismata," his Bible had labeled them. Rico flipped to the first scripture listed underneath the header. First Corinthians. He began reading in silence, as his fingers traced the indentation across the bridge of his nose.

"What are you doing up, Enrique?" his father asked from the door, slumber gripping the wrinkles in his brown face. He was still dressed in the slacks and windbreaker jacket that he had worn during the day. Why had he slept in his clothes? Rico wondered what time it was. He had been reading for several minutes…perhaps more than an hour

Mr. Gutierrez took in the setting. "Oh, you are having a Bible study! I will leave you to your studies."

"No, Dad, it's okay," Rico replied. Now that his father was up, he didn't want to return to the loneliness that came courtesy of the solitude. "In fact, could you maybe look up some stuff with me?"

"Oh, sure, Enrique. Let me go find my Bible." Mr. Gutierrez disappeared from the doorway.

Rico read until his father reappeared with his Bible and his own pair of glasses.

His father sat down on Rico's mattress, which lay flat on the floor. He eyed Coda's place on the floor, perpendicular to the bed.

"You know he is welcome to come for Thanksgiving dinner," Mr. Gutierrez spoke.

"Yeah, but I think he plans on eating with his family."

Mr. Gutierrez nodded.

"Probably best, anyway."

Even though Rico knew exactly what his father was referring to, he said nothing.

"What are we reading? ¿*Tobías?* You loved stories about angels when you were young. You and Renata were always reading those stories."

"Renata likes Esther, too."

Mr. Gutierrez glanced at Rico's Bible, placing his glasses upon his nose.

"Ah, the twelfth chapter and first book *a los Corintios. Nuevo Testamento.*" He began to turn the pages. Upon finding the scripture, he began to read silently. Rico read as well.

---

[1]Now concerning spiritual gifts, brethren, I would not have you ignorant. [2]Ye know that ye were Gentiles, carried away unto these dumb idols, even as ye were led. [3]Wherefore I give you to understand, that no man speaking by the Spirit of God calleth Jesus accursed: and that no man can say that Jesus is the Lord, but by the Holy Ghost. [4]Now there are diversities of gifts, but the same Spirit. [5]And there are differences of administrations, but the same Lord. [6]And there are diversities of operations, but it is the same God which worketh all in all. [7]But the manifestation of the Spirit is given to every man to profit withal. [8]For to one is given by the Spirit the word of wisdom; to another the word of knowledge by the same Spirit; [9]to another faith by the same Spirit; to another the

gifts of healing by the same Spirit; ¹⁰To another the working of miracles; to another prophecy; to another discerning of spirits; to another divers kinds of tongues; to another the interpretation of tongues: ¹¹But all these worketh that one and the selfsame Spirit, dividing to every man severally as he will.

Mr. Gutierrez turned to Rico. He spoke in English. "Are we studying the Espíritu Santo? The Holy Spirit, hijo?"

Rico shifted on his bed. "Kind of, Dad. I don't know. Spiritual gifts, mostly."

"Ah, *carismas*." Mr. Gutierrez switched back to Spanish, since it was easiest for him. "The gift of faith is a powerful thing, Rico. That is one that I desire. And healing would be nice; you would have had no sick days in school." He chuckled at his joke, and Rico saw once again how similar his poles-apart-parents were.

"Aren't there more…*physical* gifts?" Rico asked, also in Spanish.

"They are called 'gifts of the Spirit' for a reason, hijo. The physical gifts don't have their own list. They are more like blessings for chosen people."

Rico glanced sharply at his father. "Blessings for chosen people," he repeated. His mom wouldn't agree, but this was exactly what made the most sense to him.

"Yes," Mr. Gutierrez said, oblivious to his son's renewed alertness. "Like Samson and Moses."

"Is there a scripture about that?" he asked.

His father frowned. "Not that I can think of at this moment," he conveyed. "I'm not exactly an expert, as you know. Though we could read about Samson and Moses. Shall we keep reading here?" he asked.

Rico shook himself, trying to wake his brain completely, then nodded.

---

²⁷Now ye are the body of Christ, and members in particular. ²⁸And God hath set some in the church, first apostles, secondarily prophets, thirdly teachers, after that miracles, then gifts of healings, helps, governments, diversities of tongues. ²⁹Are all

apostles? Are all prophets? Are all teachers? Are all workers of miracles? 30Have all the gifts of healing? Do all speak with tongues? Do all interpret? 31But covet earnestly the best gifts: and yet shew I unto you a more excellent way.

"What are you guys doing up?" Drowsy English.

Rico and Mr. Gutierrez glanced up and looked at Renata, who was leaning on the doorpost with a hand on her waist.

"Are you asleep?" Mr. Gutierrez asked.

"Not anymore, Papá," Renata smiled through her sluggishness. "What are you two doing?"

"Just a little midnight study of the Biblios!" Rico cried.

"Shh," Renata said, putting one finger up to her mouth, and pointing another towards the snoozing Coda.

Rico, remembering, looked over, and then, content with the fact that Coda was still sleeping, turned back to Renata. "Yeah, we're just reading about gifts and stuff."

"Oh," she muttered.

"Are we too loud, or did you care to join us?" Mr. Gutierrez asked.

"Maybe," Renata said, settling herself in between her father and her brother. "What about the scriptures that say people should love each other forever?" she asked, not quite as innocently as Rico knew she planned to.

"Renata," their father intoned warningly.

"Just asking," she said, pulling off the innocence that time.

"Your mother and I have..." Their father spoke again, but in Spanish. "You two have always had a mother and a father. Your mother and I did that part very well. However, I've never had a wife and, according to your mother, she's never had a husband, so we're just considering...making that official."

"Yeah, can we not talk about this?" Rico asked, looking down at the floor.

"Sure," Renata replied, disappointed. "Let's read up on gifts."

Despite brushing off the feelings that Renata had stirred up, Rico still found himself frustrated in regards to his predicament. He felt he should be seeing more in his study than he was, that the answers should be a lot easier...however, his soul was settled with the fact that he had at least started digging. And digging was the only way anything that was buried in the Word could ever be unearthed.

• • • • •

December 7th—

The attacks on Ezekiel, Coda and Kim had definitely freaked Rico out. He sat in his dorm racking his brain for all of the tricks he'd learned when taking boxing during Plebe Summer. If only he had signed for more self-defense classes, but his schedule was too full; between learning naval science, calculus, government, chemistry, and the dreaded English course, he barely had enough time to talk to BJ (though he made time) or even join a boxing or karate or judo club. Extracurricular activities, or ECAs as they were called, would have to wait until Rico adjusted more.

Nautical colors affected everything in Rico's dorm, from the cream walls to the navy chairs accompanying each of the three desks. The room was built for three midshipmen, but their third roommate had declared on the first day of school that the academy wasn't for him and within the next cycle of the moon, only two were left in the room. The accompanying vacant area was quickly snatched up to house the drums of Rico's remaining roommate, a fellow freshman.

An elevated bed framed his organized desk-area, where his bookcase held several of the mammoth manuals required for those extensive courses. The largest book was actually one he was reading for fun, a manuscript that was filled with pictures and loads of engrossing information about the military ships and aircrafts. In the corner of his desk was a miniature Christmas tree, one that he had put up the day after Thanksgiving.

The desk was very well-kept; Gutierrezes had always been good at staying organized. All the books were on the shelves, save the ethics book he had been studying that very moment before his mind drifted back to the call that he had received weeks before from Ezekiel. His calendar was laid out to keep his dates in order, his clothes were packed up nice beneath the desk, and his two naval caps were displayed prominently above the bookcase. Pete's area was less impressive than Rico's. In-between their beds rested the door that led into the hall.

Rico was living in the second-largest dormitory complex in the continental United States. He could look out of the window and look across the large campus to the other end of Bancroft Hall, dorm building for all the Midshipmen, which trekked a lengthy bracket to where he was located.

He found himself going to the Chapel more often, to Father Gregory's spiritual pleasure, waiting for them to show back up—her more than the boy. The boy, by all accounts, he could handle, but the girl—Solitaire was her chosen name, according to Ezekiel—was no joke, proven by her appearance at Georgia Tech.

He considered everything, analyzing and picking, until he was thinking clearly. Solitaire would've found him anyway, in the same way that she had found Ezekiel, however that was. He had just made it a little easier for her to locate him. If she was anything like Kim's boy or Coda's creature, she'd have no problem popping up at the right place without other people noticing and disappearing without anyone knowing how. He just had to make a plan.

Assuming that she only knew *where* he was, and not *who* he was, he couldn't let her figure out the situation anymore than she already had. There was also the dilemma of Rico not being able to let other people see what he could do. Whatever happened, he couldn't do anything that would be a potential threat to the safety of the academy…or anything that could be *mistaken* as a potential threat to the academy.

Impolite words crossed Rico's brain. There was a costumed girl passing by *outside his window*. He could see her through the blinds. Her head was wrapped in a towering sparkling red hat like the "swaddling clothes" Rico had seen Baby Jesus wrapped in at countless Christmas programs, only far more blingy. It actually looked familiar to his mind, though as a fashion accessory it seemed just as random as her collective appearance was. She looked like she was taking a nice morning stroll in Halloweenville, but he wasn't in Halloweenville—he was on the fifth floor!

He couldn't look directly at her, what if she was waiting for it? Then a chillier thought crossed his brain, for if someone *else* saw her—an innocent person—she might—

He jumped into action. He found his black sweatpants that, like most of his pants, were too big for his thin legs, and dug for his sunglasses. He stripped out of his khaki pants, grateful that Pete wasn't there to ask any questions. As he put on his sunglasses, he yanked his sweatpants over his thermal-padded legs with his other hand, all the while looking for the right shirt to wear. It was freezing outside, but he couldn't wear anything that touched his hands, because that would initiate a fire, and that definitely wouldn't be the greatest thing in the world.

Aha! He found an old sweatshirt that he had never cared for, and painstakingly ripped the sleeves off. He put the shirt on backwards at first, but hurriedly pulled his arms inside and twisted the shirt around so that the tag wouldn't distract him by scraping against his Adam's apple.

As a kid he had imagined what it would be like to be a superhero and in all his imagining, he had worn a red and blue costume. Unfortunately, he didn't have any present option to be choosy, and the reality of the situation was, well, quite a reality.

Now the only thing left to do was to figure out just how to get his bony butt up on that roof.

Rico danced over to the window in a mix between fear and anticipation. She was further down on his wing of the dormitory, on his left. What could he do?

He opened the window and leaned out into the chilly atmosphere. His arms broke out in goose bumps, a likely effect of the combination of low bravado and seemingly negative degree temperature. He closed his eyes and breathed slowly. By focusing with a particular amount of energy, he could make the heat in his hands either shrink away or, like he was doing now, grow to warm his entire arms. Rico had figured that if he had this ability, he'd better know how to use it, so this routine he had exercised several times.

If only he could fly like Ezekiel. Please God, he wanted to fly like Ezekiel.

He turned and looked up at the roof, which was thankfully right above the fifth story—his story. Huge stones jutted out of the wall. When had architecture ever come in so handy? He grabbed the stones and began to pull himself up, out of his room and towards the roof. What if his sunglasses fell off? What if she recognized him anyway? He couldn't leave the window open! She'd know which dorm he came out of and, well, he knew he had to close it. He slammed it as quietly as possible and thrust himself onto the blue copper roof, right as Solitaire spun below, looking for the source of the noise.

He watched as she began gliding back in his direction, like a shark. A shark who was built like Jessica Rabbit.

He scuttled away from the roof's edge, observing his setting. There were the Chapel Towers, there was the baseball field… Actually, if he could just get her onto the roof, he'd be more at ease. But what was he going to do once he got her up there?

Rico needed her to notice him. He couldn't bring himself to just call her name, so he had to come up with an alternative. He stood and took a deep breath. He hadn't used this certain aspect of his powers often, but he anticipated that by the evening's end he'd be an expert at it.

"Yo," he yelled, letting a brief burst of flames rip from his hands, over the side of the roof, right over her head.

"Ah," she exhaled, rising onto the roof with discomforting ease. She seemed pretty good with *her* power. "Eli attacks?"

Rico adjusted his position to a more impressive stance, though the transition showcased his uneasiness. "That wasn't an attack."

"It was an attention grabber," she briskly agreed in a rough, hoarse voice that he struggled to place. "I get it."

She was taking him in. He did the same. As he stared, he realized that the skin around her hellish eyes was not peachy, like Ezekiel described, but rather the color of a brown egg, like his. Her eyes were un-settling…the blackness. She was not a girl—she was definitely a woman —but then there were times Rico forgot that he was now a legal man and not a boy. The hat she wore still struck him as familiar, and she had on a buttoned white trench coat that brushed against the ankles of her red combat boots. Where had she found those? Her gloves were red, but her face…was blurry. He couldn't make out a single feature but those black eyes. Even when she spoke, he couldn't make out whether her mouth was open, closed, or there at all. It was the oddest thing he had ever seen.

"Are you checking me out?" she asked him, tilting her head.

She wasn't dumb. She must have known about the repercussions of infiltrating a Naval Academy.

She appraised him. "You're a little bony somebody."

"Do you know who I am?" Rico asked. "Do you know what you're doing?" What was she doing? He really wished he knew.

"Are you afraid?" Solitaire asked, not looking for an answer, just a reaction. "Have you heard about me?" She spoke again, while suggestive-ly trailing her hand down the center of her chest. "Do you want to be what I'm doing?"

Rico froze. "What?"

And just like that, she jumped at him. In reflex he brought up his arms to shield his face, and fell back onto the roof. She hadn't landed on him, though. She had landed *next* to him, and then took of down the roof, away from him. Her jacket was open now, leaving him staring after shapely red legs, escaping up the slanted roof.

They both knew that she could fly, so why was she running? Flight must have been easier for her, what with the intense slant of the roof and especially with that towering bejeweled hat. Rico concluded that she wanted the thrill of the chase. So he indulged her.

After a few yards, she halted without warning. Rico was not as close to her as he had wished, but with her stopping he was glad he wasn't close enough to crash into her. He skidded to a stop.

She lifted her head into the air, not turning to face him.

"*Eli, Eli,*" she moaned, "*la'ma sabach-tha'nai?*"

Rico frowned. What was that? That wasn't any language that he knew, yet strangely, it sounded familiar.

She whirled around without pause or warning, just the streaking glitter of that ridiculous hat. There was a glint of metal flashing through the air and Rico dodged it, but another swing followed, then another, in a never-ending stream that had him on constant defense. She got much closer to making contact than he appreciated, as if he were a moving fish that she wanted to filet.

Eventually she stopped, bored almost, throwing her head back to cackle at the sky, sounding like a garbage disposal grinding in her throat. It was the furthest thing from attractive that he could conceive. He realized she was toying with him. He got a look at the hideous knife that had appeared earlier in her hands so suddenly. If she was toying with him, this was the most dangerous game he had ever played.

"What do you want from me?" he blurted.

Solitaire's neck popped back into place, as if he had interrupted her, and for all he knew, he had. She smiled a smile with hidden meaning, blinking those perverted eyes. She was a bundle of teasing, flirtatious mirth. "I don't rightly know. Isn't that insane? But really, is that even much of an issue? I'm here and so are you, so I'll figure it out soon enough."

"Solitaire, who are you going after?" he asked. "Who's Eli? Why were you at the chapel that day?"

"Mmm, so many questions and so little time." She placed her hands on her hips in mock contemplation. "Hey," she said, "it's no fair that you can call me names and I can't call you anything but Hot Hands." She glowered at Rico. He had almost mistaken it for pouting.

"Hot Hands will do, *niña,*" he fumed, aiming his hands at her, sending a stream of flames in her direction.

"You can't be serious," she laughed, leaping into the air. "Hot Hands just doesn't do it for me, *cabrón,*" she said, his flames passing safely underneath her feet. "Why not Inferno or Ignite?" She advanced swiftly but cautiously in his direction, whipping out that hideous knife from a very surprising place. "Or Incinerator?"

"How about N-O?" Rico said, and blazed another bonfire in her direction. She casually flew to one side, steadily advancing.

"*Perdón, Solitaria*," Rico raged. "What exactly are you trying to accomplish here? What's your story? Did a superhero kill your father when you were a girl or something? Do you hate people that get struck by lightning or are you some type of superpowered sadist? You must have some type of motivation for this. Did God even make a choice for you?"

She pulled up short, eyes slanting.

"Did God make a choice for me?" she asked evenly. "I think you should watch your mouth, angel boy."

Rico noticed that she wasn't advancing anymore and the knife had disappeared. He decided to get bold. Whatever that comment had bought for him, he'd use it for however much it was worth.

"Watch your tone, *mujer del diablo*," Rico said, not knowing why he was throwing out so many Spanish terms. "Or I'll fry you right where you float."

Her head tilted. Her blurry face…he had to see it close up. "Try it, freak boy," she said, her voice deepening.

"Skippy." Rico let it rip from his hands like he had never been able to before; he felt the pressure in his lower stomach like the abdominal crunch that came at the end of a long set. He even grunted, looking in amazement as his forearms were covered in fervid flames. The fire thundered so strongly that if it hadn't been for the fact that he could see them underneath the orange flood, he would have thought that his arms had turned into flames themselves.

Rico dropped his arms. Then he frowned in understated distress.

Solitaire was "perched" in the air above the edge of the roof, a few yards away, arms raised just as his had been. As the flames were reaching her, she was sending them back like miniature comets.

Rico froze, before realization sunk in and he jumped away from the first volley. He leapt and twisted to avoid her attack, which was in essence his own attack reversed upon him.

His feet struggled to stand. His toes couldn't find the roof, but he was still…standing upright. Could he even say he was standing? Maybe he was…

He smiled in spite of himself. He was actually flying! God had heard his unofficial prayer.

Solitaire was fuming, which was only expressed through the clenching of her fists, for her face was still blurry and her heaving chest may have been the product of the acrobatics alone.

"You all just keep pulling them out from your sleeves, don't you?" she grumbled, that darn head leaning to one side again.

"I'm not wearing sleeves," Rico responded acerbically, tilting *his* head in mockery.

"Let's see what else you have in common with Leviathan," she said, enraged.

She flew quickly towards him and punched him in the mouth. Rico punched her in her stomach instinctively.

"Returning the favor," he said, spitting the blood from the inside of his lips.

She in turn smacked him into a mid-air cartwheel, staring at him with her head tilted, effectively reversing the mockery. Rico picked himself up along with his ego and sent another ray of fire in her direction. This time, she simply whipped her hands in the air and the flames came back to him and burst upon him.

Stop, drop, and roll. Stop, drop, and roll, he repeated in his brain, and flew headfirst, straight into the roof. The flames went out, but his head throbbed. He had a power hangover. His powers, these talents and gifts that he had, they weren't meant to be used against him. It was a perversion of the Spirit.

"Roll," he moaned, turning onto is back, his face scratched by the rusting copper panels.

Solitaire sailed towards him, her face remaining incredibly indistinct with each increasing meter, and pulled out her knife. Upon glimpsing the knife, Rico's thoughts were quickly scattered.

"There's just one thing I want you to take back to Sammy and David," she purred, putting him in mind of Kim with her feline elocution. "And—why not—Leviathan, too, if he hasn't learned his lesson, yet. Tell them that they don't want to bother with me. I could care less about the others, but if you get in *my* way, there'll be hell to pay, and no *choice* of God will save you." The knife was getting dangerously close to Rico's well being. When she spoke again, it was in fluent Spanish. "Now, here's a small token of my appreciation for your hospitality."

Rico put his hands on her waist. She screamed, damaged by the heat, and twisted away. Flames enveloped Rico's hands as he swung over and punched her stomach, right where he had wounded her before. She yelled, lifting up her leg and kicking him in his groin. He moaned, dropping next to her, fetal and defeated.

"Don't do that," Solitaire spoke breathlessly. "Ever again."

And she laid her knife to his neck.

"Move if you dare," she encouraged, but he didn't have the strength. She carved a very tiny spade onto the side of his neck, just deep enough for him to feel it, though not over the previous injuries she had given him. She stood.

"*¿Dios hizo una opción para mí?*" she said curiously, before dismissing it and waving her hand uncaringly.

Rico didn't have the strength to even rise up onto his elbows.

"Creep," she muttered. "*Hasta luego, Rico de fuego.*"

And she was gone.

Horrible timing. Horrible, because her expensive-looking hat didn't keep up with her travel plans, rolling next to his torso as if looking for an owner.

Horrible timing. The thought rotated in his mind as the SWAT team swept onto the roof, guns and lights pointed at Rico like he was some big-time criminal.

"Crap," he moaned, staring down a multitude of barrels.

Horrible, horrible timing.

14.

Diamonds and Spades

"You're the best boyfriend in the world!" Kim squealed, hooking her arm into his. "I just squealed didn't I? I hate it when I squeal."

Dishon grinned, pulling her close. "I love it when you squeal."

"I'm going to pretend that I don't know what you mean," she said coldly, looking up at the ceiling of the tent as they circulated amongst the tables. "Because pressure—"

"No pressure," he said, grimacing. "I was just cracking a joke, Mary Poppins."

"Such an outdated reference," she laughed, shoulder bumping his sinewy triceps.

He glanced over at her. "I really can't do right by you, can I?"

Ouch. Oh well, she had asked for it. "Sorry, Dishon," she purred. "You did right by bringing me here. I can't tell you how long I've wanted to watch a real poker tournament."

"I need you to be my good luck charm," he said. "If I win the pot it'll book us studio time, and I may have extra to get you that diamond bracelet you want."

"La-di-da, don't wanna hear it," Kim laughed, her blue bracelets jangling on her arm in agreement. "I don't need diamonds, Dishon. Cubic zirconia will do just fine. It all looks the same under the club lights."

He chuckled.

Kim looked around her at the active tables. A guy in front of her with a really well-shaped mini-fro seemed to be getting into his game, slamming cards down quite obnoxiously. *He must have attended the Shannon school of game-playing*, she thought to herself.

"Are we late?" she asked as they moved closer to the rowdy table. "Seems like some of the games have started."

"We're not late," he said. "And that's Spades. They're not even playing poker."

Kim barely heard him. At the table, looking up from his hand at her with his gorgeous hazel eyes, was Justus.

"Hey!" he said, waving.

"Hey, Justus!" she grinned. He went to school in Macon, which was an Atlanta suburb almost one hundred miles away. It was a pleasant surprise to see him. Well, to her at least.

"Seriously?" Dishon asked. "You and all these white boys," he grumbled.

"Chill, boy," she said softly as the game ended. It seemed Justus's team had lost. "You'd feel even more threatened if the boys were Black."

Almost on cue, the Afro in front of her stood up, turning around.

"Kim?"

She would've recognized the booming voice even if she hadn't recognized the towering, titanic body.

"Eugenie!" she exclaimed, bounding over to him to give him a hug.

He chuckled. "You know, I've always gone by Gene. No 'Eu' or 'nie' has ever been necessary."

He was the same Gene, all right. A long-sleeved mock turtleneck with shorts and Timberlands. She giggled in spite of herself.

Dishon had traveled over to them, several inches and pec sizes smaller than Gene, and the cautious discomfort showed in his expression.

"Gene, this is my boyfriend Dishon." She ignored the surprised look on his face ("Yes, I'm dating now," she wanted to snarl) and continued the introductions. "Dishon, this is another high school buddy, Gene Hightower."

"She has a lot of you 'high school buddies,'" Dishon said.

"Not all of us are social Frankensteins," Kim countered.

"Nice to meet you," Gene said, shaking Dishon's offered hand while ignoring all impolite implications. "You go to school near here?"

"CAU. With Kimi. You?"

"UGA," Gene nodded. "I play football there. Second string quarterback."

"Oh man," Dishon said, eyes growing wide. "Gene *Hightower*. Number Five! I saw that game back in October where you came through in the third quarter and widened the winning score by, like, three touchdowns. The Tower of Power!" He shook his head in realization. "I didn't know you were a freshman!"

"Yay, friends," Kim said, boggling her eyes humorously. Dishon gave her a strange look. "You're growing your hair out," she said to Gene. "I like it. It's groomed."

"Checking the mirror constantly," he said. "I feel like a chick."

"Are you entering the tourney?" Dishon asked, gesturing to the rapidly filling room.

Gene shook his head, the darkness in his eyes battling the smile on his face. "Naw, man. I just came for the advance fun. I've gotta big final to study for."

"Ugh," Kim said.

"I know, right?" Gene looked at Kim, a brightness returning to his eyes as quickly as it had left. "Yo, tell your bestie I said wassup, alright?"

"Oh, of course I'll tell Maya," she mewed as he hugged her. "You take care, Gene."

"You, too. Nice seeing you." He shook Dishon's hand again in that complicated Black boy way. "Nice meeting you, Dishon."

"Nice meeting you, Gene. Keep killing them on that field."

"Oh I will," Gene nodded. "Dust. Dust, Kim."

"Dust," she sang out brightly.

"What does that mean?" Dishon asked.

"No idea," she said, looking at him. "For a second there I thought you were getting all fantastically fanatic for Mr. Mantastic over there."

"Ha," Dishon said dryly. He checked his watch. "Yo, I gotta use the bathroom and buy in. Meet you near the Michelob poster at ten after?"

Kim glanced at the clock on her phone. "Sounds good."

He kissed her on the cheek and became a lingering scent of cologne in the air. A new, equally delicious scent swooped in to replace it.

"What are you doing here, Kim?" Justus asked her, surprising her with a hug. "Did you see Gene?"

"Yeah, I just talked to him," she said, squeezing back. "Are you playing?"

"Definitely," he said, letting her go and tousling his honey-gold hair. "I haven't missed a single one yet—here for these every month. It's worth the gas money. I used to see Gene here all the time, but last month they banned him from participating."

"What?" she asked, eyes growing wide.

"Hey, you want some ice cream?" he asked, raising his voice to cover the preposterous growling of his stomach. "My treat. There's a stand somewhere near this tent and I've been cravin' like a raven. Plus I could benefit from some air freshery."

One double scooped strawberry cone and a Volcanic Fudge Sundae later and Kim's questions began to occupy her mouth instead of her spoon.

"I'm confused," Kim said, pulling out her phone to keep mark of the time. "Why were you guys playing Spades at a poker tournament?"

"Oh, we were just waiting for the tourney to start," he said, crunching on the end of his cone as they strolled down the sidewalk back towards the giant poker tent. "Passing the time and all that. Just a fun game. Not as intense as poker."

"Oh, okay. Dishon's been talking about this tournament all month!"

"Dishon?" Justus asked.

"My boyfriend." She ignored the look. "He's gonna play tonight."

"Ah, I see," he nodded. "So you're not playing, I take it?"

Kim giggled. "I can't even play Go Fish without getting confused about the rules."

He nodded again. "It can get a little wild. And I never figured out I Declare War."

She had forgotten how silly he could be.

He knew of her way before she knew of him. They were both schooled at Marshwind Middle School, and Kim had performed in a talent showcase that Justus had attended in the sixth grade. He had struggled to enjoy the bad soloists, unsynchronized steppers, and loud, bad rock bands. The show did not get any kind of special until one of the show's performers, a four-foot pixie with long, black curls, stepped onto the stage, decked out in a lavender gown, white lace gloves, and—just for the occasion—contacts, launching into a spit-fire recitation of "Phenomenal Woman" that blushed the cheeks of every face in that cafeteria. Her delivery was powerful, and it was hard to forget her face afterwards.

During their eighth grade year, they both were placed into a gifted class that was taught by a Mrs. Frizzle wannabe. In this class he learned her name—Kim—and he got to glimpse the real pixie: silent and intelligent, with just a hint of quirki-slash-dorkiness. She had a hidden fierceness that was released almost exclusively under the bright lights of the stage, but in nearly every moment, Justus's eyes saw her as he first did: a complete boss.

On the Atlanta street, he gazed down at her with those eyes and for a moment she mistook him for handsome.

"So you met Dishon at school?" he asked her.

"Yeah," she said. "We had a class together."

"Oh, your semester's over already?"

Darn her and her word choice. "Well, he's not really in school right now. Long story."

"Oh, okay." He didn't press and she appreciated him for it. "Did Gene tell you about how they're thinking of making him first string?"

"No way!" Kim said happily. "He's acting like he's serious about the thing! That's awesome."

"Yeah," Justus said. "He'll go pro for sure."

She remembered the question she had planned to ask earlier. "Why exactly did he get banned from the poker thing?"

Justus made a face that she couldn't quite interpret. "He got in a fight with one of the players last time. The guy cracked a 'your momma' joke and Gene just went ballistic."

Kim inhaled sharply. Gene's mother died of cancer when they were freshmen. Benny Commons had ignorantly cracked a similar joke once when they were sophomores and his entire body was one big wound for the next week. "Oh, man. Did they—"

"Get to him in time? Not quite. I think Gene dislocated the dude's shoulder."

"Oh man," Kim said again. "I'd hate to be on his bad side."

"You know he's roommates with Shannon Crescitelli?" Justus asked. "Doesn't that sound like a match made in hell?" he cracked.

Kim laughed. "I'm surprised that's worked out this far."

Justus nodded, looking at the shops as they passed by. "I talk to Shannon occasionally. Seems like those two are growing really close."

"Good for them. I'd like to be a fly on that wall," Kim giggled, before wearily waiting for Justus to add some innuendo like, "I bet you would," but she had momentarily forgotten which ex-classmate she was dealing with.

"I missed you, Kim," he said, hugging her as they walked. It was quite awkward, and that made it all the more endearing. "How's the crew? Maya and Coda? Coda calls me like all the time, but I'm always studying for something. I need to call him back one of these days…"

"You and I both, love," she said. "I catch up with Maya sometimes. She pledged some fraternity and got in."

"A fraternity?" he asked. "Is that even allowed?"

"When you go to an all girl's school it is," she smiled.

"Jacuzzi," he said. He inspected his watch.

"How much time do you have?" Kim asked. "I've still got twenty minutes before I have to meet up with Dishon."

"I have all the time in the world," he replied. "Why? Wasabi?"

She pointed to one of the shops they were near.

"Madame Endora," he read in his best ghoulish voice. He looked at her, question marks in his stained-glass eyes. "She's like a fortune-teller, right? Fortune-tellers are maizey."

"Let's see how bad she is," Kim said impishly. "I've always wanted to check one out. Life is a banquet, yeah?"

"You're crazy," he said, uncomfortable with the idea.

"I've seen her commercials," Kim said. "She's supposed to have the 'second sight' and all I have is Miss Cleo flashbacks."

"You want to?" he asked her.

"Let's do it," she said, almost delirious with delight.

He shrugged in noncommittal agreement. Within a few short moments (he paid for both of them though she asked him not to, giving the money to some bored looking lady named Lorena) they were inside. It was just as she had imagined, with Persian fabrics draped over the comfy seats and shimmering beads hanging from the ceiling. They were the only two in the tiny room.

"I guess business is slow," Justus quipped.

"Probably because of the prices," Kim muttered. The charges were ridiculous. "Where's the crystal ball? With the dough we spent, I think we deserve a crystal ball."

They sat in silence for a while until Kim delivered a random, "Sam Wheat?" and dissolved into giggles.

"Endoraaa," Justus said, letting the word fill the air.

A thoughtful look crossed Kim's face.

"Hmm, Endora. Like 'Bewitched'?" she asked.

Justus giggled. "Yeah. Like 'Bewitched.' Sure."

"'Sam,'" Kim said in her best Darren voice, "'don't expect your mother to be gracious. She doesn't do imitations.'"

"You can quote 'Bewitched'?" Justus asked.

"Today I can," Kim said. "Just popped in my head. 'I Dream of Jeannie' is far easier. 'Yes, Master.'"

Justus cracked up. It was nervous laughter, she knew. Her stomach was as unsettled as his mood.

"You know," she sighed, "I think Madame Endora stole some décor tips from inside of Jeannie's lamp."

"See, you're thinking old Nick at Nite shows," Justus said softly. "And I'm thinking more Witch of Endor."

"Why have you come to see me?"

The teens both jumped.

A woman stood where Kim had assumed a wall was, but now she saw was a doorway. Her hair was blond—that was the first surprise. That she was wearing Nikes and jeans was the second, but she was draped in enough fabrics to almost blend in with the surrounding room. Enough jewels—fake or not, Kim couldn't tell—draped from her ears and iced her fingers that it was borderline obscene. Aside from that, she appeared normal. Around fifty, Kim thought, but white people always seemed to age faster than their years.

"That was a question, not the Emergency Broadcast System," she spoke again. She pointed to Justus. "You."

"Uh, I guess a palm reading," he stammered. The psychic's implication of Justus wasn't fair, Kim thought. This had been her idea.

"Both of us, actually," she spoke. "Just palm readings. Or whatever you usually do."

Madame Endora stared at Kim for a moment without speaking, no expression decipherable. She turned back to Justus.

"Read your own palm, cross-eyed dreamer. You close your eyes and see more than you do with them open. Sleep and read the cracks in your feet and the wrinkles in your knee. I won't read your palm. I have nothing to tell you."

"Okay," he said standing, looking at Kim as if to say, *Let's get OUTTA HERE*.

"And you, Starchild," the psychic said to Kim, her voice eerily toneless, "never set foot in here again. I see your stardusted eyes and I hear your earth-anchored thoughts. You bring trouble and warfare to me, to my very door and I'll have none of it. Go where you belong and leave me in mine."

She turned and waved a dismissive hand as she withdrew back through the fabrics. "Lorena will give you a full refund."

Back on the street, as Justus was stuffing folded twenties into the pocket of his khakis, Kim tried to still her reeling consciousness.

"That was, uh, not fun," the berry-blond commented.

"No," Kim said, shaking her head. "The exact opposite of that."

"I think she destroyed my poker face," he remarked as they headed back to the tent, and, even if he was being facetious, Kim found no laughter.

"Go where you belong," the psychic had said. What had she meant by that? And how did she know about Kim's starry eyes?

"I feel like I need to get baptized again," Justus said, and again there was a possible joke in there. Clowning or not, Kim wholeheartedly agreed.

• • • • •

"*Beautiful* church," the doctor said hammily, leading her team down the aisle inside of the Chapel. "It's like… the *Mr. Clean* of churches. I hope I didn't tell my age with that. Haven't seen one of his commercials in *ages* if that counts for anything."

She turned into a pew, gesturing to the architecture around her.

"Seriously, this is just *gorgeous*. I should have my next wedding here."

Three of them sat there. Damn government, they said it would just be the boy waiting for her and her crew. "We haven't met," she said archly.

The chaplain stood. "Commander Scott Gregory. Midshipman Gutierrez requested my presence and his request was approved by the Vice Admiral."

The doctor nodded coldly. The other uninvited guest just sat there, staring at her with placid eyes.

"Patricia Preacher. Pat. Doctor." She scrunched her face and waved a hand as if dissipating a stench from the air. "Whatever."

She handed the encrusted hat to the chaplain. "The Atlantis Diamond Cap. Are you familiar with it, Commander Gregory?"

"Only slightly, I'm afraid," he answered, frowning.

"I wish our little cadet here could say the same," Patricia said.

"That investigation is over," Gregory said, tightly. "Midshipman Gutierrez has been cleared of all charges."

"Yes, yes, indeed," she said. "And it was so *quick*, wasn't it?" She observed the boy, his anger simmering beneath the surface.

"You graduated from Wilbanks Academy, didn't you, Enrique?"

His expression changed ever so slightly.

"Yes, ma'am."

"Hmm, either you're a southern gentleman or this Navy thing is working out for you." She reached for the cap and Commander Gregory returned it silently. "My daughter attends Wilbanks. She'll be a senior next year. Time does fly. And so do you, I hear."

Another shift in expression. "Excuse me?"

"I didn't want to talk about this in front of just anybody, but you've left me no choice, you see."

"What is this about?" the chaplain asked.

"Hold thy peace, Reverend!" Patricia exclaimed. This was fun. "As you see," she gestured to her fellow doctors, "my guests have managed to do so."

"You asked me a question," Commander Gregory began.

"Indeed. Indeed I did and you gave me an answer. Utter boredom ensued. My interests now lie completely with Enrique. If he's comfortable with lying, that is." She looked at the boy again. "Have you heard the history of the Atlantis Diamond Cap? I'm sure you know *something*, I hear it's part of cadet hazing these days."

"There is no hazing—"" the commander began, and Patricia cut him off with a steely delivery of "You're really starting to annoy me. From a Preacher to a chaplain." Back to the boy. "Humor me, cadet."

"The cap's supposed to be from some military expedition during World War I," he spoke disinterestedly, "when a ship was lost for three and half months in the Bermuda Triangle. Mermaids gave them that hat, decorated with the 'red diamonds of Atlantis.' Everyone knows some lame American hat designer made that story up. The history books say nothing about that specific ship, even." His voice was dripping with disdain. More cad than cadet. "And I would know; I had a project on World War I naval watercraft."

"It's a true story, Enrique," she said softly. "I've examined this cap myself."

"What?" the boy asked, committing her to the asylum with his current expression.

"That fabric is full of DNA. Have you ever seen mermaid DNA, Enrique?"

"What is this?" the chaplain asked, growing just as perplexed as she'd expected.

"I study mermaids," Patricia continued. "I study fairies. I study Tinker Bell for Christ's sake."

"This is the House of the Lord," Chaplain Gregory spoke up, as the silent guest glared at her.

"Tell Him to send me His decorator, because, again, this place is *fabulous*." She leaned in towards the boy. "What I mean is, I'm a Wendy. I'm perfectly normal, which unfortunately means there are virtually no perfections in me. I can only get so far. You're damn Peter Pan. You're a *convert*. You've adapted somehow. And that girl who was on the roof with you doing your Think-Happy-Thoughts ballet, she's one of the Lost Boys. I know you're part of a group, don't bother denying it. You all should come to me. Come to Wendy's place."

"I don't like fast food," the boy said, glowering.

She steadfastly continued. "It'll be painless. No *E.T.* type trauma. Just simple things like occasional blood tests and tissue samples. Nobody's gonna be cutting you open."

One of the doctors with her coughed. Probably that Lemming, but she ignored the impulse to cut her eyes in their direction.

"So you're telling me that I'm a mermaid, Dr. Preacher?" Rico asked, thoughtfulness in his eyes attempting to disguise itself as laughter. "Or that I'll never grow old?"

"How'd you get up onto that roof, boy?" she asked quietly.

"I climbed," he replied, apparently forgetting to add a "Duh" at the end of his sentence.

She soldiered on.

"Why are there burn marks on that copper roof? How did *this cap* get out of—Hubbard Hall, is it? How did it get out of Hubbard Hall with no signs of tampering on that booby-trapped-to-hell display case and no video of anyone going near it and end up on the three-story-high roof of a military dormitory with a twig of a teenager out past his curfew?"

"Did you read the report?" he asked.

"I did and it's all bull."

"No, bull is what you're spitting to me right now."

So he hadn't bought the mermaid schtick. Unfortunate.

"Do you know how far my jurisdiction reaches?" she asked. "I sign a few papers and I could have you out of here tonight. Back home in Brunswick, with your parents—because your Lord probably knows that *someone* needs to be there pulling them back together—aiding research that could change the course of this country."

"I'm serving the country just fine right here," he said plainly. "Plus there's this whole spoken bit about me being Peter Pan that still isn't sitting nicely on my ears."

"Damn the metaphors. Erase the metaphors. In black and white, you're not normal, Enrique. You're *gifted*."

For a moment, his Jericho wall crumbled, but it was back up in a hurry.

"Show him the chart," she said, and Lemming handed him a clipboard.

"Your friend Lakota Crenshaw decided to give blood for a lovely fifty dollar donation. He's on rough times, I'm sure you know. I hope he spent it on a season's supply of Ramen."

"This is his blood?" Enrique asked softly.

"Yes. See the difference in his hemoglobin levels compared to a normal subject's?"

Enrique looked up and Patricia saw something she hadn't been expecting.

Fury.

"Are you stalking us?" The boy stood, scrawny chest threatening to burst, and the chaplain quickly followed, clamping his bewildered mouth shut long enough to formulate words.

"Calm down, Midshipman Gutierrez."

The boy was spitting out cuss word combinations faster than most teens could formulate them in their heads. As she made her way around the vulgarities to make out the threats and the promises, she realized that what she had hoped for would not come true, at least not at this meeting.

"Anger in the temple..." Wearily she signaled her team and they moved as quickly as the boys words. "I needed your consent," she sighed. "You have no idea the pain you could have saved me."

The injections were completed within seconds and the military men dropped back on the pews with looks of surprise on their face.

"Hate to go all *Men in Black* on you," she said, gathering the spilled papers from the clipboard, "but you won't remember the reality of this in about two minutes. I should be so lucky."

If she had gotten the boy, her chances of getting that girl would have doubled. How did the girl get inside of that protected case and get that hat?

"Would you like us to extract some of his blood, Dr. Pat?" Lemming was asking.

Patricia shook her head in declination. "We don't have enough time or equipment to draw a useful amount."

She lifted her painstakingly-duplicated version of the cap, trying not to think of all the funds wasted on the replica, on flying her SWAT team so far north, and on the pretentious simulated investigation. "If you had just given me your consent," she sighed.

She moved her team towards the aisle. They'd leave the base tonight, it was best. Time to draw up a brand new blueprint. Maybe one that wasn't entirely legal. Consent was quickly becoming overrated.

"Until we meet once more," she said, waving. "Because we will."

She spoke again once they were outside. "Get the name of the silent one from the Vice Admiral, Lemming." She pulled up short. "Wait, did he get injected?"

"They both did, Dr. Pat."

All the doctors were looking at her with great interest.

"What do you mean 'both,' Lemming? What happened to the third man in there?"

"What third man, Dr. Pat?"

"The *other guy* flanking that Mexican kid. With all those pink ribbons."

"There were only two guys in there, Dr. Pat."

She glared at him. "You're telling me that I made up a guy?"

"You can ask each of us, Dr. Pat, but I promise you there were only two guys. The chaplain and that cadet."

The other doctors were nodding.

"Oh, I know who you saw," one of the older doctors spoke up after a moment of confusion. "He was another officer, right?"

"Exactly!"

"Yeah… That was Captain Hook."

And her team was in stitches. Patricia found no humor in it.

15.

Developmentally

Winter swooped into Brunswick as intense as a newborn's stare. The wind felt like invisible ice, while clothes, no matter how layered, were only a temporary postponement to the inevitable chill.

After the first semester of college, Karol Roach had come back a lesbian with electric blue hair. BJ told Rico about it, knowing this because Karol was her next-door-neighbor. No one was really surprised. It was always the quiet ones and the sweet ones that went off the deep end. Like Kim Hamilton, BJ said. Rumors of her drug use and trouble-finding boyfriend had gotten around quicker than the seasonal flu.

Kim didn't think she was off the deep end. She was just swimming near the waterfall. She liked the adventure. She rebelled against stability.

Coda's dad had warned him about situations like Kim's. Kids that go off and try to live like adults because they think that's what they're supposed to do. They are the ones who come back alcoholics or addicted to drugs or worse. It made Coda just a little happier that he had stayed in town. Just a little.

Coda had slugged through the first semester of college. He didn't really care for it, and felt that it was a waste of his time. He figured that he'd move back to California in January. Be stupid and chase his dreams. Things like that.

Renata Gutierrez was maturing into a lovely young lady, though she was still just as twiggy as her brother. She was in the Holiday Heart pageant at GWC High and came in third place. She wrote about it to Rico in a three-page letter in which she seemed determined to refer everything to Rico with the obvious exception of life at home. After all, with him coming home for winter break, he'd be unfortunate enough to experience it all firsthand.

Ezekiel had been flying all over Atlanta in the middle of the night, reading minds and doing little things. He had gotten a mention in The Atlanta Journal, once, when three homeless orphans showed up on the steps of the best orphanage in town with an anonymous and quite significant monetary donation. They said that the Ninja helped them. Ezekiel laughed when he read it.

Wayne Emerson had lost one of his babies before any of them were born. Rumors said that the mother planned it.

• • • • •

It was a gray day in Maryland. The snow had combined with the clouds to block out the sun and make the day dreary beyond saving. The courtyard below wasn't viewable through the weather, so Rico had shut his blinds, content to allow his dormitory to be the extent of his world. His hands were sore and his arms were sore and his legs were sore and his butt was sore and his abs were sore. Too much exercise. Too many things he felt like he had forgotten. He remembered the undercover investigation, and there hadn't been any reprisals, but there was more…lingering on the edge. He stretched out across his bunk, trying to shut more of the curtains across his mind. All of it was just too much.

"Do you miss me?" BJ brightly asked him.

"Yeah, baby." Rico smiled into the receiver, as if BJ could see him. "I miss you all the time. I miss running my fingers through your hair and across your skin—"

"Yeah," she cut him off. "I miss you, too," was her easy response to his unasked and not yet thought about question. "Shannon called me yesterday."

The changes in conversation always seemed much more random than they actually were, although BJ had gotten Rico used to them.

"Shannon?" Rico smiled. He hadn't talked to his soccer buddy in a while. As their senior year of high school drew to a close, they'd have these unofficial breakfast hangouts, all of the team captains. Rico would be there, as well as Shannon, Gene and Benny, who was the baseball captain. The captain of the basketball team was a junior, so he was essentially not expected to participate. It was an elite Class of Conviction thing, just like how the seniors on the student council and Student Advisory Board were allowed to skip to the front of the line in the cafeteria the last two weeks of school (but by then, no self-respecting senior was still on campus by lunchtime). They had all bonded very tightly, but over the course of this first year of college, due to distance, maturity variations and this minor supernatural issue Rico was dealing with, he had grown apart from all of them.

"Yeah," BJ said in her slightly scratchy voice. "One of his sisters—Skylar, I think—is a freshman at KWA, but they're not the Class of Conviction anymore."

"What do you mean? There's been a CoC since the eighties!"

He heard the shrug in her voice. "Get this, though: due to Saint Kim's speech, the freshman class was dubbed the Class of Accomplishment."

"That's cool!" Rico wondered if Kim had heard about her imprint.

BJ laughed. "Shannon called the designation wishful thinking. I think they've already had fifteen dropouts this year."

"The Italian Stallion would," he mused. "How's *he* doing? He's hanging in there?"

"By a thread," BJ said, laughing. "He's less annoying these days."

"He must be getting sexual satisfaction."

"You would go there," she laughed. "We're all hanging in there, tho. First semester down."

"Yeah," Rico murmured. "We're all changing, too."

"What do you mean?"

Rico heard the slight concern in her voice. "You know: things." He was sure he wasn't yet making sense. "Not like we're growing apart or anything, but we're all growing."

"Growing together," BJ pursued.

Rico guessed she was right, but all he could say was, "Growing."

She had gone to college and become such a chick. She hadn't been so girly in high school, caring what he thought so noticeably. She also hadn't worn so many skirts. Every time they video-chatted, she was in a skirt, or a dress. He approved, but he didn't get it. He was still satisfied with his polo shirts and hoodies.

"Let's go to Poland."

"What?" Rico asked, wondering where the conversation was turning to now.

"Like for spring break one of these years. I mean, who goes? If we go at least we'll be different than everybody." BJ was laughing, but Rico knew that she was serious. He could hear the excitement in her voice that came at the most outlandish suggestions and inquiries. She was neck and neck with Justus as far as weirdness was concerned.

All he committed was, "We'll look into it," tracing the groove on his nose with a thin, lazy finger.

When he was four, the one rule in his house that he was always tempted to break was the "no jumping on the beds" rule. He had heard his schoolyard friends chanting the "four little monkeys jumping on a bed, one fell off and broke his head," but since he had never heard of four-year-old-boys from California breaking their heads, he decided that there was no harm in it.

One day when his parents had stepped outside to watch the starry Bakersfield night sky, he went for it. He jumped and jumped and thought he was going to reach God. Then, he came down on his left foot at the wrong angle and plummeted downwards, his face careening dangerously towards the sharp wooden edge at the foot of his bed. Right when the wood met his nose, two hands grabbed his right arm and two hands grabbed his left arm, plucking him away from certain harm faster than the opposing gravity could pull him. He remembered being sat down on the bed and feeling foreign, yet friendly fingers running through his mullet. By the time his young mind realized he was still alive and thought to look for his mysterious saviors, he found himself alone in his room.

Little Rico rediscovered fear in that moment of sudden isolation, and he wailed at the top of his lungs. His parents rushed at the alarm, becoming so frightened that they didn't even admonish him for jumping on the bed. They knew—like he did—he'd never do it again.

He was grateful that God didn't let him break his head then, and he still had the reminder. Yet, God had saved him from destruction numerous times now, and it had to be for a reason.

He didn't think he was fulfilling his purpose living the way that he was.

Later, once he had gotten off the line with BJ, he stared at his webcam, eventually moving his gaze to the Rico in the mirror.

"Growing," he said to his reflection. And in the mirror, as Rico had recently become accustomed to seeing, an angel sat on his bed, placidly watching him with gold eyes.

$$\bullet \quad \bullet \quad \bullet \quad \bullet \quad \bullet$$

"Have a great winter break, Ezekiel!" a classmate called, and Ezekiel acknowledged them with a wave.

"Ezekiel!"

He turned to see Jordan Vang running down a hill towards him, breathless.

"Hey, Jordan!" He hoped she wasn't standing there when his parents arrived. They'd assume she was his girlfriend. "Don't you have a plane to catch?"

"This will be real quick," she said, hitching her traveling bag back up over her shoulder. "Holiday spirits and such." She handed him a thumb drive.

He observed it dubiously once he had taken it. "Does this have all of next semester's test questions on it?"

"I had Phil do me a favor."

Now his befuddled gaze was on her. "Are you actually talking about test questions? Because I was kidding."

"He knows some of the campus security folks."

Ezekiel rocked back on his heels, still not understanding. "Ok. So what's this in my hands?"

"The only remaining copy," Jordan said, not bothering to elaborate. She knew he was smart enough to make the proper realizations.

The wind blew through his hair, but apart from that he was still. Jordan smiled.

The last sentence she said before she walked away was, "Kick her ass next time."

· · · · ·

"What are we listening to?" Coda asked Kim, sitting in the backseat of Maya's giant green piece of machinery that some called an SUV, and others called a tank. Between Coda's two-wheeler that some called a bicycle, the ginormous red truck tiny Kim drove around whenever she was in town, and Maya's truck/tank/van hybrid ("It's a Toyota Sequoia," she had groaned, annoyed when he had exhaled, "What is it?"), they were quite the team in transportation.

It was a random December night and they were out "re-bonding" as Maya called it.

Kim laughed. "Listen to it! This song is *evv!*" She had beautiful lustrous braids framing her face and was wearing a red and black sweater over black, red and white pants, with her white sneakers and a white belt, and jeweled white earrings hung from her ears.

The last few months seemed to have been good to her, developmentally. Her arms, currently hidden beneath her heavy sleeves, rippled when she moved, even when she breathed. Her legs were much shapelier than they had ever been. Coda had joked to her upon seeing her that he'd call her Kim-burly in honor of her new physique.

Coda turned to Maya, who was driving. "What are we listening to, Maya-ya?" he asked her.

"Hmm-mmm," Maya mumbled, noncommittally. The Bio major was braided up also; auburn hair that wasn't hers tumbled down her back and brushed her waist. A beautiful lavender sweater, grey slacks, and lavender heels were her choice of wear for the evening, even if they hadn't yet gone anywhere. They probably wouldn't end up anywhere, but they were attempting to go eat out at whatever restaurants might still be open.

The night was not exactly young, and the three friends were subconsciously asserting their adulthood by staying out late, though both Kim and Maya knew that it couldn't be too late. Coda's father didn't quite care, but Mrs. Delia Hamilton and both of the Sierra parents weren't having it. The girls were milking it though. It was the first time they were able to hang out since Maya and Gene stopped seeing each other.

In the car, the song got worse. With each ensuing line of the song's chorus from "I'll call you out" to the triumphant, if misguided phraseology of "I'm my hero," the song's singer would rhythmically belt out an accompanying vulgarity that was once used as an alias for canines of the puppy-birthing persuasion. Kim sang and bounced along with disconcerting zest.

Coda didn't know what to say.

"Ye-as!" Kim purred, as the song fell to higher lows.

"The music is nice," Maya allowed.

"Yeah, if you go for crap," Coda muttered, tugging on the Annapolis Midshipmen football jacket in his lap that Rico had given him. Maya silently glanced over at him, searching his carriage.

As his shoulders heaved a sigh, his long-sleeved tee, a souvenir from the cross-country trip to Orlando, undulated with the passing air. His large shoulders still gave him the allusion of being bigger than his twenty-five inch waist. Coda had gotten wirier over the past months. Some would assume it was the bike riding or the karate class or the Body Conditioning class, but the reason that Coda couldn't keep weight on was because of the amazing things he found himself doing, like dodging attacking dogs with the ease of a seasoned escape artist and the artistry of Evel Knievel. That and the fact that he was too poor to eat more than two meals a day.

His hair was braided back into simple cornrows so old they looked like dreadlocks and his face was covered with a rough beard, betraying the lavish life he had lived his senior year. He was dealing with everyday issues that his friends weren't stressing over, like jobs and bills. Their scholarships paid for their dorms. He had to give his father one hundred fifty dollars a month, as well as pay other bills around the house, plus buy groceries. He was seventeen now, and Rev. Crenshaw was not playing.

"'I'm my hero,' Coda!" Kim managed to quote and rave at the same time. "Surely you get the significance of it!"

"That's why the world is getting thrown into the lake of fire, right there," Coda asserted.

Kim leaned back in her seat, giggling. He could be so overly dramatic at times, especially when he didn't need any help being undermined.

Kim remembered how he had sounded during their sparse phone conversations. All lonely and whatnot. She had empathized at first, and then the empathy turned to fading sympathy as she made her friends and found her niche, like he should have. She wondered why Coda allowed himself to be so tormented.

Maya reached an intersection and stepped on the breaks.

"I was thinking of becoming a vegetarian," Kim said randomly, probably to fill the void of silence.

"I don't encourage that, Burly," Coda said. "I mean, if we aren't supposed to eat animals, why are they made with meat?"

Maya and Kim shared a look. They weren't going to touch it.

"I was kidding," he spoke flatly.

Maya chuckled and stared out the window at some garish Christmas lights.

"Whoa," she said, staring at a girl walking around the yard who was trying too many of the current looks at one time. The multicolored flashing from the bulbs she was stringing through the fence did her no favors.

"She looks like my girlfriend," he observed, attempting to look away.

"She looks like whom, Coda-da?" Kim asked carefully, while Maya coughed.

"My girlfriend, Dyna-na," he replied, apathetically.

"Who?" Maya and Kim questioned in unison. Maya chuckled again.

"My girlfriend," he said again.

"Coda: your girlfriend?" Kim repeated incredulously.

"Is this one of those games where you see how many times you can get me to say something over?" he accusingly inquired.

"When did you get a girlfriend?" Maya asked, smiling.

"Tasha? We became official last week."

"Tasha?" Kim asked. "Is this that girl who goes to your church who you were telling me about? The one that everyone says you'll marry?"

"Yeah," Coda replied with a grin.

"Spicy," Kim commented, managing to plaster a real smile onto her face.

"How old is she?" Maya asked.

"Fifteen," he replied, ducking. Maya reached back and hit him anyway.

"Ooo, Lakota. Robbing the cradle," Kim mewed. "That's nasty."

"You're going for a record, apparently," Maya declared, in a statement that required an answer.

"It's not like I'm going to *do* anything, Maya," Coda avowed, deciding not to remind them that the age difference wasn't that drastic. He looked at Maya's face and could see her silently questioning, *Are you?* "I'm a righteous virgin, one-hundred percent!" he asserted. "A prude! You guys know that better than anybody."

"That's true," Kim said, mostly because she was just having trouble imagining Coda with a love life, no matter how controversial. She looked across at Maya. "La Sierra, Do you remember the night that we watched *Heaven Sent* in Mrs. Donahue's room?"

"Segue much?" Coda muttered.

"Yeah," Maya laughed. "*Heaven Sent…* Is that the movie where the lady's bumper sticker reads 'If you love Jesus, tithe. Any fool can honk?'"

Kim began to laugh. "Yeah."

Coda chuckled. "And the dude sat next to that fire-and-brimstone bus rider? 'This is my son's first Halloween.' 'Oh, we don't do Halloween…'"

"'That is not of God,'" they all said in unison, and fell out laughing.

"Funny how the most extreme character in the movie was the one with the most subtle message," Coda mused.

"That was a funny movie," Kim squeaked.

"'Let's give the Lord a handclap of praise!'" Maya said in a nasally voice.

"Kim kept laughing each time that woman opened her mouth," Coda remembered.

A bittersweet laugh exploded from Maya. "I was sitting next to Gene, and he found a million and one ways to describe that woman as the most idiotic person in the world."

Kim raised her hand in imitation of the bus woman. "'We've got to pray that God will remove this traffic. Part the highway like He parted the Red Sea.'" She fell over on the window in a fit of giggles.

"And then when the traffic didn't move: 'He's just using a few minutes to make it look natural,'" Coda added. Maya was gripping the steering wheel, shoulders shaking, caught in hushed hilarity.

"It was only so crazy," Kim said delicately with a smile.

Maya let loose a thunderous snort, causing Kim and Coda to lose it along with her. After a few moments of unbridled mirth—laughter leading to more laughter—Kim shifted her weight and said, "You know what's funny, you guys? Well, not funny ha-ha, but funny…"

Kim's pause was ponderous.

"You don't even know what word to use, do you?" Maya accused, riddled with laughter. "'Not funny ha-ha,'" she mocked, "but funny…hmm, funny-what?'"

"I'm at a loss," Kim professed in nasal rigidity, and Maya snorted again. "Well," Kim started again, playing the upper register of her voice like a violin, "what's strange is that whole thing with the lightning. You know how they explained lightning as falling angels, come to torment humanity? And then that night of graduation…" As she grasped at straws, she noticed Coda shifting in his seat. She was making him nervous. "I missed what happened that night."

"I didn't," Maya hooted. "Coca-Coda here passed some gas and we made him get out of my car!" Back then, Maya had driven a very nice red sports car that had since met its maker when parked under a remarkably top-heavy tree on the side of the road. Maya had a hard time explaining that away to her parents, who had assumed that she and Gene were indeed going to meet Kim and Coda at the movies, not make a prolonged pit stop at the side of the road for any apparent purpose other than one that nobody wanted to suggest. For her part, it wasn't the way Maya knew it sounded…but it sure sounded the way Maya knew it did.

"You two were belching," Coda defended himself. "I just added to the gas."

"You ass," Maya snickered. "We weren't giving it from the other end!"

Coda glowered at her and she glowered back.

"That night?" Kim questioned, glancing at Maya. "You're talking about the night of the movie, but I'm talking about graduation. How I didn't show up to the party at Shawn Montgomery's house." Coda finally saw what she was getting at.

"Kim, I love you," Maya said. "And some of us in this car are more appreciative that you survived that accident than others." Coda's glower turned up impossibly higher. "I just don't get why you feel the need to wrench further sympathy out of us by bringing it up in such needless ways!"

"I've been feeling strange," Kim said pathetically. "I bench-pressed—"

"Kim, you do not bench-press," snorted Maya.

"I do," Kim declared.

"Whatever," Maya laughed. She turned to Coda. "Why does she always go there?"

Kim sat back in her seat, perturbed. Coda decided to begin the healing process.

"Ladies," he began, "may I point your attention to something?"

"What?" Kim and Maya asked together.

"We've been sitting at this corner for about three, maybe five minutes."

Kim and Maya glanced around to inspect the evidence.

"Oh," Maya hollered, smacking her forehead, stepping on the gas and cracking up at the same time.

"What?" Kim demanded.

Maya pointed to the stop sign they were passing. "I thought this was a stoplight."

"Hmm." Kim's face wrinkled up, trying to contain her amusement. "Crazy," she said in her strange way. "I thought so, too," she admitted.

"I was wondering why those guys over there were staring so hard," Maya chuckled, and the friends continued on, laughing the rest of their time together.

· · · · ·

Kim cried all night. She felt such responsibility. Coda was looking up to her like a school-grade kid did their favorite teacher. She didn't know when this change had occurred, but it frustrated her a great deal, because he seemed to be expecting perfection and she no longer felt capable of it. And he was not the only one. After Ezekiel got attacked on campus at Georgia Tech, the first person he called was Kim, to explain to her the goings-down and requesting her opinion and input. It was Ezekiel who seemed to know what "Steve" referenced, but it was Kim who in turn had to figure out what would be the best course of action.

Action. Action was everywhere, it seemed. She had beaten up a mugger the other day, and apprehended a would-be rapist a few weeks ago. It all just happened so naturally, but the gravity of the reality stayed with her. She wasn't a vigilante. She barely knew what that word meant; she was reading 'q' words. 'V' words were a long way off. She was perhaps a hero, but what kind? Why did God see fit to put her in such situations?

Was it that God wanted them to be vigilantes? Were they supposed to wear capes and thigh high boots? Was this a punishment? Were they supposed to bear the burdens of those less fortunate? Perhaps that was it. Who was doing for the minority if the majority of the earth's population was consumed with doing for themselves? It starts off righteous enough. Each person wants to get to a place where they can support themselves. Then, once they can support themselves, they want to get more out of life through materialistic enjoyments. Then, once they have purchased enough enjoyments, they want to be left alone to enjoy. Meanwhile, the next person is struggling with their bootstraps, attempting to get to a place where they can support themselves. Kim wondered if she was thinking like a Communist.

God loved her, she knew that. There was no question there, aside from why.

Yeah, why exactly did God love her so much? Why did He pick her, and what about the others? She wondered.

She continued to cry, tired of it, but not being able to bring it to an end. She prayed, hoping it would stop her tears.

One day in her dorm room she had just caught the Holy Ghost and sat there crying and saying "Thank You, Jesus" for no apparent reason. Maybe because He spared her life after that accident. Maybe because of Ezekiel's lightning, or Coda's suicide attempt, or Rico's firearm mishap. Maybe it was just because He saw fit to wake her up, because she hated the way she was living, deep down inside, though she liked to pretend that she didn't. God knew, however, and it was a miracle that He didn't strike her down and let her actually die this time.

She had become a stranger in her own mirror in too many ways. If she barely recognized the Kimberly Hamilton that had graduated earlier that very year, who was it that God saw when He looked at her? She wondered what Ezekiel...and the rest, Coda, Maya, Rico, Gene... Who did they see when they looked at her? With Maya rejecting everything Kim knew to be true about how she had been changing since the accident, Kim didn't have a grounding source. She needed a Ma and Pa Kent...or an Alfred.

When Rico got attacked by Solitaire, unconsciously following suit with Ezekiel and Coda, he called Kim. It was odd; she had no real connection to Rico and Ezekiel outside of this weird "choice nights" thing. In high school she never went over their houses, except the graduation party Rico threw at his house. They never came over hers. Before the weirdness, Coda had been her greatest link with those two boys, and now it seemed like God had put her together with Rico and Ezekiel for His own mysterious purposes.

She didn't know when she drifted to sleep. Her dreams were bombastic that night, especially the one in which she stood on the Brunswick marsh, watching a giant tidal wave make it's lethargic way towards shore. In the towering waters, she made out the shadow of a giant, almost pre-historically huge whale, the vacancy-having fish to her drifting Jonah, waiting serenely as she stood rooted in terror.

When she woke, she was still praying and her pillow was wet with fresh tears.

The first thing her eyes settled upon was one of the many inspirational sayings that she had pinned above her vanity during her sophomore year.

"Rule worthy of might.—Socrates."

Underneath it was one far more familiar to her.

"Don't try, just do it.—Mom."

She stared at that simple signs for a good few minutes. To whom much is given…

There was a reason the Lord had gifted her with so much strength. He expected her to do some heavy lifting.

"Okay, God," she whispered. "Okay."

16.
Providential

"I'm so excited to see you, Enrique!" Renata couldn't stop gushing, having months of verbal catching up to do with her brother, which mainly consisted of her telling stories and him listening.

They were driving down a busy street in Brunswick, on their way to the mall. They—Rico, Renata, Mrs. Gutierrez, who was driving, and Renata's friend Cassie—were planning on doing some shopping at the mall, but Rico had plans to first chill with Coda and whoever else had been rounded up by his bubbly buddy.

Once Renata turned her attentions to meek Cassie, Rico listened to the radio and tried to lose himself in the song played by the band. Renata had convinced Mrs. Gutierrez to put in some CD by a band that sang rock in Spanish and English. Renata really didn't like rock, but she said the lyrics were amazing. And they were. Rico lost himself in the libretto.

He glanced out of the window at Brunswick. It was almost bearable to be back in the little place he used to hate. The beautification of the area that had taken place during the summer had quickly become a thing of the past, for the nature that had been fixed up so nicely when the President was in town was back to the overgrown weed-and-oak-tree combination it had always been before. The cracking sidewalks, the moss, Coda, and the Christmas lights that just made it all look impossibly worse in the daytime.

Coda?

Rico could have sworn he just saw Coda scrapping in the air with that Boy that was at Chapel Towers with Solitaire. Rico had caught a brief glimpse of the two of them before they disappeared beneath the line of trees on the opposite side of the road.

What was going on?

"Ma, I have to use the bathroom," he shouted over Renata and the radio.

"Okay, well, we have a store a little up ahead—"

"NOW!"

"Okay, mijo, we'll just pull over right here and you can run—"

Rico was out of the car in a flash, grabbing his sunglasses and the sweatshirt he had removed because of the heat in the car. He looked both ways and was off, jetting into the traffic.

"Enrique, couldn't you have used it before we left the house?" Renata yelled after Rico, who was quite a sight, half-waddling, half-leaping through the traffic to the other side of the busy road into the trees. She added, "Why is he going that way?"

"Renata, I do not know about your brother, sometimes," Mrs. Gutierrez was saying with concern. "I don't think he knows how unhealthy it is to hold it in so long until you just have to go. That is not a good thing to do."

Rico was hoping that he got there on time.

· · · · ·

"What happened?" Rico yelled to Coda, shooting a flame in the direction of a boy in a tight brown unitard-looking outfit. Rico himself was decked out in his sunglasses and sweatshirt, like times before.

Coda was wearing an extremely colorful winter knit hat (originally intended to counteract the December chill) that he had simply pulled down over his face in a shoddy effort to conceal his identity. Because of the way the hat had been put together, there were enough holes in the cap for him to see as if he wasn't wearing one at all. He was wearing winter pants and a generic black coat from Brunswick's new favorite athletic store, so, aside from the glaringly uncommon hat, he was untraceable.

"Um," Coda responded, pausing enough to focus his energy and thoughts, jump the few yards between the pale boy and himself, punch the boy with an intensity learned through his shotokan class, and hop, skip, and jump back in order to place himself next to his friend and finish, "it's a long story. But he was following me."

They were combating in an area obscure from the travelers on the busy road that was right next to them, amidst tall trees and high weeds that would soon be bought, bulldozed, and transformed into yet another store for Glynn County's growing shopping district. If the city was smart, and it didn't seem to be, even on its best days, they'd have been incorporating the county long ago.

The pallid boy's face showed absolutely no emotion as it repeated Coda's exact movements with a surprising speed, punching Rico in the back of his head before hopping back into place. Coda marveled that the boy was barefoot and the harsh ground didn't seem to phase him at all.

Suddenly the boy's face was flushing. He rubbed his shoulder underneath the brown suspender-like strap, then rapidly paralleled his ripped white arms in a direct imitation of Rico and let a stream of fire jet from his hands in the direction of the gifted two. Coda, vision having long stained red, jumped out of the path of the flames while Rico slammed sideways into the dirt.

Rico whipped his head around and glared at The Boy.

"How did you do that? Only I can do that!" Before Rico had finished speaking, The Boy was upon him, kicking him in the stomach. Then, just as quickly, The Boy was in Coda's face. He moved faster than should ever be allowed.

Coda attempted to punch The Boy, but The Boy flipped safely out of punching range and kicked Coda in the stomach. Coda stooped slightly and The Boy took the opportunity to kick Coda in the head.

Rico had snuck up behind The Boy and connected a flaming fist to The Boy's jaw. The Boy promptly grabbed Rico's hand, flipping him facedown into the dirt.

Coda reached up and grabbed The Boy where Kim had once kicked him, bringing The Boy to his knees. He then slammed his leg into The Boy's chin and their adversary faded into the ground in the same fashion Kim had described. He did it with the adeptness of a cartoon.

"Well, that was easy," Rico marveled.

"Seems that way, doesn't it?" Coda commented, glancing around cautiously. "Kim said it was that easy, didn't she?"

Rico didn't have a chance to respond, finding himself frozen in shock as The Boy materialized in midair behind Coda. Flames covered The Boy's hands as they grabbed Coda around the throat.

"Whoa!" Rico hollered, attempting to kick The Boy, but kicking Coda's knees instead.

"Oh, great aim," Coda muttered as he hit the ground.

"Hey, he's not frying your throat right now, is he?" Rico asked, flying into The Boy. They tumbled into the dirt.

"Oh, yeah," Coda reflected, attempting rub the pain out of his throat and both knees while remembering the previous conversation. "How this all started: Well, you see, I was heading—"

"Not now," Rico wheezed. The Boy was kneeling on his chest, applying pressure to his throat.

"Oh, sorry," Coda said, rushing towards The Boy who in turn back-handed him with a flaming hand.

As Coda stumbled back, reeling and burned, The Boy raced into him for further confrontation, leaving Rico coughing in the dirt.

"Jesus," Coda prayed. He grabbed The Boy's fist before the punch landed, extinguishing the flame and twisting The Boy's arm. Coda hollered, adrenaline flooding the intersection of pain and determination. Rico was on the other side of The Boy and grabbed The Boy's left arm. They had him now.

Coda kneed The Boy in his throat. The Boy started to cough, chest straining greatly against the jumpsuit. Rico stomped on The Boy's foot, as Coda elbowed The Boy's spine with his free arm.

Rico lifted The Boy's head by those slimy dreadlocks and he and Coda jointly punched their antagonist in the nose. The Boy fell back, eyes rolling into his head as he disappeared.

Rico roared, staring at the spot where The Boy had disappeared.

"Dude, you okay?" Coda asked, dismayed by his friend's intensity.

"Skippy," Rico said, touching his neck softly. He turned his intensity onto Coda. "Come on. Ma'll give you a ride."

. . . . .

Ezekiel stood in his front yard, swinging his nunchucks around and minding his own business, when two figures fell out of the sky and crashed into his front yard.

"Whoa!" Ezekiel jumped back from the wreckage they made in his mother's marigolds.

"Nice, Rico," came Coda's overactive vocals as the other groaned. "You know how to fly, but you don't know how to land." The skinny Creole jumped up, pulling his winter knit off his face before brushing a mixture of grass, dirt, and petals off his shirt.

Rico pulled himself up, frowning slightly. "You try landing with two tons of Mr. Yell-and-Holler on your back screaming, 'pull up, pull up, oh, watch out for that-'"

"'-marigold patch.' Which, if I may point out, you didn't." Coda slapped a few bills in Ezekiel's hands, grimacing. His hands were still sore. "Ow, ow, ow." He had a few slight, but telltale burns on his face. "Tell Mrs. Yang whatever you want to, but we're sorry."

The Yangs had first moved from the bright and beautiful Hong Kong streets to America when Ezekiel was six years old. The first "American" thing that his mother set out to do was to plant an American flower garden. The first flowers that she ever bought were marigolds and, though they had moved since then, his mother always planted marigold seeds as a reminder that America was now their permanent home. She wouldn't take it very lightly that the majority of those flowers were crushed, so Ezekiel would have to come up with a good explanation. Rico and Coda were hoping for a lie.

"¿Que pasa, chico?" Rico asked, brushing dirt off his sweats.

Ezekiel stuffed the bills in his pocket. "What are you wearing?" he had to ask, glancing around to see if any of the neighbors in his subdivision were outside or peeping through their windows.

"Our costumes." Coda said it like it was common sense. They were wearing their fighting outfits and looked like a couple of reject bank robbers.

"Right," Ezekiel said, wrinkling his eyebrows. He was wearing a Governor's Honor's shirt, a blue jacket and some faded navy blue slack, and amazingly they made him feel inappropriately dressed. "Why are you guys here? Didn't I just see you?"

The mall affair had been a success. Ezekiel, Coda, Justus, Rico and BJ, Hanley Powell, Peppi Ortiz, Maya, and even Gene Hightower had all been in attendance. Only Kim—who had a "thing" with her mother— and Shannon Crescitelli were unaccounted for. It turned into a big catch-up period for everyone: who's still dating who, who's dating who for the first time, and who hates their roommates and/or their professors.

Coda had spent most of the time raving about Renata Gutierrez, who had been sitting at a table far on the other side of the food court with her mother and Cassie, so as to not interfere with Rico's friend time.

"I love your sister, Rico," Coda had said while shoveling down bourbon chicken and fried rice from Cajun Asian. "I'm sorry for saying it so often, but the good Lord knew what He was doing when He made her. There is something that she has that…"

"Yeah, dude," Rico had replied, not quite getting his friend but mostly wishing he would shut up. "Umm, you have a girlfriend."

Coda had looked at Rico with question marks in his gaze.

"You can't say those things anymore," Rico had elaborated.

After all was said and done, though, Rico, Ezekiel and Coda had agreed to meet up with Kim later on, to discuss the further undertakings that had occurred, then they all went their separate ways.

Ezekiel had journeyed to his home in a pristine neighborhood on The Island, where all the houses were at least two-stories and the back-yards had grass. Justus had called and they had talked for a while before he decided to have some fun with his "hapkido sticks." Unbeknownst to him, Rico had run into Kim while shopping with the lady Gutierrezes and a muy interesante plan was formed.

When Kim encountered Rico, she had been out shopping for some last minute Christmas trinkets with her parents. Passing some inflatable swimming pools, God had brought what had happened to Justus in Shannon's pool seven months ago back into her memory. Upset with herself for having pushed it so far out of her memory, she now figured that whatever occurred back then must have had some relevance to the situation involving Rico, Ezekiel, Coda, and herself. Together, they came to the conclusion that it was the perfect time to do something about it.

So that's why neither Rico nor Coda seemed surprised when Kim's red truck hummed into Ezekiel's driveway.

"Nice, boys," tiny Kim tinkled with an undercurrent of a rumble as she stepped out of the truck. "You kind of flew off the road, you know."

Her clothing was very normal compared to those of her compadres. She was dressed in a long jean skirt with a yellow and purple striped sweater and her white sneakers. She wore two giant hoop earrings, and the one in her left ear had the word "Fallen" scripted across it in blue. Her braids were pulled away from her face, hanging behind her ears. Ezekiel thought she looked nice.

"Sorry," Rico sheepishly grinned.

"I know. It wasn't my fault," Coda rectified. Ezekiel noticed how much more assertive Coda had become since everyone had been away. Coda said he had been hanging out with Terry and Hanley Powell while everyone else did their college do. It was an interesting combination: the dramatics of Coda with the loopy yet wise view of Hanley and the guy's guy antics of the redhead. Ezekiel could only imagine.

"Whatever," Kim said. "Though watching Coda race through trees those few blocks made me think that Robin Hood had returned to Sherwood Forest." She glanced at Ezekiel. "You should have seen him, doing fast-as-lightning gymnastics through the branches after Rico dropped him for a spell."

"Like I'm heavy," Coda grumbled.

"About fifteen pounds heavier than I am, Robin Hood," Rico retorted.

"Really?" Coda grinned. "Wow!" he added, proudly, inspecting his arms to see if he had added muscle, then, since he hadn't, inspecting Rico's to see if he had lost a little.

"It's the hair," Kim whispered.

Rico found humor in this, adding with a laugh, "Or the giant head." Taking a second look he walked right up to Coda, squinting his eyes. "You're still getting taller, aren't you?"

"Wait, you guys flew here?" Ezekiel asked, stupefied.

"How else would we have dropped in so literally?" Coda asked. Ezekiel frowned and shrugged, not wanting to reveal his momentary lack in reasoning.

"Kim didn't know how to get here, so she followed us," Rico replied, as if flight was the least demanding solution to that issue. Ezekiel was unconvinced.

"We wanted to feel like superheroes," Coda explained, jumping higher in the air than Ezekiel knew was humanly possible, snapping a kick with his left leg.

Kim hadn't taken her eyes off Ezekiel holding his nunchucks nonchalantly, as if it was a normal sight to see a man standing in a neighborhood like his, barefoot on the lawn with nunchucks in late December. "What up, boy? We came to party with you."

Rico reached over and lightly touched the nunchucks. "These are cool, 'Zekiel! Where'd you get 'em?"

"I'm a yellow belt in *hapkido* now," he explained, "and yellow belts get nunchucks."

"Can I see these?" Rico asked with a glint in his eyes.

Ezekiel handed them over then turned to Kim and Coda.

"So you flew here?" he asked again, trying to grasp their mental process. This was the first time that the "Rollerway four" had been together since the surprise party.

"Show us something cool," Coda enthused, fending off the primitive *nunchucku* attack that Rico had immediately unleashed on him.

"What?" Ezekiel was thrown off by the intersecting of the parallel conversations. Rico began swinging at the air.

"Like, show us some moves!" Coda grinned, breaking into a *shotokan* stance.

"I just had an operation on a hernia," Ezekiel said, and Rico dropped the nunchucks. "Not 'cause of those," he laughed.

Kim wiggled her nose in thought. "I thought you had thick skin."

"I do. Don't you guys know how a hernia works?"

"Uh, can we play ping pong?" Coda asked, rather loudly, before the conversation could blow upon the sails of a boat upon which he didn't want to voyage.

"Umm, don't you guys wanna go somewhere?" Ezekiel laughed to make it seem like a natural question.

"Like where?" Coda queried, glancing at Rico who was making distracting sound effects as he worked the nunchucks. "Can we at least go inside and say hey to Ma and Pop Yang?" He turned back to Kim, grinning stupidly and pointing his thumb towards Rico.

"Sure." Ezekiel smiled his half-smile. He strolled up the driveway and into the garage and Kim, Rico and Coda followed closely behind. Steps were located next to the Durango that Ezekiel drove whenever he was in town, leading up to a chestnut wooden door that he opened. They all trekked inside.

"Hey, Mom," Ezekiel called.

Ezekiel felt it as Rico's stomach dropped. Rico glanced to Coda with an anxious smile.

"I, too, am perturbed," Coda whispered back, his request having been made while he had temporarily forgotten about Mrs. Yang's marigolds.

"Chill, boys," Kim said, taking in the surroundings.

They had entered a carpeted hallway where Ezekiel's athletic shoes were sitting against the wall with his ankle socks folded inside of them. They all followed suit in removing their shoes. Stairs were on their right, but they turned left, entering a bright, spacious kitchen. An entryway to the living room was located on their new right and they saw the back of Mr. Yang's head as he watched a Chinese news station while simultaneously reading *The Brunswick News*. He didn't seem to notice the company, but they weren't bothered.

Ezekiel's beautiful mom glanced around the corner from the living room inquisitively. She had a short, bobbed haircut and looked remarkably like her son.

"Ezekiel, you have friends! Company!"

"Hey, Mrs. Yang," Coda said brightly, going to give her a hug.

"Mrs. Yang," Rico managed, bravely following suit.

"Hi," Kim said shyly.

"Mom, you remember Rico and Coda, and this is Kim," he introduced, touching Kim's arm.

"I remember you," Mrs. Yang smiled. "You spoke at graduation. Lady Wilbanks"

Kim beamed. "Yes, ma'am." She slid her eyes towards Ezekiel. "I like that! I feel like I should curtsy."

Ezekiel seemed to ignore her. Rico and Coda had sat at the small kitchen table with pained looks on their faces. Ezekiel turned to them.

"I'll be right back," he said, exiting with his mother into the living room.

Kim turned to Rico and Coda, purring. "Oh, boos, it'll work out. You're too timorous."

"We've got to get to Justus's," Rico muttered, his voice cracking.

Coda was staring at Kim. "Timorous? Do you just pick the oddest words out of the dictionary?" he asked.

"Now you said 'perturbed' not even a minute ago," Kim riposted, taking a seat at the table. "And you said it all dramatically in fashion. 'I, too, am perturbed.'" She laughed. "Like that."

Coda made a face.

Kim sighed contentedly and leaned back in her chair, stretching her arms along the table's edge.

"This table is as big as my dining room table," she giggled, and glanced to the dining room. "And that table's bigger than my bed."

Kim reached over and pulled a twig from Coda's braids.

"And you have a big bed," Coda remembered.

Rico glanced at them, raising his eyebrows.

"Not funny," Coda said to him, laying his head down on the table and trying to ignore the giant knot in his stomach from the anticipation. Kim pulled another twig out of his hair.

Rico's grin dropped as soon as Ezekiel re-entered the kitchen. Behind Ezekiel, Mrs. Yang leaned against the living room mantle, observing the guilty party with her large dark eyes.

"What did you say?" Rico asked Ezekiel, he and Coda leaning close in anticipation.

"I told her that you two crushed her marigolds," Ezekiel stated indifferently, glancing to Kim. "Are you ready to go?"

"How, Oh Great Unflappable One, do we make penance?" Coda asked, trying his hardest not to look up, afraid to see Mrs. Yang frowning at him.

"Those twenty dollar bills sure did it," Ezekiel laughed lightly. Kim and Rico stared at Coda.

"Those were twenties?" Kim asked.

The Creole boy looked sicker than he had earlier. "I guess." He glanced to Mrs. Yang, who smiled and gave a little wave before turning to sit next to her husband. "Tips," he mumbled.

"So where are we going?" Kim asked, resuscitating the earlier conversation.

"What about Eden's place?" Ezekiel mentioned, crossing his arms. He knew the purpose for this visit when they had shown up, but was having fun playing along.

"Eden?" Coda shook his head. "She's in Argentina for the holidays. Or Spain. Forget which."

"I haven't seen Genie in a long time," Kim mused. "Not long enough to really talk."

"Who?" Ezekiel asked. Then he looked for the answer. "Oh." Gene Hightower.

Kim was giving him a strange look.

"Gene Hightower, KWA King," she said. "But you know that now, I suppose."

"Sorry," he said, shuffling his feet. His tear-shaped eyes glanced at her, but he didn't dare re-enter her mind.

"It's okay," she said softly. "Is it getting easier?"

"What?" Ezekiel puffed.

"Controlling your gifts?"

"Yeah, I guess. Is it for you?"

"Sometimes. But when I saw Coda maneuvering through those trees, I wondered."

"That's my thing, though," Coda reminded. "It's supposed to look easy when I do that. It's easy for you to pinch people on the arm and to give them bruises."

"Do you let anything go?" she questioned crossly.

"Watch the attitude, Bethany Kelly."

"Ooh," Ezekiel said with a laugh. Kim was glaring at Coda.

"Don't push me, Coda. I could pick you up and throw you if I wanted to." She was joking. They thought.

Rico grabbed Ezekiel's hands and Ezekiel in turn looked at Rico like he was crazy, before his gaze turned to their entwined hands.

"What are you doing?" Ezekiel asked, preparing to shake loose.

"Do you feel anything?" Rico asked, staring into Ezekiel's face intently.

"No."

Rico let go in triumph. "Dude! This is awesome!"

"You tried to burn him?" Kim was intrigued.

"Well, not hurt him, but, you know…" Rico was thrilled. "His skin must be like a rhino's!"

"Whatever," Ezekiel shook his head, half smiling, half not caring.

Kim caught Rico's eye.

"What about Justus's house?" Rico mentioned, casually. "I didn't get to talk to him for long at the mall."

"Yeah, let's go see Justus!" Ezekiel enthused.

"Let's call him and see if he's there," Rico told Ezekiel.

"Oh, he's there," Ezekiel asserted. "I talked to him on the phone about…an hour ago? He's cleaning the backyard and he said he'd call me when he was done."

"Oh, chores." Kim shook her head in disgust as they all stood from the table. "You're never truly free without a headstone. Well, let's go." She glanced around at the boys and a grin overcame her face. "I've missed Justus and his Nancy Drew hair."

She wanted to get to the bottom of what had happened in Shannon's pool, and if her hunch was correct, then Justus was one of them. A Gifted, A Chosen, A Choice Night Dude. He could be another clue that this entire mass of gobbledygook was providential.

"This is only so exciting!" she exclaimed, perhaps a bit too dramatically. She had already been around Coda too long.

"I'm riding with Burly," Coda declared as if on cue, as they headed back to the hallway.

Rico opened the door to the garage, his mind occupied. He was still trying to figure out Kim's headstone comment.

"We can all go in mine," Ezekiel offered, wrinkling his eyebrows and slipping on his shoes. "I mean, there's enough room." They all stared at the silver Durango.

"How is it with demons?" Kim asked, and nobody laughed. "I still should take mine, so I don't have to come all the way over here when we're done. You boys go in the van."

As the boys piled into Ezekiel's transport, Kim moved her truck.

They were all caught in their own individual memories and thoughts —Ezekiel included—until they reached Blythe Island.

Blythe was not one of the official Golden Isles since it was located in the middle of Brunswick River instead of the coast. It was an island of suburbia, save the trees growing amidst everything as if it were Maurice Sendak drawing. At the moment, however, most of the trees and lawns were covered in garish Christmas decorations. Blowup snowmen, illusions of racing reindeer, bows and holly and wreaths.

When they reached Justus's seashell covered house, they pulled into the wide driveway on the side of the house near the back fence. Kim hopped out of her dad's truck and swooped up a red, blue and white basketball that was lying near her front tire.

"Coda-da," she called, dribbling towards the basket on the street. "Let's play, boo."

"Feeling random?" Coda asked, catching the ball when she tossed it to him.

"I feel like winning," she quipped, as Coda attempted to dribble. Inside the house, the dogs were barking like crazy.

"Oh, *cherie*." He grinned and let the ball roll off his fingers straight into—

– Kim's hands, who in turn made the basket. She turned to Coda, laughing. "Are we playing as a team or against each other?" She brushed off her skirt and her hands and turned to Ezekiel and Rico who were patiently waiting on this random deviation. "Uh, sorry. Are we ready?"

Rico raised an eyebrow, responding, "Are you?"

Coda chuckled and leaned against the fence, looking into the backyard. His throat grew tight and his eyes widened. As his jaw dropped, Kim, Ezekiel and Rico raced over to join him.

"Um, whoa," Ezekiel breathed. "No wonder the dogs are barking."

Justus Alexander floated above them in the sky, his hands pure water, his lower torso rather dissipated, as if it was turning into the sky, and his shirt, as well as the chest and stomach that should have been there behind it, appeared as solid and as clear as the ice it had become.

"I guess it's a good thing we didn't bring anybody extra," Coda commented.

Kim and Rico's assumptions that they weren't the only ones changed by God's unknown plans were correct. But what was Justus doing? More specifically, what was he?

"Hello, Hydroxygen," Kim laughed.

Justus looked down, touchingly desperate. "I hope one of you can explain this to me."

Kim glanced around to her awestruck buddies. She looked back to Justus and bravely opened the fence. "I think we can. Quite thoroughly, actually."

17.

Hysterical Faith

Justus held up his hands in confusion. "Wait, now. Who's the boy? Why was Kim fighting a boy?"

His shirt had changed back from the solid ice it had been into a nice orange T-shirt displaying some politically incorrect joke across the back. His hands were flesh and blood, his legs were all there in their khakis, but his eyes just didn't look right. For the moment, it seemed, he was as normal as could be.

"Not 'a boy.' The Boy," Ezekiel corrected, his arms crossed, "who has yet to be named."

"Just let us explain," Coda advised, waving a plastic spoon in the air. He returned to digging into a carton of yogurt Justus had been nice enough to provide.

They were all crammed into Justus's room, with Kim lounging across the bed and Ezekiel leaning against the wall next to the closed door. Rico was standing next to Justus's tie-covered vanity and toying with one of the hangers from the nearby closet, while Coda and Justus sat cross-legged on the carpeted floor.

Kim was struggling to stay focused while she counted the number of different colored crosses hiding in the flecks of Justus's beautiful stained-glass eyes. There were three green ones, two blue ones, about five golden-brown ones...

"Let's give him the basics, guys," she suggested. "When we each experienced our separate choice nights, we all changed."

"You seem to have been turning into water, which is hecka-cool, I might add," Rico allowed himself to rave, "while Miss KWA here gained super strength, as well as a few pounds—"

"Hey," Kim protested.

"—of muscle," Rico steadfastly continued.

"Oh," Kim replied, sinking back into the pillows on Justus's bed. "Sheer muscle," she clarified with a grin.

"Coda the Cheshire is agile like a—like a cat. And 'Zekiel has impenetrable skin and can read minds."

Justus's attention flew to Ezekiel. "Really?"

Ezekiel gave his half-grin.

Justus's eyes sparkled. "What am I thinking now?" he asked Ezekiel leaning forward as if that would help.

"You'd have to have a brain to think," Coda retorted, jokingly.

Ezekiel laughed, twisted his lips and said, "You're thinking about what your mother cooked for dinner last night and whether Eden would really have sex with you if you asked her."

Three sets of incredulous eyes flew to Justus. Rico whistled, then smiled big.

Justus leaned back. "No, I'm not," he said firmly.

"But you were when you were walking us into your room," Ezekiel laughed, rocking against the wall.

"Yes, I was," Justus hollered with a laugh, shaking strands of gold and ruby out of his face. "Oh, this is too cool."

"I bet she won't," Coda said needlessly, tossing the empty yogurt carton towards the waiting trashcan. Kim would have popped him, but she didn't want to break any of his bones. Instead, she helped the carton make it to its destination.

"We'll never know," Justus said, and even Ezekiel couldn't decipher that statement.

"And have you noticed your eyes?" Rico asked Justus.

Justus turned and looked at Rico, inspecting his eyes.

"No, *your* eyes, dude," Rico corrected him smoothly. Rico gestured to Justus with his hands, and just to show off, let a flicker of flame travel from the tip of his index finger up to his elbow, where it dissipated.

"Mmm, so he's been practicing," Kim cooed to no one in particular.

"I noticed my eyes looked different back in June," Justus responded. "And your eyes are just as weird, though they just changed when you did that trick." He turned to Ezekiel, who was standing facing him. "And your eyes, too! They changed when you went inside my head."

"Changed how?" Kim asked.

Justus turned to her. "I don't know, but you all have different types of eyes." He looked at Coda, gesturing with his feet. "Except you and me." He giggled. "The crosses."

He didn't mention that he wouldn't have realized the root of his weird eyes if it wasn't for his attentive mother pointing them out. Several crosses.

Coda was smiling. "Crazy…"

Justus had already revealed to them the real reason he missed Kim and Rico's party at the Rollerway. He had been too freaked out from his strange situation in the parking lot of Summer Falls to wrap his head around anything, so he went home and spent the night praying, not getting any sleep. These days none of them seemed to be sleeping.

Kim sat up. "You seem to be part of the small group of us that can fly."

"Really," Justus said in amazement. "Who else can?"

"I can," revealed Rico, raising his hand.

"So can I," Ezekiel said, with a single rock against the wall, his arms still crossed.

"And so can Solitaire," Kim declared. She seemed ready to steer the conversation into a particular direction. "Hey, guys, remember how Rico said that she froze up when he brought up God making a choice for us? What if she was gifted on a 'choice night,' too?"

"What?" Coda asked, not grasping the idea.

"What's a 'Choice Night' again?" Justus asked, though his question was swallowed quickly by another.

"If God chose her, why isn't she one of us?" Ezekiel asked.

"Assuming she was 'chosen' at all," Coda added, pulling on one of his braids.

"What if she is one of us?" Kim mused. "What if she really knows us personally, but doesn't know that we are Chosen or Gifted or whatever we are."

"You mean, like a classmate?" Coda sputtered. "Like someone we know?" Was she referring to Maya, Queen of the Amazons?

"Maybe God didn't choose her," Ezekiel said broodingly. "The devil can work miracles, too."

Kim and Coda nodded silently, though they knew they hadn't reached any type of conclusion.

"Um," Justus cautiously spoke up, "who's Solitaire?"

"This knife-wielding baddie that quite separately beat up Rico and Ezekiel—" Kim began.

"Whoa," Rico and Ezekiel spurted in unison. Ezekiel seemed to find humor in the moment, attempting to hold back a smile.

"She did," Kim said matter-of-factly.

"And that boy you asked about, Justus," Coda said, "was some possible teenager or man that baited and attacked Kim in the bathroom at Concrete Whatever downtown. But she won that fight."

"By forfeit," Rico mumbled.

"If it'll make you feel better, Rico," Kim added, bruised, "Rico and Cheshire, here," she continued to Justus, "fought The Boy today at the mall. And won. But that might mean that he's just a crappy fighter compared to Miss Solitaire."

"And I," Coda started, self-importantly, "was advanced upon by a…" His voice trailed of, catching the spark of a memory.

"Creature," Kim finished, examining Coda with an odd expression. "Though he never quite described what it looked like."

Coda bowed his head. Kim continued.

"We think the five incidents are connected somehow," she explained to Justus.

Ezekiel was in Coda's brain. "The devil is the author of confusion. He appears as an angel of light, you know?"

Coda glanced up, and then he looked down again at Justus's yellow carpet.

"Why were you at Concrete Wave?" Rico asked Kim. "I've been meaning to ask that."

It was Kim's turn to look ashamed. "I skateboard."

Rico raised his eyebrows. "Really? Wow."

"Solitaire sounds cool," Justus ignorantly verbalized.

Rico turned to Justus so quick that a few neckties were shaken off the mirror and onto the top of the vanity. "She gave me this scar, dude!" He pointed to the dark spade on his neck. Justus thought that made her sound cooler.

Ezekiel, meanwhile, was thinking, and they were hoping it was in his own brain. "It was like *hapkido*, you know?" he vocalized. "Like, she was taking her opponents' energies and using that energy against them. 'Action requires a reaction. A proper reaction exploits the action.' You see, it's the way we move. Our force, you know? Our powers. She took that and, like, reversed it or something."

"I get it, Ezekiel. And that boy actually absorbed our powers," mused Kim.

"Or duplicated them," speculated Ezekiel.

Justus and Coda were bouncing up and down, heads wriggling like twin bobblehead dolls.

"Oh, this is so cool!" Justus put into words with his deep baritone. "We're, like, solving a mystery."

"It's like The Boy is an empty shell," Rico grasped.

"A Hollow, A Hollow Shell," Justus modified. "Can Hollow read our minds if he absorbs Ezekiel's powers?"

Kim looked worried. "I hope not."

"Like, what if we're going about this all wrong?" Coda mused.

"How do you mean?" Kim asked.

He turned to look up at her. "What if these things we are fighting aren't, like, our classmates?"

"We never agreed they were," Rico interjected.

"True, but you all were thinking about it way too hard for it to be a simple thought; Ezekiel isn't the only one who can see that." That statement came out meaner than Coda meant it. "Let me give you something else to think about. What if Solitaire, and Hollow, and the Creature... like, what if they are all demons?"

Justus giggled nervously. "That's insane, dude."

"Like turning into water and ice and floating in the air? Like falling into a mirror and coming up without a scratch? Like being attacked by guys in tights and girls with knives?" Coda shook his head. "Is it more insane than that?"

"Humans don't fight those battles," Justus reasoned. He hated the idea of being pursued by demons. "That's spiritual warfare that you're talking about. Angels handle the demons."

"Just trying to make you think," Coda stated stiffly. "The conversation was getting awfully prosaic." It was an exaggeration, they all knew, but they let it slide.

Ezekiel lifted onto the balls of his feet. "Do you have a Bible in here, somewhere? I wanted to show you all some things that I've found."

"About demons?" Kim asked, surprised, as Justus stood and walked to his drawers, rummaging for his Bible.

Ezekiel laughed. "No, about our powers. I was, like, trying to come up with a reasonable explanation for all the weird things that have been happening, you know? And then some of my classmates dropped in on me and brought to mind something that Vanessa and I were studying, in the Bible, you know? And we were—" He stopped and looked at Rico.

"Pay attention, dude."

Rico brought his mind back from wherever he and Ezekiel knew it had been and smiled sheepishly. "Sorry, dude."

Ezekiel didn't turn his attention away from him. "Why don't you burn when fire is on your hands?"

Rico paused. "I don't know. Super heat absorption, perhaps, hmm?"

Ezekiel looked at Coda. "Why, if you've gotten so much better at everything, can't you do bike tricks? Or dunk in basketball?"

Coda frowned. "Dude, I don't know. And I *can* dunk!" They all gave him a look. "If I wanted to... Bad enough, that is."

Ezekiel turned to Kim. "Why do you think God gave us this...whatever it is—our powers? How do you know it wasn't pollution from the pulp mill factory or even, like, Satan?"

"Ezekiel, this is crazy," laughed Kim, in her closed off way.

"Dude, have you found it, yet?" Ezekiel inquired, glancing to Justus.

"Yeah, dude," Justus breathlessly reported, wheeling around, Bible in hand. He tossed it to Ezekiel, who in turn handed it to Coda.

"Can you find Second Kings for me?" Ezekiel asked the young one before continuing. "Solitaire mentioned Eli, Sammy, Steve, and David." He counted each name off on his fingers, holding them up for his friends to see. "Like, she was hinting at something. I don't think she necessarily wanted us to figure it out, though, but she was hinting. Playing the 'I know something you don't' game."

"What are you saying?" Kim questioned, focusing intently on Ezekiel's message.

"Who is Sammy to you, Kim?" Ezekiel asked. "I'm not trying to be vague or anything—"

"Ambiguous," Coda offered, while Rico said, "You are, though."

"Sammy?" Kim sat in thought. "Didn't we go to school with some kid named Sam?"

"I don't remember a Sam or a Sammy," Rico said.

"He went by Sam at Marshwind Middle," Kim said. "In high school he started going by Wes. He's in Coda's karate class."

"Sam Wesberger," Justus remembered. "He was huge. His muscles had muscles."

"He has a huge percentage of body fat," Coda grumbled.

"Boys," Kim purred, "how important is that information, really?" She turned back to Ezekiel. "Solitaire is looking for Sam Wesberger?"

"No," Ezekiel shook his head. "Not him. Samson. The 'Samson and Delilah' Samson."

"Whoa," Rico said, as Kim absorbed this. Justus dropped back down next to Coda, confused.

"What?" Coda asked, looking up from the Bible.

"Samson was a superhero," Ezekiel said with a smile, as he grabbed the Bible from Coda and started turning pages. "He was as chosen and gifted as Kim is. And Coda, David the King of Israel was definitely blessed if he could kill Goliath with one try."

"That was God," Coda said, discarding Ezekiel's thesis.

"Maybe that was God working through David," Ezekiel proposed. "Think of all that David did, you know? What if God simply enhanced what he could already do? The amazing songs David wrote; the amazing battles he fought." Ezekiel was so absorbed in what he was trying to convey, even his sentences were sounding like questions. "They were talents David had as a shepherd."

"David said that *God* delivered him out of the hands of a lion," Coda protested, refusing Ezekiel's theory again. His friend meant well, but in the moment Coda saw him as a newly born-again Christian, who didn't understand the complexities of scripture.

"God delivered you out of the hands of the Creature," Ezekiel pressed. "God delivered Rico and me out of the hands of Solitaire, when she very well could have killed us with that crazy knife, you know? But we didn't just stand there and do nothing, you know? God will deliver us, but we have to put in our own input. 'Faith without works'…"

"…'is dead,'" Coda finished, contorting his mouth unpleasantly. He was at a loss.

Ezekiel handed the Bible to Rico. He pointed to a spot on the page it was opened to. "In the Old Testament, there are several occasions when a 'fire from the Lord' would consume people. Yet, right here, the first chapter of Second Kings, Elijah calls down a fire himself, upon King… Ahaziah's men, and he does it, like, more than once. It's God's fire, but it's Elijah that calls it down, right? I mean, did I read this wrong?"

Rico shook his head, as if to make room for all this new information. They too were disproving his mother's theory about humans not having special abilities. The new theory was intriguing.

"And as far as why your arms don't burn—"

"God's all powerful—" Rico began singsongingly.

"No," Ezekiel said, a little chagrined now, due to the continuous interruptions, "I mean, yes, of course, but the specific mentions in the scripture to back it up are the facts that the flaming bush Moses was at didn't actually burn, and, like, the chariot that Elijah got in was definitely made of fire." He was trying not to over-talk himself. "Elijah didn't, like, burn himself in that chariot, did he?"

"Good point on the bush, Ezekiel," Justus interrupted, as Ezekiel resisted an obnoxious sigh, "but Elijah never got *in* the chariot. He went to heaven in a whirlwind."

"Really?" Ezekiel asked.

"Yeah," the four said.

"But keep going," Rico added.

"I mean, like, look at all the people in the Bible that did amazing things that weren't, like, by their own design: Moses turning his rod into a snake or when he parted the Red Sea; the healing that the prophets could do through their own hand even though it was God's work; the amazing wisdom of Solomon that he got from God after asking for it; the music of the Israelites outside of Jericho being *enhanced* enough—Coda—to bring the walls down—oh!"

He had officially over-talked himself, almost forgetting his point. "Like, Steve!"

"*Steve?*" Kim asked, thrown off.

"Stephen," Justus remarked. Everyone glanced at him. His eyes squinted in thought. "Stephen was stoned to death and didn't feel a single rock." That was his favorite Biblical story. The only recorded moment when God *stood up*.

Coda jumped up, pointing to Ezekiel. "Like you survived the mirror?!?"

Kim was riveted. "Yes. That's entirely possible!"

"Explain this," Justus spoke up, not in dispute, but in a genuine query. "You mentioned the Hercules factory. How *do* we know that it's not just some random side effect of factory pollution or something equally ridiculous? What makes this God's specific act?"

Rico seemed to wake up. "God's spoken to all of us within the past year. That was His way of expressing that, 'in today's times, I'm giving you no excuse to wonder.' He personally got to us—all five of us—so that there'd be no doubt."

"This is so cool!" Coda was repeating over and over as he marched excitedly around the room.

"Why not just whisper it to us?" Kim asked. She was upset by the thought that God's best option was to kill her in order to choose her.

"I for one," Rico offered, "wouldn't have listened. I wouldn't have known to listen, and if I *had* heard, I wouldn't've believed. I still barely believe as it is, dude."

On some level Kim still disagreed, but Rico made a good point.

"Deuteronomy 29:29 says that some things we are not meant to know, while some things we are, and what if this is one of those things that God has revealed to us, you know?" Ezekiel put forward.

"One of the few scriptures I know by heart." Coda was pleased. "'The secret things belong unto the Lord our God: but those things which are revealed belong unto us and to our children for ever, that we may do all the words of this law.' And I also know all of Psalms 122. 'And I was glad when they said unto me, 'Let us go into the house of the Lord. Our feet—'"

Kim frowned. "Coda!"

"—shall…stand…withinthygates."

Kim sighed. He always stayed just *this* side of annoying.

"You can't argue with the Samson proof," Ezekiel added.

Kim nodded. Even though Ezekiel was proving, well, attempting to prove her presumption that God had given them these gifts, she was cautious about jumping too quickly on the bandwagon that had so easily rolled up in front of her. Things were never this easy. After all, this was the same group that not ten minutes earlier had suggested that they were fighting demons. She had to be sure. "Then describe Justus. Where is there a scripture where someone is transformed into water?"

"Knock-Knocks." Rico offered.

"What?" Kim turned to him, inquiringly. Ezekiel, too, seemed surprised.

"That's what the Creature called us," Coda explained to Justus.

"Enoch." Rico looked to Ezekiel for approval. "Is that right?"

Ezekiel nodded.

"Enoch?" Justus was desperately trying to grasp his piece in the puzzle that was being assembled so quickly.

It suddenly struck Coda's ego that as the pastor's son, his résumé implied that he should have been the one to figure all of this out. When was the last time he had picked up his Bible?

Rico said, "Enoch walked with God 'and was not,' or something like that."

Justus was flipping furiously through the Bible, suddenly on the bed next to Kim, who had relinquished a good portion of elbowroom to the wild man. "Where is that? New Testament? Old Testament?"

"Genesis," Coda said.

Ezekiel explained, "If you go to Hebrews the eleventh chapter, there's a whole listing, from, like, Enoch to Moses to Joshua, about how their faith made all kinds of things possible, you know? It was the book I started with. It says that Enoch was 'transformed' so that he didn't see death, or something like that."

"We are probably paraphrasing horribly," Coda commented, shaking his head.

"Here's what I think," Ezekiel stated. "If Enoch could be 'transformed' into something so that he didn't have to die, why can't Justus be transformed into water, you know?"

"I see that," Kim said, still not sure if she was buying it. She got a visual of Enoch as a wave, crashing on the coast of St. Simons Island, waiting for God to turn him back into a human. She giggled.

Rico, like the rest of them, still struggled with part of the theory. "What would make me, Rico Gutierrez—or you, Ezekiel Yang, or Coda, or Kim, or Justus—special enough to be… superheroes? *God's* superheroes on top of that! It's not like I have the faith of Moses or anything."

"Moses didn't have 'the faith of Moses' at the beginning of his story arc," Justus commented. "I mean, think about it: few of the biblical heroes raced towards their destiny the way we've assumed or been taught they did. If Mary or Peter or Abraham knew the specific routes they were gonna take, they would have drafted contracts full of clauses."

"True," Coda agreed.

"My youth pastor calls it 'hysterical faith,'" Justus said.

"My chaplain uses that phrase," Rico nodded.

Ezekiel asked, "Hysterical faith? Like spiritual adrenaline?"

"Exactly. Like hysterical strength," Justus explained, "you need it and suddenly you have an abundance of it. You get the job done and then marvel at the why's and how's of it all once it's over."

"Hysterical faith," Rico nodded. "A beautiful theory. That explains so much about the Bible crew."

"Who's to say that we're supposed to be on that level anyway?" Kim asked her comrades. "Are we merely chosen to be gifted, or do the gifts have some purpose? I mean, Samson just walked around killing animals and telling riddles until he got himself into a hot mess."

No one seemed to have an answer. And Ezekiel was looking amongst them for one.

"God's superheroes," Rico mused. "What a freakin' trip, dude!"

"Superheroes?" Kim asked. "You've said that a few times now, boo."

"That's what we are!" Rico defended. "'Zekiel even has a name, don't you, Leviathan?"

"Leviathan?" Justus was impressed. "That's a good one, dude."

Ezekiel just puffed with that little half-smile. "I had to come up with something on the spot."

"But that's really good," Coda lauded, wrinkling his forehead. "What's yours, Dyna-girl?" he asked, twirling a braid around his finger absentmindedly.

It didn't escape her that that was his attempt to pin one on her. He wasn't as slick as he thought he was. "I need some time," she replied, looking at Justus. "Do you have one?"

"What's that word you said when you saw me floating up there in the sky?" he asked her.

Kim frowned. "Hydrog-oxy…Hydroxygen?"

"Yeah," he said, his eyes lighting up. "Hydroxygen."

"That's cool," Ezekiel concurred. "Hate to have to read that in a book, though."

Rico was frowning. "What would mine be?" Solitaire had called him many things, but he didn't like the idea of being named by a bad guy. Well, a bad girl. A bad girl who could fight like a grown man.

"Fire," Justus shot out.

Kim shot it down. "Too plain."

"Fireman," Justus suggested.

"That's lame, dude," laughed Ezekiel.

"Firefly," Kim slyly stated. "That's cool."

"That's taken," Coda announced. "And so's Fire."

"By anybody real?" Kim asked, adjusting her sweater.

"No, but we don't need the copyright infringement in case our story hits the Wonderful World of Disney," Coda said. "Ooo, Firework!"

They all shook their heads.

"Flame?" he continued.

"No."

"Flamer?"

He got a look from every person in the room.

"Okay, that one was stupid, I'll admit that."

"Pyromaniac." Justus looked proud of himself.

"Sounds dirty," Ezekiel said.

Rico grinned.

"Look at Rico!" Kim exclaimed, pointing. "Dirty is his style."

Rico straightened up, pointing upwards in honest humility. "But not His."

"Py-ro-main-i-ac," Coda muttered to himself. "Romaine!" he shared with everyone, glancing around eagerly. "Get it?"

"Lettuce?" Ezekiel asked.

"Forget it," Coda mumbled.

"Pyrotechnic?" Justus was still trying.

"Eh." Rico didn't like it.

"Pyro?" Kim selected.

"Taken," Coda rejected. "What about Third Degree?"

"Sounds like a boy band," Rico laughed. "I like Torch."

"Taken," Coda informed.

"Scorch," Rico countered.

"Too close to Torch," Kim grieved.

Justus's eyes lit up. "Hey, guys, what about—"

Ezekiel cut him off. "No."

"Dude," Justus protested.

"No," Ezekiel mandated.

"Redzone," Kim breathed. "Like Frozone from *The Incredibles*."

"Greatest superhero movie ever," Coda said, wistfully.

"Redzone is a body spray," Rico informed Kim.

"Really?"

"Old Spice," he affirmed.

"Wow," she said.

"Burn?"

"Blaze."

"Boiler!"

"The Ashtray."

"Oh, *gracias*, but I'd sooner go with Flamer, thank you very much."

"Boiler? Did you really just say Boiler?"

"Sparky. Heh, heh."

"Ash...*maker*."

"Ash*kicker*, heh, heh."

"Your name suggesting privileges are revoked, Coda. Otherwise I just might kick *your* ash."

"Sparkplug."

"And it gets better and better."

"Furnace!"

"Radiator!"

"Magma."

"Ooooo! I like Magma!"

"I don't. It sounds like a degenerate drag queen."

"Where are all your minds at right now?"

"In the gutter with Magma, obviously."

"Skylight?"

"Heat."

"Heater."

"These are so maizey," Ezekiel laughed.

"Something Spanish?"

"Oh, yeah," Coda snorted. "The Mexican dude gets the Spanish superhero name? I guess I should look up a Swahili superhero name since I'm Black and there'd better be a way to say Leviathan in Chinese for Shen Long."

"Lakota, chill."

"Spontaneous Combustion. Oh, what about Ice? That's ironic!"

"And yet: taken."

"The Chiller?"

"Flamethrower?"

"Bernice!"

"Bernice?" Rico asked.

"Burn, Furnace…duh!"

"Yeah," Rico sighed. "'Duh.'"

"Hot Flash," Justus offered.

"Okay," Kim spoke out, giving Justus a dismayed gaze. "Apparently we won't all get our names today. They should come naturally, like Leviathan did. And like Hydroxy-gen did. I've got to get used to that." Kim stood. "And I've got to get home and change; Maya and I are going out tonight."

"Cool," Coda said as he stood. "And any parting thoughts?" he asked as they all stood and stretched.

"I love you," Justus said.

Coda reached over grabbed Justus around the waist and planted his lips atop Justus's peach smackers.

"I love you, too, Justus," he said breathily, pulling away before cracking up.

Ezekiel was laughing, too, and Rico's mouth dropped open.

"Whoa," Rico said. Justus rubbed his mouth in reflex.

"Coda!" Kim said, very surprised. "Tasha is going to be very jealous," she intoned.

"I'm sorry. He told me he loved me!" Coda pointed to Justus accusingly, laughing so hard that tears were rolling down his cheeks.

"Remind me never to say that around you," joked Ezekiel.

Rico chuckled. "Kim, I love you," he whimpered as he held his arms open to her.

"I'm easy to love," she said with a smile, walking out of the room.

"Ooo, rejection" Ezekiel said.

"Dude, I am sorry," Coda said, turning to Justus.

"It's okay, dude," Justus said shrilly.

"Any other parting thoughts?" Kim said from the door.

"I'm afraid to say anything else," Justus said, giggling. His cell began to ring. He reached for it, holding up a finger so they would wait. "Shannon," he mouthed.

"Hey, Shannon!...Yeah, I'm here with some people...Ezekiel and Coda and—"

Suddenly, an unnatural burble escaped from his throat. His eyes began to fly around the room in panic, and then, as his friends watched in confusion and dismay, he burst into gas.

As Ezekiel and Rico hollered, Coda ran out of the room into the hallway and straight into Kim, who was standing static in disbelief.

Kim hollered to Rico. "Pick up the phone!"

Justus was already beginning to liquefy on the floor.

"Whoa," breathed Ezekiel.

Rico grabbed Justus's cell, wide-eyed. "Wasabi, Mr. Shannon?...It's Rico, dude...Yeah, we just played a prank on him; we didn't know he was on the phone...Yeah...um..." He looked to Kim in panic.

She hurried over to him, stepping over Ezekiel, who was on the floor, watching the liquefaction process with much interest.

"Stop watching!" the puddle squealed, causing Ezekiel to jump back and Kim to scream.

"Sooooo, hey, Shannon," she began after procuring Justus' cell, her eyes repeatedly averting themselves from the puddle.

"It's Kim...Long time no see indeed...That's just dirty, Shannon." She gave a disconcerted look to Rico and then gazed off into space. "Oh, *that's* what you meant." She laughed. "I can't with you, sometimes...No, just us...Justus, Ezekiel, Rico, Coda, and me...and I, I guess...Oh, well, we're leaving now...So, why weren't you at the mall?"

"Why weren't *you*?" Coda muttered, and Kim ignored him.

As Kim continued to ramble with Shannon, Justus's hands became flesh, and he pushed his liquid form out of the carpet in order to materialize fully. His face appeared encased in some type of liquid husk, like a plastic bag over his head, as his upper torso attempted to return to human form. The room was quiet, save Justus spitting a little carpet fuzz out of his fleshing mouth.

"No, I'm still here, Shannon-baby," Kim chirruped suddenly.

"It's like a horror movie!" Coda commented.

"Shut up!" Justus squeaked.

"Why is your hair black?" Rico asked.

Justus stared into his mirror in shock. "It's purple!" he hollered.

"Oh, dear," Kim cooed.

Ezekiel laughed.

• • • • •

"Poor boy," Kim smiled, shivering against the sudden chill that had hit the Georgia air. "I don't think it's fading."

Justus was hopping back and forth on the pavement of his grandparent's driveway, rubbing his arms to stay warm. "Really?"

Behind them, leaning over the metal fence drenched in Christmas lights, Ezekiel, Rico, and Coda were playing with the two pub canines.

"Yeah, boo," Kim nodded. "I'm sorry."

"Nothing you can do," Justus nodded, glancing to the sky. "I wonder if there's anything I can do. Pray, I guess."

"Yeah," Kim frowned. Her braids were pulled back atop her head to hang down the back of her neck, but she shook her head as if to shake them out of her face. "I thought you were afraid of dogs!"

Justus glanced into the backyard. "Oh, Jennifer and Poopsie?"

Kim snorted. "Jennifer and Poopsie?"

Justus grinned. "Yeah. My grandparents' two dogs. It took me years to get used to them. They're the only dogs I even tolerate."

"Look, Justus," Kim said, leaning against a plastic snowman, "I'm sorry for getting all freaked out at Shannon's house that day."

After a short pause, he nodded at the memory. "I would have freaked out too." His teeth chattered. "I did," he added as she said, "You did. Twice!"

She smiled at him.

"Sorry for making you break Shannon's pool," he said.

"What?" She was mystified.

"When I went all watery and you slammed into the concrete." He tilted his head. "You don't remember that?"

"Don't tilt your head like that, dude," Ezekiel said, walking over from the fence. "It makes me think of Solitaire."

Justus tilted his head further, confused like Kim. "What?"

"Hey, dude," Rico called to Justus, bounding over. He grabbed Justus's hands. "What do you feel?"

"Ow!" Justus's hands burst into gas.

Ezekiel shook his head. "Crazy."

"Dude, does my hair look better?" Justus asked, glancing from Ezekiel to Rico.

"No. It's almost pitch black," Rico said, shaking his head.

"Purple black," Kim said. "The best kind."

Coda asked, "How long has it been?"

"Twenty minutes," Ezekiel informed, glancing at his wristwatch. "Maybe it'll go back if you burst into gas again."

"I can't go all gassy on purpose," Justus said.

"Stop drinking so many sodas," Kim cracked. She laughed alone.

Ezekiel looked at her oddly and she looked right back. He turned to Justus.

"So you had never burst completely into gas like that?" he asked.

"No," Justus stated, almost sadly as his hands liquefied. "The most that my head has ever done is turn into water."

"My guess is that the temperature change affected the chemical makeup of your hair or something," Kim said, attempting to sound educated in such details. "Like when hair lightens in the summertime."

Rico and Ezekiel shrugged in unison, while Justus's eyes squinted, watching his hands re-tissue.

"Shannon probably thinks we've gone insane," Kim laughed, thinking back on the phone call.

"He already knows that," Ezekiel replied, plainly enjoying Justus's creepy fleshing process.

"All of this is like chess," Justus murmured. "It's like we're pawns in something greater."

Ezekiel snorted. "Like chess, like *hapkido*, like a comic book, like *life*," he said, momentarily tired of all metaphors.

Justus looked hurt.

"Well, boys," Kim said, "it's been mighty real like Sylvester, but I *must* be going, *really*. We should talk about all of this again, though. Soon."

She headed towards her truck.

"Take it easy, Kim," Justus waved.

"See you later," Ezekiel murmured.

"Bye, Kim," Rico drawled.

"Kim!" Coda cried, running over to her. "Where are you and Maya going tonight?"

"Umm, just around," she sighed.

"Can I come?"

"Coda, this is just Maya and I," she explained as she climbed into the truck.

"So you two go off to college and you're back to normal, huh?" He seemed disappointed. "And I'm out of the loop?" That must have been the reason.

"She's my BFF, you know that!"

Coda did know it, but what bothered him was the fact that he had figured he was her BFF, too.

"I wanted to hang with you," he pouted.

"Hang with them." She pointed to the trinity formed next to Ezekiel's minivan. "Though I can't tell if they're the three kings, the three amigos, or the three stooges." She laughed at her newest little joke, then couldn't stop laughing. Coda just stood and stared at her.

Kim tried another tactic. "Why don't you do something with your college friends or something?"

Coda's eyes widened in astonishment. "I didn't go to college to make friends," he clenched indignantly. "I already have friends."

"That's one way to look at it," Kim grumbled. She hated when Coda got self-righteous like that, so she returned to sender. "What do you want to be Coda? What are you going to school for? What's your plan?" Her neck was beginning to roll against her will. "Are you achieving any goals? Are you achieving anything? Why are you even going to college?"

Coda just glared at her wordlessly.

She held the gaze, waiting for some type of answer. Looking at his eyes, she realized Justus had been mistaken. The gold in his eyes formed stars, just like hers.

"Your earring, Dyna-girl," he said, gesturing to the hoop that Dishon had given her. "Fallen?"

"It's a rock band," she said sharply, her eyes narrowing.

"It's a mindset," he hissed. "Tongue ring that nobody's supposed to know about, alcohol-drenched nights that you type about on your online journals, and now getting high with that dropout boyfriend—"

"Are you determined to be unhappy, Coda? Because I'm not."

Coda stared at her hands and she followed his gaze. She had unknowingly gestured to his wrists.

She sighed and sat back against the grey seat, but he wheeled around and stomped off towards Rico and the rest before she could make any peace with him. She started her truck and pulled out of the driveway. At times, Coda was almost as dramatic as she was.

At that moment, Rico and Ezekiel were comparing their individual encounters with Solitaire. Coda walked over and stood next to Justus, crossing his arms.

"What's wrong?" Justus mouthed, noticing.

Coda just shook his head, looking away.

Justus nudged him, moving his lips again. "Are you sure?"

Coda nodded, but looked away again.

"The voice was scratchy," Ezekiel was agreeing, rocking back and forth on his staggered feet, "but her skin was peachy. I know I remember that. Didn't you see her at night?"

"With the light of flames illuminating her face," Rico said, meditatively rubbing the invisible stubble on his cheek.

"Illuminating," Justus repeated, as if learning the word for the first time and enjoying it a little too much. He stuffed his hands into the pockets of his khakis, relieved he had put on thermals that morning.

"Oh well. I saw peach skin," Ezekiel said with a chuckle.

"And I didn't," Rico shrugged, attempting to keep the dispute from sliding into argument.

"Her voice was like BJ's," Ezekiel stated.

Rico paused. "What?"

"Wasn't it?" Ezekiel asked.

"Yeah…" Rico didn't like the newest turn of conversation.

Ezekiel shook his head. "But the body…"

Rico brightened up. "Yeah, the body…" He visualized Solitaire's features. "BJ's stockier. The just-right size."

"Yeah," Ezekiel half-agreed, still wondering. He glanced around at the golden sky. "Well, I'd better be going." He glanced at Coda. "Am I taking you home?"

Coda looked to Rico. "I was wondering if I could spend the night at Rico's."

"That's cool," Rico nodded. "You can stay at my crib, but no hitting on my sister." It was made light, but it was a warning nonetheless. "Do you have your stuff?"

"What stuff?" Coda asked.

"That's okay;" Rico said, patting Coda on the back, "we can just go grab it later."

As his friends turned the corner on Justus's drive to drive onto the Blythe Island highway, Justus held up his hands above his face, carefully turning them to water. He clucked in upset. The reflection on his palm proved that his hair was still black. Purple black.

How unreal could things get?

18.
The Powers That Be

Christmas came and went and Kim didn't get the one thing that she really wanted for Christmas, not that she told anyone. She got clothes from her parents, however, so in their mind she had nothing to grumble about, though her complaint list seemed to be growing each day. Decent clothes were better than synthetic jewelry, she admitted, though the blue plastic things had grown on her.

Hanley Powell threw a Christmas party at her place out in the boon-dock-marshes and, surprisingly, many people showed up. Kim and Maya showed up together, of course, and Coda showed up with Tasha. Tasha, Kim and Maya, the only Black girls present and the only cheerleaders invited, escaped to the upstairs billiard room where they talked more than they shot. Justus, whose hair had changed back to blond after a long twenty-four hour period, showed up as well.

To Hanley's disappointment, Rico and BJ left the party rather early, though it didn't bother Kim one bit, considering the fact that BJ was beginning to stomp on Kim's nerves. Kim didn't know why she was developing such a violent allergy to the girl. Secretly, Kim liked to imagine that BJ was Solitaire so that she'd have a good excuse not to like her... and maybe throw her around a bit.

Kim didn't think she liked Vanessa anymore, either, especially when Ezekiel left the day after Christmas to head up to Cedar City to spend New Year's with Vanessa. Justus called to check up on him, making sure no demonic activity was going on in the area, "because," he professed adamantly and repeatedly, "I'm looking for the opportunity to show my stuff!"

Rico spent most of his winter break days curled up with BJ in her den, watching foreign films and participating in BJ's culinary enjoyments. BJ was into baking suddenly, and Rico liked having her version of she-stuff coming into play. She baked muffins, bread, cookies, and cakes. Rico was glad to put on more weight, considering he had worked off more pounds than he knew he had in the first place. Once he realized that the weight he was gaining was fat, however, he was quite upset. He would stand in front of the bathroom mirror after his morning showers, pinching and inspecting the areas that needed the most help.

Maya called Coda when he was at the mall with Rico and she used the green-eyed one as the middleman to talk to Rico. Coda got so red in the face, he handed his phone over to Rico so that the two horndogs could flirt in their dirty ways without him having to hear both sides of the conversation. One was bad enough. Rico really liked Maya, but Maya wouldn't let him say it, since they both were linked to other people (not officially, of course). But both of them liked to think about each other, and often.

Terry Bozzo, fresh from his mission trip, asked Kim and Coda to come over his mother's place. It was a nice gesture from the returning Terry, and Maya, of course, showed up as well. Terry and Kim started playing cards while Maya and Coda flirted (though their flirting was nothing compared to the way Rico and Maya would flirt), and eventually they all ended up playing Egyptian Rat Screw. Maya won all four games that she played. They rented a few foreign films from Videoville that Rico and BJ had recommended. "Aside from all the sexiness," Coda had proclaimed, "they were very good."

Shannon was absent from most of the get-togethers over the winter break. Justus is the only one who saw him and it was one time at the mall. Justus, Rico, and Ezekiel all talked to him on the phone several times, while Coda, who could never get anything but Shannon's answering machine, pretended he didn't care.

Gene Hightower announced he was throwing a joint New Year's party with Brandon Evans at Brandon's grandparent's house. Kim said it—"a Black people party"—smelled like trouble and stayed far away. Sure enough, the police showed up at the Evans house and shut it down. Interestingly, Gene had left a few moments before they showed up and he wasn't linked to the mayhem in any way. All the police did was end the party, but a certain Brandon Evans decided to challenge their authority and ended up behind bars. He called Kim to bail him out. She did.

Justus called Kim late one night, waking her up. He sounded distraught. She attempted to calm him down, but he was unstoppable. He described a dream to her that he said had been recurring. He described their high school graduation and a chilling car crash. Kim was silent and told him that she'd call him back in the morning. She never did. And for once, Justus tasted what Coda was eating for breakfast, lunch and dinner. Eventually Justus got the details from Rico, leaving him to wonder why Kim found it so impossible to just tell him the full story.

Shannon Crescitelli decided to follow Brandon Evans's example and throw a holiday bash in the marsh that got the police hopping. Benny Commons and Gene (again) avoided getting jailed, but Shannon wasn't so lucky, though he was out in less than an hour. Bethany Kelly said that that's the last time she would ever stick her neck out for them, but they knew she was lying. Her father was chief of police.

Bethany had invited Terry to the party, but he passed it up to attend the movies with Coda. Bleach couldn't wipe off the smile on Coda's face once he found out about Terry's "sacrifice."

Rico's neighborhood was several corners away from Bethany's, out in the county, and a nice suburban neighborhood it was. Peppi Ortiz was his next-door neighbor and he hadn't even found that out until their senior year. Everyone in that neighborhood generally kept to themselves and seemed to like it that way. The front yards were decorated with palm trees and had no boundaries (none were needed), but concrete fenced in the back yards.

Coda's tendency to sleep over at the Gutierrez house each time Rico came home was becoming a nice little tradition that both looked forward to, since there were few things better than face-to-face contact with friends. In early January, they sat up into the wee hours of the morning, just talking. First they talked about recent events, then girls, then family, then girls, and eventually started talking about their adventures. It was around two o'clock in the morning, but they weren't even considering the prospect of shutting down for the night.

"So what do you make of the bad guys complication?" Rico asked.

Coda frowned and shook his head. "When I was attacked, the Creature just said, and I quote, 'Stay out of my way.' Now what that 'way' is, and which direction it's heading, that's left to interpretation. Technically, we still don't know if they're really 'bad guys' though."

Rico chuckled. "Yeah, 'cause who's to say that we're the good guys?"

Coda looked alarmed.

"No, no, I don't mean like that, Coda. I just mean, what makes us good by definition? We're all pretty horrible people when it comes to doing the right things."

"You're not horrible, Rico," Coda said in his child-like way. "We all sin."

Rico smiled softly. "Tell me about it. And we *like* it." He looked deep into Coda's eyes. "Moses was a murderer. So was David. And Saul." He could tell Coda was biting his tongue. Rico was purposefully needling his friend. "Give Kim a break, Cheshire. And remember forgiveness. Not everybody stays on the highway to heaven without stopping for diesel or taking a few detours. Don't hate anybody for it."

"I don't hate," Coda said quietly. "Though sometimes I think if I didn't love you guys so much, all this would be easier for me to take."

"You just need to relax," Rico said seriously. "Do you masturbate?"

Before Coda could sputter a response, someone tapped Rico's window. Rico and Coda froze. They looked over at his window and it came again. A small brown hand rapped softly and briefly on the window.

"That crazy girl," Rico heard Coda mumble as he headed over to the window. "Why couldn't she just call?" Coda made motions at the window before heading out of Rico's room.

"Kim's here," he said over his shoulder. "Don't ask me why, though."

Rico stood perplexed for a second, then hurried to his closet to snatch two sweatshirts and followed after Coda.

"Kim's here?" he repeated, as Coda slipped the door open and disappeared outside. Rico glanced around the living room, but his father wasn't home and his mother was in her bedroom, probably deep asleep after another one of her busy days.

Rico closed the door behind him as he stepped into the chill.

• • • • •

"Hey, boys," Kim smiled, so layered in warm clothes that she looked like an ebony snowman. Her father's red truck stood out in the bland surroundings of white-lit peach and sea foam green. "I was hoping you wouldn't be asleep."

"¿Que pasa, chica?" Rico greeted her, slipping his sweatshirt over his head and tugging it over his black sweater. Coda, in a green turtleneck, reached over and grabbed the other grey sweatshirt and followed suit.

Kim and Rico embraced. "Why didn't you call?" he asked.

"I did, but neither of you has your phone on."

Coda and Rico glanced at each other.

"Oh," Rico said.

"What phone?" Coda asked with a bitter grin.

"Mine's on silent," Rico added.

"Is there any way I could come inside?" Kim asked.

Rico shook his head. "My parents would kill me."

"That's okay," Kim said, rubbing her gloved hands together and watching her breaths dissipate into atmosphere.

"We can sit in the car, though," Rico offered.

"Ooo, good idy," Coda said.

"Just let me go get the keys," Rico said, slipping back inside the house. He tiptoed into his room and slipped into his boat shoes. While looking for his car keys, he found the camera BJ had given him and slipped the attached cord onto his wrist. After finding the car keys, he grabbed his cell phone, making sure the ringer was turned on, and slipped it into his pocket. He headed out of his room, leaving the light on and closing the door.

When he got back to the front door, he paused. Kim and Coda were whispering an argument.

"We have responsibilities, girl! Responsibilities."

"It is not that serious, boy, and you are not my father anyway."

"I'm your friend—that's family, it's close enough."

"It is not."

Coda was breathing hard, like he was trying to control his temper. "Okay."

Rico heard Kim sigh. "Why do we do this? Do we have to argue?"

"It's the only way you and I seem to communicate."

"That's not true," Kim said reproachfully.

"Okay."

"Stop doing that!"

"I don't want to argue."

"Fine. We don't have to."

"Okay." Coda was being extremely curt. Detached for his own good, maybe.

Rico exited the house, tossing his keys from hand to hand, looking at them strangely. Coda was looking at him, his eyes pained. Kim's eyes roamed across the expanses of the Gutierrez lawn, just as tortured, but covered by a glaze of blankness. Rico was beginning to figure her out.

"Let's go," he said.

As they settled into Rico's little brown car, Coda laid himself down in the backseat. Rico was behind the wheel and Kim sat across from him in the passenger's seat.

"I saw Mrs. Donahue today," Kim said. "All the teachers are back at the school, so I went to say hey."

"Cool," Rico grinned.

"She is the best teacher in the world," Coda said drunkenly.

Dinah Donahue was the AP Literature teacher that had rescued them from the angst, confusion and suspicion of English-language literature that Mr. Georgeson had instilled in them the previous year. She had exposed the pulsing vein of each author, scene, character, and page that crossed their palms. Without even trying, she caused them to see themselves in each book, poem and occasional song lyric that was examined. She, perhaps, had turned teaching itself into an art of the likes of which her students studied. It was at her Monday Night Movie fellowships—MNMs—that Rico had gotten to know Kim, Ezekiel, Justus, Maya, and Coda much better than he had before, even if he did spend most of his time entwined with BJ.

"Why are you here?" Rico thought to ask, suddenly snapping a picture with his camera.

"Boy!" Kim squealed, instinctively smoothing down her braids.

Rico was looking past her.

"Is that Ezekiel's minivan parking behind your truck?" he asked.

Coda sat up, following Rico's gaze. "It is," he said, as Rico's phone began to ring.

"Umm, yeah," Kim hummed, with the type of forced nonchalance that betrayed her pretense of innocence. "I felt the need to call a little meeting."

"What?" Rico asked. "Here?"

"Sure. I mean, no one was asleep, and my parents would not have it—boys in the house in the middle of the night—and neither would have Justus's or Ezekiel's or—"

"Justus is coming?" Coda asked, crunching into a pear that seemed to appear from nowhere.

"Yeah," Kim replied.

"My parent's wouldn't like it either!" Rico croaked, as his phone kept ringing. "All these people in the house…"

"If I wasn't a girl, it would be fine, right?" Kim asked.

"Yeah," Rico admitted, staring at her. Everyone knew his parents were cool with anybody who was cool with Rico.

"Well, everyone else's parents just wouldn't have liked it, period. No matter the gender. The hour kills it, thanks to the powers that be.—Are you gonna answer that?"

Rico's phone had already stopped ringing. Coda hopped out of the car and waved to Ezekiel, motioning for him to join them.

"No one was asleep?" Rico asked.

"Nope. Not a single one of y'all," Kim said.

"How'd you know?" Rico asked.

"Nowadays, are there any questions that don't have spiritual answers?" Kim asked.

Rico shrugged. "I don't think there ever were, you know. We always say, 'something told me…' when it was Somebody."

Ezekiel was laughing as he headed over to the car. He hadn't been asleep; he had been working on an idea. During the holidays he usually didn't get to sleep until around three in the morning, so he was in good spirits when Kim called.

Coda led Ezekiel back into the car, finishing off the pear as he slid over to the far window.

"What is this?" Ezekiel asked, amused. "A car jam?" He looked to Rico. "Is your phone on silent?"

"Scoot over, Ezekiel," came another voice, smaller, lighter, and this time even Kim was taken by surprise.

"Are we having a superhero meeting?" Renata Gutierrez asked, standing right behind Ezekiel in her woolen pajamas.

Kim, Coda and Ezekiel all had the same panic-stricken expression on their faces when they looked at Rico.

"I told her," he said.

Renata laughed at their faces as she slid in next to Ezekiel. "Chill, people. I'm not gonna tell anyone."

"Who all have you told?" Ezekiel asked Rico.

"Just Renata," he coolly responded. "What about you?"

Ezekiel hemmed and hawed. "Well, uh, I've tried to tell my girlfriend, but she…doesn't believe me from the lightning, you know? Then there are two kids at school that know I have a friend who was struck by lightning and suffered weird side effects…and they were there with Christopher Nyberg when I slammed into the mirror."

"Mirror?" Renata asked. So Ezekiel, with ample help from Kim, Rico, and Coda, told of his encounter with Solitaire. Then they had to tell Kim's story and Coda's story, since Rico had conveniently left all of those colorful historical tidbits out of his exchanges with his sister.

"Who have you told?" Renata asked Coda.

Coda looked forward in dismay, unable to make eye contact with the girl who he considered so attractive and was now familiar with part of him that he hadn't exposed to many people.

"Umm, just Maya."

"You told Maya?" Rico asked.

"Yeah," Coda replied, as Kim said, "Of course."

"Not that she completely believes us," Coda added.

"She doesn't believe a thing," Kim corrected.

"You guys didn't tell your parents?" Renata asked.

They all puffed and snorted and sucked their teeth in response.

"My parents would preach to me," Kim said.

"Mine, too," Rico said, while Coda said, "I think my dad was born preaching."

"I told my parents," Ezekiel said.

"Really?" Kim asked. "What do they think?"

"Like, they just tell me to be careful and to not get caught by the government."

"Sometimes I wish I was you," Coda said breathlessly.

There was a knock on the window, causing them all to jump.

"Relax, guys. It's Justus," Kim said, hopping out.

"Just who?" Rico quipped.

"Hopefully, that's tonight's last surprise," Coda said.

"Yeah, I can't take much more, dude," Rico said.

They all watched as Kim explained why they were all in the car. Justus got in the front seat of the car while Kim squeezed in the back. With Coda and Renata so skinny and Kim and Ezekiel so small, they didn't feel too crowded. It was hot enough, however, for Kim to remove her jacket and her gloves. It started a wave across the car where all, save Renata in her sleeping clothes, took off their jackets.

Justus hadn't been asleep either. He had woken around twelve-thirty after having more dreams and was relieved with the prospect of doing anything other than closing his eyes again. The novelty of their situation hadn't yet left the blond and he took private fascination with each meeting he had with "the other four."

"What's crackalackin', everybody?" he asked when he got in. Rico took a picture.

"Dude!" Justus squealed, rubbing his eyes.

"We were just revealing to each other who all we've told about our secret," Renata explained.

Justus did a double take.

"She knows," they replied in their various and simultaneous ways.

"Oh, really?" Justus looked excited. "Who all have you told?" So they repeated the previous train of conversation.

"What about you?" Kim asked Justus.

"Well, I told my granny the full story, as far as the water and flight stuff, you know." He gazed out of the vehicle into the night. "I didn't update her on…all of you."

"Well, Maya knows about all of us," Coda said. "But once again," he continued as Kim joined him, "she doesn't believe."

Kim shrugged, watching her breath briefly fog the mirror. "Not that it matters."

"I know everything," Renata said. "Except the cool stories that is. I just know about Enrique's thing with that crazy red girl, and now Ezekiel's thing with the mirror, and Kim's thing with the Hollow boy and Coda's thing—whatever Coda's thing was, anyway. And I haven't spoken a word of it." Her eyes twinkled.

Nobody added what many of them were thinking. *Yet.*

They all looked at Kim.

"Oh. I guess this is my turn," she giggled.

"Oh, no! How many people?" Justus asked.

"Oh, no, it's not that," she said slowly, smiling. "Aside from Maya, I only told my brother Azari. About all of us. He's a pastor and I needed his input. That was spiritual guidance and brotherly love all in one swoop."

"Good choice," Justus nodded.

Ezekiel watched Coda stare out of the window into the cloudy midnight sky. He wondered what Coda was thinking… "You know, the first time I saw lightning after I was struck, I felt it right to the center of my bones, as if it was striking me again… Reminding me of its existence. Sometimes it seems like it's following me. Like I'm leading it to something."

"What do you think you're leading it to?" Justus asked.

"I haven't figured that part out," Ezekiel muttered. "I have, actually, gained a lot of weight."

"Huh?" Kim asked, turning to him. "What exactly are we talking about now?"

"I mean, like, do you know why the mirror didn't cut me?" he asked.

They went along with him. "Why?"

"Like, my skin isn't dying according to the usual lifespan of skin cells. It's not falling off, washing off, flaking, none of that, you know? I just have this thick layer of skin, now. I checked it under one of the biology microscopes this month. Like, I'm literally thick-skinned."

"You don't look like it," Rico said.

"Good," Ezekiel laughed.

"I wonder how thick it gets before it begins to come off," Justus mused.

"I don't know," Ezekiel said. "I don't want to turn into Goliath. Or the Thing."

"How much do you weigh?" Kim asked.

"One hundred and eighty-five pounds."

Coda's mouth dropped open and Rico whistled.

"Wow," Justus managed.

"You almost weigh more than Justus!" Coda marveled, then cackled as Justus threw an empty soda cup at him.

"I'm not fat!" Justus said, almost succeeding in not squealing.

"You *aren't* fat," Coda agreed, prepared with the comeback. "In *some* areas."

Kim was nodding, realizing. "That's why we were all wearing sweaters in your yard and you were in just a T-shirt. And barefoot."

"Well, that and the fact that I'm developing a lightning flower scar on my back. Months after I was actually struck."

"Can we see?" Justus asked, before wilting in Ezekiel's non-blinking stare. "Dumb question."

Rico grabbed the steering wheel, pretending to drive. "So why are we here, Your Cheetah Majesty?"

Kim turned to look at all the faces in the car. "I feel like we should be together, right now. Whenever I have a question, I wonder if perhaps we all have pieces of the answer. Facets of the same situational jewel. I mean, it's obvious that we all have some bond…this thing that connects us all."

She continued. "You ever wonder about the scriptures on Jonah and Moses and the Hebrew boys and all kinds of people who should have been dead, but were spared? My brother said in a sermon a few weeks ago, that many things happen in our lives and we don't know what they all connect to mean until years, maybe decades later." Kim looked at the faces of her comrades in the car. "I was spared because I have a job to do still, and one day I will know what it is. My brother said that God gives the devil permission to torment us, but only God can kill us."

"I thought that Coda's creature was trying to kill him," Renata commented.

"No," Coda scoffed. "I doubt that."

"Could Kim's creature be Coda's creature?" Justus asked.

Coda thought about the blue eyes and Kim's description.

"Is that what he looked like?" Kim asked.

Coda shook his head in negation. "And I really don't want to talk about it right now."

"Come on, Coda," Rico said, swearing. "We're here to put this thing together."

"Well, let's put the rest together first," Coda sulked. "Like, what was up with Hollow and Solitaire at that church when Rico saw them? I mean, what were they up to?"

"Cool, Coda," Rico said, staring at him with dangerous outward tranquility. "Have it your way. You are the seventeen-year-old, right? I guess that makes you the baby of this group and the baby always gets its way."

"Geez, Rico," Ezekiel muttered.

"So you're gonna lay into *me*, now?" Coda asked angrily. "When we've already got crazy people coming out of the woodwork, now I've got to deal with *you*, too? Forgive me for being born in the wrong year. I apologize for skipping the second grade! Maybe I should pray that God makes me stupid!"

"What, that hasn't happened yet, Mr. Oakwood *Community College*?" Rico baited. "Maybe I was mistaken... Maybe it was recent, and 'the Creature' infected you with 'the stupid.'"

"Boys!" Kim yipped.

"Tell him to back off!" Coda exclaimed. "Not all of us can hide behind ROTC in order to get a nice fat scholarship!"

"Annapolis is *my* dream!" Rico said. "Just because you've lost yours—"

"*¡Hermano!*" Renata squeaked.

Coda shook his head, voice growing quiet. "You know what, you can keep on ranting, Mr. Gutierrez. Keep misdirecting your anger."

Rico hesitated. "Coda..."

"Don't," Coda said, still quiet. "You're right. You hit the nail on the head, sir."

After a brief silence, Ezekiel began to whistle. It was an interesting decision to whistle at all, but "Bananaphone" seemed like an unusual selection.

"Fellas, I have a question," Justus spoke up, relieving them all. "What if God is only *allowing* Hollow and Solitaire...and the Creature to attack at the times and places least opportune for them? Maybe they were allowed to come out and attack—or pretend to attack—that chapel up in Maryland because God knew Rico would stop them."

"Rico didn't *stop* them," Kim said.

"Well, his appearing did," Ezekiel countered. "But why would they attack churches? Wouldn't they do more damage, like, attacking other things?" He snickered. "Us, for example!"

"Solitaire knew my name," Rico spoke up. "And, as a side note, they weren't attacking the church. I think they were looking for this ridiculously expensive hat... I don't really remember what happened with all of that, actually." He paused for a moment, looking lost before regaining his footing. "Hollow seems to have targeted both Kim and Coda. And Coda's…creature referred to a princess. It was probably talking about Kim, right? I mean, she's the reigning pageant princess. And after fighting Ezekiel, er, Leviathan here, Solitaire knew who she was going after next, though it's not clear if she knew who he—I—anybody truly was at that point. Well, she definitely knows me now."

"Well, Hollow was certainly following me," Coda said. "On the way to the mall that day. I kept sensing something watching me, though it kept moving. First I'd feel it behind me, then to my right, then over in front of me to my left. I was riding my bike, right? I got a flat tire. When I stepped off to inspect it, I saw the flash of his shoulder behind me in the trees and I took off after him. He was fast, but I'm limber and that made it pretty even. At first. Anyway, it's like he was keeping tabs on me."

"Hollow's look never changed, right?" Rico asked. "I mean, Solitaire has looked two distinctly different ways so far, from the costume to her skin color and her *ojos*."

"Rico!" exclaimed Justus.

"That means eyes," Renata said, rolling hers.

"Oh," Justus said. "What about her breasts?"

"Two boobs," Rico nodded. "Exquisitely sized both times."

Ezekiel laughed and Coda muttered, "Here we go, the demonstration of utmost maturity."

"The Hollow boy had white, white, white skin," Kim said, looking at Rico and Coda.

"Yep," they nodded.

"He was insanely fast and barefoot with nasty thick dark dreadlocks. About seven of them."

"Yep."

"A brown jumpsuit straight out of some bad seventies television show."

"Yep."

"Did he talk?" she asked.

"Not a word," Coda said, as Rico shook his head.

"Then it's the same guy," Kim concluded.

"Wait, you think that there are two Solitaires, Kim?" Renata asked.

They all paused.

"That's not where I was going," Kim said, "But that's a possibility. A good one."

"No, it can't be," Ezekiel said, "because she implied that she was going to fight the fire guy—you know, 'Eli'—next."

Justus spoke now. "What if she meant 'she' to reference the entity of Solitaire? The being, not the person behind it."

Ezekiel responded with, "You're weird."

"What if they're not even interested in us, really?" Coda asked.

"What?" Kim said. "What do you mean? Why else would they attack us?"

"To get us focused on one thing, while they accomplish something totally under the radar."

Silence grew in the car as they all pondered notions in the hush.

"Why don't we attack *them*?" Rico said. "Attack the Hollow thing and Solitaire and the Creature and what-not."

"How would we find them?" Ezekiel asked. "and when would we have the time to plan something like that? I go back to Tech in, like, two days."

"I leave tomorrow," Kim said.

"How would we find them anyway? And what would we do with them?" Justus asked.

"Well, what do you guys suggest we do?" Rico asked. "Here we are, chosen by God to wield superhuman abilities at our inclination, sitting in a car in the darkness of the freakin' morning while three supernatural muthas follow us to the mall and to our schools? And we don't know their motivation or their identities. They have us at a disadvantage, you guys. A freakin' *large* disadvantage.

"It's been six months. Six whole months since Kim got attacked! And what have we achieved? We don't even know their motives or what our purposes are!"

"And what if they know our families?" Justus asked, pointing back to Renata.

"Great," Renata mumbled. "That makes me feel real good."

"Sorry," Justus said sheepishly.

"I tell you what," Rico said, "until we figure it out, more mess is gonna go down! We're gonna get more bruises and we're gonna get more scars and we're gonna get more and more upset! I don't like the odds of them using my own anger as a weapon against me."

"Well, anger is a sin," Renata began.

"It's not a sin," Kimberly corrected. "The sin is letting the sun go down on your anger, which just means don't hold grudges. And I would add not to get mad over stupid stuff."

"Well, what do we do?" Rico asked again, looking at Kim.

Kim swallowed, running her hand over the large beige beads covering the passenger seat. It had happened again. They were all looking at her, like they needed her guidance of all things.

"Mmm," she offered.

Give me the words, Lord, she prayed. *Please don't allow me to lead us astray. Let us rely completely on You and Your wisdom.*

"Well," she began, "we study more and pray more. We ask God to reveal things to us. He said that He'd make our enemies our footstool and I believe Him! I'm gonna ask Him to fulfill His promise. I mean, y'all, this isn't your run-of-the-mill Hardy Boys situation."

"Or Encyclopedia Brown," Coda spoke.

"Or Encyclopedia Brown."

"Or Cam Jansen."

Kim sighed. "Now's not the time, Coda. Focus, here."

"Sorry, *menina.*"

"We are not fighting against 'Hollow Boy' or 'Solitaire' or the 'creature' when we face off against them. We're being used by God to fight the evil powers of this world. So don't think we're fighting alone. We've got angels fighting right alongside." A yawn came to her and she surrendered, knowing that it spoiled the affect of her speech.

"Darn it," she said, glancing at her cell phone. "It's four o'clock in the morning. I'm leaving for school in three hours, so I'd better get home. I still haven't taken down those New Year's decorations and if I don't attend to that, my mom will attend to my behind."

She began to put her gloves on, but the words kept coming to her.

"We need to communicate. The devil is the author of confusion. That's why most of our problems as people, human beings, are communication issues, especially with our families. If we don't communicate, the devil will infiltrate."

Renata moved her lips absentmindedly, noting the words. "If we don't communicate, the devil will infiltrate."

"We need to let each other know that we're there for each other and that we will try to help in whatever way we can. We need to visit each other. Email, call, and deal with each other and put up with each other. God placed us together for a reason and Jesus said that what God has placed together, let no man put asunder. Though I think He was talking about marriage there."

"He was," Justus nodded.

"But it applies. And don't just communicate with each other. Remember, this isn't Captain Planet and the Planeteers. This is God and His disciples. So feel free to talk to Him, too." Kim looked around at their handsome faces. "Let's do this thing, y'all," she said softly. "Let's do this thing."

"Let's do it!" Coda cheered, and they all joined in, Ezekiel more-or-less so, before Rico quieted them, saying that they might wake his mother.

Renata spoke up once more. "You guys see that haze in the car?"

As the gifted ones glanced around the car, they noticed she was correct. It seemed as if a fog had settled in the car only. Perhaps a sacred Spirit, made manifest to their eyes.

"Where two or three gather in My name..." Coda murmured.

"No," Rico shook his head. "That's just Justus's rank gas."

The girls grabbed their noses while Justus said proudly, "I couldn't have timed that any better."

"I think I swallowed it," Ezekiel said, making a face as Renata gagged.

As they all poured out of the car in laughter, Renata made quick rounds to say goodnight to them all, before hurrying towards the house to get out of the chill.

Rico pulled Ezekiel to the side. "I should apologize to Coda, huh?"

"He already forgave you," Ezekiel said, watching Renata thoughtfully. His eyes eventually met Rico's. "Still, I guess it would be a nice gesture."

"Yeah," Rico said, trailing off, lost in his own thoughts as Ezekiel travailed in the thoughts of others.

"Goodnight, Kim-burly," Coda said to the pixie, who gave him the most amazing hug he thought he had ever received in his life. Their bodies melted together as she pulled him in close to him. He felt soothed. Loved. A tear left the corner of an eye and Kim was forgiven.

She whispered in his ear, "I miss Dishon."

Coda frowned, but she couldn't see it. When they pulled apart, he quickly wiped his eye and turned to stare at the stars.

She turned to Justus. "Praying man."

Justus raised his eyebrows slightly. "Yeah?"

"Send up some special talks for me, okay? I'm not a whole lot of hero."

Kim waved to the rest of them and headed towards her father's truck. The boys exchanged handshake/hug combinations, high-fives and holy kisses, and they all returned peacefully to their respective abodes.

From a beneath a palm tree in a neighboring yard, a hooded figure stood, usually a glimmer of white and ebony, but tonight a subdued shadow, silently watching them depart.

19.
Purple Roses

And lest I should be exalted above measure through the abundance of the revelations, there was given to me a thorn in the flesh, the messenger of Satan to buffet me, lest I should be exalted above measure. For this thing I besought the Lord thrice, that it might depart from me. And He said unto me, My grace is sufficient for thee: for My strength is made perfect in weakness. Most gladly therefore will I rather glory in my infirmities, that the power of Christ may rest upon me. Therefore I take pleasure in infirmities, in reproaches, in necessities, in persecutions, in distresses for Christ's sake: for when I am weak, then am I strong.
> – 2 Corinthians 12:7-10

If we live in the Spirit, let us also walk in the Spirit.
> – Galatians 5:25

Coda's vision was red, while violet, amethyst and wisteria rose petals rained down on the KWA Auditorium steps. *The night wasn't supposed to be like this,* he thought as he plunged the thorny stems of the bouquet that was meant for Kim into his opponent's face.

The Miss Wilbanks Pageant had already begun, and there was a possibility that Kim's replacement had already crossed the stage. Not that Coda cared about some senior prep. His heart was with the incumbent. His fists, however, were still in this strange parallel universe of the past few months that saw him battling unknown adversaries like a comic book character.

Hollow had come out of nowhere, as if having followed Coda to the high school knowing that the boy would be running so late that he'd be alone outside in the dark.

Worst of all, Coda was losing.

Hollow was as agile as he was, crawling across Coda's back as if manipulated by Andy Serkis, gripping him from beneath his armpits and setting Coda's balance on a tilt. Coda's feet lifted in front of him as his shoulders were pulled down. Hollow used his handy trick of disappearing into the ground, leaving Coda to meet the dirt as if it were concrete.

His head felt like it had been jackhammered—as if cracking his skull would actually alleviate the pain. On top of that, his clothes were ruined. It was his last decent outfit, red stitching in the slacks matching the vibrant crimson shirt detailed with Chinese dragons along the now-ripping seams.

Hollow was on top of him now, punching him in the face while using his legs on Coda's sides like a nutcracker. Coda managed to grab the pale one's right arm, twisting it and flipping him. Using the momentum he created, Coda stood and stomped Hollow's ribs with his dress shoes. Hollow, almost seeming to not feel any pain, grabbed the arm that Coda held him with, bringing him forward until their skulls connected.

Stumbling, Coda whipped the roses across Hollow's face before falling onto his butt next to him.

As if replicating the quality of the stems, thorns sprouted from Hollow's knuckles, and he slammed his prickly fist into Coda's chest.

Grimacing, Coda thought, *Kimberly Hamilton. The things I go through for you.*

He should have just stayed home.

Next to him, Hollow suddenly went rigid. As Coda turned to look, Hollow's shoulders were pulled at an unnatural angle, before a silver boot tagged him in the back of his head. As the dreadlocked one rolled away in agony, and Coda looked up in apprehension.

It was as if the figure was a shadow of light, moving just as slickly and undercover as if it wasn't robed in ivory. It stood Coda up and pointed a silver glove as if to tell him to go.

Hollow was rising, however, and Coda felt like this battle was his to turn. He ignored the strange robed figure and rushed towards Hollow. Within moments, he was on the ground again. The figure had grabbed Coda's foot and tugged him backwards. By the time Coda could get his bearings, the Silver Sentry was in deep fisticuffs with Hollow, boxing Hollow's ears with its elbows before slamming them into Hollow's shoulders. It then brought a single elbow up into Hollow's nose, and blood began to flow.

It was fast, yet methodical, as it seemed to be working its way through each region of Hollow's body—smashing, snapping and denting. Its blows were all the more affecting, it seemed, due to the silver armor that kept appearing from beneath the flowing robe. Hollow struggled to get away almost comically, reminding Coda of a professional wrestler. The sentry just grabbed Hollow's hair, pulling him back in for a continued beating.

Why wasn't Hollow pulling his disappearing thing? Coda took a quick look around and, catching his breath, he realized that the Silver Sentry wasn't alone. There was one in white and green, hands raised towards the battle, hood pulled down so far that Coda wondered if it could see through it. This sentry seemed to be preventing Hollow from going anywhere with some kind of force field.

Oh crap. Maybe that's why the Silver Sentry had told Coda to get out when it did. Coda realized he couldn't get off of the ground at all. The best he could do was turn his head, and when he turned it back to the two alabaster adversaries, Hollow lay in a crumpled heap near the Silver Sentry's boots.

Both of the Sentries had turned their gazes to him. Crap, again.

The Silver Sentry raised its hand to point once more, and, again feeling the use of his extremities, Coda rose quickly.

"Are you guys angels?" he asked breathlessly.

The Emerald Sentry swung its arms wide, and a gust of wind knocked Coda back a few steps. He realized that he no longer cared for an answer.

His teammates on the cross country team would have been proud of him. He had never ran so fast in his life.

· · · · · ·

She liked to think of it often. The strong arms that could be rough at the same time that they were gentle and how they would grab her as if she belonged there and nowhere else. She didn't have to be strong. He was her strength.

He had walked into class on the first day and caught her attention immediately. He had long hair, but it wasn't girly, and he had the eyebrows of an animal. This was a man. He wasn't a whiny high-schooler;

he wasn't a male constantly trying to prove his manhood to cover up his insecurities. His insecurities proved his manhood.

He was trying to be cool, and she naturally assumed the dorky role. She wanted to know his name. She wanted his attention. He wanted her to have his number. He was so smooth with giving it; she loved it.

"Dishon." His name was in the Bible, she remembered. She hadn't been able to find it, but she promised him that she would. That was all before the rest of the saga…

The first time they danced together was quite spicy. They were both at Peaches, the hangout for kids attending Clark Atlanta. The former club of choice for all of the college students was The Card Shop, but too many toothpick-chewing old men, bald heads covered in wide-brimmed straw hats, scamming on fresh flesh sent the crowd searching for a new spot, and the forefathers hadn't yet discovered it was Peaches. There were other clubs, like Volume Six, which catered to the older crowd, and The Alley Cat, which had become so much like The Sex Kitten strip club/book and video store, that both places were avoided by the more pristine demographic that was the non-admitted majority.

Peaches was the spot, so she wasn't surprised to run into Dishon there two weekends after that night his crew had picked her up outside the corner store.

He was wearing a sweatshirt broadcasting some popular name brand worn by aristocratic Black folk. It was worn out of pride, not vanity, though she admitted that there was a thin line. Upon glimpsing him gazing at her, she began to wish that she had gotten her hair rebraided sooner; she was scheduled to have it done the next day, right after church, if she ended up going. She knew she was cute that night, though. She had on some jeans, white sneakers, and a short-sleeved green, blue, black, and white shirt. By adding a white belt that had green strings handing from it, she was almost doing too much, but she had caught his attention.

She walked over to him, chaffing him in her irresistible and annoying way. She wanted him to know that she was interested. He asked her why she hadn't called him; what could she say? He asked her to dance, and he was a gentleman. They got down, grooving like Jesus was right around the corner and they'd never be able to be wicked again. Nothing was old, back then. She loved that boy. Still did.

Life was good, she liked to tell herself. His strength was her comfort. Her strength she tended to ignore. She was a college girl. Her power connected her to the people she spent high school with, and she wasn't there. Anymore. Many times she didn't want to be there, then other times she missed Maya and Coda.

She still thought of Coda and Maya as her best friends, but now she had a new crop. Franklin Griffin was a boy her size, with light skin and light brown eyes that he professed were his real color. Sometimes he had a tiny Afro and sometimes he had tiny twists, but his mean sense of humor was permanent. Exactly how Frankie, Dishon, and "Kimi" as they called her, became a tight unit was alien to her, they just were. Coda and Maya were jealous, she knew. They wouldn't admit it, but they were, she felt it in her bones. High school hadn't allowed them to go through the things Frankie, Dishon and she had.

Clark Atlanta. She loved being the only person from "Brunswick and the Golden Isles" to be at that school. Not that she wanted to reinvent herself for college, just that she wanted to distance herself from high school. Sometimes she attempted to connect the two lives, but the results weren't always good. When there was a break during the fall semester, Dishon and Frankie had accompanied her back home. Dr. and Mrs. Hamilton weren't so sure that it was a good idea to have the boys journey with their daughter across such long distances. Sure, her parents were decent enough to their guests…maybe she didn't *want* them to be so accepting. Maybe she had wanted some controversy. Well, whatever they didn't give her, dramatic Coda-da sure made up for it.

It was only so crazy. Coda had invited her over to give her a belated birthday present, which he actually had ready for her before she left in August, but they kept missing each other and she left for college without it. They agreed that on that particular Saturday, months later, they would get together and she'd pick it up. He had later insisted, quite adamantly, that she hadn't told him a thing about having guests in town, and his only clue was when he had called her that afternoon and she said that "they" were on the way. When he opened the door, she felt it. Tension. She bravely gave a bright hello, yet he kept repeating the anti-gospel that she had brought "boys" over his house. If it wasn't for his sister, Cheyenne, pointing out his rudeness, his dismay would have kept them outside on the porch. The tension. When he asked which one of them she was dating, they all just grinned. She wasn't going to let him jump to conclusions, no matter how correct they might have been. He let it go for the moment, and gave her the present he had prepared for her: a self-illustrated homemade book that displayed the lyrics to a beautiful Stevie Wonder song. He also gave her a book on "I Love Lucy," and bouquet of teeny-tiny purple fabric roses, which she accidentally left at his place. He never apologized for his behavior, not that she expected him to.

On the trip back to Atlanta, they had stopped at a restaurant across the street from a gigantic mural, full of the most vibrant colors. Kim had several minutes to spare while the boys visited the restroom, so she stepped out of the restaurant and crossed the empty street. Shivering in the cold, she stared at that mural wishing that she could take a picture.

Purple roses came in the mail. A shabby Christmas card bought on a struggling collegian's budget, along with a teeny-tiny fabric rose. She smiled when she got it.

She had spent Christmas missing Dishon, wishing he was under her tree instead of the wrapped clothes. She was at the house with Dr. and Mrs. Hamilton, and Azari came with his fiancée, Autumn, and surly Shirley came with her husband and their brats. Ah, the holidays. She was ready to pull her hair out. It was made a bit better by a drop-in from Ezekiel.

So, Ezekiel was nice. A very nice guy. Sure, he was Asian, but he was nice. Not that she'd ever think of him that way. It's just that her mind would jump around, and she'd start thinking like Maya, correcting herself as if she had misinterpreted herself. She knew what she meant. She liked Ezekiel because he was a good person. She could say that she liked him. It was only so chill. He was dressed like he always dressed. Khaki pants, a white long-sleeved t-shirt, stylish brown tennis, and a blue jacket with some random insignia. It was before the car jam, and they talked about everything and came up with nothing. So she gave him a snack cake and he was on his way. They were accomplices in this venture, though not willingly—not to say that they wouldn't be happy working together, just that they were put in this strange situation without knowledge of the reason. But at least now they knew who had put them there.

Ezekiel had felt that perhaps they were looking in all the wrong places for their clues. He also mentioned that at Shannon's party, with so many people in attendance, "like, someone must have seen something." "Like." Ezekiel said "like" a lot.

In her spare time back at Clark, she'd do bench presses with her bed piled high with all the contents of her room. Her roommate was never in. That was a fact she could count on ever since her first weekend at Clark Atlanta, when her roommate disappeared early one morning and didn't show up till four days later, without even attempting to offer any type of explanation. With the recurrent freedom, Kim would bench-press her sofa, and do calf raises while carrying her recliner on her back. She was toning her body beautifully, yet she felt that her *life* should be changing more. She was super-strong, but what did that mean to her on the real? On a day-to-day basis? She didn't quite know. And if she didn't know what it meant to her, she didn't know what it meant to the world.

Frankie would call sometimes to see if she wanted to go shopping. Sure, sometimes she had to study, but most other times she said yes. She liked having something to do. Something else to think about. They'd go and shop together, lunch together, laugh together. Somebody lend that girl a quarter to buy a clue. Do these shoes come in brown? Are you hungry? You see that outfit? I must have it! There was always something else to think about.

They both worked at a nicely styled sit-down restaurant. A steak, shrimp, and bread roll type of place. She was the hostess and Frankie cooked. Dishon worked there sometimes. She was praying for him, really praying for him. She loved him. She would smile while remembering how upset Frankie and she had gotten with the news that their friends, like Stasia and Nicholas, felt that they (Dishon, Frankie and she) kept excluding the rest of the "group." There was no "group!" It was just Frankie, Kimi, and Dishon. That's all it had been, that's all it ever would be. When the saga began, it was just Frankie, Kimi, and Dishon. When Dishon got kicked out of school for gambling—who knew it was a seriously enforced misdemeanor at Clark Atlanta?—it was just Frankie, Kimi, and Dishon. When Dishon got thrown in jail, it was just Frankie, Kimi, and Dishon. The only time there was a "group" was when either marijuana, alcohol or money was involved. That's no group. If she had asked Stasia or Nicholas to pray for her, they wouldn't do it. They wouldn't even know what to pray for.

Purple roses came in the mail. A few scriptures on a card and two purple fabric roses in the seal. She had friends praying for her.

Her mother knew all about Kim's dancing. (*Why were parents right about everything?*) Her father would flip if he knew. Her tongue was pierced, she was an inch taller, and her breasts were larger. She was a different person. She didn't know. Maybe she was the same.

She kept rereading the Biblical story of Samson and Delilah. She wanted to see the mistakes that he made. What caused him to fall? Beyond Delilah...it was beyond Delilah. What was the true source of his strength—"Why hair?" she always asked—and what made God give it back? She wondered. To know his true strength would be to know his true weakness. Whenever she went to church, it was in hopes to get some more answers. Anything, a word, a phrase, a message that would enlighten her as far as God's will.

Most Sundays she went to Curly's church. She called Azari "Curly" now, in honor of his hair, and in reference of her new nickname of

"Burly," and her long-standing name for Shirley. It seemed appropriate: Surly, Curly, and Burly. Like Goldilocks's three bears. She didn't even know if the three bears had names.

It was a long drive from the Clark Atlanta campus to her brother's church, and she generally made the trip with Frankie, but one particularly rare morning, she borrowed his tiny car and journeyed by herself. His car reminded her of her old car. She missed that car.

Curly preached a sermon. "Ergo, Forgo the Ego." He preached that sermon. He had a way of jumping and leaping up and down like he had bouncy balls in his soles. He was so skinny. Like Coda. Like Dishon would be too if he didn't have that home gym. It was a phenomenal message. Sometimes God puts people in situations for them to see how dependent they are on him, and so they can show Him how humble and righteous they are.

Azari asked, "Are you so high and mighty that you can't PRAY? And when did faith become lazy? Lazy is for losers and I'm a winning warrior. Can't entertain laziness. I gotta punch that clock and get my faith hustle on. And arrogance tells me I'm above having to get my hands dirty. Arrogance, ego tells me that I need a desk job at the faith corporation. Maybe I can be an executive at Faith Co. Let me break it down for you. Ain't no executive sinking rocks into Goliath's skull. Ain't no executive walking on dry land out of Egypt. Hello, church! Ergo, *forgo the ego!*"

• • • • •

"Curly Bear," Kim sang out.

"Burly Bear," her brother responded, reaching up to her. "You had some questions about Dr. Stone's book?"

Kim plopped down on the rug next to Azari amidst his sermon notes. "Brother, this man says a lot of borderline crazy things."

Azari nodded, smiling wisely. "I know."

Kim read aloud, "'What keeps us from laying hands on that angel?' She glanced to her brother. "Umm, probably because angels are spirits and holy. Why would I get physical with one? And if he's being metaphorical, why can't I tell? I mean, I get his point about settling for less, but he's a little... extremist, wouldn't you say?"

"Discern, Kim. What is backed up by scripture, and what are just the ravings of a mad professor?"

Kim ginned. "I know all about mad professors."

"Exactly! What are the things you retain simply to pass, and then what are the things you retain for life?" Azari looked off as if into his memories.

"The one line I'll never forget from that book is 'Why don't we follow David's example and take off the king's armor in order to stand in the King's glory?'"

Kim flipped a few pages. "I don't think I've gotten there yet. He's still talking about whooping the behinds of angels."

Azari laughed. "Look at the life-context, Kim. In your unique position of being gifted with a strength similar to Samson, you are going to take some of Dr. Stone's words more literal than, say, our parents and our sister would."

Kim nodded. "True."

"And I've met Dr. Stone," Azari added. "He meant every word literally. But maybe his life-context is much different than yours and mine."

Kim was surprised. "Wayment! You've met him? Is he like, the theological Cornel West?"

Azari sighed. "These days he's considered a radical. But once upon a time, his possibilities of effecting change were quite… Well, John Singleton made Boyz in the Hood *once, right? And since then…"*

Kim nodded. "Wasted potential."

"Misguided output," Azari amended. "You can do revolutionary things. But the scale can be increased or decreased depending on thoughts and guidance. Stay in The Book. That's the meal. This other book is just a bag of chips. A bag of highly recommended and not necessarily terrible for you chips."

"I'm hungry now!" Kim whined, grabbing her stomach.

"Let's go eat!" her brother exclaimed, bounding from the rug.

Kim was happy to oblige. "Something more filling than a bag of chips," she said hopefully.

• • • • •

Kim's classes kept her hopping. They were only so intense. Her history teacher, bow-tie wearing Professor Jabar, was intently Islamic, like Malcolm before he went to Mecca, and seemed to believed the Black race was superior to all other races. Ironically, her public speaking class professor was only as boring as Frankie's love life, and her music appreciation class included only one other student. Introduction to Theatre was not the golden hill she had dreamt it to be. She only hated it. Pure hatred. She had never felt so misunderstood in her life. She didn't get the teacher's references, she didn't understand why she was constantly singled out, and she didn't see why they had to do things the teacher's exact way. She had approached the teacher many times in an effort to "rectify the situation" like her parents had recommended. Many times that class made her cry on Dishon's shoulder. Maybe she wouldn't become anything that had anything to do with being an actress or reading lines or even standing on stage. Maybe she'd switch her major to aerospace engineering like Ezekiel. If Clark Atlanta had aerospace engineering.

So Stasia's car, the one Nicholas always seemed to be driving, broke down one day. A trivial situation that should have stayed trivial, but the next thing everyone knew, whenever Stasia needed to go somewhere, she'd ask Frankie to take her. Dishon didn't have a car. He had his hands full paying rent on the apartment that he shared with Nicholas and buying whatever drugs he wanted. Frankie, however, didn't appreciate Stasia's appreciations, and one day refused to take her to work. So, it was only the seventh day that she missed of work when she was supposed to go in, and the Dynasty Dog fired her. Then, she had trouble finding another job, even though Frankie decided he would chauffeur her finally. And she lost some scholarships and couldn't afford student housing, and then she had to find an apartment, so she kept asking Kim to move in with her. Kim recommended the company of Leeza Marcus. Kim was not gonna live with Stasia if she could help it. Stasia liked boys too much.

She and Dishon had gone on a little date later that week. They dressed up and it was only so spicy. Professor Jabar had assigned the class to go see some Gael García Bernal picture, so they made the best of the situation. It was the walk back to her dorm that was bad. They argued about their situation and the level of their love and she found herself emotionally wounded. Once he left, she popped in a Whitney Houston CD, wished that she had a tub of strawberry mint ice cream, and buckled down.

There was a fabric rose in the book that Coda had made. A teeny-tiny purple rose.

Maya had gotten Kim hooked on an online journal website, and only everybody was on there, including Rico, BJ, Coda, and even Gene. It was supposed to be a simple way of keeping in contact with everybody. The only issue was the "journal" aspect, where people wrote their innermost thoughts and feelings and activities, and other people got hurt. Or disgusted. But it was nice to see how everyone was doing, especially Maya, who loved her college more than anybody else seemed to.

They had met years ago in middle school, where Kim was the freaky tiny girl with glasses and big-time stage presence, who only hung out with white girls. Maya was the freaky Amazonian cheerleader who was from New York City and loved being half Puerto Rican and only hung out with white girls. They both knew of each other, but one dork had never met the other. Then in the eighth grade they both made the cheerleading squad, and their legendary unbreakable bond was formed. She knew that they were growing apart, now. They were both expanding their horizons by drinking, partying, and such, but they weren't experiencing the changes together, causing skewed views on how the other was changing.

One weekend in early February, she had to make a trip back to Brunswick for the Miss KWA pageant. As the holder of the crown, it was her job to co-host with the previous year's winner as well as to pass on the crown to the new recipient. She was only so hyped, because she had gotten a random call from her drama-bosom-buddy, Terry Bozzo, who had asked her when the pageant was. Out of the blue, a muy interesante call. He wanted to know how she was doing, how everybody was doing, where she was, was she enjoying it… It was so sweet, and it was like finally pouring in the sugar with the rest of the pinch of salt. Suddenly life was bigger and sweeter than the negativity she found herself sometimes bogged in. So Terry was back in town for a few, and he and Coda were planning on coming to see her, and she got so excited. In her I'm-about-to-give-up-the-crown speech (which some of those chickenheads on that stage had the nerve to rush her on), she even gave Terry and Coda a shout out. Afterwards, only Terry was there. Coda hadn't even shown up.

One by one they were all losing faith in her.

Did she believe that? She didn't believe that. She wanted to believe that. Maybe she was hoping it was so, so that she could excuse herself when God asked her why she hadn't treated herself better. Now she knew what those overly dressed ladies who gave testimonies in church meant when they said that "He's been better to me than I could *ever* be to myself." And now when they said it, she could join in with the congregation's majority in saying amen. Amen.

Sometimes she hated it. Why did everyone have to care so much? Frankie thought that she got caught up in the wrong things and much too deeply, Maya thought she was moving too fast and for the wrong reasons and that Frankie was gay, Coda thought that Dishon was all wrong for her but not in a way that would make him seem jealous he hoped, and Dishon thought she thought too much of what everyone else was thinking while pretending she didn't care. Kim thought they were all wrong, and hated the fact that she thought about it so much. She was an individual. They did not make her. They didn't even know her.

Purple roses came in the mail, combined with a letter. She cried.

Dear Dyna-na,

Sorry I missed speaking with you at the pageant. I was there, contrary to what Terry and you believe, but you'll recognize my excuse: Hollow. Something was weird around the campus and I got caught up. I swear I'm being stalked. AnTways…

I saw some pics online. You looked crazy beautiful in the green. A pretty flytastic choice.

What's happening to us? Are we still friends? If it wasn't for the C. nights, would we even talk as much as we do now?

Well looky here. I usually never run out of anything to say. Enjoy the pictures, mi cielo,

Coda-da

Drama. Sometimes she wondered if it was a class or a way of life.

20.

Jacuzzi

...Mr. Flint, whose name implies the later-proven fact that his heart is stone cold...

Justus Alexander was writing complete crap. Off the top of his head it was coming and into his laptop he would type it. He had a "periodical" due for that class about the novel that they were studying and he hadn't completely finished the assigned chapters. It was seven-thirty in the morning and English 1102 began at eight-fifteen at Mercer University. Previous situations similar to his current predicament ensured that he could skim enough to come up with an "A" essay. Of course, he didn't consider it crap; it just wasn't his best. He wasn't challenging himself.

His flecked hazel eyes were coolly fixed on the computer screen. His peach lips were slightly parted, as if they should've been mouthing the same words that his fingers were typing. He glanced down at the problematic novel in his lap, bit the inside of his bottom lip, and then glanced back up at the computer screen. He still had to put on some clothes; he was wearing the same royal blue shorts that he had worn to work the night before.

"Admonishment? Admonition?" he vocalized in an attempt to find the right word. He bit his lip again and scratched his ribs, fingers sinking into the softness of his flesh. "Exhortation."

That last sentence capped it nicely. If it hadn't been for Mrs. Donahue's timed writing drills his senior year, he didn't know how well he'd be faring in this college course. He instructed the computer to print.

Brushing his golden-red hair out of his eyes and making a mental note to stop at the barber's first thing when he got back to Brunswick for spring break before his grandparents would fuss, Justus glanced at the digital alarm on the floor in front of the dressers that framed the mirror. Eight-zip-five. Perfect.

Justus stood up from his computer and stretched a long, grunt-worthy stretch. His dorm was empty; well, even excluding his sleeping roommate, to say that his room was empty was not quite correct.

Clothes, appliances, papers, and trivial things like cans of shaving cream were scattered all across the room from the door to the back wall, not to mention all over the floor: their shared vanity, the table that housed Justus's laptop, the huge dresser, and the closet and bunk beds that were across from the dresser. Save the tiny walkway from the door to directly in front of the television at the foot of the bunk beds, there was no floor space. The pile of video game equipment and CD players and DVD players piled up right along with the clothes atop the ten-foot-long dresser and led to a green poster hanging on the wall that read "When the chips are down, the buffalo's empty." There was a tasteless illustration accompanying the quote. His mother had practically fainted when she saw the way he was living during her visit the previous semester.

Justus crossed the room and grabbed a sky blue shirt off the top of the dirty clothes hamper that he shared with his roommate. He dug under a pile of clothes that seemed to have materialized overnight in order to find his flip-flops. Slipping into his shoes, he smoothed the shirt down over his skin and took a few seconds to stare at the slight pooch leaning on the shorts he was wearing. Was it getting smaller? He shouldn't have eaten that last slice of pizza the night before.

Turning his attention away from his one-pack, Justus grabbed the newly printed pages that were only going to be important for the next twelve minutes and slid them into his one-strap backpack.

He glanced nervously towards the bunk above his, listening for his roommate's light snores. Content with the sound, Justus began to focus.

Mind over body over mind, he reminded himself. He never knew which muscle would start first, but there'd be a chain reaction to follow. This particular time, there was a twitch in his thigh.

Okay, he struggled. *Liquid*.

His legs exploded into gas, and Justus involuntarily kicked his flight into gear. As his head smacked into the ceiling, his roommate grunted and adjusted himself in the bed. Justus froze, listening intently while trying to ignore the throbbing coming from directly above his ear. Hearing the return of the slight snores, Justus returned to the complication at hand. He had to focus the energy. That's what Rico had recommended after Ezekiel had pulled him out of the sky months before. Rico should know. Their powers were similar. They were elementals.

Focus the energy. Just like the ShowChoir days…when he and Terry and everyone else would be joking and playing around before the show, either Coda or Bethany Kelly would holler above the cacophony, "Focus the energy!" So he did. The gas had to be made liquid. He watched as balls of liquid started to form in the air around the door. He began to pull them into him.

He didn't quite understand how his gift worked, but he equated it to bodybuilders who could isolate and move specific muscles, like the dudes who could bounce their pecs. The H_2O *was* him, even if it was gas. He could always feel it, sense it, because he was it. Or it was he. As if proper language mattered.

He felt like he was pulling his knees into his chest. The water droplets hit his shirt and it happened. His body liquefied, clothes included, but that wasn't his finale. Flesh. He had to become flesh.

He glanced at the clock. He knew this was taking too long, but he hadn't expected half of his body to burst into gas. He had created a trick that would clean him and his clothes at the same time. When his body had turned completely to water, the dirt that had accumulated during the day would not turn to water, nor the extra oils he had procured during his daily activities, so right before he'd change back to his original form, (he didn't say natural, because he figured that with God, the line between the natural and the supernatural was one that humans couldn't quite see) he would maneuver all of the nastiness to the center of his liquid fist. When he was flesh, he'd release his fingers and wash all of the gook off his palm. His clothes would be clean and his body would be cleaner than any bath or shower could ever make him. It was supposed to be a quick thing—the clock read eight-thirteen!

All calm was lost. He burst into gas from top to bottom.

Everything immediately succeeding that was considerably murky. He remembered racing down the hallway and across the street and into Willingham Hall and into the bathroom.

What the heck! Justus stood there for a moment, attempting to catch his breath, unsure of what had just occurred. He couldn't remember when his trick had ever gone so wrong.

He glanced into the mirror, and sure enough, his hair had changed color, back to that odd, yet peculiarly handsome blackish-purple, which in turn turned his eyes to a forest green. "Hydroxygen returns," he muttered with a smile.

• • • • •

Hydroxygen was the name of somebody's superhero, superhero being Rico's new favorite word, but Justus certainly didn't often feel like one. Superheroes, first of all, should have attitudes like Coda, all outgoing and happy and prudish at the same time. They should have bodies like

Shannon Crescitelli. Shannon had a lifeguard's body, or maybe a Roman soldier, or something similarly iconic. Because of the way Shannon was built, he could do the most ridiculous things and make it look masculine and powerful. From a ping-pong stroke to a swimming stroke, or from dancing the salsa with Eden to dancing dirty with Maya, every move was confident, even if Shannon himself was not. Justus, on the other hand, would feel comfortable while he did something, and then look back on it disconcertedly.

Once, the summer before, he had taken Coda over Shannon's house for a "friendly" game of ERS, and Lena Park's popular debut jam came on over the radio. Justus got up from the table and began to boogie. Coda shook his head, something between a frown and a smile latched tightly onto his face, while Shannon just sat there with raised eyebrows. It was not the effect he was looking for. Later, Shannon announced his plans to go running and Coda remembered other plans he had made for that particularly hot July afternoon, so they decided to part ways. Leaving his shirt inside, and escorting them to Justus's car in bare feet, Shannon found a long switch in the front yard, and proceeded to whip it around in the air with an insane grin stretching his face. It was ridiculous, but watching Shannon do it, Justus couldn't help noticing that he made it masculine. And powerful. And Coda was laughing, which was more than he had achieved. So Shannon should be the superhero.

Plus he had that darn thing with dogs. Justus had been afraid of dogs for as long as he could remember, and there was no shaking it. It took him two years before he would even attempt to pet Poopsie or Jennifer, his Granny's pets, and then it took another two years before he realized that if they wanted to eat him, they would have done it long before. But if Hydroxygen came face to face with a nefarious dog, he'd wet the lawn in a different way.

Oh, and superheroes should be able to fight! Rico knew how to box, Coda and Ezekiel had taken up karate in college, and if Justus believed the stories, Coda used to fight all the time before he moved to Brunswick. Even Kim knew kickboxing. The last time Justus laid a violent hand on someone, he had been in diapers and just wanted his stuffed dolphin back.

Superheroes should have all the time in the world, and he couldn't think of a single example of somebody who had all the time in the world that wasn't unemployed. Justus himself not only had school (which takes up about seventy-five percent of one's life), but he played catcher for an intramural softball team, worked at a school office and attempted to have some free time on top of that. And maybe sleep deep and dream-lessly every now and then.

After he'd heard the fullness about Kim's crash, Justus's dreams went to other places. Flying in clouds above snowy mountain ranges, driving buses, running through jungles, many things he did not understand. However, the dreams didn't disturb him much these days. He was a college student; he hardly slept anymore.

· · · · ·

Walking out of the bathroom into the hall, Justus bumped into a hair tree.

"Sorry," he trilled, thrown off-balance.

"Justus!" greeted Maggie St. John, purposely oblivious to Justus's display of amateur acrobatics.

Maggie was a subconsciously beautiful young woman with a build out of an Archie comic: long limbs, slender yet squared shoulders, and a thin nose that waited till its tip to extend away from her face. Her mop-like brown hair had recently been cut into the shape of a bowl, albeit a shaggy one. Her face held a small mouth and sandy brown eyes that were staring at him without a trace of widespread suspicion.

"What's up, Maggie?" he squeaked, righting himself at last. He realized that he had left his backpack lying on the carpet in his dorm, right in front of the door. His periodical was in his backpack.

Justus froze. That meant that he had flown through his door! In his gassy state, he must have filtered through his dorm room door, as well as the cracks in the windows at the end of the hall on his floor, and soared through the air, materializing in Willingham Hall's bathroom. He hadn't raced there after all. What had he gotten himself into? What had God gotten him into?

"You dyed your hair!"

"Huh?" Justus came back to the scene at hand. "Oh, yeah. It was on a dare."

"Oh, yeah? Who dared you to do it?"

"Nobody, really." He flashed a wide, cheesy grin before removing all traces that a smile had ever been there. "It'll be back to normal tomorrow."

"Oh," she said, and proceeded to exuberantly relay a story about what happened on some teen soap the night before.

Justus had been to a few of the soap-loving get-togethers Maggie and her girlfriends held every Tuesday, and the effect was quite phenomenal. The girls all knew character's middle names and former places of residence. They knew who should be together versus who *would* be together, and they loved each cliffhanger as if it was completely unexpected. It was easy for Justus to get caught up in the hoopla in such cases, and he found himself asking the girls the next week about whether Jamie had hooked up with John, and if Jessica took Jack back. He asked them once, and only once, about whether or not they'd considered the fact that if the ratings were down and the show was cancelled, it could possibly be their fault for watching as a group. He hadn't been asked back since.

They entered the room that housed their English course and took their places on the desks against the wall beneath the large windows. The English classroom was arranged into one big ring, which Justus still hadn't figured the purpose for. Four large tables connected to make a digital zero, while the actual desks flanked the outer walls. It's not like Professor Sanford stood in the center of them all and rotated around to face everyone; at times she'd place her lectern directly against the foremost table, and lecture from there, but for the most part, she'd actually sit at the makeshift "round"-table.

She entered: a frazzled mass of well-styled old school curls, papers, books, and suitcases, followed by an unwilling assistant in a pink fraternity shirt, just as loaded down as the professor.

"Hi, hi," she spoke with her naturally soft voice. Justus liked the days that she'd get passionate and cuss a little. Such words coming from such a voice box: pure entertainment.

As Professor Sanford got settled in, Justus slid Maggie's book between them, to make it less obvious that he was completely unprepared for the class. He remembered a day during senior year that the majority of Mrs. Donahue's second period class hadn't done the assigned readings, and Mrs. Donahue had abandoned all hope—and all students—and left the classroom in an attempt to find her daily passion once more. It wasn't a great feeling to be the cause of that type of emotional reaction.

"Okay," Professor Sanford's susurrations began. "Harriet Jacobs writing as Linda Brent. We'll get to *Incidents in the Life of a Slave Girl* in just a moment, but if you could, go ahead and pass last evening's periodicals to your left and I'll collect them."

Justus smiled lightly and rearranged his now dark eyebrows with his forehead muscles in an attempt to look casual and indifferent.

"I have some tissue," Maggie whispered, as she received and passed a collection of papers down the table.

"What?" he asked, looking at her. It was at moments like those, when his face was blank and his mouth was closed, that he looked like he could be a model for Abercrombie and Finch. Well, Eden Enamorado had told him that once, so he used that look to his advantage.

"Do you have to sneeze?"

Justus grimaced lightly. "No."

"Oh," she said, and turned back to Professor Sanford.

"Now," the professor was saying, "there's a speaker coming to the school…well, that was yesterday, so never mind." Professor Sanford set the reminder to the side.

"Well," she spoke again, glancing around the tables, "I was going to quiz you all on this recent reading, but it seems that I ran out of time to come up with one, so we'll dialogue instead, shall we?"

Justus hated when people threw "shall we" on the end of sentences, as if the receiving party actually had a say. He sat back in his chair, content to let Professor Sanford recite a monologue while he pretended to pay attention, like Pink Fraternity Shirt did every day.

Professor Sanford wriggled her fingers as if she was preparing to feast on her seven-year old copy of the literature at hand. Her book was full of neon page markers, scribbles, inserted cards, and highlighted passages. If made Justus think of a different Literature teacher from high school, and from there, his mind did not cease to wander.

• • • • •

Political Science: Poly Sci. Professor Charles Henderson. Nietzsche's theories. Not boring.

The purity with which Professor Henderson was presenting Nietzsche's argument was grating.

As much as Justus respected a clear-cut presentation, whenever the ideas worked so directly against his personal beliefs, he wanted to scream out and correct the fallacies. Perhaps he wasn't as different from the people on Fox News as he thought.

Nietzsche's argument was basically that nobility, strength, power, and (sin-induced) happiness characterized the original definition of "good," which was displayed prominently in aristocrats, nobles, and knights, while "bad" was defined by all others who were weak and powerless, and thus unhappy…like the priests of the time.

In contrast, as a counter effect of the *master morality*, the weak ones, or the priests according to Nietzsche began to equate good with peace instead of war, and idealize sufferance in the place of mercilessness. So in essence, the "bad" created morals and "good" became evil, referred to by Nietzsche as *slave morality*.

All in all, Justus saw it as a weak theory by someone who did not understand the purpose of Christianity, in fact, it bordered a downright attack against Christians of Nietzsche's time, but, like in most of his classes, Justus kept his mouth shut. He understood that in current times —his times—most people found something wrong with Christianity. Justus did not know how he could change the mind of the common man.

"Here Nietzsche is saying that the resentment of the priests against those that were powerful and at ease engendered a movement to make the good…bad," Professor Henderson was saying with a wide smile. "It takes impotence to grow hatred."

Justus, hair back to its normal orange, wrote that down. Impotence grows hatred.

Everything Professor Henderson was throwing out, Justus's brain was spinning into a more acceptable direction.

"Priestly vengefulness" came from the professor's mouth. *Priests shouldn't be vengeful,* Justus thought. *It's devilish vengefulness.*

The phrase "hatred of impotence" entered the teenager's ears.

No, Justus corrected internally, *hatred of carnal-minded leadership.*

"So much Christianity in two days," the girl next to Justus moaned. He glanced at her.

"Were you at the lecture last night?" he asked.

Her face flushed a bit, and she nodded, feathers in her hair flirting with her cleavage. "Wasn't it the epitome of boringness?" she asked, pronouncing "epitome" so that it rhymed with "Rome" instead of "sea."

Justus disagreed, but instead he asked, "Are you a Christian?"

The question came naturally to his lips as if he was asking her name. Inside he panicked, because he had not planned on even asking the question.

"I'm a sinner, baby," she said with a smile.

Justus couldn't enjoy the rest of the class.

After class he caught up with her. She was pacing up one of the concrete walkways, holding her folders and textbooks at her breast, auburn hair swinging in braided curls across her back. Her hair was almost as long as Hanley Powell's.

"Hey!" he greeted as he fell into pace with her. "Professor Henderson is a tough one, isn't he?"

"I'm surprised to hear you say that," she said with a light smile. "I think you're his favorite."

"You think? I'm alright, I guess, but not too special," he said.

"Don't say that, Justus," she laughed.

"You know my name?" He was surprised. Professor Henderson never called anyone by his or her name. He just pointed and you jumped to it.

"Justus Alexander," she nodded. "Valedictorian. Don't you know mine?"

Justus wrinkled his brow. "Should I?"

She chuckled. "Sometimes I'm Cheyenne Crenshaw."

"Cheyenne! Coda's older sister!"

"The one and only," Cheyenne nodded, looking remarkably like her brother now that Justus's brain had made the connection. Her eyes were brown, her skin was darker, but she was her brother's sister.

"How is that brother of yours doing?" Justus asked.

Cheyenne's face hardened. "So you haven't spoken to him either."

"Nope, not super-recently," he said, faltering to turn that conversational aside into anything fruitful.

"Flirting or stalking?" she suddenly asked him.

Justus's eyes widened. "What?" He realized that she had caught on to the fact that he had no real reason for chasing after her outside of class. Since he didn't really know why he had followed her, he just kept yakking, hoping that she'd come to her own conclusions. "Oh. So you're a…sophomore?"

She laughed again, but her mood still seemed somber. "You're quite the conversationalist."

Justus realized why he couldn't shake the craving to chat with her, so he went with his impulses, saying, "I thought you guys were Baptists!"

Her face tightened. "Sinner is the word I use to describe myself. Others call me an atheist."

"So, you believe in Him, but you've rejected—?"

"I don't believe He exists," she said matter-of-factly.

"Really?" he said, unable to keep the soprano incredulity out of his baritone voice. "Why?"

Cheyenne didn't sigh, didn't pause, didn't ponder. "Let's just say that the one time I needed Him, He wasn't there for me. And if He isn't there when you need Him, then He isn't there."

Justus had a million questions racing around his mind, but she didn't give him a chance to start.

"No way will you change my mind, Justus," she said soothingly. "So don't even attempt to start. Many before you have tried to kill this dragon and rescue the princess inside, but she likes the dragon. The dragon… well, the dragon's always there, isn't it?"

Justus was unsettled.

"But," the woman next to him continued, "save your holiness for Lakota. He needs a swift divine kick in the ass if anyone does. Trust me."

She stopped, looking him in the eyes, a coldness in her own.

"And you're cute. But don't preach. That ruins your attractive qualities."

Justus stood frozen to the sidewalk as she moved on, hair swaying.

Justus looked around to make sure no one was near before trying to see if he could turn the ice blocks beneath his pants back into feet.

• • • • •

"Oh how cute!" Patricia exclaimed, entering the room. "They sent Baby Doctor."

The gentleman sat at the table across from her in a sharp black suit, tousled locks the only part of him that seemed to express himself instead of his organization.

"We have nothing for you," Patricia said. "So I'm not sure why you rejected my request to cancel this touch base."

"*I* have something for *you*," he said pleasantly, pulling a photo from his breast pocket and holding it up for Patricia to see.

Her face grew tight. "How did you get that?"

"That, Dr. Preacher? That is a human being, despite your best efforts, and human beings are referred to as either him, her, or who."

"Spare me the unneeded attempt at some lesson, Baby Doctor. I was referring to the picture."

"We had your *project* in our holding cell on the mainland until just yesterday, when a magnificent escape was conducted."

Her expression changed. "Until yesterday?"

He nodded, observing her closely.

She pulled away from the picture. "Then you have nothing for me."

His eyes slanted. "Why do you say that, Doctor?"

She made a show of a sharp inhale, replying, "If this was what you had and you no longer have it, then what exactly do you have for me, Baby Doctor? They should have sent the old guy this time. Adults have a more advanced form of communication."

The man stood, smoothing down his tie. "The Vice-President requested me to come instead of my mentor."

Patricia's jaw went slack. "Colton? He…"

"This is a matter nearing the levels of national security, Dr. Preacher. You know my allegiance is not with the American government or any corporation."

"Spare me the sermon," she spat.

"The Word I carry is not for you," he said, "but my actions are. The President supported you through Annapolis in hopes that you could make a solid gain and you failed him. Now the ball's in my court, because they know I can deliver. And I intend to. Your facility is a quick drive for me. Almost faster than a flight. Almost."

He slid the picture across the table to her.

"Get a handle on this within the month, Doctor. Or I will. And then I'll get my handle on you. Promise, INC."

• • • • •

Justus dreamed again, and it was violent, intense and he worried if he would ever wake. When he finally did open his eyes, he was content to find himself in the haven of his dormitory. His bunk and pillow were soaked with his sweat, and he found that his heart was banging against his ribs as if it was partying in some bodily mosh pit. He was universes and lifelines away from where his dream had taken him, yet he found himself disturbed nonetheless.

He was wide-awake, so he sat up and rolled his head around on his shoulders, telling himself to calm down. He rubbed his lips, and looked into the mirror. He blinked slowly. All around his reflection was a grey haze…a fog, maybe. Smoke.

Yes, it was smoke. He had noticed it in a few pulpits, and several weeks ago in Rico's car. It was the presence of the Holy Spirit! God was letting him know that He was there; Justus was protected! His heart swelled with a new focus.

Justus dropped to his knees and began to pray. There was something that God wanted him to know or do…or maybe both.

• • • • •

Post-midnight fog wasn't the greatest thing in the world, but Hydroxygen was enduring it. He was sitting on top of Newton Hall on Mercer's campus, wearing a blue bathrobe over his blue shorts and a white tee that he had put on just for this occasion. Sunglasses disguised Justus's hazel eyes, only a tuft of reddish hair showed at the base of his cap-covered head, and his black track shoes were on his feet in case he had to run.

"Okay God, you know your business, and I'm not doubting you, but —"

He glanced up and thought of all that God had done already in his life.

"Right. Never mind, Lord." He reminded himself that he was protected. "Just keep the campus police away, please, Lord! That's what I ask. You're in complete control."

Sure enough, moseying up the sidewalk was a muscled boy with achromatic skin and about seven large dreads adorning his head. As the boy whistled a tune, the sound reverberated inside of him as if he was full of nothing but space. Justus—Hydroxygen—figured that this was the "Hollow" he had heard so much about.

Hydroxygen dropped to the sidewalk, landing quite loudly behind the Hollow and struggling to stand steadily. Hollow spun to face him.

"Knock-knock, who's there?" Hydroxygen belatedly announced himself.

Hollow just stood there, his muscles tense, ready for combat.

"Okay, let's talk this over, Hollow—" but he didn't get to finish. Hollow had taken off running up the hill. And he was fast!

"Hollow is super-fast?" Hydroxygen asked himself, before it came to the forefront of his mind that he hadn't come this far just to let the boy escape. "Mind over body over mind," he mumbled, and his legs fluidized, and he propelled himself after Hollow.

His legs were dissipating behind him. He was going too fast for his own legs to keep up with him! This was another of God's miracles, this dissipation, but that did not prevent him from being a bit unnerved.

In fact, it felt as if the fog that was smacking his face was actually becoming part of him, as if to make up for the pieces, the droplets of himself that he was losing. Hydroxygen was amazed. God was freakin' amazing!

"This new feature on our model allows increased speed, as well as an increase in confidence," he projected in the voice of a car salesman, before the joy fizzed like soda pop in his veins and he was reduced to girlish giggles.

In the night's fog eclipse it was almost impossible to see. Hydroxygen threw out his hands in front of him. As he flew, the vapor melted into his hands and de-misted the view in front of him. The word "amazing" came to his mind once more.

"Thank you, God!" he said inside, half honored, half focused.

Where was the Hollow kid?

As something just a bit more concentrated than mist himself, Hydroxygen sailed silently past dormitories and fraternity and sorority residences, and he could hear the pounding of Hollow's dense body up ahead in the fog.

They were passing the gigantic University Center. He heard Hollow racing up the sidewalk, then suddenly, there was nothing.

Darn, Hollow had switched over onto the grass! Hydroxygen could still hear him, but barely. Why hadn't Hollow just done the disappearing trick Hydroxygen had heard about? Surely Hollow was working much harder by running up an inclined slope when Hydroxygen was just racing like Seabiscuit behind him.

Hollow had turned behind the UC, perhaps heading towards the expanses of the sports field below the hill. Hydroxygen turned behind him, the UC a few steps to his left and the empty parking lot several feet to his right. Yet Hydroxygen still couldn't hear his adversary-to-be, even on the rock foundation, so he continued using his vision-increasing de-vaporizer trick.

Hydroxygen gained his vision too late, for Hollow had stopped, and Hydroxygen flew straight into him!

As they tumbled to the ground, Hydroxygen dissipated into the air as quickly as he could. He wanted to observe this Hollow a little closer, remembering Kim's comments about how their antagonists could actually be somebody they knew. He was going to analyze Hollow's facial features and body type.

Hydroxygen drifted around Hollow towards his face. The boy was surreally pale. That was a given. His nose was straight and his mouth was thin. His smallish, dark eyes were roaming the fog, looking for the person that was concurrently looking at him. His eyebrows were a little roughly arranged, and his dark dreadlocks were brown, not black. His upper torso was long, and he had freckles on his arms, though not too many. Hydroxygen realized that Hollow really wasn't a "boy" per se; he was probably the same age Hydroxygen was.

Hollow waved his hands in front of his face and Hydroxygen had to back up. Hollow must have sensed the slight change in the air current, and his swiftly reddening face began to smile.

Hydroxygen froze, dumbfounded. Hollow's legs had begun turning into water. How could Hydroxygen have forgotten? When he tumbled into Hollow, Hollow had absorbed his powers and was now capable of duplicating them. Hydroxygen was left dismayed, unsure of how long Hollow would be able to use the stolen powers.

Hydroxygen lowered himself onto the sidewalk, creating a dense fog around Hollow's fluid calves. He hadn't gone unobserved, and just as Hydroxygen condensed completely into a puddle, the spectral being liquefied his body entirely.

What happened next would have been so cool to a boy named Justus Alexander, had he not been fighting for his life. The two puddles of water ascended off the asphalt and began to battle, with upper torsos of water and fists of ice, while their lower torsos were still lying as puddles on the pavement.

They were fighting near one of the upper service entrances, located near a guardrail that was designed to prevent someone from falling onto the monolithic blacktop a full floor below, where the first floor service entrance was located.

Hydroxygen quickly realized that he and Hollow weren't getting anywhere with the sidewalk wrestling. He was being sloppy. He was afraid; he didn't have experience with such violence.

He thrust himself into the air, becoming full flesh, and levitated above the sallow rogue. He was breathing heavily; the brawl had taken a lot out of him. That fear was rising inside of him again, and he countered those worries with the hope that his adversary was just as tired.

Hollow, whose dreadlocks had changed into a greasy orange, shot from the ground and was in solid form before Hydroxygen could blink. Before Hydroxygen could scream, Hollow, who apparently was not very tired at all, sent a solid ice fist into the features beneath his opponent's cap.

His regrettably reincarnate face began to run blood as the force of the sledgehammer blow sent Hydroxygen flying back into the side of the brick building, striking the unyielding surface with a sickening sound.

Hollow flew closer to look him in the eye, then, smiling with malicious triumph, clawed into Hydroxygen's shoulders and detached him from the wall. They were suspended over the drop, the railings of no help unless Hydroxygen could reach them.

Hydroxygen liquefied with the plan that he would rain out of Hollow's grip. However, once Hydroxygen turned to water, Hollow did so as well and when the first rain began to form as a hand around the railing, the second torrent washed it away. Hydroxygen formed into flesh and grabbed blindly. He gripped the railing, and swung there for a second, to get his bearings. Without the slightest delay, Hollow was behind him, on the second floor level, pounding his hands with velocious fists of ice. Hydroxygen didn't know how he could win against someone that had more tricks than he did. He let go of the railing, and dissipated into the air.

As he floated up to look at his opponent, who did not look happy in the least, Hydroxygen felt dizzy. His first full-blown fight being one fit for a Saturday morning cartoon was not something he appreciated.

Somehow he had turned into flesh. Why did he let his mind drift? Hollow was already flying into him, knocking him back into the wall. Blood was in Hydroxygen's eye, and he heard something crunch, though he did not know if it was building or bone. Hollow was back in his face and on his body, punching him over and over in various places with those sharp fists of ice. The blows kept Hydroxygen suspended in the air and hammered against the side of the building. What usually flowed through Justus's veins now poured from his mouth.

Hollow quit pummeling and floated back to get a look at Hydroxygen, who felt like he was glued to the bricks with his own blood.

Hollow, who looked impossibly worse with his orange dreads compared to the brown locks, made an offensive gesture, then translated into gas and was no more.

Justus tried to smile in relief, but his face hurt, and whatever grip his body had on the building, or vice versa, was lost, and he slowly slid down the side of the edifice—each millimeter down blasted pain into the few unaffected regions of his body.

After he hit the ground, Hydroxygen faded in and out, thinking of the biblical martyrs who had taken worst human punishment for their God. He remembered seeing red hair leaning over him and feeling soft hands cradle his face. He remembered a conversation, but it wasn't in English, and he remembered being picked up by a man—an angel who was wearing a pink tank.

Pink tank—God had a strange sense of humor.

21.

The Skyboarder & the Leviathan

"There are things that we've been setting ourselves up for since God set us apart," Ezekiel mused, moving the hangers and dressers underneath his dorm room bed in order to reach an item that was covered in a sheet. "Things in God's divine plan, you know?"

"Mmm, no," Kim smiled.

She was sitting at his roommate's computer desk, sporting jeans and an orange tee that read, "Maybe." With the roommate out, Kim was busying herself by playing war games with his packaged anime toys.

She eventually set Hiroshi on the opposite end of the desk from Katsuro and Takehiko to prevent further violence, spinning herself astride the nifty desk chair to better examine Ezekiel's rummaging under his bunk.

All that she got was an eyeful of khaki booty.

"I would ask if what you have for me is heavy," she mewed, "but I guess I don't have that liberty anymore."

Ezekiel chuckled, Adam's apple bouncing. "What?" As usual, he wasn't asking a question.

"So, Ezekiel… you're saying that on my last free weekend until the weekend that school lets out for spring break I backed out of a trip with my friends to Underground Atlanta—which, as I get older, becomes remarkably closer to the earth's surface—and borrowed tokens from my boyfriend causing a brand new debt to him (as if I needed another) and hopped on the city transit, sandwiched between an old lady that smelled like the Hercules factory and a dreadlocked dude with dirty fingernails, teeth the color of American cheese, breath that smelled like Hennessy and cancer sticks, a mouth that wouldn't quit flapping—and did I mention his yellow teeth?—all because of God's divine will or because you asked me to come and said that I couldn't say 'no?'"

"Both," Ezekiel grinned, turning around to face her and holding the sheet-wrapped article.

"What's that?" she asked warily. "It looks like Komodo dragon road-kill."

"What?"

Kim placed her fingers over her face, her strange laughter causing her shoulders to lurch forward.

"It was the first thing that popped in my brain," she explained, eying Ezekiel's gift. "Just 'cause of the sheet, not whatever it is underneath."

"Oh," Ezekiel said, setting it in her hands. He stepped back. "Okay, safety issues."

"What is it?" Kim asked again, carefully removing the sheets.

"Rule number one: Obey the rules."

"Ezekiel…" Her hand flew back up to her mouth.

"Rule number two:" he continued, grinning. "Go as fast as you want, but, like, if you need to stop quickly, you'll be, like, launched at high speed in any possible direction, you know? If you want to stop it regularly, and, like, more safely, just stop the engine."

"Ezekiel," Kim murmured, as she looked down at it, "does it really work?"

"I know it looks kind of bad," he said, referring to the crude artistry. It was one thing to create something on a computer, but in order to bring it to life he had to relinquish some of his hopes of beauty. "But it works very well."

Kim took in the oblong plastic board in her hands. Sections of the board were saturated in various shades of purple. On the darkest shade, Ezekiel had written "FAST" in white. On the lavender section was written a black "SLOW."

"It's purple," Kim remarked brightly.

"Coda told me you like purple."

"He knew you were making this?"

Ezekiel put his hands in his pocket, then pulled them out and crossed his arms, leaning back against his bunk.

Not pulling of the nonchalance, Kim thought, amused.

"No, I didn't tell him. No one knew, actually," he said.

"It's great," Kim said, at a loss. She sat—and he stood—in silence.

"Ezekiel," she purred.

"'Sabi?" he asked.

She began to giggle again, pulling at the sleeves on her pink hoodie. "Mmm, what's rule number three?"

He continued to explain its functions. It required a cushion of air to stay airborne, not unlike a helicopter. It could hold up to four hundred pounds before it refused to lift off the ground, and it could carry up to five hundred twenty-seven pounds before it snapped in two—those were just clear-cut guestimations. It could be handled like a skateboard or a surfboard, controlled by shifting weight from side-to-side. Increased pressure on the purple shaded sensors triggered either an increase of a decrease in speed.

"In, um, more traditional hovercrafts and stuff," Ezekiel detailed, "you can stop the engine, and it slows down to a stop, and if you keep the pressure on the lavender long enough, it will stop, though you probably should give it a few meters, you know? You can also stop by turning..."

Kim grinned at him. "Have you tried it?"

Ezekiel puffed a smile. "No, but Leviathan has tested it for you. And he thinks you can handle it better."

Leviathan? Oh, his superhero name. She still hadn't given herself one. Kim looked at the board again.

"A hoverboard," she whispered with a smile. She glanced up at Ezekiel. "That's sweet." She beamed at him and he smiled back, awkwardly. "Umm..."

She placed the hoverboard on his roommate's desk and Hiroshi toppled over. She stood up and smoothed her jeans.

"Come 'ere," she smiled, and he couldn't read her. She stepped closer and enclosed him in a dainty hug, despite the fact that if she squeezed him, he wouldn't have felt a thing.

"You are going to be such a good aerospace engineer!" she raved, squeaking huskily. "You really will build the first hotel on the moon if you choose to. I mean it."

Ezekiel's peach cheeks were tinting pink.

Kim slanted her eyes, biting back her smile. When she spoke, her voice was gruff and her eyes fluctuated as if they had briefly changed their mind about existing.

"I wanna surf the sky."

$\bullet \quad \bullet \quad \bullet \quad \bullet \quad \bullet$

"You wanna play a scene..."

"Hello?"

"Hey, Shannon. It's Maya."

"Oh, what's up, baby? You were singing to me?"

"Don't start. I was singing along with the radio."

"Oh. How are you?"

"I'm good."

"What have you been up to, lately?"

"Oh, trying to survive, that's all. Enjoying it here, though."

"Good. Are you partying?"

"Not much."

"That's not fun!"

"No, it's actually okay. I called because—"

"You wanted to *talk* to me, didn't you, Maya? I mean, you wouldn't want to call just to get something from me, right?"

"Actually, sweetie, uh, you're wrong."

"Ooo, Maya. You shot me right through. Don't laugh! I'm slumping over in my seat right now, destined to breathe my last."

"You're driving somewhere?"

"Oh, don't pretend that you want to have a conversation with me, now, Maya. You called for a reason; let's not drift off the subject."

"Shannon…you idiot."

"Nice to meet'cha. What did you call for, ninja?"

"Do you happen to know where Kim is? I haven't had any luck reaching her and I just read on her online journal that she was going to visit a friend in north Georgia this weekend, but she didn't say where. I'm off this weekend so I figured I'd meet up with her, but that depends on where she went."

"Are you and Gene not speaking again?"

"Please, boy."

"Uh-huh."

"…don't tell him I called you, Shannon."

"I knew it."

"I'm *serious*."

"Have you tried calling her? Is her phone off or something?"

"Or she has it in her purse on vibrate as usual. And I don't have Eden's new number or Ezekiel's number or Justus's *and* I seriously doubt she went to visit anyone else I know in that area."

"Oh, so I'm last on your list on top of everything else, hmm?"

"Silly. Are you gonna help me or not?"

"I guess I will. Well, she's not here with me in Rome. I don't have much new to add to what you said. It's Justus or Ezekiel, though I didn't know that they were close with Kim like that. So good luck with that. I dunno, maybe she's heading to surprise you."

"Are you laughing at me? You're laughing at me. Thanks for the encouragement."

"Anytime, baby. And you know I got something for you when I see you. Sticky, but high in protein."

"Nasty. I belong to someone."

"If it isn't Gene then you're lying."

"Shut up."

"Or it's *Rico!*"

"Bye, Shannon."

"I don't mind sharing. I guess BJ doesn't either."

"Shut up."

"Speaking of BJ—"

"Shut up!"

"I love you, baby."

"Shannon. Bye."

"Peace easy."

• • • • •

"Kimi, are you reading this?"

Kim glanced up at her boyfriend. He stood in the door holding up her now-worn copy of *The Days of Awakening*.

"Just skimming through it," she responded. She shouldn't have left it on the kitchen table when she finished her supper.

"You're using your I Love Lucy bookmark. You're not just skimming." She sighed. "So what?"

If he was a chick, his hands would have been on his hips. "All this stuff is prophecies and hocus-pocus. Do you really think that the Bible was so literal? When's the last time you saw angels descending in a ladder, for example? Did God not know that man was gonna invent the elevator? Escalators, even." He began to read from the bookmarked page. "'What keeps us from laying hands on that angel? Why don't we demand our blessings?'" He tossed the book on the bed. "Babydoll, don't tell me you're gonna start wrestling angels now."

"Do you have a reason for bothering me right now? I'm trying to figure out what I'm going to wear to Peaches tomorrow."

"Like those plastic things?" Dishon asked Kim, gesturing to the blue bracelets she had laid out to go with her blue and silver outfit. He made a ridiculous face.

"Baby, I'll buy you some bracelets, but you can't wear those," he pleaded, looking undeniably sexy.

"My parents gave these to me, Dishon," she resolutely responded. "And I've worn them out before."

"Yeah, like constantly. Why you wanna go and wear those again tonight, Kimi? You're impossible sometimes."

She retaliated.

"I don't want your misdemeanor-money bracelets," she said, suddenly ghetto.

Dishon blinked in hurt.

"Oh, and I supposed you didn't want that dinner last night, or those earrings, all bought with 'misdemeanor money,'" he said, and she reached up and touched the shimmering strings. Dishon continued, "I suppose that you suddenly wish you hadn't smoked that marijuana that *you* asked me to get that we *all* smoked last night that I bought with that same 'misdemeanor money.'"

Kim punched his chest and he grabbed her arm and pulled her into him. She tried to ignore the feel of his muscles and the heat of his body. She stared into his russet eyes instead.

"Look, Miss Hamilton, I'm sorry if I offended you, but gambling isn't a sin."

Kim called him a nasty name and began to struggle against him, telling herself that she was not getting pleasure out of the friction.

"Baby, let's not fight," he rumbled sexily. "Let's do that other thing. Sin is only fun when you have someone to do it with."

"I guess you'd better name your hand 'Someone,'" she began, and he kissed her to silence her. She struggled to hold on to her anger—struggled to find the root of it. Finally she pulled away, calling him something particularly evil and stomping off. Deep inside of her, she wondered if this was the collegiate decadence she had been looking forward to. It was the poison in the poppy.

As if nothing was upsetting her, Kim sauntered into the living room, where Stasia was blasting Christina Aguilera and hollering over her CD to talk to Frankie, who was sitting on the couch with his violin in his lap.

"Mmm, I love this song!" Kim squealed, and began to dance. "Ye-as!"

"Ooo, stop the madness!" Frankie giggled. "Girl, you are nothing but a trip. Ooo, stop the madness I *say!*"

Kim joined Stasia in dancing the dances that were popular when they were in the eighth grade. Frankie kept ragging on the girls as Dishon prowled in and sat next to Frankie, laughing at every joke, taking every opportunity to smile.

It was a display for Kim's benefit just as her careless dancing was for his. They both knew it, so she ignored him with as much might as she could muster. Sure she was offended, though she was no longer upset with her boyfriend for asking her to leave the bracelets at home. The offense came from a much closer place. Kim had gone ahead and allowed Dishon's comments persuade her to leave the bracelets out of her outfit.

She wouldn't admit that fact, however, and he had better not take it as a victory.

· · · · ·

"Hey, Ezekiel," Kim whispered with a big grin as if she hadn't seen him for months instead of that very afternoon.

Riding the Atlanta transit system alone in the middle of the night was a little nerve-racking no matter how strong she may have proven herself to be, but she had made it to the doorway of Ezekiel's dormitory building with no mentionable problem.

"Hey," Ezekiel nodded, handing the re-wrapped hoverboard over to Kim.

He was dressed in his black gi pants and a white undershirt as well as the gloves that he wore when he rode his bike. He tossed a smaller pair of gloves to Kim.

She had changed out of her bright orange tank into a midriff-bearing black blouse, though she still wore her jeans and she wore the blue bangles. Her hair was pulled back into a ponytail, and her customary white sneakers were all that made her stand out in the dark night.

"Samson and Stephen, together again," Kim sang.

As she pulled on the gloves, which were still rather big on her despite their small size, and they began walking. While Ezekiel wondered what to say next, Kim took sidelong glances at him.

"Don't you have a dark shirt?" she asked him.

"No," he said, glancing at her out of the corner of his eyes. His gaze fell to her feet. "Don't you have darker shoes?"

"Not that I could wear on a hoverboard," was her response.

She had given Ezekiel the conversation starter. "It's crazy how much information was already out there on those things, you know?" he said, gesturing to the hoverboard Kim was lifting above her head on her ring finger, attempting to keep it balanced. "It just required some tweaking."

"Oh, yeah?" Kim mumbled, tucking it underneath her arm.

"Yeah," Ezekiel continued, wondering about Kim's sudden disinterest, but resisting the temptation to enter her mind. "They're really simple, but I had to complicate it to get it to do the things I needed it to do, you know?"

"I know," she mumbled.

"I mean," he pressed on, "a hovercraft is just a vehicle that needs a cushion of air. It uses pressure, though most people would think it needs suction or something."

The lack of a "you know" grabbed Kim's attentions.

"How high off the ground could this thing get?" she asked. She had an image of boarding around the steeple tower of Curly's new sanctuary.

"Only about seven inches for me," Ezekiel said, with a trace of sadness. He was sure she was only feigning interest in the mechanics of the hoverboard. "But you could probably manage eight or nine."

Kim smiled in the dark. They walked on in silence. Kim glanced up at the stars and Ezekiel followed her gaze.

"Sometimes it feels as if they're watching," Kim murmured, more to herself than to Ezekiel. "Trying to convey a message."

Ezekiel's gaze returned to path ahead of them.

"When I was little," Kim remembered with a sad smile, "I would ask my mom to sew me a silver dress decorated with stars—real stars—and I said that I wanted to ride on the moon." She laughed. "Like a pony in the sky. I wanted to get away from all of the brutal piano lessons and baby beauty pageants and perfect report cards and present a play for God, starring Jupiter and the asteroids. Then I would recite 'The Stars Journey' for God in my pretty silver dress made of stars with a matching bow and my favorite white Easter heels, and Jesus would be sitting next to him with long, pretty braids, and the Holy Ghost would be on the other side with white hair poking everywhere like the Cowardly Lion from *The Wiz* and they would clap. God would tell me that I never would have to go home again and I would stay there on the clouds... That's where I thought Heaven was, you know. I think every kid does. It was only so beautiful.

"Every day, for the rest of my time in Heaven, I would recite 'The Stars Journey' and put on more plays."

Kim took a deep breath, too far gone in her memory to stop. Her neck popped her head back as she squared her shoulders, gazing self-assuredly down the street. Her mouth opened and a deep, compelling tenor boomed from inside of her tiny physique.

"The stars journey from Heaven above,
into human sadness, from God's great love.
Into the pain, from the gladness.

"The stars' journey—a flaming fall!
The flight: their existence; the landing: their all.
Into the pain, from the gladness.

"The stars journey to do His good will.
Elusive like sky, strong like steel,
into the pain, from the gladness.

"And here alone I want nothing more—
whether the fall, whether the chore—
than to endure the stars' journey."

Ezekiel glanced over at her. "How old were you?"

"Ten."

"You were a weird kid," he commented, chuckling.

She was silent. Ezekiel respected her by leaving her rushing river of thoughts inside of her own head.

"Yeah, I was peculiar," she agreed, after a few moments. "Peculiar, INC."

"INC?" Ezekiel asked.

"'In the name of Christ.' My father used to use it shorthand until I began using it vainly." Her reflective laugh turned into a shiver. "Ugh, it's still cool here! In Brunswick I bet it already feels like, oh, I don't know, the spring, maybe?" She giggled.

"It's not that bad," Ezekiel said.

"No, I guess it's not," laughed Kim. "You just refuse to have an outright negative view on anything, don't you?"

"You know, like, Coda's keeping something from us, right?" Ezekiel asked.

Kim swallowed and blinked, attempting to catch up to wherever this was heading.

"What?"

"The Creature he talks about. You know why he won't describe what it looked like?"

Kim wrinkled her forehead. "Why?"

"He doesn't know what it looks like," Ezekiel said.

Kim stopped and put her hands on her hips.

"Why not, Ezekiel?" she asked, and there was an undercurrent to her question. "Coda said he got in a battle with a creature. How can he not know what it looks like?"

"It was a spiritual battle with physical side effects." Ezekiel stopped and looked back at the halted Kim. "The Creature was *in* Sam Wesberger. You know, inside of him."

"It was a demon?" Kim asked, feeling cold squeezing her chest.

"Coda thinks so, and that's all I have to go on."

"Did he tell—" she began.

"I looked for it," he answered.

Kim's face became vacant.

"You don't suppose that's what Solitaire and the Hollow boy..." She ran over everything that she had every read about demons in her life.

Ezekiel shrugged, crossing his arms.

"Why doesn't he want to tell us himself?" he asked.

Kim stared at him, star-dusted eyes seeing Coda instead. "Sam Wesberger wasn't dressed up, was he?"

Ezekiel shook his head. "In normal clothes, I guess. What do you mean, dressed up?"

"Like in a costume..."

Ezekiel shook his head again.

Kim flashed back to the demon that caused her accident.

"Why doesn't he want to tell us himself?" Ezekiel asked again, shuffling his feet, because he had an idea why.

"There's a story there," is all she said. She resumed walking.

"He's not the only one who's keeping things from people," Ezekiel said softly.

Kim glanced back at him. "What? You're talking 'bout how I've smoked pot? No...everyone in our senior class seems to know about that, so you've got to be further along than that. Maybe you're referring to the fact that I can't get high at all anymore! That the magic of pot seems to have left me; that's true. That power of yours is quite a character trait, sir."

She continued walking, and he stepped vigorously to catch up.

"There's more to it, though," he probed. "The reason it all started. I don't know what it is yet, but...but I would like it if you told me."

Kim didn't make eye contact, focused instead on the stadium ahead.

"Dangerous territory, Ezekiel. Back off."

• • • • •

"Okay," Kim was muttering for the twelfth time. "Here goes."

She hopped back onto the hoverboard and reached underneath it to click the on switch. As the hoverboard began to, well, hover, Kim slowly stood.

"I'm going to try this again," she announced, looking straight ahead.

"Go ahead," Ezekiel chuckled, amused. Arms folded, he was leaning against the brick wall that separated the stands from the fields.

Kim pressed her feet down on one of the lighter purple sections, and the hoverboard took off gently, gliding over the grass. She advanced her speed slowly, experimenting in turning the board and changing its direction. She could make it turn, but wasn't having much luck in making it slide, and when she tried another slide, she flew from the board into the grass of Georgia Tech's football field.

"I'm gonna make that thing slide," she grumbled, brushing the dirt from her face and turning off the overturned hoverboard.

"Are you okay?" Ezekiel asked, striding forward with his demi-grin.

Kim shot him a dirty look. "Somehow, I'm not convinced that you care."

It was water off a duck's back. Ezekiel had seized the hoverboard and was inspecting it for scratches.

"I'm glad it worked," he mused, "because I was afraid that the dirt would be lifted and mess up the air pressure."

Kim sneezed.

"Bless you," Ezekiel said, not taking his eyes off the hoverboard.

"Thank you, my child," Kim said, retrieving the hoverboard before Ezekiel forgot whom it now belonged to.

"Well, the ground is even and compact, so everything is working to our favor here, but if we as a group ever have to go up a hill...I'm legging it all the way," she finished with a disapproving frown and shake of her head.

"You could hitch a ride on Rico's back," Ezekiel grinned. "And hope he doesn't crash," he added, unnecessarily including a noise of obliteration.

"What about water?" Kim asked, shaking out the image Ezekiel had encouraged into her brain. "I've seen *Back to the Future*."

"You can't generate much air pressure over water, but it can glide over wet areas...perhaps a large puddle, but I wouldn't try."

"This is only so frustrating," Kim began, but the lightning went off in her head, blinding her and silencing her all at once. Another one followed quickly, keeping her off balance.

"I got—caught a thought..." Ezekiel was whispering. "I *saw* a thought," he corrected, and by the tone of his voice, Kim could tell it wasn't a nice one.

Kim froze, glancing around intently as her vision returned. Could there be someone up in the stands? The giant stadium lights weren't revealing anyone...

Kim pulled on a piece of cloth that she had wrapped around her ponytail and proceeded to wrap it around her head. Ezekiel did likewise with his mask that he had clipped to his waistband.

"Come on," Kim encouraged the unseen enemy. She flipped the switch on her hoverboard, turning it on. It had been too long since she had faced one of their mysterious enemies, and she felt ready to take them down.

A man rose out of the ground like a vampire rising from a coffin. His skin was like moonlight in the lights of the stadium and he was still wearing a simple brown jumpsuit, causing Kim to wonder if he had ever changed since their first encounter months ago in the skate park bathroom.

Leviathan recognized him as the Hollow boy he had heard so much about.

"Interesting," Leviathan muttered as Kim bowed her head in a word of prayer.

Hollow just stood staring at them.

Kim raised her head, glaring. "Well, well, well, Hollow. You could barely handle me, but you *definitely* can't handle the Skyboarder *and* the Leviathan." She hopped onto her hoverboard and rose into the air.

Hollow didn't move. Leviathan went in with a thrust punch, which Hollow blocked with his palm.

Skyboarder swore under her breath, knowing that Hollow had just absorbed his own version of Leviathan's invincibility, as well as the stolen gift of flight and (this shook her confidence a bit) possibly the ability to see thoughts.

Hollow now stared at Skyboarder, Leviathan's blows non-affecting.

"You're not getting my strength," Skyboarder said determinedly.

Hollow leapt at Skyboarder and she fell off her hoverboard in her effort to avoid him. The board caught Hollow in the shins, and he fell onto the ground.

"Skyboarder!" she heard Leviathan yell.

"Huh?" she said distractedly, watching Hollow push himself off the ground.

"How long can he keep the borrowed powers?"

Skyboarder was backing away towards Leviathan slowly. She tried to focus on what he was saying. "Uh, I don't know. Not forever, I know."

"Let's find out," Leviathan recommended.

Skyboarder shot him a sideways glance. "Okay," she agreed. This time, as Hollow advanced, Skyboarder and Leviathan avoided his blows and his attempts at getting touched.

Skyboarder waited until she felt the inner nudge, and then she whacked Hollow for all she was worth. He, in turn, went flipping across the field and crashed into the stadium wall.

"That was about two minutes," she hollered to Leviathan. Then, to Hollow as an afterthought, "And that was for Hydroxygen! And Ri—Blaze!"

Hollow rose and raced over towards them, an ugly purple bruise forming on the left side of his white face and blood trickling out of his nose.

"We can last that long," Leviathan said, and they stepped out of Hollow's reaches again. When Skyboarder smacked Hollow the next time, he blocked the blow. He reached to strike her in the face and as she threw up an arm to block him, her bracelets were shattered. She withdrew her arm in time to prevent her wrists from being just as easily destroyed, kicking him in his side. As he fell towards the ground, she helped him along by kneeing him in the face.

Skyboarder glanced down at the remnants of her wristlets. "My bracelets…"

Hollow jumped up, aiming a well-placed kick towards her knee. Leviathan leapt in the path and Hollow's foot bounced off his brawny thigh. Leviathan got his bearings quickly, punching Hollow dead in his eye.

As Hollow disseminated, Leviathan turned towards Skyboarder with a shrug. "Figured the eye would be a pretty vulnerable spot." He didn't continue his explanations.

The small woman stood there with tears dropping down her face, her mask in her hands. She looked up defiantly. "I know you can hear me, Hollow!" she screamed into the emptiness of the air. "You're not fighting against human beings here. You're fighting against God, and where human beings fail, God never does. Do you hear me? God does not fail!"

Teasing applause echoed around the stadium. Kim tied her mask back on quickly as she and Leviathan looked for the source of the sound.

Leviathan nudged her and gestured towards the stands.

Solitaire was the one applauding. She was sitting halfway up in the stands, in a red body suit and black trench coat. She wore black newsboy cap and it appeared she had on black biker boots that they caught a glimpse of as she stepped up onto the bleachers. Her face was blurry as it had been when she faced Rico and her eyes were still their demonic obsidian, though Leviathan was stunned to see her skin a dark brown, not unlike Skyboarder's.

"I had heard amazing things about your ability with drama, Miss Wilbanks/Hamilton/Skyboarder/whatever," Solitaire said, though Skyboarder couldn't make out any evidence of a mouth, "but the *melodrama* must be a new foray for you." She lifted off the metal seat and began to glide towards the field. "I'm just not sure yet if I like your method approach."

"What do we do?" Leviathan spoke under his breath, not taking his eyes off the chameleon-like Solitaire.

"I get on my hoverboard, you take to the wind, and we beat her down," was Skyboarder's firm reply.

"It's not polite to whisper, Mr. and Mrs. Yang," Solitaire said, grinning.

Leviathan rose into the air, accelerating quickly.

Skyboarder picked up her hoverboard, turning it back on.

Solitaire began to advance at the same speed as Leviathan.

When Skyboarder stepped onto her hoverboard, she felt a hand grab her around the ankle. She turned in horror, seeing Hollow armpit deep in the ground, no expression as always on his face. It was as if he was climbing up out of hell.

She felt foolish. The lightning in her head hadn't triggered when he had disappeared earlier. It didn't trigger because he hadn't left.

He pulled her off the hoverboard.

Skyboarder screamed in spite of herself, twisting to get out of his grasp, but he did not let go, and he began to squeeze. Furious, she turned on him and applied her hands to his ivory throat and began to strangle him.

Above them in the stands, Leviathan and Solitaire slammed into each other with all the graceful fury of battling bucks. He was punching and she was blocking. She was striking, though he wasn't being harmed. She was actually a better fighter than he was, though he had the indisputable advantage of strength. He couldn't get over her dark brown skin, though he was beginning to wonder if his mind was playing tricks on him. Her round eyes seemed to be stretching into an angular shape the longer they kept fighting, and her skin didn't seem so brown…a light bronze, maybe.

Below them, Skyboarder pulled Hollow out of the ground calmly, hands still around his neck, every once and a while giving him a good shake. He released her ankle and she threw him on the ground. He reached up and smacked her thigh and she hollered in pain. He was holding back on the stolen strength in hopes that she could fight him longer, suffer though she might.

"Let me ask you something," she fumed, kicking him in his stomach with a good portion of her own strength. As he doubled over on the ground, she leaned down and inspected his face.

"We haven't bothered you yet. I thought we were supposed to stay out of your way. Why did you come aft—"

Hollow's eyes glinted as he reached up and slapped her face.

She stood back, hopping around like a mad rabbit.

"Get up! Get up!" she screamed.

Solitaire had pulled out her knife. Leviathan paid it no mind. He elbowed her in the stomach and proceeded to pummel her into the seats. She kicked him off her onto one of the seats beside her, tossing her knife towards the field.

Leviathan stood and raced to get in front of the knife. He supposed that she aimed the weapon towards Skyboarder, but she hadn't. When Leviathan saw the knife clatter down amidst the seats, he turned to Solitaire in confusion.

She was gone. He turned back to the field.

Skyboarder was managing to beat Hollow like a rag doll. Solitaire materialized behind her, definitely a lighter brown than Skyboarder was.

"Excuse me," she said calmly. Skyboarder turned, as Hollow lay on the ground beside her, groaning.

"You want an autograph?" Skyboarder asked.

"No," Solitaire said, flying into Skyboarder and tackling her to the ground, only to fly off her and stand next to her, deceptively dainty as a dragonfly.

Skyboarder reached for the back of Solitaire's knee, knocking her to the ground beside her. She spun over to punch Solitaire in the face, but her arm shuddered a few inches in front of Solitaire's face excruciating pain reverberated up her arm and into her chest.

That must have been what Ezekiel was talking about, she thought. *A proper reaction exploits the action.* It was only so infuriating.

As Skyboarder flopped back beside her in deep pain, Solitaire, darkening again, turned over onto her elbows and her stomach, kicking her feet into the air as if they were having a casual conversation at a sleepover.

"Who knew?" the rouge rogue asked, her gravelly voice teasing. "I would have thought that 'tough' and 'strong' were synonymous. I guess you haven't been guided or instructed in using yourself to your full potential. Midnight meetings inside of small cars don't amount to much, do they? Funny! No one made a 'choice' for me and look what I can do!"

Skyboarder wanted nothing more than for the red girl to shut up.

Hollow had recovered, but Leviathan had reached the grass and the sides of the battle were equal once again. As Hollow brought up an arm with the plan to do some damage to the female hero lying catatonic next to him, Leviathan grabbed the arm and bent it up behind Hollow like Master Thomas had once done to Jordan Vang. Once he made Hollow uncomfortable, he continued to tug the arm just enough for Hollow to screech.

Skyboarder had begun crawling away on her hands and feet, trying to get enough space between her and Solitaire so that she could stop and attempt to figure out what exactly was happening and what her reaction should be. She started praying.

Solitaire stood, just watching Skyboarder with an impassive face. Leviathan watched Solitaire, and, thinking he had done enough damage to Hollow, suddenly pounced on her.

But she was gone. Just like that: looking at Kim one moment, out of the stratosphere the next. Skyboarder saw the flash inside her eyes when Solitaire disappeared, so she was forced to stop her movement for a few moments, repeating her prayer over and over.

Leviathan looked back to Hollow, seeing the boy run at breakneck speed towards Skyboarder.

Skyboarder was a little worried. What had happened to their two-minute research? They hadn't kept track of that in the least. If she hit him, it would do no damage. If he hit her, he could kill her. She looked around desperately.

"The hoverboard!" Leviathan yelled.

Yes. She jumped back and reached for the hoverboard, which had been overturned once again. When Hollow came in with a furious kick, she held up the buzzing hoverboard. As Hollow crashed through it, knee first, the voltage shrieked through his body.

He landed on his feet, bone protruding from the knee that had symbiotically destroyed the hoverboard, though he crackled with the voltaic energy.

Skyboarder marveled, shouting to Leviathan over Hollow's screams. "He absorbed that, too!"

While Skyboarder and Leviathan watched in amazement, Hollow spent the next two minutes jerking about unnaturally due to the convection, staring at his hands and his body as if he didn't know what to do with his being. His chest strained against the jumpsuit straps and his hair extended from his body like living snakes. When the electric activity ceased, he sighed in relief and fell back into the ground, disappearing into the grass.

Skyboarder stumbled a bit due to the internal flash of light, but restored her equilibrium quickly.

"That was the weirdest thing..." Skyboarder said, ripping off her mask and wondering why she wore it if Solitaire already knew who she was. Maybe Hollow did as well, since it was now painfully obvious that the two annoyances were working together.

Ezekiel had removed his mask as well, having flown above her into the stands, searching.

"She threw her knife..."

"She probably grabbed it during one of her disappearing acts," Kim said dismissively as Ezekiel dropped down next to her.

She looked briefly at Ezekiel, inspected herself for bruises, and finally turned her attention to the broken hoverboard, lying like a mutated corpse.

"For him to be 'hollow,' he definitely crashed through that thing like it was a football placard."

She shook her head and glanced towards her naked wrist. Ezekiel stood stoic next to her, thinking, ignoring the throbbing pain emanating from different regions of his body.

"How'd they know we were here, anyway?" Ezekiel asked.

"I do not know," Kim said through clenched teeth, though her anger was not directed at Ezekiel. She turned to glance at him. "Next time I see them, though, will be the last time they bother us. Promise, INC."

And she turned and stalked off towards the exit off the field, with her tears looking not unlike stars as they dropped off her brown chin and sped towards the grass.

• • • • •

Patricia was not pleased. She was becoming upsettingly used to the feeling.

"I won't speak to the subject in 'Hyde' form. Make the injection."

It wasn't so much that she didn't desire to speak to this incarnation. She wondered what could be inside of a person when the outsides appeared in such a way. But the fact remained that speech didn't seem possible in this form, so she had to wait.

It was a lengthy process, but she was patient, polishing her gun.

The words finally came. "I can change back on my own."

She cocked the gun, her patience gone. "Bring them to me."

"You kill me and you're back to square one."

The gun apparently wasn't impressive enough. No matter.

She aimed casually, shooting off the good kneecap. Once screams surrendered into whimpers, she spoke.

"You're the one strapped to the chair." She placed the barrel of her gun on the protruding bone from the other knee. "Do you see how quickly this escalates? Do I look like I believe in a square one?"

After a moment, she stood, removed her gloves, and let the nurses in. She handed one her gloves and her gun, while the others worked quickly. Both knees would be perfect by week's end. No matter. Patricia's point had been more than made.

"Looking forward to our next talk."

22.

Inconveniences

Many of the spring vacations were premature to the Easter celebration. It was impossible to map out who was coming back to town, when, or for how long. Some people had their spring vacations and returned Easter weekend whereas others seemed to be in town for a full month with no qualms about returning to school.

Wayne Emerson had two healthy boys born to him in early March. He named both of them Wayne Jr., causing Coda to comment that everyone involved should be committed to the crazy house.

Gene Hightower received a horrific football injury and his grandmother asked everyone she ran into to lift him up in prayer. Most people wondered if he would play again. If he couldn't, according to former lackey Brandon Evans, he'd lose his scholarship to UGA.

Coda hadn't returned to OCC for a second semester. Justus and Rico thought it was a smart decision, agreeing that Coda wasn't the "college type" if there ever was an example. Ezekiel and Kim, on the other hand, worried. Kim contemplated the reasons why Coda had never listened to her mother Delia's advice and came to Clark Atlanta with her. Then she thought of the possible outcomes and realized that it was for the best that she wasn't going to the same college as her friend. In fact, the last bit of communication between them had been the letter Coda had sent her concerning the Miss KWA pageant.

Rico's powers seemed to have expanded, enabling him to see the spirit world in conjunction with his natural vision. He saw the demons crawling on the skin of one of his restless, trouble-making classmates. He observed the angels flying winglessly across campus. In every class, at every function he attended and whenever he retired to his room, there was always at least one there, watching him watch them with their golden eyes and red-gloved hands. It was unsettling in a Japanese horror way, but by the same token, the angels warmed his soul...they put him at ease.

• • • • •

"Oops, got to go, boys," Peppi Ortiz said, lifting soft pink lips to Coda's cheeks before encasing Rico in a strong embrace. "I promised Hanley I'd meet her for coffee."

She adjusted the straps on her sundress.

"Call me later, okay?" she said, exuding a clumsy sexiness just by standing and speaking. Just by living. "We can relax in my jacuzzi?"

Rico nodded. "Love to."

"Bye, lady," Coda said.

"Happy St. Patrick's Day!" she called out as she hurried off towards the house next door. The skinny boys watched her sashay.

"You, too," Rico burbled.

Coda exhaled audibly; Rico ripped his eyes away before Peppi reached her house.

As he turned to Rico, Coda's eyes took hold of the sign staked into the Gutierrez lawn and he stiffened.

"For sale?" His head snapped around to Rico. "You guys are selling this house? Where are you guys going?"

Rico knew Coda's mind was racing. Wondering how far they were going, if they would write, if he were at fault somehow. All the absurdities of thought that came from a kid who thought only of himself…in an odd, low self-esteem sort of way.

"Yeah," Rico replied casually, "my parents are finding new places to live."

"Places as in plural?" Coda asked, newly befuddled.

"Yeah." Rico responded with the simplicity of ease from one who had allowed circumstances to run their own course. "They're getting a divorce."

Coda's mouth fell open. He became aware of this and closed it. "They're getting a divorce?" he repeated.

"Yeah, dude," Rico responded, humored at Coda's astonishment. How could his friend not have noticed how his parents were rarely in the house at the same time, let alone the same room? Rico glanced down at the driveway beneath his feet, enjoying the chilly spring wind as it nipped at his face. Brunswick chilly was always better than Annapolis freezing.

"How'd you find out?" Coda asked.

Rico glanced up at Coda. "They came up to the school. They told me during one of their visits."

"Dude."

"Yeah," sighed Rico. "Renata was there. She couldn't even look at me." He turned his face away from the wind, looking down the short street towards more of his unfamiliar neighbors. "She didn't handle it well, at first, but she knew it was coming, and so did I. All of us did, really."

"And…"

Rico looked dead into Coda's eyes. "It's the best thing that could've happened. I mean, it sucks, but both Dad and Ma will be happier. Asi es la vida…y hay que seguir adelante."

Coda nodded, and Rico watched him thoughtfully.

He walked over to Coda's overnight bag that was sitting on top of his pop's car and began purposing himself with nothing. The bag was green. Everything was green. It was St. Patrick's Day. Rico hated green. He hated St. Patrick's Day.

Rico pulled his camera out from the front pocket of his sweatshirt and snapped a picture of Coda as he stared at the "For Sale" sign.

"Dude!" Coda exclaimed, as Rico laughed.

Later, when they were battling in the backyard, Coda asked, "Did you get any pictures of Solitaire?"

Rico shot a stream of what looked like liquid fire in Coda's direction, and Coda rocketed a few meters in the air before flipping into a roll and kicking Rico's legs out from under him.

"I was fighting, dude," Rico panted as he latched his ankles around Coda's neck. "No time for *fotografía!*" He sprayed teasing streams of red fire around Coda's face.

Coda brought his knees into Rico's back, then forced his shoulders between Rico's ankles, pushing the twiggy legs apart and leaping free.

He landed in a *shotokan* stance, slowly tossing a low punch towards Rico's head as Rico climbed to his feet. Rico blocked the punch, and brought an open flaming palm towards Coda's neck.

He stopped short, and Coda said, "I think Kim thinks that Maya is Solitaire," twisting Rico's arm to his side with his left hand and brought his right down towards Rico's forearm as if to snap it, "but that's as logical as Renata being Solitaire."

Rico laughed, as they stepped apart. "How so?"

Coda looked at Rico strangely. "Renata's your sister and Maya is, like, like mine."

Rico flew a few inches off the ground, and created a spade of flames in the middle of the air. "But Renata *could* be Solitaire," he reasoned, knowing his long-haired friend was dumbfounded by his reaction. "She knew that Spanish really well. And the Solitaire I fought looked just like me."

Coda waited for the spade to dissipate, appraising Rico suspiciously through the lingering ripple of heat. "Yeah, but Kim and Ezekiel say that her skin color changes, remember? And Maya knows Spanish."

"So does Peppi," Rico put out.

Coda looked down, but his mind wasn't on the pavement. "So does Eden. And Kim…"

"But Kim isn't Solitaire," Rico said. "Even if she hadn't've fought the girl, yet," he added before Coda could. No need for them to waste time on more unfounded theories. He kicked Coda in the shoulder, but Coda quickly grabbed his leg and flipped him around, bringing him down into the backyard lawn.

"So you're not gonna defend your sister's honor?" he asked.

Rico kicked Coda in the ribs from his position on the ground. "At this point, what does it matter? If it comes to it, I'll kick her ass as easily as I'm kicking yours. But if one of you touches her, I'm breaking necks."

"Could it be BJ?" Coda asked, balancing his body on his right hand, left hand casually placed on his hip. He kicked wild propeller-like legs whenever Rico stepped too close.

"BJ doesn't know Spanish, brobe," Rico answered, watching flames twist down his arms.

Coda flattened himself in the grass so that the flame balls flew above him. He asked, "Can we be sure?"

"I get it, Slick Rick. I get it, but that would open up all kinds of possibilities," Rico said, placing a foot softly on Coda's neck. "And there's still the prospect that we don't even know whoever the real Solitaire is. It could be some man-chick from Bogotá." He sighed, crossing his legs beside Coda on the grass and rubbing his hands over his buzz cut.

"At least we know who Hollow is," Coda said, propping himself up on his elbows.

Rico paused. What was Coda talking about, now?

"What makes you say that we know who Hollow is?" he asked.

"Rico. Hollow is Shannon." Coda said this as if it was old news. "Obviously. His build, his stunted athleticism. His size, his hair, his eyes…"

"But why would it be Shannon?" Rico said, attempting to shrivel Coda beneath his unwavering gaze. "I mean, come on, dude."

Coda glared. "Why would it be Renata? Or Peppi? Or Maya? Or some man-chick from Bogotá? Why would any of the good guys be Kim?"

"Skyboarder."

"Or Ezekiel?"

"Leviathan."

"Or Justus!"

"Hydroxygen."

"Or me? Or you?" Coda asked, raising his wild eyebrows.

Rico was silent.

Coda's moss-colored eyes were flying around the backyard without seeing. His brain was miles away. "What if Shannon was meant to be one of us, but he's just traveling the wrong path?"

Something was nagging in the back of Rico's mind as he caught sight of an angel perched on the neighbor's fence…watching, of course. "Shannon is not Hollow. If it is some white guy, since we can't be sure even with the skin—"

"Well, look at Solitaire's skin," Coda shrugged.

"Exactly. So it could be anybody."

"But it has got to be Shannon, Rico," Coda reasoned, propping up onto his side. "Haven't you heard about it from everybody? Haven't you heard how pale he's gotten?"

"Coda, this is stupid," Rico said. The nagging hadn't stopped. What was he trying to remember? "There are countless pale people in the world. Heck, as skinny as she is, Renata could be Hollow!"

Coda slanted his eyes. Like Renata had a physique like Hollow. "You're right, dude. This is dumb. And if we keep going, you might pinch me because I'm not wearing green."

Rico shrugged. "Neither am I. And I'm Catholic. You got the green eyes, though." Rico was peering at them a little too closely. "Justus was wrong, wasn't he?"

"Huh?" Coda asked, watching Rico web his fingers with purple blazes. "Wrong about what? And whatever you're doing with your hands right now is *pretty* creepy."

"You don't have crosses in your eyes like Justus does," Rico said, extinguishing his hands. "The closest thing I can compare it to is the flames I see in mine."

Coda laughed. "I barely see anything whenever I look for myself, just a haze of gold."

"Maybe that's it," Rico nodded. "A haze, not a flame." He motioned for Coda to get up. "Enough training for today, Freckle Face. Let's go watch some videos. Somebody's bound to have dropped a new one."

"I have a better idea," Coda said, looking at Rico's wooden fence towards Peppi's unseen house.

"What are you thinking?" Rico asked.

"What would Justus say at a time like this?" Coda asked as the cool spring wind blew the sun a little further towards the horizon.

It wasn't until his friend cleared the fence with his insanely developed gymnastic abilities that Rico understood, beginning to laugh.

"Jacuzzi!"

· · · · ·

Peppi's giant hot tub was ready for them.

"Dude, like half of KWA could fit in here," Rico said, kneeling over the water, testing it with his hands.

Coda exhaled loudly while immersing himself into the bubbles. "Who all did you invite over?" he asked Rico.

On cue, someone crowed from the back porch. Coda clenched his teeth. *Great*, he thought.

"Stallion!" Rico bellowed, as Shannon leapt over the wooden banisters, kicking off his sandals in mid-air.

"Ricochet!" Shannon said, and their bodies slapped together.

"Your hair's longer," Rico observed, tugging Shannon's curls.

"Your face is browner," Shannon said, lightly slapping Rico's face. "You're almost Blacker than Coda."

"I missed you so much, Shannon," Coda said dryly as Shannon slipped into the water next to him. "You and your pleasant abuse."

"Dude, you get tramp stamped?" Shannon asked, looking at the thorn wounds on Coda's chest.

Coda slipped a little further into the water. "Fell into some unfriendly brush on the beach," he said, staring at the deepening blue of the sky, waiting for the stars to show their faces. "I'm sure you know absolutely *nothing* about that."

Shannon looked at Rico with questions in his eyes, but all he said to Coda was "Sounds painful."

"Gene's not coming?" Rico asked, joining them in the steaming waters. "I got his voicemail."

Shannon shrugged. "The real question is what's Peppi's reaction gonna be when she finds these fine sausages boiling in her backyard. Her parents are out of town you said?"

Rico nodded. "She couldn't go because of school. But they went to Florida for the week or something."

Coda wiped sweat out of his eye. Once Rico had joined them in the pool, the temperature had increased noticeably. Coda wondered if he would have noticed had he not known of his friend's special abilities.

"Peppi's brother is auditioning for *Dancing Dynamos*," he said. "The casting is happening in Jacksonville."

"Oh, that reality show?" Shannon laughed. "I didn't know he danced that well."

"He doesn't," Coda muttered. "But even if he did, it's impossible to make it in those things. *Singing Star* auditions were the biggest crock..."

Shannon and Rico stared at him.

"You auditioned for *Singing Star?*" Shannon asked.

Coda smirked. "This is something you'd know if you kept in touch."

"No," Rico said, "'cause I talk to you all the time and I didn't know this."

Coda faltered, upper hand slapped down. "Oh, you didn't?"

Rico shook his head, eyes almost poisonous in their brightness. Coda shrank.

"Well, I obviously didn't make it," he muttered.

"What was it like?" Shannon inquired, so Coda told them about the experience. The cattle call, the way he was sized-up immediately as a cookie cutter R&B singer with a great voice but no individuality.

"That sucks," Rico said.

"No individuality?" Shannon seemed dumbfounded. "There hasn't been an out of the closet soul singer, like, ever."

Coda's gaze sharpened.

Rico seemed to be solving some mental puzzle. "Is that why you dropped out of school? To go on auditions?"

Coda shrugged. "I need to focus on something I'm passionate about."

"You shoulda gone to singing and dancing school or something, then," Shannon said, putting his two cents in where it wasn't needed. He was visibly sweating too. Rico was the only one dry. Coda found that interesting.

"I don't need to go to school for something I already know inside and out," Coda said, closing his eyes as if willing the conversation away.

"If you were still in school you wouldn't have had to move out of your dad's house," Rico said, and Coda's glare was now focused on him.

"Why are you bringing that up?" he asked.

"Dang, Shawshank. Where are you staying?" Shannon asked.

Coda didn't answer, though Rico gave a knowing glance to the stocky jock.

Shannon continued, nodding at Rico's silent communication. "Not getting a degree is dumb."

"You're dumb," Coda retorted immaturely, swallowed up by a scream coming from Peppi's house.

"Perpetua!" Shannon shouted, hopping out of the jacuzzi. He seemed to land roughly, grimacing and grabbing his knee. He hobbled over to the shellshocked girl standing in the doorway.

Peppi hit him as he hugged her. "Boys, you scared me!"

Coda and Rico were laughing. "You invited us over," Rico defended.

"You were supposed to tell me before," she said through her accent.

"Ah, where's the fun in that?" Coda asked.

"Join us!" Rico said with a glint in his eyes.

"My swimsuit's upstairs," Peppi said, turning back towards the house.

Shannon grabbed her hand, pulling her back towards the jacuzzi. "So?" He stepped out of his trunks and cannonballed into the water.

"Oh my God!" Peppi laughed.

Rico wiped water out of his face, while Coda grumbled, "Seriously?"

Shannon surfaced, sweating and naked and grinning, eyes on Peppi.

"I owe you a punch to the face," Rico said, quite seriously.

Shannon smiled at him. "The water of life, my friend. High in protein."

"You're naked," Coda said, disbelieving.

Shannon turned to him. "Have you met Lil' Coda? I call him that because when he gets wet, he has curls like yours."

"That's disgusting," Coda said as Rico started laughing.

"Or maybe because, like you, he's not straight."

"I'm getting some *bottled* water," Coda said, climbing out.

"Can you grab me—" Rico began.

"Grab your own," Coda said.

Rico furrowed his brow, but followed begrudgingly, as Peppi began to remove her sundress.

Shannon was still going. "I used to call him Jolly Green, because… well, that doesn't matter because they found a cure."

"White boys," Coda was saying as Rico joined him in Peppi's kitchen, both of them dripping wet.

"You're white," Rico said, his laughter finally subsiding.

"Tell that to my father," Coda muttered.

Rico frowned. "Whatever your problem is, I'd appreciate it if you'd get over it and let yourself have fun."

Coda didn't make eye contact, raking his eyes over the contents of Peppi's fridge. "You get around him and you act like you're just like him, but you're not. Even he's not really like that, he's just putting on one of his obnoxious shows."

"What are you talking about, now?" Rico asked. "Clue me in, because I got no memo that we'd be arguing all day."

"You're different now, Rico. *We're* different. From him. Unless, of course, he's the freak who's been kicking our asses."

"It's not Shannon," Rico said tiredly, hands on the refrigerator door.

"Well your detective work has been so thorough, especially just now in that jacuzzi," Coda sniped.

"Yours was great, too," Rico said, purposefully bringing a bright tone into his words. He had finally recalled what had been nagging him. "Shannon was at a party with Ezekiel and BJ up in Atlanta the night you fought Hollow at Wilbanks." He looked out the window, remembering to keep his voice down. "You remember parties, right? You used to be social, once. In fact, you're nowhere near as fun and vibrant as you used to be. You were a freaking butterfly in high school. Did you climb back into your cocoon?"

"Who out there is gonna understand us?" Coda asked. "That's the reason why I can't just be as open as I used to be. How will anybody understand our condition?"

Seriously? "We're not lepers, Coda."

"Oh, that's right." Coda's eyebrows were arching. "We're aiming for other 'jolly green' diseases."

"You're making it very hard for me to remember why we were ever friends," Rico said seriously. "If I wanted to hang out with a bitch, I'd hang out with Bethany Kelly."

Tears were swimming in Coda's eyes. Drama King.

…damn it.

"I'm *sorta* sorry, Coda," he sighed. "But seriously, this whole Virginia Woolf attitude is not becoming. We're allowed to have fun. You love a lot. Now you need to live a little."

"Fine." Coda gestured through the window out to the jacuzzi, where Shannon had Peppi pinned against the side, back muscles flexing as he made out with her. "Let's go get jiggy like your naked buddy there."

Rico sighed, closing the refrigerator door. "Let's go. Mood successfully killed."

As the left Peppi's house, Rico wondered if he was blaming his unsettled spirit on the two outside or the one walking next to him.

Hours later he would realize that their entire disagreement had been in Spanish, a language that, to Rico's knowledge, Coda had never spoken as fluently as he had in Peppi's kitchen.

• • • • •

"This is cute," Cheyenne Crenshaw said, sprinkling pepper on her sub as Justus joined her with his tray, "but for a date you could have taken me off campus."

Justus smiled, setting his backpack next to his chair. "You don't like the University Center? I figured the ambiance was worthy of your beauty."

Cheyenne lowered a finger in his direction. "You promise that you didn't bring me here for romantic purposes?"

Justus frowned. "You're not my type, so, yeah."

"Nice," Cheyenne commented dryly.

Justus figured he should've presented his answer in a different fashion. "I'm sorry," he said quickly. "Please don't be offended. You would've cut me down in a similar style had I taken a split-second longer to respond."

Cheyenne shook her head, as if in disbelief. Her thick hair bounced with each shake, feathers and beads rolling gently against her cheekbones. "You are one of the oddest birds that ever flew anyone's coop."

Justus laughed. "With my luck, I'm probably one of the flightless ones."

Cheyenne leaned back in her chair with a cool stare, shredding the layers of Justus's presentation off in a few quick seconds.

"Justus, let's not pretend that all of our recent talks about nothing in Poly Sci are the reasons why we're having this late-night summit."

"We couldn't have done it earlier," he shrugged, digging into his chips. "You were busy today; I was busy."

"And I could be dead tomorrow and you don't want me burning in hell."

Justus was silent.

"Come now, don't falter at the altar, Rev. Alexander. I'm sure you have your sermon prepared." She bit into her sub. "Let's hear it."

That's all he needed. The dam was busted.

"How can you grow up in the church and not experience Jesus for yourself?" Justus asked ardently. "In any fashion? You're telling me that for twenty years—"

"Nineteen," she corrected with a wiggle of her fingers.

"In nineteen years you were never exposed to the wonders of Jesus?"

She giggled, left hand playing with mustard packets. "My family's not Pentecostal, Justus. They're Baptists. We believe in the Holy Ghost, but miracles seem to be increasingly staged to raise money at church revivals."

"Your brother's experienced Jesus! He's been blessed! I don't understand how you can be blessed and not see that it was God!"

Now Cheyenne was laughing loudly. "My brother's been blessed? My brother, the runaway, is blessed? Read a book. Tell me how it ends up."

"You don't care?"

"I care, Justus. Does your God? Because where was 'He' and where were 'His' blessings when my boyfriend—the love of my life—was in the hospital for two months?" The venom in her voice choked out her laughter. "Ask Him where I was! Go ahead! If He exists as you say and answers you—and if He noticed, which He better have because I spoke to Him every day…

"I was at the hospital, that's where I was! Justus, I was with Kevin every day after school and every morning before school. I prayed in every way I could think how and Kevin still died. You tell me where the blessing was in that! And don't give me that crap about how maybe his life wouldn't have been satisfactory after the accident and that he might have come out of it with no legs or without full mental capacity. If Jesus Christ can rise from the dead and create the world and keep it turning, explain to me why Kevin couldn't have been woken from that horrible sleep with no permanent damage done!"

"I'm not saying that there was a blessing in his death," Justus said earnestly. "That's a situation I know nothing about, but I can tell you this, Cheyenne. It's unfair to expect to understand everything."

"Justus," Cheyenne intoned warningly.

"We look for Jesus in the big things, while He embraces us with the small! Nineteen years of constant breath, waking up, clothes to wear, a voice to speak with and people to talk to, food to eat or to choose not to eat, those are the miracles!

"I never knew my father. I don't even know his name! I've been practically raised by my grandparents. My mom holds odd jobs and has had different men that have meant different things to her at different times! If I constantly look at that, I'll overlook the fact that I'm here. I'll overlook the fact that I'm warm in the winter and cool in the summer and I can buy a pretty girl food at the UC if I want to. How dare I take God to task because of inconveniences, when the conveniences far outweigh those?"

Cheyenne pushed her chair back and stood, pulling her purse over her shoulder.

"Excuse me, Justus, but I can't sit here while you tell me that—no, sit back down, because if you try to walk me out I may pay you some very violent attention so sit the hell back down—while you tell me that the love of my life dying slowly over two months is an 'inconvenience' and that I should be grateful because I can chomp on a dry teriyaki chicken sub with you, the dork, who considers me a 'convenience'! And excuse me if I think that you attempting to speak to me ever again in Professor Henderson's class or any other time you see me is perhaps the most worst possible idea you could come up with!"

She gestured to Ezekiel who was sitting far off, now aware that her attention was directed towards him. "This goes for you, too, other-friend-of-my-brother, lest you come at me with fear that the Easter Bunny is gonna skip my dormitory this spring." For a moment, she paused, but her sardonic tone filled the air before either of them could seize the opportunity of her silence. "I would tell you two to go to hell, but I don't want to see you there."

She marched away, refusing to acknowledge him as he called after her. When he took a step forward, a hand on his arm pulled him back.

Shaking his head, Ezekiel said, "Let her go. That's the best thing to do at this point."

Once she disappeared through the doors of the UC, Justus sat back down, and Ezekiel sat adjacent from his friend.

"Did you hear that?" Justus asked, trying to ignore the horrible knot that had grown in his stomach. "I think I screwed up, big time."

"Yeah, this was a terrible idea," Ezekiel said. Justus's face fell, but Ezekiel continued. "Not that I can back up how she took it with any extrasensory knowledge. I think God deliberately drew the curtain on that one."

"Oh, really?" Justus was pained. "Lot of good it did, then, me inviting you here. I guess I'll have to wait it out."

"Like normal people," Ezekiel joked.

"Normal does not exist," Justus professed. "Never has."

"I guess… Man! Like, we could've handled that *way* bet—"

"I know," Justus moaned. "You might as well eat with me," he said then, gesturing back to his Philly cheesesteak. "She won't be coming back in here to dine with an idiot."

Ezekiel brought his tray over from a nearby table and the two traded thoughts, information and ideas. Mostly, Justus apologized for having Ezekiel stop through Mercer on his way home for spring break and Ezekiel continually reminded him that Christopher Nyberg, who had driven him, made plans to stop through and visit some friends anyway. Ezekiel used to opportunity to mention the lightning scar that had waited almost a full four months to show up on his back. "It's like it was there originally, but maybe really subtle, and now that my skin is getting thicker, it's gotten more obvious."

As the night wore on, the UC closed up and Justus took Ezekiel on a tour of the campus, taking great care to paint the picture of his vicious battle with Hollow as they passed back by the UC.

"I can't believe we've been so easily distracted," Ezekiel commented, staring at the wall Justus pointed to while elaborating the bloody details of that fight several weeks ago.

"What do you mean?" Justus asked, forgetting about his tale and hooking his thumbs on his backpack.

"We never asked you about your 'choice night,'" the Tech student replied. "We were so ecstatic that you were one of us, we never asked how."

"You guys never told me what a 'choice night' was," Justus said.

Ezekiel turned to him. "Wow. I get it now. You haven't had a near death experience have you? Nothing big, life re-affirming in the past year or two?"

"You mean aside from the night I thought Hollow was gonna kill me?" Justus asked, looking back up at the wall. "No, of course not. You can read my brain, can't you?"

"It's a blank slate," Ezekiel ribbed.

Justus laughed. "Well, for starters, I've been having these crazy dreams of mine for as long as I can remember. Before fifth grade for sure. They used to be exclusively metaphorical, but lately they've been exact replications…exact circumstances. And the water thing is something that I look back on in retrospect and wonder about."

"What do you mean?"

Justus shrugged. "Near the end of senior year, I'd wake up on the floor sometimes. Directly underneath the bed. I figured I had fallen off and rolled under there without waking up. Now I wonder if I just soaked straight through the mattress."

Ezekiel shook his head. "Amazing. How long do you think that's been going on?"

"I feel like it's been happening since at least freshman year," Justus said, before stopping in his tracks.

Ezekiel froze right beside him, glancing around at the near deserted walkway. Then, after following the slight jerk of Justus's cranium, he spotted the all too familiar figure in brown. The dreadlocks hadn't changed, the spotless skin was the—well, his arms were freckled, but maybe Ezekiel hadn't noticed that before. He wondered.

Hollow began advancing.

Justus yelped. This was not good. The expression in Hollow's eyes was one of malicious intention.

Ezekiel began to pray for the first time that week. It looked like things were going to get ugly.

"In my backpack," Justus whispered.

"What?" Ezekiel asked.

"Weapons," Justus said, assisting Ezekiel undo the zipper. With wide eyes, Ezekiel removed a cast iron skillet and a giant silver frying pan.

"You carry kitchenware in your backpack?" he asked incredulously.

Justus nodded vigorously, while removing the last two items, a carving fork and a large silver pot. "If you had been beaten as bad as I was beaten, you'd come up with all kinds of interesting ideas when you know there's a chance that person might come back."

Ezekiel wondered where the blond kept his books.

When they looked again, Hollow was gone and the boys didn't know why they were surprised.

Justus's eyes took in the surrounding area. There were too many trees!

"I don't see him," he said.

Ezekiel put a finger to his lips and pushed the iron skillet into Justus's arms. Stepping cautiously into the grass with only the silver pan as his weapon, he moved slowly down the length of the building, staring out around the trees. He could see snatches of Hollow's thoughts, so Ezekiel knew that the dreadlocks were still around, even if he didn't know what Hollow had planned. What did Ezekiel have planned? Anything? Or was this just some type of pointless ordeal?

Suddenly, the pale boy materialized directly behind Ezekiel, tapping the back of his neck.

"Ezekiel!" Justus called.

Ezekiel paid Justus no mind, busy trading useless blows with Hollow. Not even the frying pan was having an effect on him.

"Don't touch him!" Justus reminded Ezekiel. "He just uses it against you!"

And with that amazing speed, Hollow was in Justus's face, smiling nastily, raking the back of his hand across Justus's face.

Then, his face blushing as he rose into the midnight air above his two adversaries, he turned both hands onto Justus, pelting him with sharp hailstones. Justus liquefied his torso, allowing Hollow's ice bullets to pass through him and dissolve into the air behind him as Hollow's loins pulled water molecules from the surrounding atmosphere.

Ezekiel shot quick eyes to Justus and the elemental understood. Securing his baseball cap, Justus rose into Hollow's view, leveling with him without attempting a return strike, but the distraction did not work.

Hollow laid a gnarled claw of ice around Justus's throat and turned to greet Ezekiel as Ezekiel rose, plummeting him with a geyser of water.

He's virtually invincible, Justus marveled. He was also doing a great job at cutting off Justus's oxygen supply. Why couldn't Justus evaporate himself? Why was he not panicking enough for his body's composition to go berserk?

Ezekiel was having trouble with his attempt to maneuver out of the seemingly inexhaustible thick torrent of water that Hollow had laid upon him. The pan fell from his hand.

"It's too much," he exclaimed to Justus over the pounding liquid, being pushed further and further away from Hollow as the pale one choked the life out of his translatable friend. "I'm not strong enough to barrel through!"

Hollow smiled evilly, before lifting a thick foot of ice and slamming it into Justus's chin.

Then the stream of water narrowed. It was a powerful jet, pushing Ezekiel back even further as the water pounded against his chest like one miniature brick building. Unending. Pounding against his throat and almost destroying his balance. Against his chin and bringing a natural brand of water to Ezekiel's eyes. Ezekiel turned his head. Hollow was going for the eyes. It was obvious now. By becoming like them Hollow acquired their weaknesses along with their strengths. When they defeated him, he marked it—however they defeated him was how he could defeat them.

And that's when Ezekiel realized that he shouldn't struggle through. Hadn't that boy on the sidewalk that he and Christopher had met told them, Ezekiel in particular, that there was a time for war and a time for peace? This was a time for composure, not combating. How far could Hollow stretch his hydro-oxygen abilities? There was no water source around, save from the air, so his geyser of water had a limited range.

Ezekiel dropped to the ground and Hollow followed, keeping a good icy grip on Justus, whose face was turning purple. Justus's punches and kicks were non-affecting since Hollow still had Ezekiel's thick skin and had also stretched his mass to the limit, leaving no body beneath his chest.

Sorry, Justus, Ezekiel thought, as he continued backing away from Hollow. *But I want this turkey to try to reach me. Just try to reach me.*

Justus's khaki covered legs were flailing about as he attempted to land just one good kick, knowing it was futile. *Oh, God, don't let me die tonight!*

And he burst into hot steam, forcing Hollow to release him. Hollow ignored the condensing liquid of Justus and charged full force towards Ezekiel.

Justus rained down onto the concrete, gasping for breath as he fleshed.

Stay away from him, Ezekiel. Without your power, either one of us can do some serious damage. Where's the iron skillet?

Hollow was fast, but Ezekiel was fast as well, so with Hollow as stretched as he seemed to be, it was a fairly even match. Ezekiel kept faking him out, sometimes doing so vertically since he had the option. Hollow couldn't fly without Ezekiel and Justus's unwilling assistance, so it was becoming easier to put distance between them as Hollow's appropriated gifts left his shell. If only Ezekiel had gloves, then he could plant a solid one…

Justus found the skillet and turned back to the fight. This pan was heavier, more dangerous than the one he had originally kept for himself. Just the thing. *Fake him out, Ezekiel. Just a little longer.*

Ezekiel dogged Hollow and flew around one of the gigantic oaks. He might have to fly into the branches, but the roaches and the birds—it would be a bit much, even for him.

Hollow's grey eyes were scanning the branches. Since when were this creep's eyes grey?

And Justus was upon him, banging that skillet on Hollow's knee for all it was worth. Hollow grabbed his injured leg and Justus connected again with his exposed side.

"I don't want to have to hurt you, but God has told his servants to kill before," Justus said, with a ferocity that he didn't know he had. "And I'M HIS SERVANT!"

He continued both speaking and striking.

"TOUCH! NOT! MINE! ANOINTED!"

Hollow opened his mouth in a gruesome roar which echoed inside of him long after his mouth had stopped producing the noise, and Justus took a risk and brought the skillet down in the same spot he had connected with originally, this time smashing the hands that held the wounded knee. And Hollow departed.

Ezekiel floated gently down from the tree, wary of Justus's recent outburst and wishing that Kim was there so that he could know if Hollow was really gone.

He chuckled as he noticed that both he and Justus were sporting their black and gold cross country tees. They were almost uniformed, especially now that Justus's hair was as black—if not more—as Ezekiel's.

"One of these days I'd love to know what goes on in *your* head," the sometime-blond said, shaking his head at Ezekiel's laughter.

"Are you okay?" Ezekiel asked, appraising his friend's abused neck.

"I'm fine," Justus nodded, feeling slightly woozy. "That was jacuzzi. How are you?"

"I'm good," Ezekiel was saying, when Justus keeled over suddenly.

He gripped the side of the UC as his eyesight betrayed him right along with his balance. His vision was focused, but not seeing, as if filtered through a kaleidoscope.

"You okay?" Ezekiel asked. "Your eyes are going crazy, dude."

"I feel a little light headed, Ezekiel," Justus muttered, reaching for his head.

Ezekiel rushed to his side as Justus dropped unconscious towards the ground.

23.

Principalities and Powers

"Dreamer, open your eyes."

Justus did as he was told.

In front of him, maybe standing, maybe floating, was an impressively molded figure, brown skin drawn taunt by muscles necessarily formed for the toil of a warrior. Pink cloth in various shades and textures cascaded and seemed to fade into the air around the mysterious individual as if the fabrics were merely an aura instead of a covering. Its eyes, youthful while ancient, were the color of the late afternoon sun, warm and pleasing.

"Walk with me, Dreamer," the angel spoke, left hand fitted with a red glove and outstretched in Justus's direction.

"I know you," Justus realized, grasping his bearings as he took the hand, trying to figure which senses were available. "You saved my life."

The angel shook its head, as its gold eyes crackled. "I merely carried you to your bed and ensured no more harm came to you. It was another that saved your life, Dreamer. Now walk with me."

The muscular being turned, and Justus was allowed to take in his new surroundings.

Mercer, it was not. Justus stood surrounded by myrtle grass that stretched across an extensive meadow, blooming with giant, marble patterned flowers. The petals alone were the size of human faces. Dancing a hand across the soft flora, Justus curved his neck to marvel at the majesty of two setting suns that painted the sky green and silver. Along both sides of the shamrock pasture, mountains rose until they faded into the emerald of the sky.

Most marvelous of all were the creatures, unnamed by Adam and undreamed by mythologies, trotting happily amongst the massive flowers and flying placidly through the troposphere. Some had horns and feathers, others had scales and fur, and only one third of the animals in the air had wings of any sort.

Surrounded by such wonders, Justus had forgotten to walk, and the angel had turned to wait on him.

"Is such a creation beautiful?" the angel asked.

"Absolutely," Justus nodded, wishing he could put it all into words. "It's beyond anything I've ever seen. Beyond anything I've ever heard of!"

The angel seemed to smile without moving its mouth, and Justus dipped his head.

"I apologize for stopping," he said.

"Do not worship me, Dreamer," it warned, causing Justus to lift his head. "There is room for one King, and I am not That One."

Justus observed the angel with renewed interest. "Where are your wings?"

"Where are yours?"

He couldn't tell if the angel was joking. Did angels joke at all?

He began to stammer, but the angel's kindly, yet impenetrable expression eased the words out.

"I don't have any."

The angel stared a little longer, before saying, "One of you does." Without elaborating, the angel turned and moved on through the field, Justus following.

Justus had many more questions now, but elected to keep them to himself until they had come to an appropriate stopping place.

As they traveled, the angel guided Justus towards the sole tree in the meadow. The trunk was slender and white, stretching like an ivory cyclone several feet above Justus's head before an impossible amount of branches grew out wide, pregnant with leaves and fruit. The branches were so full that they swelled and dipped until they were merely an arm's reach overhead.

Justus turned to the angel, his heart swelling with the prospect of devouring the otherworldly fruit. "May I eat of this tree?"

"You may, Dreamer," the angel responded.

Justus reached into the branches and plucked a fruit, sparkling and pink. Biting into it, he quickly realized that all of the fruits he had ever tasted were merely poor imitations of such fruit that grew on that very tree. The skin of the fruit was not tough, and the interior tissues were filled with inexhaustible flavor. The fruit held no seeds; since the tree was of the everlasting sort, there was no need for reproduction.

"Do you enjoy such fruit?" the angel asked.

"Absolutely!" Justus exclaimed, taking another bite. The juice that swirled on his tongue and flowed down his throat did not spill onto his chin. He swallowed, adding, "It's so yummy! It's like the tastiest of tasties!"

Later, Justus would remember his words with embarrassment, but when faced with the most unimaginable essences, impressing the angel with his vocabulary was not his primary focus.

Once the fruit was devoured in its entirety, the angel walked on and Justus followed, until they heard the music of a rushing river. It did not go unnoticed to Justus that the closer they drew to the river, the fewer creatures that appeared crawling amongst the grass roots and gliding through the silver-green air. No more beasts jumped from flower petal to flower petal, and eventually, even the flowers went into hiding. At the crystal-clay bank of the river, the angel pointed.

Justus was breathless. The river flowed as red glitter, and crouched beside it, he beheld another golden-eyed angel, blue and shimmering. It was glorious to behold, jeweled and crested in the purest of molecules, though its countenance was…afflicted.

"Is such a creature beautiful?" the escort angel inquired.

"Perhaps the most beautiful in this world," Justus exhaled, afraid to disturb the environment with his movements or words. There was a level of fragility here, a dissonance in harmony that he didn't understand, and perhaps that is what made this particular angel so beautiful to him. Fragility was one thing that, as a human, Justus could consummately grasp.

One of the unnamed creatures of the air flew near the Blue Angel, and Justus willed it away. The delicate balance was surely to be tipped somehow, and Justus was afraid of any new addition to the equation. However, as unbidden as the presence may have been, the Blue Angel was appreciative of the company, even seeming to smile.

The Blue Angel held out an ivory hand, the left one, and the aerial creature perched on its palm, two cinereal feathers quivering atop its opalescent and encrusted head.

As Justus watched, the Blue Angel's expression changed on some spiritual surface. Just as the Blue Angel's smile was not quite manifest, Justus couldn't quite make out what this new visage intimated.

It was proven to be something ugly. He watched in revulsion as the creature on the Blue Angel's finger collapsed into newer dimensions, creating something smaller, less beautiful, and uncomfortably familiar to Justus's eyes. The balance had been broken; something was sucked from the area—a bit of love that had to be transferred elsewhere.

Justus shuddered at the ruination, as the cockroach fell from the Blue Angel's finger. The Blue Angel seemed to shudder as well, and Justus saw the angel for what it was. It was a renegade.

They observed the angel for a few more moments in silence, though Justus no longer wanted to cope with the conditions that had rolled over the area like a psychic thundercloud.

On cue, cracking the air like a perceptive bolt of lightning, yet another heavenly creature arrived from the sky. Resplendent in garments similar to those of the Blue Angel, it was adorned in colors unlike any colors Justus had seen in his existence. The one color Justus could even recognize as an earthly one was the red on this new arrival's left hand.

This was the emissary. It towered over the Blue Angel, noticeably taller, watching the cockroach crawl away with those now recognizable honeyed eyes.

The renegade spoke, voice beautiful, but something less than pure…a copy of something truer and former, equal to a cubic zirconia in a world where diamonds no longer dwell. "The ill is in me, Baraqiel."

Baraqiel the emissary turned its discerning gaze to the renegade. "Ambriel, it is known over all creation that the ill is in you. You have invited it in."

"It won't leave," Ambriel spoke, looking up, its golden eyes flickering with a color that matched its attire. "One moment, just to see how it would feel, and now I belong to the ill whenever it wants me!"

Baraqiel leaned close to Ambriel in a blameless fury. "Why would you want to feel anything other than the closeness of El Roi?"

"El Roi," Justus whispered. *The God who sees.*

Ambriel rocked back on its heels, wailing, ripping at its clothes and skin as if ripping at the ill that had raped its being.

"I cannot drink from the river!" it cried, golden hair as distraught as its owner, shaking loose from beneath its shawl. "I have waited here, but the river still tells me I am not welcome! Is my fate changed for me because of one moment?"

Baraqiel stepped back, observing Ambriel with steady eyes. In a testament to where the emissary stood in God's eyes, it dipped a hand in the sparkling river, and the melody of the song in the stream changed ever so slightly. Holy still, yes, but foreboding and severe. Baraqiel brought the palm of crimson liquid to its own lips and drank deeply.

"Everlasting joy is what I have chosen," Baraqiel spoke, now holding a flaming sword in the ebony hand that had been shrouded in a red glove moments before. "El Ruach is my Refresher. El Vahr is my Weapon!"

Justus was translating this as if he could speak their language. The Wind of God, or the Holy Spirit, was Baraqiel's source of being, and the Word of God Himself was its safeguard and its ammunition.

Ambriel shrieked and covered its head in its bare hands, one indigo and the other white. "I no longer have the Weapon."

Baraqiel spoke with finality. "And now your place is among the ill. Leave or I shall send you there. You may not hide here any more."

Ambriel crawled away, shrieking like a wounded animal, leaving ripped ribbons of blue cloth on the riverbank.

It was difficult for Justus to watch.

"I shall stay, Baraqiel," Ambriel screamed. "El Rapha is my God, my Master, my Source forever! El Rapha can take this ill from me!"

"You invited it in, Kamiskas," Baraqiel said again, pointing the sword at the blue one's body.

Ambriel gazed up, immediately alert to the new name—or title—that had just been used. Justus was not fluent in the way of angels, but he was sure that this signified another shift, similar to when Ambriel himself had 'created' the cockroach.

Baraqiel continued. "Inside of you there is only room for one or the other, Kamiskas. Once you send El Roi out, El is lost to you forever."

Justus understood now. The angel Ambriel no longer had God inside of it, so accordingly it was no longer allowed to bear a name with God, or El, in *it*. Ambriel would now be Kamiskas.

On the river's bank, Ambriel scurried away from Baraqiel, falling out of layers of clothing until it was no longer clothed in its angelic garments. "You are aware that El is going to allow those humans to have Possibility and Opportunity! These are the most guarded gifts of El!" Its voice had topped out with desperation. "Baraqiel, they shall have even Redemption! Look at what we, the very hosts of heaven, have done with Free Will! Imagine what those who abide far from the presence of El shall do with Redemption!"

Baraqiel spoke softly, still able to be heard over all of Ambriel's wailing.

"If the Accuser had not invited in the ill, there would be no reason for El to release Redemption on the earth. You, Kamiskas, joined the Accuser in the ill. And now you shall join the Accuser apart from heaven."

At Baraqiel's final word, Ambriel leapt off the ground, eyes flicking to blue and hair catching the atmosphere as if the strands themselves were preparing to strike Baraqiel in their anger.

"Then may you join us as well, Baraqiel. *May we all—*"

Seven branches of electricity leapt from Baraqiel's sword, and with sickening sizzles and pops, the skin of Ambriel burned, flayed from its bone by the whips of voltage. Justus would spend the rest of his life trying to shake the visual of the screaming angel getting whipped out of its heavenly worth.

The blue eyes were wide with fever and insanity and once the whips sheathed themselves back in Baraqiel's sword, Ambriel was no longer recognizable with its hair burned away and its body appearing as the worst version of a childhood boogeyman. All that was left was… Kamiskas.

It remained still without movement, crazed beyond the point of pain.

"To their eyes," the fallen one hissed, eyes now permanently blue, "I will still be pleasing. And you, Baraqiel—you and your kind will be inaccessible."

Justus couldn't see how such a thing could be considered pleasing to any eye, but upon closer inspection, he realized that the creature…was *the Creature*. The beautybeast. Blue and skinless and hairless, yet still supernatural and seductive to the ignorance of the human mind.

Justus realized that there was a balance. In their earthly bodies, humans could never achieve such beauty, yet they had chances, choices and options. Justus would not have traded that gift for all the pulchritude in the world.

"Is such a creature beautiful?" his angel asked once more.

After the non-superfluous splendor of angelic voices, Justus's voice sounded so one-dimensional to his own ears. "No, I see no beauty in it."

"That is sin that you see," the angel said. "That is weakness; that is pride, fear, sloth, and all manner of wickedness. That is the anti-God. Are such things beautiful?"

"There's no God in such things," Justus replied. "How can there be beauty where there is no God?"

On the riverbank, Baraqiel spoke again.

"It matters not if I am accessible. *El Roi* is accessible." The emissary pointed its sword towards a distant twinkling planet. "Just no longer to you."

Kamiskas was lifted off the ground and violently jerked in the direction Baraqiel's sword had chosen, joined in mid-flight by a flurry of cockroaches and weeds that the fallen one had spawned during its time on the planet. All together, they were sent crackling like lightning through the cosmos towards their new home.

"God is in the Word," the escort said.

"Amen," Justus agreed. "And the Word is thereby beautiful."

Instantly, Justus was streaking across the starland, faster than he believed it was possible to travel. When he was able to register his new surroundings, he stood on the side of the causeway, watching a familiar vehicle pulling to the side of the road.

"Ezekiel," Justus mouthed, glancing to the amazingly ripped angel at his side.

The escort nodded, just watching. Justus also watched, as Ezekiel climbed out of the car with his cell phone at his ear. The sky rumbled in pain and darkness, bringing Justus's eyes far above the causeway.

Suddenly the coal colored clouds came alive, a war raging on the inner side of the atmosphere. A host of brilliance burst through the clouds; a rainbow of glittering fallen angels were on the defense in the battle, underfoot the robed agents of the Lord. The devil's hosts dusted the heavens with distracting sparkles shaking from their neon swords. The gleaming warriors had come up with their own weapons in place of the word of God, and their irradiant swords were hooked and jacuzzi looking. The attitude sourcing their attire was disconcerting; the failing combatants had a bloated self-confidence which made them foolish, and even more dangerous.

With the battle arrived rain, and Justus rocketed his gaze back to Ezekiel, who braved the torrents in order to inspect his fender, folding his head against his shoulder to shield his cell from the rain.

For every move Ezekiel made, the celestials made one hundred. Justus had never seen such combat. With every shriek of their swords, they were moving closer to the ground.

One of the fallen ones, glittering pink and pearl but with eyes as brutally blue as Kamiskas's, caught sight of something on the causeway and broke free of the melee, racing towards the ground in a streak of the hottest pink, over-saturated in comparison to the pink that dressed Justus's companion.

A golden-eyed angel took notice of the bolting fallen one and followed without hesitation. The hellion turned, hearing the approaching angel, and glee stretched across its face. It wanted the violence. It invited the mayhem.

If Justus hadn't already been dreaming and thus unconscious to the world, he was sure he would have fainted.

Ezekiel seemed to sense the approaching powers, looking up in the sky as lightning appeared to strike him.

It wasn't lightning, though. In fact, Justus was sure that it was the angel emissary Baraqiel, shooting past the pink demon and gripping Ezekiel's shoulder. In fact, that's when Justus was able to understand what the color was that Baraqiel wore. It was the color of lightning, a magnificent shade fused so utterly in the spiritual that Justus's naked human eye had never before been able to see it.

It appeared that the angel's grip knocked Ezekiel unconscious with a spiritual intensity. The heavenly warrior continued sparring with the hellion while keeping Ezekiel safe from traffic.

"Was that demon going after Ezekiel?" Justus asked his escort, a bit confused.

The angel turned to him, its gold eyes sharp from viewing the battle. "What can a spirit do to a body but make suggestions that lead it to either Life or death?"

"What is this battle?" Justus asked. "Why is it happening in Brunswick?"

"Because it needs to," was the angel's response, and Justus asked no more, content to observe in the knowledge that he was safe with his angelic guard.

He marveled as Baraqiel defeated the demon, who seemed to be... changing. If the demon was even remotely corporeal, Justus would call it shrinking. However, his attention was soon taken by two other spirits, angels, as they placed Ezekiel in his car and drove back onto the causeway to take him home and away from the combat.

"God really is all around," Justus said.

The next movement was so swift, Justus didn't initially realize that one had occurred. Three unfamiliar faces, certainly human, were in front of him, draped ornately in opalescent capes. One, a female several years older than him, secured an emerald armored boot on her left leg. Another, redheaded and male, was securing all manner of weapons to his black vest. The third sat calmly in the corner, fingers around what looked like a rosary.

They were set up in some type of warehouse. It looked like one of the countless abandoned buildings located in downtown Brunswick, though the architecture was different. A little less port city and more central Georgia. At the far end of the warehouse, a door opened, and a gentleman in a black suit stepped in, walking swiftly. The other three seemed to be expecting him, turning towards him in anticipation.

"If she calls me 'Baby Doctor' one more time," the guy in the suit said, unbuttoning his jacket, "I promise you I won't be so nice."

The one sitting tucked his rosary and stood. He was much smaller than the rest. "You couldn't be mean if you tried."

The suited gentleman sputtered. The small one laughed.

The redhead asked, "Did you tell her that he has both of her serums?"

"It seems she suspects as much," the gentleman said. "I didn't tell her, but it was obvious that she was beginning to understand the reach of this."

"But that's all she knows?" the woman in green asked. "The end of the ocean?"

"She's a pond, with all she knows," the gentleman said. "And a pawn, with all that the Vice President has told her."

"A pond and pawn," the redhead said. "Great. So she's a dead end. Where does that get us?"

"She gets us nowhere, currently," the gentleman said. "The Vice President, though… He gave me coordinates." He pulled a folded piece of paper from his breast pocket. "We're going to have to put our protection of the county, Kim, and her friends on pause."

They gathered around as the gentleman began unfolding the paper. Justus was amazed at how easily they moved in their armor and those capes.

Looking at the unfolded paper, the small one grunted. "You've got to be kidding me."

"As tantalizing as this is," the woman said, "your sister is in the middle of a hurricane that she knows nothing about. Shouldn't one of us stay here at least?"

"We can't afford it," the redhead spoke. "And those kids are developing fast enough, considering they don't have the resources we had."

"That demon has an interest in them, though," she argued.

"What can a demon do?" the gentleman said.

"Seriously? We've seen what a demon can do."

"We're not demon hunters," the gentleman groaned, "despite our reputation. And that demon is a legionnaire. It just serves as a distraction."

"It and Patricia are like gnats," the small one said, taking the paper. "We're going after the real deal."

"And with demons about," the gentleman added, "then surely there are angels."

The woman sighed. "I get the idea of greater and lesser evils; I do. And I believe that the angels haven't revealed themselves to you for reasons we aren't yet to know, if ever. I just..." She turned intently to the one in the suit. "I wanna know if you'll be all in if we go?"

The gentleman broke away from the others, loosening his tie and removing his jacket. "I don't appreciate the doubt, Michelle, though I appreciate the concern." He removed his shirt, revealing an assortment of wounds and scars. "Everyone has their day of judgement. And it's not Patricia's yet."

He picked up his silver battle armor. "Nor is it ours."

Before Justus could register the meaning of what he had just seen and heard, the angel took him elsewhere, and this was the visit that stayed immediately with him when he woke.

It was Coda this time, alone on the campus of Oakwood Community College.

As Justus began considering the reasons that the angel had brought him to this particular place and time, Justus quickly saw that the boy was not truly alone.

Hollow and Solitaire appeared amongst the trees, violently interrupting Coda's run.

Justus couldn't protect or rescue his friend, resigned to watch helplessly.

He turned to the angel next to him.

"When is this?"

"This is tomorrow," the angel replied. "You cannot prevent it, but it was said for you to see it."

"What can I do?" asked Justus.

The angel raised the red glove, saying simply, "Everything," and the dream released him.

24.

Griefs

The Saturday after St. Patrick's Day brought Renata home, and she walked in on her favorite skinny boys stuffing down a mountain of breakfast tacos and making exuberant plans for the day. Coda became aware of her first, and, as was the new habit, immediately clammed up.

Renata noticed. She always noticed. Wondering briefly what his damage was, she decided not to sweat it, but her mouth betrayed her. Her mouth often betrayed her.

"Constipation of the mouth?" she inquired, secretly wondering if she had the opposite condition.

Coda cracked a wan smile. "What time did you get up?"

Renata was confused for a second, until she realized that Coda probably didn't know that her mother had moved out already.

"I just came from Mommy's place," she said.

Coda nodded, glancing at Rico. She found more in that gaze than she expected. They had been discussing things. She wondered what.

She headed over to the sliding glass doors that led out into the backyard, opening the baby blue blinds so that the late morning sunrise could spill onto the white kitchen tile. She noticed a small stain on the floor and snatched a paper towel off the counter, stooping to clean it up. Her papa was doing a good job of keeping the house clean, but it was the little things like that that her mother would have never let last more than one moment.

"The cookie woman's in town today," she notified Rico, wiping until there was no trace of whatever had been. She stood and brushed a mutinous strand of hair out of her face. "She called earlier, 'cause she couldn't reach you on your phone."

Rico slapped his forehead. "That's right. I'm supposed to pick her up from the airport." He began patting his khakis in search of his cell.

"The cookie lady?" Coda asked, looking back and forth between the siblings.

"BJ," Rico and Renata answered in unison.

"Would you like to know why I call her the cookie lady?" Renata was more than willing to offer the information.

"Sure," Coda said, ripping into another stuffed tortilla.

"That's BJ's new bit of slang. 'Cookies,' she says. She says it all the time."

"Oh," Coda managed.

"I think it means drugs," Renata said brightly, depositing the used paper towel into the white wastebasket adjacent to the refrigerator.

"Renata!" Rico exclaimed, giving her his trademark wide-eyed glare. Renata returned a withering gaze of her own before skipping into her room, singing some T.V. commercial jingle.

"BJ doesn't do drugs," Rico assured Coda, pulling his phone out of his pocket. "I'll be right back," he said, slipping into his room and closing the door behind him.

When Renata assumed it was safe, she headed back into the kitchen to help Coda displace the mountain of tacos.

"He always says he'll be right back," Coda muttered. "But with girl-friends…"

Renata took the opportunity to dig into her brother's friend a little more. "Coda, I heard you're single now," Renata said. "What happened to…what's her name?"

After letting the question settle, Coda answered. "Tasha wasn't ready for our relationship."

"What do you mean?" Renata pressed, flipping her brown ponytail over her shoulder and taking a massive bite out of her second breakfast meal, chewing vigorously.

"She never wanted to…talk to me, greet me, hug me, smile at me, dance with me, listen to me, hear me even…"

Renata swallowed. "You don't sound bitter at all," she teased.

"And you couldn't possibly understand why," Coda tartly replied. "I've had a long history of relationship problems."

"What you mean is you've had a long history of almost-relationships," she said, leveling with him. "You're high maintenance."

Coda raised his eyebrows. "That's a lot to assume coming from a high school freshman."

Renata snorted pleasantly. "We are an all-knowing generation."

Coda ignored the interjection, asking "What do you know about re-lationships?"

"I like my boyfriend, but if he wants to break up with me, no biggie. I only have one God, and *His* name isn't Mario. *He* doesn't take me to the lame-behind movie theatre each time *He* wants to connect with me." She took another bite.

Coda wrinkled his nose. "What kind of relationship is that, Renata? If you won't even mind breaking up with him, what's the point of having the relationship?"

Swallowing, she countered, "It's a realistic relationship, singing friend of my brother. Just about everyone breaks up, unless there's serious money involved." She bit into her burrito again.

"Now you sound jaded for real."

"Divorce'll do that to ya'," she managed through the mouthful of food. She reached for the bottle of Tabasco.

"Don't use that as an excuse."

"Oh, it's not an excuse, Coda. It's an explanation."

"Sure." Coda had forgotten all about his breakfast.

She raised her eyebrows, looking like her brother right down the the flames threatening to jump out of her eyes. "I'm serious. I mean, look at you! You've got to cut your losses if you ever plan on moving forward."

Coda shook his head. "Young minds." He raised the taco to his lips.

"Delusional minds are worse."

Coda pulled the taco away from his lips, waving it dispassionately, sausage and salsa dropping onto his placemat. "Oh, okay, Renata. So my outlook is counterfeit because I believe in love?"

"Wow, you could have said that much simpler, Coda."

"But you don't think love is as beautiful as I see it to be?"

Renata cackled. "Listen to yourself! You're a Disney character, Coda! Someday your princess will come and be a part of your whole new world. But I, I won't say I'm in love."

"That was ridiculous."

Renata lowered her eyelids. "You wish you had thought of it."

Coda spoke with a ludicrous accent. "It's not what I wish. It's what you wish!"

"That's not Disney. You just went all Broadway on me, didn't you?"

Coda nodded with embarrassment. "*Into the Woods*."

Renata shook her head. "Yeah, can't follow you there."

They continued to eat in pulsing silence, though it churned thoughtful, and not bitter.

"Why do you come over here so much, Coda?" she asked.

"You don't like me coming over?" he asked, staring at the backyard sky through the blinds.

Renata actually growled at him. "Don't answer my question with a question. I guess I'll answer my own question. I think you hate your house, so having Rico home is an excuse for you to have a home away from home."

Coda grinned. "Has anyone ever told you that you talk too much?"

"Yup, but I'm usually talking over them when they tell me, so a lot of good that does," she said, brown eyes shining. "Why do you hate being home?"

"See, you're jumping to conclusions, baby."

"That's because you're not giving me any, pookie."

Coda chuckled. "Rico's one of my closest friends."

"So are several other people, but you're always here," she said, looking pointedly at their brown kitchen table, "and not with them."

She couldn't read his mood. Coda was leaning forward, his chin raised high above his plate and his elbows just off the corner of the table, expression as far away as his thoughts.

"What about Kim?" she asked.

That sparked something in him. "Tell me something. What is up with that good-girl-falls-for-bad-guy stereotype?"

"What do you mean?"

"There has to be a reason. Kim's so awesome and she's just flouncing around in the mud. Like an angel in an oil spill."

"There's a thrill there," Renata suggested. "A challenge that doesn't come as easy to her as other things, maybe."

Coda twisted the sweatbands that hid the scars around his wrists. "That makes certain sense."

"Yep," Renata said. "But that's not too bad, you know. I mean, I've heard about her becoming a wild child and stuff—"

Coda's eyes slanted. "You and everybody else."

"—but one dastardly dude and a little college wing drying doesn't mean Kim needs an intervention or something. You know her better than I do, though."

She was cut off with a flourish of Coda's burrito.

"Can we not talk about Kim anymore, please?" he asked softly.

And thoughtful silence reigned yet again.

Rico exited his room, snapping his phone shut. "Are you ready?" he asked Coda.

"For what?"

"We've got to pick up the cookie lady, then drop Renata off at the college for some training thing she's doing."

"I'm tutoring in Spanish," she announced proudly, before holding up a hand, mentally processing something. "Wait." She squinted at Coda. "Have you always spoke Spanish this good?"

"What?" Coda asked in English. He looked over at Rico in confusion. "I haven't spoken Spanish since I took that last high school final. I switched over to French last semester and bombed."

Renata looked to Rico for support.

"Yeah, dude," Rico spoke up, "you've been speaking Spanish for a couple of days."

Renata was as dumbfounded as Coda appeared to be. "Wait, you don't speak Spanish?" She turned to Rico. "You haven't said a word to him about it?"

Rico shrugged. "I figured it was a power thing."

Renata swung her head back to Coda. "What is your power again? Does your flexibility apply to Romance languages?"

"*L'anglais n'est pas une langue romane*," Coda said, cluelessly. "*C'est une question j'ai manqué pendant l'examen de fin de session.*"

"*That* wasn't any language I speak," Renata said, while Rico offered a simple, "Whoa."

"Actually," Coda mumbled, thoughts seeming to race, "I think I'm just gonna grab my stuff and head out."

Rico glanced quickly at Renata before returning to Coda. "You sure? You want me to drop you off somewhere?"

"Did you bring your bike?" Renata asked.

Coda shook his head, careful to speak in English. "My dad borrowed it last month without my permission, even though he owns two cars, and now the tire is perma-flat no matter what I try, so I've got to get enough money to replace it."

"Don't you work at that restaurant on The Island?" Renata asked.

"He quit on Valentine's day," Rico said, not taking his eyes off of the Creole boy. "You sure you're gonna be okay?"

Coda stood, stretching. "I'll be fine. Promise. I like obstacles. Gives me purpose."

When he was gone, Renata looked at her brother. "He doesn't know the extent of his powers..."

Rico stared thoughtfully at the door where his friend had just been. "Maybe none of us do." He creased his forehead, adding, "That was crazy."

"It's not just that," Renata said. "He also doesn't seem to know he's gay."

Rico glanced at his sister. "What's it matter?"

"It matters because he thinks he's in love with Kim. And he thinks he likes me."

"He'll get over Kim," Rico said, putting on his jacket. "And he knows you're off limits."

Renata redid her ponytail. "All of this stuff with you guys and your powers is just starting, isn't it?"

Rico gestured to the door. "Sometimes I think it started back way before we'd ever guess."

"In the beginning, God created the heavens and the earth. And then He created Rico and his superpowered friends." The corners of Renata's mouth turned up just like her brother's. "And He said, 'Well, this is a peculiar group of dudes. Good, yet peculiar.'"

He smiled, too, for a moment. But something in the atmosphere didn't feel right. He glanced down the street, not liking the unsettling of his spirit.

"Get in the car," he told his sister.

· · · · ·

Lester Hamilton stared at the ugly Easter basket his grandchildren had sent him by way of their mommy, bubbling over with bath oils and candles and upscale chocolates that were probably their mommy's idea. The Hot Wheels, SpongeBob SquarePants lunch boxes and the pack of sour gummy worms were probably ideas purely their own. They had their moments, like most children, where they could be so sweet and thoughtful that you could forget all of the pounding headaches that they had caused. Lester chuckled to himself. Parents were the same way. His parents supplied him a good dosage of sweetness and headaches until their passings. 1973 and 1985. The hardest years of his life.

Kimberly was very different from her older sister, bright and bubbly in personality but very introverted in thought. Whenever Shirley had an opinion or an emotion it was right there in her disapproving expression. Kimberly kept her expressions under control to a scary fault, causing Lester to sometimes wonder exactly where her mind was and what exactly her mouth had meant. Like her unbroken habit of calling Lester "Dr. Hamilton" when he hadn't been a practicing ophthalmologist in near a decade.

Curled up next to her husband, Delia Hamilton thought back on how strict her mother had been. How she had warned against the snares of the devil, and Delia had dived perfectly into most of them, knowing quite well what she was doing. Her first husband had been the same way. And now her beautiful daughter, the light of her world, was making the same mistakes. And it worried her.

Things had changed, however. As times got worse, so did the devil's snares—at least the terminology. And the tongue ring. If Lester found out, he'd have a fit, even if it was the least of Delia's worries. She wanted to call both of her children. Well, all three. See how they were doing. See if older sister was handling the kids. See if brother was looking out for younger sister. See if daughter had survived another week.

Tears came to Delia's eyes. She had parented—was parenting the way God wanted her too, so why was her daughter going down the opposite path? And the answer was plain. Because she wanted to. Not because she was ignorant to the results or had been brought up wrong. Kimberly just wanted to live through her mistakes, in order to say she had made them. Delia had done the same thing, but she saw how foolish her plan had been in retrospect. With age comes wisdom, so what comes before that?

Lester was humming a little song. *"What a friend we have in Jesus. All our sins and griefs to bear."*

He heard Delia chuckling. He knew that he was atonal. Kimberly had gotten all of her speaking talent from her mother, but the lack of singing talent and the dramatics: that was all Lester's doing. Shirley was just as dramatic. Two daughters and a son. All grown. Lester sighed. The song was no longer on his lips. He missed his daughter.

"Everything to God in prayer," Delia said, standing and heading into the kitchen to refill her mug of coffee. "Everything to God in prayer.

• • • • •

Coda collapsed, leaning against the trunk of a pine, in amidst the decaying fallen leaves from the tall surrounding trees, as well as the carpet of pine needles, rotting brown limbs and prickly green bushes. Running the long distances through the convoluted trails at the community college was not what had gotten to him. It was the surprising March cold that had pitilessly clenched his chest and began chasing his nose.

He sniffed; Lena Park's early autumn jam was rotating on his mind's turntable and his brain had been far from the bodily suffering he was forcing upon himself, yet once he collapsed to recoup, his muscles began to make him pay. He decided that on account of the steadily increasing complacency and soreness, he would hop up and keep going, just taking some medicine once he got home.

He stood and brushed the damp dirt off his butt and attempted to shake off the bits of bark on his shirt. Ignoring the pounding in his head due to the fact that he had forgotten to eat any type of breakfast before heading to the college, he took off again, trampling the grass into the ground, He was alone with his song and his demons. And God was there. Somewhere.

Coda reached an opening in the pines and the oaks, and the large man-made lake opened up in front of him. He swung to the right and continued his out-of-the-way trek back towards the track that was lay-ing ahead of him to his left. He admired the stillness of the brown water as he loped around the grassy shoreline.

What was that noise? Coda turned around, disturbed by the rustling of dried leaves behind him. He saw some of the leaves flicking off the ground, and assuming that it was due to the draft he was kicking up, he turned back around, maneuvering through a thin section of the trail. Then he heard it again. A patter. A whir. Rustling. As if it was a tiny snake racing along behind him. He turned again, still only seeing the leaves being lifted again. Something still wasn't right.

But noise was coming from in front of him as well, and the leaves were stirred there as if by a ghost's desperation.

Before his vision could turn red, a rock to his head turned everything black.

• • • • •

"Why didn't *you* go home?" Stasia asked Kim out of the blue.

Kim was standing in the kitchen of Dishon's apartment, boiling some noodles, and Stasia was letting the cold air out of the refrigerator as she nosed around.

The emphasis on the "you" was not misplaced. At Clark Atlanta, Kim seemed to have bonded with classmates just as anti-everything-related-to-home as she was, though they all had different reasons. Fun-sized Frankie had endured an impossible childhood, so no matter where the future led, she couldn't see him ever actually looking forward to going home again. Dishon's parents had let him have it when they found out about his arrest and consequential expulsion from school, and his pride kept him from going back to let them know that he was doing better. He didn't even answer their phone calls. Stasia's parents had told her that it was about time she learned how to handle herself and her finances. She was not allowed back into their home until she had one of her own, and since she hadn't found an apartment quite yet, she was marooned in Atlanta as well. And there was Nicholas, Dishon's gold-toothed bandmate and roommate, who didn't have a home or family that he spoke of.

Why *hadn't* Kim gone home? She didn't feel like putting up with parents who would only treat their children like adults when it was self-beneficial. She should have gone back if only for the sake of her fellow peculiar people: Justus, Coda, Ezekiel, and Rico. But she didn't go back, because they'd be looking to her for leadership and she didn't feel like leading. She felt like just being one of everyone else.

But you're not, she heard, clear as day.

Ah, imperfection is indeed what she had gotten. But she had learned to embrace it. Love it, even. She'd get drunk and pass out—her attempt to escape the silence of the night, left alone with her thoughts. Maybe she was reneging on responsibilities, but that was between her and God.

It is, she heard, distinct and explicit.

"Hey Kimi, you know what you and corn have in common?" Stasia spoke up, pulling a beer from the refrigerator with her chubby hands.

Kim's interest was spiked. "No," she said, turning out the fire beneath the pot of noodles. She knew one thing, though. If Stasia didn't get Dishon's permission to drink that beer, there'd be an ugly situation later that Kim would have to smooth over. He was specific about his brews.

"Absolutely nothing!" Stasia exclaimed, laughing hysterically as if she had just cracked one of the funniest jokes of all time.

Kim glanced upside Stasia's head, searching for clues that would cement the theory Kim had just developed that the girl had been dropped on her head several times when she was younger.

"Sagacious today, are we?" Kim asked while pouring her noodles onto a styrofoam plate, deviously satisfied with the knowledge that doofy Stasia had no idea what 'sagacious' meant.

Kim had surrounded herself with an outer core of kids that weren't as smart as she had grown accustomed to. Sure, there were kids lacking common sense that had attended Wilbanks, but everyone had that vocabulary down, at least in her dealings. Coda used to be able to keep up with her toe to toe as far as the rare usages went, even going so far as to shout out to "Glynn Academy's Lilliputian First Lady" when he and Terry hosted Wilbanks' Talent Extravaganza.

Coda. Why did Kim think of him and Maya so much? They weren't thinking about her. They were all leading their separate lives now, and

Kim knew that it would never be the same as it was during high school, even though she wondered if that was an improvement.

Coda had been very offended when Maya had pushed them aside in favor of Gene. It seemed so trivial now, but Kim remembered the argument she and Coda had about being overtly friendly with their self-ostracized friend.

"Why wouldn't we talk to her?" Kim had asked innocently. "She's just being evil, that doesn't stop her from being my friend."

"She's still my friend, too," Coda had corrected, "but evil, no matter how slight, must not go unpunished—"

Sure, Coda.

Then there was that sad argument they shared on the porch of Rico's parents' house.

"Is it true that you get high nowadays?" Coda had asked.

"What?" Kim had asked. "Umm, Coda, boo—"

"I was talking to Gene the other day and he was telling me—"

Kim had sighed and swore. "Why did he have to open his big mouth?"

Coda had been trying to speak softly. "Kim, don't you think that with our specific blessings—"

"Coda, just stop. Like, really. Quit. Not right now."

"We have responsibilities, girl! Responsibilities."

The severity in his attitude made her feel so icky, and she retaliated as if he was Dishon.

"It is not that serious, boy, and you are not my father anyway."

"I'm your friend—that's family, it's close enough."

It was not. "It is not."

Coda had bit the insides of his cheeks, his white boy nose seeming to sharpen further. "Okay."

Kim had sighed. "Why do we do this? Do we have to argue?"

"If we didn't, we'd have nothing to talk about, apparently."

Seemed true enough. "That's not true," she lied.

"Okay."

Great. He had gotten himself angry. "Stop doing that!"

"I don't want to argue."

Then we wouldn't ever talk. Just like you said. "Fine."

"Okay."

Okay. "Don't say 'okay' anymore."

"Sure thing."

Poor emotional boy. "Good," she said immaturely.

Rico had exited the house, then. By the look on his face, she knew that he had heard them.

She had told him once, through the online journal, "Coda, you can't spend your days pining away over us. It's ridiculous. Grow. Expand. *Change.*"

And he didn't acknowledge her existence for about two weeks, and the whole ordeal was more hell on him than it was on Kim.

It was his fault for being so immature. All sexless and pure and wanting to be perceived as more than he himself thought was. And having the ability and the talent to go so far beyond what he knew.

Why did she think of him so much?

In the apartment, she had finished her noodles, so she shook off the memories and pushed back her chair to deposit her plate in the trash. She stood, realizing that stupid Stasia must have left while Kim ate.

Her boyfriend, however, was staring casually at her from across the table. Startled, Kim jumped.

"Can I help you?" Kim asked rudely, placing a hand on her hip. She tried to antagonize him for the sole reason that it was near impossible. Well, perhaps there were other reasons.

Dishon smiled darkly, speaking brightly. "Hi! Haven't seen you all morning."

Kim waggled her head. "Were you supposed to? Because I can't seem to come up with any reasons as to why."

Dishon stood, laughing. "Didn't we go on a date once? Or was it twice? Or maybe I'm your boyfr—"

Kim waved him off, making her exit from the kitchen. "Must've been once, 'cause I never make the same mistake twice."

Why was she so mean to him sometimes? He didn't deserve it. He did right by her. For the most part.

Her mind drifted to Justus as she passed through a living room full of strangers and smoke. Bothered by revealing dreams that he couldn't understand on his own and trying so hard to prove his worth on a team that didn't need him to prove anything to them. He was the only one of them that didn't have *some type* of training in fighting, but he was what Kim's brother called a prayer warrior. Kim could actually *feel* him praying whenever she was around him, and her spirits would lift. Everybody brought something different to their group.

Rico. Rico was actually becoming more eruptive than Coda. Once Solitaire scarred that boy's neck, it became a personal battlefield…

"Does this song ever end?" Stasia asked, bringing Kim out of her reflections and into the disheartening present.

It was a windless afternoon outside and Stasia was sitting out on Dishon's porch with more strangers, smelling like their shared high and all drinking cans of beer and playing cards as they watched the little project brats play makeshift kickball.

"Lena Park songs never end," Kim said, staring at the motionless trees behind the complex across the cracked concrete and worn-down grass. She was vaguely aware of Dishon stepping out onto the porch behind her...watching her. Her mind was far away, remembering her brother's first sermon, entitled "Red Plants." Curly had poised the question that if someone loved you, would you appreciate them as much if they gave you a blood-stained tree instead of a red rose as a token of love. He took the church to Calvary and back. He had a gift for The Word.

That night, she had a torturous nightmare, one that was lost the instant that her eyes opened. She had woke in a bit of hysterics...feeling the green flakes of her past fall again from her memory onto Dishon's sheets.

Her phone was lighting up. She glanced at the screen, then promptly got out of bed.

· · · · ·

Stepping out on to Dishon's porch, she squinted against the light of the moon.

"Ezekiel? What are you doing here?"

He mirrored her confusion with concern. He was tense, dressed for action and levitating. "I heard you screaming. In your head."

"I was dreaming." She stepped down to the sidewalk where he levitated. "How were you even close enough to pickup my brainwaves or whatever?"

"I actually was coming because there's something you need to know." Oh, good. He wasn't being a creeper. "I just looked for your most frequently used photo tags and started from there."

Welp. Maybe he was being a creeper.

"But I have to say this first," he said. "I heard what you were screaming in your sleep. And I get that you have complicated emotions. But, like, stop taking every circumstance and turning it into a burden. You have to learn what you need to ask forgiveness for and what's okay. And if you need to ask for forgiveness, one of the steps is forgiving yourself, too. You can feel sorry, but don't *be* sorry. We need you, and we don't need you sorry."

Kim looked at his apparel, his tenseness. "Thank you for that, but I'm sensing that the other message you have for me is a little more important…"

"Sort of," he said, before admitting, "yeah, actually. Last night, Justus collapsed after we were attacked by Hollow. It wasn't from the injuries; it was because this dream he had. Premonitiative, if that's a word…"

"Premonitory." Kim was still. "Is he okay?"

"Yeah," Ezekiel nodded.

"Did you win?"

His gaze turned a little withering, so Kim quickly asked another question.

"What did he dream about?"

"He saw Hollow and Solitaire capture Coda."

Kim caught her breath.

"But we can't be sure, can we?" Her heart was clenched inside of her like a fist. "Aren't dreams supposed to be metaphorical?"

"His dream about your accident wasn't."

True enough. She bit her lip. "Did anyone call his dad's house?"

"Yes," Ezekiel nodded, "but that didn't do much. It's not like he's been there that much recently anyway."

Her look of naïveté must have clued him in, because he added, "He moved out in January. Didn't he tell you?"

Of course not. "Out of his dad's house? Without at least getting a cell phone first?" Then the bigger question. "Where's he been living?"

Ezekiel shrugged. "Here and there. He's been with Rico for the majority of this week, and Rico last saw him this—well—yesterday morning. He left; he went walking somewhere. No destination. That's not it though, Kim." He stared at her until she reestablished eye contact with him. "The situation is much more complicated than that, but Justus should be the one to explain it to you, you know?"

Kim bit her lip again and Ezekiel watched her eyes ripple gold.

"Where's Justus?" she asked.

"He headed on into Brunswick. He and Rico are going to follow some leads together."

"I want to hear about this dream," she professed. "I need every detail."

Ezekiel's own eyes crackled gold, and for the first time during their conversation seemed to brighten up. "Exactly how much do you weigh?"

"Oh, dear," Kim muttered. "I'm gonna grab some clothes. While I'm doing that, you come up with a plan to get me another hoverboard."

Ezekiel smiled.

•　•　•　•　•

"And you're sure they're at Oakwood?" Kim asked, staring out the window of the Gutierrez kitchen.

Justus nodded vigorously, holding a pack of ice to his forehead. "It's the only actual trail I've ever known Coda to run. Rico just called Renata who's on the campus for some tutoring stuff and told her to be on the lookout for anything strange."

"They threw a rock at him," Kim repeated in amazement. "They actually threw a rock at him!"

"They're cautious about taking him on," Justus explained. "He doesn't realize his capabilities, but they don't want him to discover it to their disadvantage."

"Like Ezekiel and Rico discovering they could fly while they were fighting Solitaire," Kim said.

"Yeah," Justus nodded. "Something similar to that."

"He...channels powers?" Kim asked. "Explain that part to me again."

"In the dream, it was obvious that Solitaire and Hollow's powers were...enhanced, you know?" Justus shook his head, keeping all other memories from the dream at bay as he attempted to recall the details of that particular segment. "As they carried Coda away, Hollow's feet were turning to dirt. He was absorbing properties of the inanimate objects around him, basically becoming a replicating capacitor, if that makes sense."

Kim mulled over this. "Enhancement? Enhancing...replication. That's wild."

Justus continued, "Coda channels...he streamlines their powers. He intensifies everything that they're capable of. He sort of magnifies their potential."

"Tell her about Solitaire," Rico said. To Kim, he added, "You think *that's* wild."

"Solitaire." Justus squeezed his eyes shut, putting himself back in the dream. "Her entire body was...warping visually. She was reflecting light waves or something. Everything that we know them to be, they were the extreme, jacuzzi version of that!"

"Jacuzzi," Kim nodded, not mocking him intentionally. She turned to Rico. "You're the only one who's ever displayed your powers around him, correct?"

Rico shrugged. "Nothing strange happened to me."

Kim nodded. "I guess I should have found it strange that the rest of us have these very specific powers, and all I've noticed in him is the way he can balance on tree branches and do cool flips that he wouldn't have been able to pull off a few months ago."

"His singing's better," Rico offered. "Much better, actually! I mean, his voice is just about beautiful lately."

Ezekiel had been calming his heartbeat up to this point, since flying almost three hundred miles from Atlanta to Glynn County with Kim in tow had been the most extensive, strenuous flying he had ever performed. "Good thing I've been practicing," he had commented to Kim, referencing his midnight flights around the Georgia capital. In Rico's kitchen, however, he had found a reason to laugh.

"What?" Rico asked. "His singing *is* better!"

"No, not the singing," Ezekiel chuckled, looking at Justus.

The marine teen was turning red. "Don't say it, Ezekiel!"

"The kiss," Kim realized, understanding Ezekiel's laughter. "Ever since that kiss, you've been better at the gas transfer haven't you?"

"I can do it on purpose now, if that's what you mean," Justus said, attempting to maintain his dignity. "But was that really Coda who did that? I mean, haven't we all touched him at some point since he developed powers?"

"I dunno," Kim murmured, "but there's got to be a bad side to this. Them being enhanced, I mean. The devil cannot use God's gifts for good."

"True," Rico nodded. "So if they're enhancing their abilities with Coda's gifts, there's gotta be…"

"There's gotta be a perversion somewhere," Kim said. "A wrinkle in their otherwise foolproof plan. If we can exploit that…"

"You mean the fact that now Solitaire's gonna reverse at random?" Ezekiel asked. "That probably won't go in her favor."

"And Hollow's just a giant emptiness waiting to be filled," Kim said. "And we can make that possible."

"That's what they're gonna expect," Ezekiel said. "They know we're gonna come for him."

Kim laughed. "So? Of course we're gonna come for him! Their mistake is in thinking that they'll be able to handle us when we get there."

She was their leader for a reason. Since she had joined them that day, the boys had sensed a change in her. They approved. Well, almost.

"This is the part where I'm supposed to ask why we don't just call the police, but it seems we should fast forward through that bit of idiocy." Justus seemed queasy, dropping the ice pack. "So *we're* the ones who are gonna save him?"

Kim shook her head. "Not us. We have college and families to think of. But we do know how to reach—" She pointed in turn "—Leviathan, Hydroxygen, Ri— Blaze, and Skyboarder."

Rico raised an eyebrow.

"Reblaze?" Ezekiel asked.

"Sure," Kim said. "I mean, if Rico likes it." She shrugged. "That's not at all what I was originally gonna say; I always start off saying his name and end up just kinda making it up as I go along."

Rico chuckled. "I'm sure that name has no copyright infringements."

"Didn't you say BJ was visiting?" Justus asked Rico.

"Don't worry," the soccer player said. "I gave her my car and sent her to the store. She wants to bake muffins or something. This is more important."

His brow was creased. "You know, with Coda coming over my house so much, there's gotta be some change that I just haven't noticed," Rico said, as an angel watched from the counter.

"Whatever it is you're probably used to it by now and haven't realized that it's something Coda may have enhanced in you," Kim replied.

Rico nodded. "Probably," he said, not understanding when the angel seemed to smile.

"Let's get down to business," Kim said, cracking her knuckles. "I've got an idea."

"You can tell Coda's not here," Justus said, sadly. "He would have started singing *Mulan*."

· · · · ·

"They're coming," Coda was ranting, knowing he sounded like Lois Lane. "And you won't be able to stop them!"

He was chained quite awkwardly to a large tree on the OCC campus, far from the trails and isolated cabins. His captors had found a wonderful place to hide him, though it was obvious to him that they were fairly inexperienced with the type of job they were attempting to carryout.

They had chained him with bike chains. It was almost an insult!

There she sat, lounging beneath the nearest adjacent tree with her chin to her chest. She hadn't left his side since he had regained consciousness. (Surprisingly, his head did not hurt from the rock.) She seemed to Coda to be the punk rock, flashy version of everything his comrades had described her as. She wore a dark red bustier and a matching belted, black Xena skirt over a fishnet catsuit. Black combat boots adorned her feet, some type of black armor protected her shoulders and wrists and her hair shimmered white instead of the red he had expected. Her mouth was hidden behind a maroon veil and her skin was white… filmy. It didn't make sense to him; since she was supposed to mirror her opponent, her skin should be light brown like his. He didn't waste time on theories, however. He was too busy preaching.

"You see, they won't just be coming to you as men. They're coming to you with the power of the Holy Ghost, Solitaire! They're coming to you united in Jesus Christ and carried by our God, our Father, our Maker, our Buckler, our Shield!"

Solitaire yawned, rubbing her hands across the grass, changing the color from brown to green to brown again. "Are you still talking?" she asked, her throat sounding dry.

"There is hope in our God," Coda continued. "He is almighty! Undeniable strength and power is wielded in His hands. Not only does He have the ability to bring us out of whatever the devil has planned for us, He has the inclination to do so!"

He stopped speaking, listening to an approaching sound.

"Now that the Power Ranger action figure has had his say," Solitaire muttered, still not looking up, "Rita Repulsa will go and kill herself before he has the chance to charge his battery."

The sound was growing closer, but Solitaire didn't seem to mind. She muttered something about Beetleborgs and Jay Leno.

The sound belonged to Hollow, who was actually whistling. The whistle seemed to bounce around his insides for a few rounds before dispelling itself completely. The boy ambled up from behind the tree, never facing Coda and patiently waiting for…Coda had no idea. Distressed, he kept his brave face on and continued.

"Where God is, there is power! Where God is, the devil has got to flee!"

Hollow spun, snarling in Coda's face like a rabid animal. The sound rumbled through him like distant thunder. Coda flinched, put off by Hollow's velocity.

"Be careful, shepherd boy," Solitaire warned, looking up with her demonic eyes for the first time. Coda caught his breath at the sight. She didn't notice, continuing on with deceptive simplicity. "You know nothing of the devil."

Coda's trembling body betrayed his voice. "I know he loses." He looked into Hollow's brown eyes. "And so will you."

The mud beneath Coda's feet became strawberries and fudge, and he was overcome with searing pain, ripped across his throat, far delayed from the actual moment of injury.

He felt the life bubbling from his neck, and he realized that death was not as cold as most said, only life—life was just so hot. It was life that pumped in his veins, composed of pain and happiness and laughter and injuries and the songs and the solitude. It was life that Coda desperately now wanted to hold on to.

Calmly handing a slack-jawed Solitaire back her knife and moving at a much more human speed than he had used to steal it, the dreadlocked villain whistled once again.

25.

Super Heroics

Hydroxygen wheezed. It seemed his respiratory system had forgotten how to breathe. He watched as Skyboarder struggled to be patient and as Leviathan tried his hardest to pretend that she hadn't gotten that heavy during this additional flight from Rico's place to the Oakwood campus. Rico…Reblaze had his eyes closed, but Hydroxygen could tell by the rivulets of flame dancing among the hair on his arms that his friend was hungering for the fight.

"You about ready?" Leviathan asked him, gloved hands on his waist, chest rising and falling rapidly.

In response, Hydroxygen wheezed.

The four were decked out in their superhero attire. Hydroxygen was in blue from head to toe, with a blue ball cap over his lemon rust mane. Reblaze was bit more put together, black sweat pants and a black tank top, with sunglasses in his hand that would shortly be on his face. Leviathan was wearing a spare black gi, which he used for such occasions these days, plus a matching eye mask. Kim wore a dark purple running outfit, her white sneakers, plus safety guards including a purple mask over her eyes. They weren't beautiful, but they were ready. Well… three of them were ready.

Reblaze shifted his posture, appraising the water-powered male with half-raised eyelids. He sighed and glanced at Skyboarder. "Maybe we should go on ahead and he can just join in when he can."

"Give me a minute," Hydroxygen squeezed out. The bushes that surrounded the tree providing him support stabbed and jabbed through his fighting costume, but he managed to pull himself away, slucking through the mud until he stood again in grass. He inhaled the chilly air, before releasing it through a coughing fit.

"Give me two minutes," he amended.

The flames on Reblaze's arm turned violet, and began to sear his arm hair. Hydroxygen felt bad, knowing that Coda was in trouble, but it was better to take a breather now rather than later when he wouldn't be able to. Sure, Reblaze had flown there on pure adrenaline, but if they wanted to save Coda, they had to use more than adrenaline…they'd need each other.

"Take whatever time you need, Droxy," Skyboarder said. "If we're gonna save Coda, we have to do it together." Justus made a mental note to tell the other boys that he liked having her as their leader.

Reblaze put his sunglasses on, biting back many comments.

After his wheezes had turned back into breaths, he said, "I'm ready," and Reblaze erupted into the atmosphere, not slowing until he was far above them and scouting from the treetops. Leviathan rode the air like a humming bird, dodging through the upper limbs of the trees.

"God be with us," Skyboarder said, hurrying silently through the brush to the right.

Hydroxygen was supposed to take the left, but before he could follow the plan, a dart struck him in the back. As he reached for it, the trees around him grew into nothingness.

•   •   •   •   •

Solitaire rushed over to Coda and quickly laid a hand across his throat and the blood gushed between her gloved fingers. She closed her demonic eyes, swallowing hard.

Coda felt the blood in his throat return to its conventional course. He felt his neck sealing itself back up, veins and arteries reforming to the way they had been minutes before. Most importantly, the hotness of life was no longer pouring out of him, but simmering naturally inside.

Then his tissues ripped once more and the blood was flowing again. Solitaire swore, jumping back from the spray.

"How did—" she exclaimed, rushing back over to him to seal him back up once more.

The wound wasn't quite as bad as before, but that fact didn't cheer either of them much.

Hollow was observing all of this with a blank expression, showing only marginal interest now that Coda's neck was performing its bloody encore.

Solitaire removed her gloved hands from his throat and again there was no blood there.

"I don't know what happened there, but ease up, okay?" she whispered. After a pause she continued, much quieter. "You really have no idea what he's capable of."

Hollow was playing macabre games. He had known that Solitaire would heal Coda.

Life still simmered inside of the braided boy, but anger had now begun to boil.

In front of him, Solitaire stared at her hands with a perplexed expression. Her hands rippled as if there were waves of heat between them and Coda's eyes.

Solitaire, the reverser.

In the way that Coda saw it, Solitaire just may have a soul. And her power actually had a spiritual source. In fact, Coda realized, Solitaire was not merely a reverser.

She was a healer.

• • • • •

Skyboarder crouched in the bushes, breathless as she watched Solitaire heal Coda, bringing him back from the brink of death. The poor boy had just decided that life was worth living and that no good twosome had decided they could just take it away and give it back for sport!

She was livid, feeling those green flakes falling from her hands. Fingers merged into fist.

Hollow paced silently, no longer watching the other two and not disturbed in the least. There was something about his stance that was familiar to Skyboarder.

She looked across the thickets, hoping to make eye contact with Hydroxygen. Where was that boy? She looked up and saw Leviathan, silently hovering in the branches of the tree that Coda was chained to. She raised her eyes to find Reblaze, but identical jets of flames interrupted her vision.

Just like that, they were engaged in battle. It was completely not the plan.

Oh, well.

Solitaire shot towards Reblaze, but Leviathan met her halfway. Pummeling her with his fists before she even realized what had happened, he drew blood quickly, and they plummeted towards the ground.

Hollow, distressed to see Solitaire actually on the losing end, sped to her aid. Skyboarder had anticipated this, and knocked him back fourteen feet with a giant log she had lifted from the brush.

"No, bro," she announced loudly, patting the log with her free hand. "I have a date with you."

As Hollow struggled to rise to his feet, she pounded him once again, head on with the other end of the log and forcing him against another tree, blood escaping from the fresh scratches on his arms.

"Uh-uh! I made a promise, didn't I?" she asked, taking the wood to his torso once more and grunting with her exerted force. "I keep my promises!"

. . . . .

Once Reblaze saw that Skyboarder and Leviathan were in place, he decided to go for it. He had a clear shot at Hollow and figured he'd take it, despite the fact that he couldn't make out Hydroxygen's placement. For all they knew, Justus had forgotten the plan and decided to sneak into the clash by way of gaseous matter. He had slowed them down enough for Hollow and Solitaire to do some serious damage Coda, and Reblaze wasn't ready to let anything else nearly as bad go down.

Once the fire left his hands, however, something new caught his attention.

He turned to his left, trying through his sunglasses to make it out more clearly...whatever it was.

He could only see snatches of it, for it managed to blend in quite well with the green and brown of the trees and the growing darkness of the sky. It was odd, though, because whenever Reblaze could positively identify a visual, it appeared in an ivory color, something that shouldn't be able to blend in at all... Like a white shadow.

Purple flames cascaded from his elbows as he moved further away from the approaching presence. Waiting.

Suddenly it was in front of him, white and furious and unmistakable. Before Reblaze could even prepare to fight back, the sallow-skinned boy was behind him and had him in a chokehold.

As the situation registered in Reblaze's mind, his attacker drove him into the wind, flying forward and slamming him into a tree.

They're ruthless, Rico thought, as his thoughts faded with his vision.

. . . . .

Skyboarder had Hollow pinned to the ground with the log, and as she debated what her next move should be, suddenly the log became firewood.

She looked up, expecting some explanation in the form of Reblaze, but instead was amazed to see-

Hollow dropped in from the sky with fire rushing over his muscular arms. As Kim turned back to look at her captive, she was punched dead in the face—feeling an electric zap as if static electricity had jumped between two bodies.

Intuitively, she fell to the ground, letting a brown-and-white blur of a body fly over her head. She grabbed another log, tossing it, but Hollow disintegrated it underneath his flames just as easily as he had disintegrated the other. Then he pulled a large piece of concrete pipe out of the ground, hurling it at Kim, who shattered it into concrete crumbs.

At that moment the confusion cleared and she realized what she was up against.

Hollow was not attacking her with super strength and producing flames out of his arms at the same time. Hollow *was not* in two places at once, preparing two separate attacks on her.

One had somehow gotten Rico's fire powers and the one who had punched Kim now had her strength…for there were two of them.

There were two Hollows.

• • • • •

Hydroxygen came to, and his surroundings gradually settled back into his vision. He couldn't recollect what had happened since his friends had charged into the brush, but that wasn't his pressing concern.

Hearing the sounds of battle, he leapt back into action.

• • • • •

Each floor of the facility was resplendent with bustle. Patricia was too tense to enjoy it.

"The tracing agent has been administered in conjunction with the RiD substance," one of the scientists reported. "Would you like us to send the team in?"

"No," Patricia said. "We can't afford any slip-ups or half-done jobs. Follow the Alexander boy and once we've verified that the entire group is centralized, I'll give the order."

The scientist cleared his throat. "Can I get verification on who is included in that 'entire group' that you mentioned?"

Her teeth clenched, she replied, "I want. Them. ALL. If I have school you at this point in the project, I will be happy to offer you new avenues of employment."

The scientist slunk away. Patricia's palms were sweating. Damn that Vice President.

• • • • •

Leviathan had taken such an advantage by surprising Solitaire with his attack that she had barely been able to gather her thoughts in order to reverse anything on him. He was in her brain easily, trying to figure what her next move would be. Trying to figure out what she was.

And then he was pushed out. She had finally gotten a grip, and he lost his.

"Sucks for you, doesn't it?" Solitaire asked, as Leviathan's next blow landed on his own thigh. "Maybe you should come up with an alternative fighting style, *Hapkido*-baby!"

Her words were mocking, but her tone was not. Leviathan had been inside enough to know the source of her panic. She was losing control over her power-reversing, just as he had speculated.

He was thinking too much, for she had just landed a kick upside his head and she was quickly bringing her foot around to his face, aiming for his eyes.

Leviathan slid into her, his feet knocking her standing leg off balance, and they tumbled into the bushes.

"My, my, Stevie," she murmured through her mask, as he pinned her beneath him. "You really do know how to get off on the right foot."

Was she serious? That joke wasn't funniest in the least.

A few yards away, Skyboarder began screaming something about there being "two marshmallows." Leviathan glanced her way, and the horror of the moment splayed panic across his face. Solitaire observed his expression.

"Secret's out, huh?"

Leviathan sprung off Solitaire, catching the wind until he was by Skyboarder's side.

"You shouldn't have come over here," she hissed. "They're faster than they've ever been. We've gotta get Coda away from them!"

"How are there two of them?" Leviathan asked. He grabbed her shoulders, pushing her to the ground so that he alone was caught in a rain of fire, leaving his gi blouse in tatters.

"Thanks," Skyboarder replied, leaping into the air and kicking the fiery, freckled Hollow in his stomach. He fell over, spitting up blood, and while Leviathan braced a punch from the strong Hollow, Skyboarder raced over towards Solitaire.

A single volley of fire split the makeshift battlefield in half. The fiery Hollow was in pain, but he used the focus that he could to create flames that prevented Kim from getting close to the tree where Solitaire stood guard.

Leviathan rushed upon the Hollow despite the flames, but then his world physically turned upside down. He felt the ground beneath his back, but couldn't make out what had just happened to him. He heard Skyboarder scream. Where were Rico and Justus? What had happened to their plan?

Skyboarder was still screaming and Leviathan tried to turn the constantly changing blur of grey, green and blue into an actual visual. He felt an electrical pop in his neck as a brown-and-white blur passed over his face.

Then Solitaire was in his face and he could suddenly see. The strong Hollow had flattened Leviathan beneath a giant slap of concrete and Solitaire was stretched out on it atop of him now, like a cat content to play with a mouse until it was dead.

"Poor Stevie Wonder," Solitaire clucked, her voice as abrasive as sandpaper. She had lost her mask at some point during the fray, and he could almost make out the shape of her lips. "Your girl, Sammy, she's strong, but not tough. You're tough, but not strong. So that means you can't lift this giant piece of rock! With great sarcasm I add, what a shame." She pulled out of his frame of vision and he felt the ground beneath him beginning to give way to his body. His breathing was labored.

She was still talking and his eyesight began to blur once more. "Let's see how long you last.

· · · · ·

Reblaze came to, suspended across several pine branches. His face felt like it had been injected with bark and his neck was wet. A quick inspection showed his chin was bleeding, probably other body parts as well. He sat up, sunglasses falling in broken fragments from his face, feeling like his chest had been used as a bass drum.

The cacophony from below reached his ears and he bent to look, holding his ribs. So he *hadn't* been crazy. There were two Hollows, and one of them had attacked him in the trees while the other was down with the others.

There was no time to think further. He had to get down there.

"Mr. Gutierrez."

It wasn't even a voice. It was the intoned form of a Saturday afternoon soccer game followed up with two Dynasty Dogs with extra coleslaw.

A demon was perched on a nearby branch, muscles taunt as if preparing to pounce.

Reblaze froze, completely taken aback by its vicinity and its beauty. The descriptions he had been given by Kim and Justus did not compare to the lustrous vision that now faced him. It was as beautiful as its voice, maybe even more so.

"Get thee behind me, Satan," Reblaze said, gliding slowly away.

"Come now, Enrique," the Creature spoke again, and Rico heard waves crashing on the Florida Panhandle. "I am not Satan."

Reblaze shook his head as if to get the ocean water out of his ears. "I know what you are, demon, and I'm not gonna talk to you."

"Then you shouldn't be so quick to turn your back on me," the demon said. "I know what you are, too."

Down below, Skyboarder screamed as Hollow set her ablaze again. She dropped to the dirt quickly, rolling the fire out before she kicked at the strong Hollow, who was suddenly there, reaching for her face.

She reared back and socked him, hearing something crunch beneath his skin.

But he was crazy, feverish with power lust. He grabbed the fist that she had just socked him with, breaking two of her fingers and causing her to scream even more.

Deliver me, Father, she prayed, and Hollow snapped another finger.

• • • • •

"Coda, it's Justus."

Coda looked away from the distressing battles raging around him, trying to get Hydroxygen in his peripheral vision.

"They keep touching me," he notified his aquatic friend, "as if I'm home base or something!"

Hydroxygen ran fingers through his black hair as he collected his thoughts and began turning his other hand to water. "Let me try to explain this to you, Cheshire," he spoke quickly, diddling with the chains. "We thought your power was just that crazy agility, but it seems that it's more specific because you've enhanced your own abilities, the things you were already good at. If Hollow touches you, he enhances himself and whatever other powers he steals until, of course, that time span runs out. And by being near you, Solitaire can keep you incapacitated by reversing your own self-enhancement, limiting your strength and adroitness. And you enhance other people's abilities, too, including theirs. That's why they keep touching you."

"What? So I'm like a steroid?"

"Kinda." Justus was growing frustrated with Coda's bonds. "What are these, bicycle chains?"

He slipped the chain through his liquid hand. He didn't know if he could freeze it and bust it or if he could only rust it, but he was going to figure it out.

"I'll have you out of here in a jiffy," he whispered to Coda.

"I doubt that very seriously," Solitaire spoke up from behind him.

Before Hydroxygen could react, she reversed the liquefaction of his hand, refleshing the limb with the chain running right through the muscle and bone.

Hydroxygen stared in repulsion, panic slowly bubbling inside of him.

He couldn't liquefy; he couldn't dissolve into the air and it was her doing. Solitaire grabbed the chain and began to shake it, ripping the tissue in his hand.

"Ah, God!" Hydroxygen exclaimed, and Solitaire lifted her knee, connecting between Hydroxygen's legs. As he doubled over, she continued bringing up her knee until she rammed it into his face.

"I call that move 'one knee, two heads,'" she quipped, and Hydroxygen wailed from the pain, blood springing from the intrusion in his hand.

The freckled and fiery Hollow bounded over energetically, his face redder than the blood pouring down the chains. He laughed heartily at Hydroxygen's situation, the noise rebounding inside of him as red flames poured over his arms.

The other Hollow watched as well, gripping an overwhelmed Skyboarder with quickly fading interest.

Coda turned his head upwards, scanning the branches for Rico.

Fiery Hollow caught sight of Coda's neck and his laughter faded. His grey eyes flew to Solitaire, who noticed too late the wounds on Coda's neck. Usually there would have been no marks, but due to the lack of control Solitaire now had on her own powers there was an obvious scar stretched across Coda's throat.

When Solitaire looked to Hollow, he was looking at the knife she had hooked beneath her shoulder pads.

"No," she began, but Hollow was in her face, backhanding her into Hydroxygen, who screamed louder, his hand tearing wider.

Coda wanted to struggle with the chains, but remained still, afraid to harm his friend's hand any further. The situation however, disturbed him immensely. Their enemies had just turned on each other, for whatever reason.

Hollow's lips curled to his pernicious thoughts. He now had Solitaire's powers.

She rose, holding out pleading hands. "Don't do this! I don't want to have to hurt you."

This comment made Coda more nervous. They were reaching the moment that would decide whose power trumped whose, and Coda wanted to be far from the repercussions.

Hydroxygen had disappeared. He was no longer prostrate next to Coda's tree. Coda hadn't noticed him translate into any other form of matter, so he was without answers and quite possibly without any protection.

Solitaire seemed nervous, though her pleading hands were curled in anticipation towards Hollow's direction. Hollow, face flushed a deep maroon, raised an arm nonchalantly.

Solitaire was lifted off of the ground, twisting in the air above Hollow's head. The more she struggled to return to the ground, the easier Hollow could reverse her body's attempts and keep her in the air.

Very deliberately, Hollow reversed every joint in her limbs, cracking her fingers backwards, bending her elbows in and snapping her kneecaps.

Fear and limitless pain drank the evil from Solitaire's eyes, as the irises shrunk to normal size and returned to brown. As her body went into shock, she quit trying to reach the ground, and it was then that Hollow sent her smashing into the rough bushes.

True shock came to Coda when Solitaire spoke again, and it was a hoarse whisper. Despite the pain that must have been ripping through her body, something more important required her energy.

"Terry," she managed, "it wasn't me..."

• • • • •

Skyboarder refused to dwell on the pain that was attempting to monopolize her thoughts. She couldn't dwell on the pain. She had to keep everything together, continue pushing for their goal.

She rolled onto her back, looking to the sky for assistance and finding a fetal Reblaze instead. She could make him out a few feet above them in the branches of the pines. What was he doing?

She had heard Hydroxygen's unmistakable shrieks coming from the direction of the tree Coda was chained to, so she knew he was back in the game, even if it sounded like he was on the losing end. She now had a handle on everyone's position. There was a way to salvage this.

She could not dwell on the pain. Ensuring that she only put weight on the palm of her hands and not her fingers, she slowly brought herself to a seated position. It didn't help much, for at that moment her right hand belonged completely to the torture, and not to her.

Help me, Jesus, she prayed.

She turned her head towards Coda. Solitaire was laid atop the bushes like a discarded bear rug and the freckled Hollow stood over her with a perplexed expression. Skyboarder saw the scars on Coda's throat and understood that Hollow had caught sight of them. He had reacted nastily, punishing Solitaire in only the worst way…though the truth had just been spoken.

Nearby, the other Hollow's breathing had increased with worry. He had forgotten all about her, and Skyboarder was beginning to understand why. Division had grown among their enemies. She saw how she could play this to their advantage.

"She wasn't lying, Terry," she spoke up, and both of the Hollows turned to her. "She's not the one who slashed Coda's throat."

Terry's lips were pursed and his fists had clenched. She was beginning to think his two-month disappearance had nothing to do with mission work. Well, not his church's mission.

The other Hollow was the one who had been breaking her fingers, the sadist. Now he seemed to be gearing up for battle with Terry, his shoulders tensing and his achromatic face flushing crimson.

Kim wondered what powers he was calling on. He had her strength, but Terry had Solitaire's reversing power and one of them had touched Leviathan, but she didn't know which. Did it matter who had what power? She considered what the effects would be if their weird power-sucking abilities ever came in contact with each other. And having Coda in such close vicinity possibly providing involuntary enhancements wouldn't help either.

In fact, with the two Hollows focused on each other, maybe she and Leviathan could figure out a way—

Ezekiel! She had forgotten all about him. She turned towards the giant slab of concrete that was hiding her friend.

"Let the dead bury their dead," she muttered, as the Hollows charged towards each other.

26.

Padre Nuestro

They were upon each other with a stunning fervor, and their roles were drawn markedly. One wanted retribution and the other simply could not turn down the prospect for more carnage. The formerly blue sky was now gray, emulating the increasing heaviness of the developments on the ground.

Terry landed the first blow, cracking the other's jaw, and his second punch was to Hollow's gut. They were now equal. Their borrowed faculties had established redundancy and the atmosphere changed as if the power cycle had been broken. They had borrowed, and thus increased, their own power of replicating power.

Hollow flew into Terry, thrusting his knee into the freckled one's abs.

Terry roared, an echo ensuing as with all of their sounds, but Hollow grabbed Terry's dreadlocks, smashing face against knee and effectively canceling the noise.

Terry dug his fingers into Hollow's side, reducing the other to feline-like screams. Hollow retaliated by applying his fingers to a few of Terry's pressure points. That didn't satisfy him, however, and he raked his nails down Terry's face, eyes lighting up as the blood began to flow.

With them sharing both Kim's super strength and Ezekiel's thick skin, they didn't hurt each other on any astronomical level. Even the air was silent, since they absorbed the blows as if they were simply more abilities. It was as if two demonic Supermen were facing each other there on the OCC campus. It was a draw, but the side effect was that their power was growing too strong for their human bodies. They continued to pass their competencies to each other, strengthening their absorption capabilities. It was more effective than if Coda had ever touched them.

A very low hum vibrated across the thicket's floor.

The Hollows had begun to reverb.

• • • • •

Leviathan gasped for breath, no longer attempting to move beneath the giant slab of concrete. His vision was now an entire blur and darkening in places. Where had Hollow found such a large slab? Justus had mentioned something about OCC being built where a factory had once stood. Perhaps their enemies were more prepared than he had given them credit for.

Help us, Lord, he prayed, not having the breath to speak aloud. *Don't let it all be in vain.*

He tried to focus on everything but the crushing pressure on his body. He fixed his attention on the strange tingling across his back shoulder…an electric tickle that caused him to recall the shock he had gotten when one of the Hollows made physical contact with his neck. It wasn't the first time he had been zapped by a Hollow, so that in itself caused him no disturbance. How, though, was it possible to shock with no static electricity? It was as if (if indeed that was the Hollow from that night in the stadium) the voltage from the hoverboard had somehow—

"Hey, boo." Skyboarder's voice rested on his ears like the whispers of angels and the weighted burden on his body was lifted.

Air rushed back into his lungs and his vision worked itself back to its rightful health.

Skyboarder stood there, skin welting and blistering from burns, holding her right hand with her other palm as tears flowed down her face.

"Yeah, so my fingers are broken," she notified him, sniffling and still beautiful. She shook her head, as if she could will the pain away. "Can you tell if Justus is nearby?"

Leviathan scanned the thoughts in the area. "Yeah, he's here. It seems that watching Terry…do that to Solitaire seems to have freaked him out a bit."

Skyboarder sighed. "We've got to rely on God, not on what we see," she said. Glancing over at the fighting Hollows, she added, "Let them fight. This is our opening. You go get Reblaze and I'll set free the power-channeler over there."

Leviathan held up a hand, causing pain to rush across the front of his body. "Ouch," he winced, lowering his hand again. "Where's Reblaze?"

With her able hand, Skyboarder pointed to the upper realms of the tree branches.

"Find out what's up with him," she said, "and then please get him down here. The Hollows are gonna destroy this whole area if we don't step in."

• • • • •

Reblaze panicked when he saw Leviathan approaching.

"Stay away, Ezekiel," he called down to his friend, never taking his eyes from the blue ones of the demon.

Leviathan pulled up short, staring up at him concernedly. Reblaze wondered if his friend could read the demon's thoughts, while it continued to talk, spitting all sorts of perversity and indecency…details it had pulled straight from Rico's own life.

"What do you see, Rico?" Leviathan asked. Rico barely heard him.

The demon still spoke. "I know all of the workings inside your twisted little head, Enrique."

"*Protégeme*," Rico prayed.

• • • • •

Hydroxygen had reached liquid form by the time Skyboarder reached Coda. She wanted to be angry with him, but she knew she had no sufficient reason. They were all doing what they could. Plus she saw the gaping wound in his hand was still bleeding.

"Yo, your little gas bursting thing," she said, stealing a glance at Solitaire—good Lord, what did Terry do to her?—before turning back to the task at hand, "you've got to get control of that!"

"I know," Hydroxygen said, watching as she knelt in order to bust Coda's two bottom chains with her good hand. "I'm sorry." He flexed his fingers, staring at his wound.

It happened too quickly for Skyboarder to register it, but at the exact moment that Hydroxygen finished his apology, Terry slammed his counterpart into the tree right above her head at the precise spot Coda was chained to. Coda, however, used the fact that Skyboarder had freed his legs to flip out of the way with his amazing reflexes, clinging to the tree inches above the ghostly doubles grappling against the timber.

As Hollow crashed into the tall oak, his shoulders cracked and browned, absorbing the properties of the bark. Terry's own face turned to bark beneath his eyes, but before Skyboarder could take in any more details, they were off again, knocking Solitaire to the dirt as they rumbled past her. Hydroxygen rushed over to her.

"Let me loose, please," Coda panted. "Before they aim higher next time."

Skyboarder punched another of his chains, shattering it beneath her force. Coda fell to the dirt, hanging from one arm.

"Ow," he said.

Skyboarder turned to Hydroxygen, whose eyes were on Solitaire.

"How is she?" she asked, holding her damaged hand.

"Not dead," was his reply.

"Take care of her, Droxy," Skyboarder said. "She may not be at death's door, but we don't want her going much closer to it."

Hydroxygen nodded, turning away, and Skyboarder busted Coda's last chain.

• • • • •

Hydroxygen stared down at Solitaire's broken body and hot tears splashed onto his cheeks. The air seemed sad as well, smelling like impending rain.

"Who's your god, that they would let you suffer like this?" he asked.

Her eyes turned to him, all normal and brown. Her face was still pale, perhaps due to the stress on her body, and was wet from her own tears as well as the sweat that had come from her body responding to its new extensive injuries.

"Help," she managed.

And Hydroxygen knew what he should do.

"Focus," he reminded himself. "Focus the energy."

His tears flowed into his cheeks as his cheeks poured into his lips and his lips melted into his chin. As he collapsed into himself, he felt his way along the ground until he reached Solitaire.

I gotcha.

He surrendered to the dirt, rushing around the rocks and roots of the grass and pushing his way back to the surface. Straining every muscle he had, he did not yield again to the dirt, nor to the woman, holding Solitaire in a liquid cushion.

And once again, he reminded himself. *Focus.*

• • • • •

"You see it, don't you?" Leviathan asked. "You see Kim's demon!"

"Demons don't see inside us, right, Ezekiel?" Reblaze hollered. "They only see our actions?"

"What is it saying to you? Don't listen to it, Rico! It's trying to get you all confused. That's not where you should be focused right now!"

Reblaze was flustered. "Where should my mind be right now? Why is everything so backwards?"

Kamiskas turned an evil glance to Leviathan, sensing his words.

"Keep your mind on Jesus!" Leviathan's voice was strong now, calming. "You've got God right here and right now. His angels are all around, but you're just not seeing them. Remember how God has protected you in the past. His blood still covers you."

"We have an expert," Kamiskas said, seeming to snarl. It wasn't so beautiful anymore. It looked the same, yet…burned. "Are you sure you want to believe the newblood? He can't even see me."

Tears streamed down Rico's face. This was torture.

"I'm here, Rico," Leviathan repeated. "You've got me right here, too, dude. And He's with both of us right here and right now. Remember that."

"He wouldn't want to help you if he knew you," the charred demon said, keeping its eyes on Rico. "You're not worth what he thinks you're worth."

The demon's words triggered something within Reblaze, who swallowed the blue creature in purple flames.

Leviathan reached through the mini-inferno, grabbing Reblaze's hands. The remainder of his seared blouse caught fire, but his thick skin didn't burn.

"God said I'm worth Calvary!" Reblaze screamed to the empty air where the demon had previously been, as Leviathan pulled through the trees to the woodland floor. "I'm worth EVERYTHING!"

* * * * *

The fight between the void villains was getting out of control. Skyboarder pushed Coda back up against the tree as he attempted to charge into the fray.

"What are you doing?" he hissed at her. "Terry!" he called.

"Coda, listen to me! You've got to be careful!"

Coda glowered at her. "Of course I'll be careful, Sky! But I've got to stop this! Terry hurt the other one because the other one hurt me!"

"You touch either one of them and this place could become a virtual black hole," Skyboarder exclaimed.

Coda sputtered, looking at the two Hollows through his red-stained vision. The two, all bloody and waxen and pulling apart from each other, were bracing for another round.

"You can make this thing worse," she said, lifting her hand from his chest and freeing him yet again. "Any one of us can."

As if on cue, Reblaze and Leviathan landed on the floor of the brush, directly between the two Hollows.

"Oh no," Skyboarder mumbled.

Leviathan ripped the seared, glowing remains of his karategi blouse, letting them fall to the dirt. His Lichtenberg scar was exposed to his friends for the first time, decorating his back like Spanish moss.

He glanced in Skyboarder's direction, as if to put her at ease. She turned back to Coda.

"Do you think you can get me up there?"

Coda raised his eyebrows. "Up where?"

She pointed to the branches above the clearing. "Directly up there." Anything to get him away from the fight.

Coda motioned for Kim to climb on his back. "Let's see. Watch that hand, chica."

The Hollows rushed towards Leviathan and Reblaze, but Leviathan wrapped his arms around Reblaze's waist and lifted him into the air, allowing Reblaze to focus all of his energy on producing blinding flames. Each of the Hollows lost their way, colliding into each other.

Reblaze let the flames lapse and Leviathan let him go.

The one without freckles looked up with cerise flames pouring from his eyes. He had absorbed the properties of the fire so strongly, his clothes hadn't even burned. Black dirt rained to the ground where his fingers should have been.

"He's getting out of control," Leviathan said. "If they keep fighting each other both of them will be near-unstoppable. They'll be non-human."

"I can distract him," Reblaze offered, doing his best to ignore the pain emanating from the giant bruise of his body. "But I have no idea how to—"

The same giant slab of concrete that had been used to immobilize Leviathan earlier was now sailing through the air with the evident intent to immobilize Rico. He flew back in time and the slab found Leviathan again, swatting him through the woods instead.

The flames subsided from one of the Hollow's eyes as he roared in satisfaction. Reblaze flew towards him, but Terry—the freckled Hollow—reached his bookend first and the hum grew louder. Terry's hair began to fluctuate continuously between orange and dark brown. His fists pummeled into the duplicate's face and the prostrate one returned the volleys with one concrete arm to the skull.

Gravel rippled across Terry's scratched face, his grey-blue eyes turning to rock before reverting back to tissue. He attempted to return the favor, but his arm turned to terra and grass, collapsing in the soil before it could do any damage.

Panic was evident in Terry's eyes as he climbed off his look-alike and backed away to the center of the small meadow. His body emitted a hum so strong that it overpowered the hum from the other Hollow. Yellow flames burst briefly across his shoulders, singeing the straps of his jumpsuit.

The other Hollow smiled, enjoying the show.

Coda saw this and paused on his journey through the branches, crouching.

"Kim, check this out!" he hissed.

Skyboarder looked over Coda's shoulder as Hollow brandished the singed log Kim had taken to him. He swung it towards Terry, who caught it, and both of their arms crusted over with bark.

"I'm going down there," she said, carefully taking her arms from around his shoulders and biting back a cry when her fingers tapped against his shoulders.

"Why would you want to do a thing like that?" Coda asked. "Especially after telling me that I can't—"

"The situation has changed. I have an idea."

"Your idea is sounding stupid."

Reblaze flew past them, scouting for Leviathan. Thunder rolled, closer than Skyboarder anticipated. The sky was rather dark, she realized.

"Trust me," she said firmly. "Please, just trust me. One of those two is about to collapse from the strain on their body and whichever one does, I need you to keep that one away from the other one."

"I think I know who the other one is," Coda whispered, as if their enemies were in the tree with them.

"It doesn't matter," she said, shaking her head. "Not now. But listen to what I'm saying." She took a fervid glance over her shoulder at the two Hollows who were now shakily making their way back to one another. "Get whoever it turns out to be up and out, you got me? Away from things he can touch. I just pray to God that he doesn't turn into sky or something like that. But you can't touch him at all and whatever you use, let it be minimum contact."

"I'm lost," Coda said, searching her face for unspoken answers.

"You are not," she said without the usual coddling patience. "You have to do this, Coda. You're the only one who even can!"

She dropped through the trees, solid as an anchor.

• • • • •

When Skyboarder landed, she was several feet away from where she wanted to be and she landed, roughly, on her butt near busted pieces of pipe. No matter. She had gotten down there without breaking anything. Her fingers throbbed, swelling her hand into a paw. *Dishon wouldn't recognize me,* she thought bitterly.

She watched as the Hollows, not concerned with her, tried to walk towards each other. They moved slow not due to weakness; they were actually too potent at this point. They had already passed so much to each other on account of their incestuous endowments that Skyboarder couldn't even be sure that the orange-haired one was Terry.

Whoever he was, he was in worse control of his powers than the one with brown hair, and he soon collapsed.

Instantly—that was her boy!—Coda swooped in, propelling himself on a nine-foot timber staff. He landed between the boys, lifting the orange-haired one off the ground with one end of the staff and punting him in the air as if he were playing lacrosse. He dug the staff into the ground, pushing off into the air. Once free from the clearing, he used the staff to scale the branches and prod the fallen Hollow closer to the woodland roof.

Beyond them, the sky was growing black with clouds.

Reblaze and Leviathan flew into view. Reblaze appeared concerned for Leviathan's well-being, though the shirtless one seemed indifferent towards his condition and more anxious with what was going on between Kim and the remaining Hollow.

"You," Skyboarder cried, tossing a broken pipe piece to the Hollow that remained. He caught it in his hands, rapaciously absorbing its properties. His hand turned to concrete as he tossed the pipe away.

Having his attention, Skyboarder continued. "You have looked for fulfillment from everything but the Holy Ghost. And that's an issue, because you see, fella, we've got a direct line to the Holy Ghost."

She gingerly stepped onto larger pieces of pipe, shattering them in the process. Hollow cried out in his deathly, unnatural voice and the concrete crumbled from his skin. Skyboarder began to advance.

"That's right, 'Hollow.' You will not go away empty this time."

The words came to her easily, for she had been reciting scriptures in church school for sixteen plus years. They were emboldened by a strange sort of foolishness, a worthy nonsense, for the infancy of her audacity was in no way ignorance. It was the reality of someone who had lost sight of what her eyes could see, keeping her sight on an invisible, spiritual view. She was again that girl in the sky who waded in stars and took up conversation with rapturous Music.

"'Let mine enemy be as the wicked,' Job said, 'and he that riseth up against me as the unrighteous.'" Her chin was high, her eyes level.

A growl grew inside of Hollow's body and he began to circle Skyboarder as if she were his prey. She was not abashed.

Leviathan and Reblaze settled from the air onto the grass, watching. They split the sides of the clearing, keeping their eyes on the dreaded one.

"'For what is the hope of the hypocrite, though he hath gained,'" Kim continued, "'when God taketh away his soul?'"

Hollow took a leap towards her. Reblaze had anticipated his move, and for this Skyboarder was grateful. He sent a torrent of flames, forcing Hollow back several feet.

Skyboarder took the opportunity to take a fervid glance around. Leviathan stood nearby, watching and silently digging for whatever was beneath Hollow's surface. She didn't see Hydroxygen, but she did see Solitaire lying useless on the ground. She turned her attention back to the seething pasty-face in front of her.

"Job continued and said, 'Will God heareth his cry when trouble cometh upon him?'"

Thunder bellowed yet again, and the darkest cloud now crouched over their heads. Indeed, trouble had now come, but it hadn't come for her.

• • • • •

As the darkness swelled to a harrowing black, Skyboarder's eyes seemed to shine brighter and deeper, if such a thing was possible. Reblaze had never seen anything like it. Her eyes were virtually solid gold, and the more luminous they grew, the more Reblaze's spiritual vision increased.

Her skin and her clothes were as sprinkled with glittery gold as her eyes were. Everywhere on her body that a shadow fell, the shimmer was brighter. It was the spiritual manifestation of her strength. There was a protection over her being, Reblaze now saw, dressing her like a fabric starfield.

He saw the demons swirling around them in the darkness, each a varied version of the beautybeast that had been tormenting them— gaudy with indulgence and ugly with impudence. They were bright within themselves, but spread no light to the darkness around them. There was also a hungry energy about them, trying to pull every bit of assurance and faithfulness from the area.

There was a source of protection, however, beyond the illumination from Skyboarder's eyes and the powers swirling through their bodies. A barricade of angels comforted his vision, standing between the battle in the clearing and the demons swirling amongst the trees in toxic darkness. Their swords were blazing a type of fire that Rico had never seen, as if the very air was being burned, but instead of being burned to uselessness, the troposphere was finding renewal. It was wild.

Comparing the glitziness of the demons to both Kim's brilliant radiance and the untainted glow surrounding the Stonehenge of angels, Reblaze had no doubt what was sun and what was moon. The demons were merely a lame reflection of their former glory.

If Kim's eyes were bright like the sun, then Hollow seemed to be as dark as the mounting storm. He was a direct contraposition to Kimberly's consecration, a reprobate embodiment. Reblaze found himself awestruck at the fact that the sin itself, in one such as the blue creature and his fellow demons, presented itself so beautiful, while the effects of it were so gruesome. Hollow's body was no longer a human body in Reblaze's eyes, but the hulking body of a beast; his dreadlocks appeared as twisting worms and his pale skin was merely a marble prison.

Yes, a prison disguised as a body, and Reblaze was shaken by his vision. Inside that prison, tormented but not possessed by undersized hellions, was a prostrate figure that was at once familiar and also alien to Rico. The figure howled as Kim's eye-light shone through the marble and burned the human skin, leaving oozing black wounds.

"Deliver this person, Lord," Reblaze prayed without pause. "Whether friend at heart or a true enemy to me, please deliver them out of the devil's hand and bring them into Your kingdom."

Suddenly the demons on the figure turned to shriek their ingratitude at Reblaze.

"Bring them back to Your love and care. Cover them in the blood of Your Son Jesus, and fill them with peace and passion and charity and wisdom and Your heavenly power to resist Satan! Fill them with Your Love, Jesus, in Your holy name!"

The demons were shrieking in their ungodly language, no longer in anger towards him, but announcing themselves to something else.

Reblaze glanced towards Leviathan and his mouth went dry.

The blue creature sauntered out of the blackness, just as superficially beautiful as always, right past the angels and their swords. No one moved; even the angels just watched. Reblaze felt in his spirit, as sure as if he had been told, that the angels had been instructed to wait. So Reblaze waited as well, though his muscles were tensed for unknown warfare.

The Creature walked past Leviathan without care and Ezekiel did not see it, kneeling on the ground either in prayer or peering inside of someone's head. The closer it got to the Hollow monster, however, the calmer the tiny demons seemed to get. It's presence shaded the demons and their captive from Kim's illumination. It waved its hands in front of the marble face, and Hollow, an entire being once more, gave the cobalt beast his attention.

The Creature pointed to the moving figures in the trees above them: Coda and the freckled Hollow.

Hollow's eyes followed and the vision registered. With a spring, Hollow was in Reblaze's face, punching him. As blood began to flow out of Reblaze's nose, Hollow took to the air, bound for the two in the trees and leaving Kim's spiritual assault beneath him.

Reblaze clutched his face, his tongue finding a loose tooth.

Then that illicitly beautiful voice spoke directly into his ear.

"Shame on you, Enrique. There is no god. What is it that you are really fighting for?"

Reblaze trembled in anger. The Creature was wrong. Reblaze knew beyond his spirit into the depths of his soul that the Creature was wrong. He thought back on all that God had done for him in his life and he knew that the Creature was wrong.

He could feel the supernatural energies flowing within his body, no longer content to stand idly by. He couldn't stand there as God's existence was challenged and rejected by this demon, that, despite its allegiance, was still one of God's creations.

And that other one… Hollow had punched him in the face!

His ego had been purified. And the righteous anger blistering in Reblaze's soul rippled through his neck and across his shoulder blades. Rico felt the flames erupt from his back, his tank falling in charred pieces to the dirt.

How dare Hollow touch God's anointed!

On wings of flame, feeling pain no more, Reblaze lifted into the air.

• • • • •

Skyboarder saw Leviathan clutch his head and drop to one knee, but she had no time to wonder. She was in the middle of a spiritual showdown with one of the Hollows. As long as Reblaze or Hydroxygen was praying, perhaps Leviathan could find whatever he needed inside of Hollow's mind. She could only hope that Coda was managing with the other.

Another scripture came to her. "It is said in Isaiah, 'It shall even be as when an hungry man dreameth, and, behold, he eateth; but he awaketh, and his soul is empty: or as when a thirsty man dreameth, and, behold, he drinketh; but he awaketh, and behold, he is faint, and his soul hath appetite: so shall the multitude of all the nations be, that fight against Mount Zion.'"

Hollow had stopped moving. Skyboarder really hoped someone was praying.

"'Hell is naked before Him, and destruction hath no covering! He stretcheth out the north over the empty place, and hangeth the earth upon nothing!'

"Listen here, Hollow! For, 'Lo, these are *parts* of His ways: but how *little* a portion is heard of Him? But the thunder of His power who can understand?'"

Hollow strangely took this moment to turn an inquisitive face to the atmosphere, as if to respond to the thunder rolling across the sky.

Skyboarder looked up as well, immediately understanding. He had spotted Coda. Her attention returned to him, but he was no longer in front of her. Only when Reblaze reeled backwards, clutching his face, did she realize Hollow had snatched power from him and taken off into the sky.

Leviathan's instincts were on point; while Reblaze and Kim were flailing about in surprise, he had already lifted into the wind.

"Keep ministering with the Word!" he yelled to her, flying after Hollow.

Kim looked to Reblaze, and caught her breath as she saw the blood gushing between his hands. It was time to end this

"'Let us hear the conclusion of the whole matter:'" she screamed, "'Fear God, and keep His commandments: for this is the whole duty of man! For God shall bring every work into judgment, with every secret thing'—oh geez."

Skyboarder lost her words as flames, a raging violet tipped with orange, sprung from Reblaze's back, flapping with some semblance of organization just as naturally as bird wings. In seconds Reblaze had gained on Leviathan, passing him completely seconds later, leaving only the ashes of his shirt in his wake.

"'Every secret thing,'" she continued, almost perfunctorily, "'whether it be good, or whether it be evil.'" As an afterthought she added, "Finito in Cheeto."

•   •   •   •   •

The rest, though extensive, happened very quickly.

Coda saw Hollow approaching and panicked. He overextended his arm, chucking Terry too far with the wooden staff. Leviathan noticed the orange dreads disappear into the clouds and, deciding not to get in the path of the now-winged Reblaze, took off after Terry. Coda saw this and clung to the trunk of a nearby tree, watching Reblaze and Hollow warily, waiting to be needed again.

"¡Padre nuestro," Reblaze prayed, sending a cyclone of flames in Hollow's direction, "que estás en el cielo!"

Hollow turned, shocked to see the purple fiery wings but easily dodging the flaming volley. In doing so he found himself within Reblaze's reach, which was the thin one's plan.

"¡Santificado sea Tu nombre!" Reblaze cried, blood caking on his chin. He grabbed Hollow by the hair, swinging him away from the open expanse of the blackened sky. "¡Venga Tu reino! ¡Hágase Tu voluntad en la tierra como en el cielo!"

He wrapped his wiry arms around his alabaster adversary and fear stretched in Hollow's dark eyes.

"May this be a taste of how it will feel for you to burn in hell," Reblaze hollered, allowing the purple flames to rip from his arms. "And may you change your life so that you will not go!"

Hollow, consumed in the flames, wailed in his unsettling rumble. The flames he attempted to produce were nothing compared to the ones Rico could. It was the difference between spiritual fuel and a carbon copy.

Coda observed this, clinging to both his timber staff and the tree. He tried to ignore the pain-filled howls and focus on Hollow's features…if the other was Terry, who was this one?

"¡Danos a nosotros hoy," Reblaze hollered, continuing his prayer, "nuestro pan de cada día!"

He violently released Hollow, whose skin had now tinted pink all over. He wasn't burned physically but…Reblaze's fire had taken on a spiritual facet. Hollow had been scorched to his soul.

And he spoke.

"Perdona nuestras ofensas," Hollow said softly, his voice ringing dully through his internal canyon, "como también nosotros perdonamos a los que nos ofenden."

Leviathan appeared within the vicinity once more, agitation showing in his brown eyes. He sailed to Coda, holding out his hand.

"I can't find him, Coda. I can't find Terry."

The sky spoke again as Coda reached for both the staff and Leviathan's hand, and the air was shaken.

Reblaze continued his prayer, observing Hollow with wide eyes.

"No nos dejes caer en tentación y líbranos del mal…"

Leviathan pulled Coda onto his back and rose again through the trees. Coda attempted to maneuver the staff so that it would not catch on any branches.

"Ezekiel, slow down!"

Hollow repeated Reblaze's words. "Líbranos del mal…"

Rico's purple wings faded into an orange.

As Leviathan sailed through the timber, the staff almost knowingly embedded itself into a tree hollow, jerking Coda off Leviathan's back and slinging him into the air.

"Porque Tuyo es el reino," Reblaze professed through the crack of intensified thunder from the cloud above them. He didn't hear Leviathan yell Coda's name.

"El poder y la gloria por todos los siglos."

Leviathan flew towards Coda, who grasped wildly for any source of support. The branches, instead of yielding to the skinny boy, snapped back and whipped him on his forearms. He threw an arm in front of his face, using only one hand now, which still couldn't grab hold of the surrounding bark-bearers.

A tear formed in the corner of one of Hollow's eyes, as his ivory skin slowly received its pigmentation and his hair slowly began releasing the locks.

"Almost there," Leviathan muttered to himself, dodging the branches as they whipped towards him in Coda's wake.

Coda's flailing hand found Hollow just before Leviathan could reach him.

"Amén."

The sky opened.

As Coda grabbed a hold of Hollow's heel, the surrounding atmosphere buckled like the unclogging of a pipe. Reblaze was sucked towards Hollow as if towards a giant vacuum.

Lightning reached past Leviathan like a supplemental arm grabbing what Ezekiel himself could not reach, leaving the boy without sight or control of his flight, spinning into the entanglement of the timber below.

The lightning split through Hollow's skull, cracking him as if he were a walnut and ripping through his body, filling every crevice. The current shocked Coda into letting go, and he fell quickly through the oaks and pines until one branch met him that was firm and big enough to break his fall.

The lightning flowed out of Hollow's foot, shattering across the treetops. Rico was blinded, grabbing onto the nearest limb, dangling and awaiting the return of his vision and situational sanity.

The rest wasn't meant for him to see, for at the moment he was blinded, an arsenal of angels entered the area from the raining clouds, swirling and soaring down to catch him, Coda, and Ezekiel, toting them to the ground.

Some moved as liquid, blessing the air and surprising the enemy with each shift in the tidal currents of wind. Most moved with the lightning—staccato with purpose and speed.

The preexisting faction on the ground, visible to Rico earlier, battled the iridescent defectors with fury, their hallowed swords of red flame keeping the sparking blades of the demons on the defensive.

The towering Baraqiel was a fury of electric motion, holding onto Hollow by his hair and casting the collective of his tormenting demons against a pine where four of the angel's proxies swiftly surrounded them. The malicious creatures shrieked and whined, collared.

With its non-gloved hand, Baraqiel pointed towards a blue form darting through the trees beneath them. Three of its proxies followed the wordless command, cracking thunder in their quickness to obstruct the eternal renegade.

"Delegates of Raphael," Baraqiel called, and five angels appeared before it, resplendent in greens and another color that was heavenly in nature. Baraqiel pointed to them one at a time. "Dreamer. Dyna. Shen Long. Coda. Rico. El commands."

The angels enkindled the air with their movements.

Baraqiel hadn't relinquished its grip on Hollow, walking on air towards the shrieking miniature demons.

"Bring them," it instructed

In the next moment they were gone, along with their captives, their plasmic heat lingering in the air.

• • • • •

Skyboarder watched what she could from the ground, unsure of what she was seeing. The presence of the angels was almost strong enough for her to detect them, but what she could physically see overwhelmed her senses. Rico fell to the ground a few feet from her and, before she could move towards him, another figure approached her in a rush of golden-green wind, healing energies flowing only so thick.

"God is pleased, Dyna," the angel said, reaching for her maimed hand with a gloved hand of its own.

Kim offered her swollen extremity almost subconsciously and when the angel took it, she screamed in surprise and alarm. The flames leapt from its glove to her hand, lighting her up inside, stirring metaphysical flames throughout her body.

"The battle," the angel said, "has prepared you for the war."

The combustion flared about her spirit to the point of being unbearable and she allowed herself to feel nothing more.

• • • • •

Kamiskas's screams would have been damaging to the human ear.

"Just give me the girl!" it exclaimed. It was referring to Solitaire, who lay on the ground just beyond its reach. One of the healing angels administered to Justus in the distance.

The angels that blocked Kamiskas from his target remained silent. Behind them, an angel materialized above Solitaire, massive and formidable, pink melting into gold.

Kamiskas wailed all the louder.

"IN THE NAME OF EL." The voice ripped through the clearing like a father's cry. Kamiskas turned warily.

Facing the demon was yet another angel, no bigger than it had appeared in Justus's subconsciousness those few months ago, and slightly bigger than the starving child it had appeared as to Kim. Blue swirled around its golden frame but it did not move.

The demon snarled, an electric blue triton-styled weapon appearing in its hand.

"Kamiskas," the tiny angel spoke, red glove peeling from its hand until it had lengthened into a sword of flame. "El Elyon can always reach you."

Without another word, the angel's sword shattered Kamiskas's weapon and just as quickly, it wore its red glove again. With the gloved hand in conjunction with the triton, the angel struck Kamiskas continually, causing the demon's baubles and opals to fall from its body and dematerialize on every plane of existence.

The angel was reducing the demon, its authority and abilities shrinking along with its perceived mass. When the small angel finished, Kamiskas was no more than one of the miniature demons that had been tormenting Hollow.

"Go now, demon," the angel spoke again. "Understanding that there is nothing lower than you in the eyes of El Roi. If you torment a gnat, it shall still be far greater."

· · · · ·

Overflowing with tears, Solitaire's eyes followed the angel as it sat her up. This was the same angel that had sat at Rico's side in the chapel as stealth protection against the doctor's evils, and the same angel that had shown Justus creations beyond imagination.

It now waved a hand over Eden and commanded, "Speak."

"I'm sorry—" she began, and another wave of its hand silenced her.

"When you healed Justus of your own will, you did the Lord's will. You saw then what your power can be used for. Now God commands that you wield the power in the way from this moment on, and never turn back to the evil that corrupted you."

It waved its hand again and the pain instantly vanished from her body.

"Your tongue is loosed," the angel spoke, almost friendly, "as is your body."

"God is worthy," she said, overcome.

"God is indeed worthy," it agreed.

It stood, motioning for her to follow its lead.

Once she was standing as well, it laid a hand on her shoulder.

"Never be sorry again, Eden-in-Love. Dios te creó para ser más que eso."

She understood. God had made her.

He had made her more than.

27.
Shock Round

Hello, my delightful Dyna.

Kim stood, surrounded by a strange blackness above her. Black, yet it was the furthest thing from dark. She looked down to find that the ground beneath her was comprised of stars. Fine as sand, while white and green and blue and blinding. They extended limitlessly in every direction she turned. She gazed back up into the blackness, smiling.

"Hello, Daddy. I crashed and burned, huh?"

You're learning, Dyna.

"I'm doing, Lord."

That you are, came the pleased reply.

One of the white specs beneath her rose slowly into the air, like a snowflake falling the wrong way.

Continue doing even greater, my daughter. In My name. Knowing that I am with you.

Another glowing speck joined the other, rising into the black.

I am with you.

More miniature beings began to drift upwards and Kim lifted her arms in prayer. He was telling her exactly what she needed to hear.

The atmosphere was full of shimmering spirits, dancing like dandelion seeds as Kim began to sway and spin. The stars floated up all around her, all the way out to the assumed horizon of cosmos.

I am always with you.

· · · · ·

Terry stared down in concern while Coda opened his eyes. When Coda moved to prop himself up on his elbows, Terry took purposeful steps back across the muddying soil.

"Malvolio," Coda said weakly.

Terry, hair a neon orange instead of the Crayola red it had once been, didn't speak for a few moments, lowering himself to his knees. His thighs embraced the muck and he quoted, "'Thou canst not choose but know who I am.' You saved my life back there. I owe you one, I guess."

Coda was regaining himself quickly, his braids dripping water. "Terry. What the hell is your damage?"

Terry's voice and face hid his emotion. It was purposeful to a fault. "You don't know how deep it goes, Coda. There are truths that you can't handle."

Coda cocked his head, attempting to understand, while staving off the righteous fury that had built.

"Truth is meant to be handled," he hissed. "It's deserved."

"Coda, you're innocent to this kind of corruption," Terry said, a new current in his tone. "That 'doctor.' She's devious, man. You're special. Kim's special. You're both stupid, but special. Every single one of you guys needs to avoid this. That doctor is gonna rain down something horrible on this place."

Coda was exasperated. "What doctor? And if there's evil, why does it seem like you embody it?"

"I can't fight this on the side you're on, Coda. Can't win that way."

The rain pounded. Coda broke.

"We're friends," he said through trembling lips and collapsing lids.

"Until this moment, we were, dude. But the tide's going out."

Coda's eyelids fluttered up and eyes began to sharpen, remembering the jellyfish—baby jellyfish stranded on the increasingly exposed sandbar. Terry's goal was to become a fully developed Man O' War.

Using the moment he had created, Terry pounced, discharging the syringe in Coda's neck. Coda slumped over, his body already reacting.

Terry tucked the needle back in his busted overalls. To the swiftly distant Coda, he continued. "It's better for you that we're not friends anymore, Cheshire."

He stood, orange Medusa dreads soggy with precipitation and perspiration. His emotions were now as evident as his tentacles. His voice cracking, he allowed himself the closure he couldn't permit to the boy who had been his kindred spirit.

"Nobody loves you more than I do," he said, fingers lingering near Coda's face. The air thickened and cleared, pulsing with a supernatural vibration. "Change that." And he was gone.

When Justus located Coda, the serum had already done its work. Coda sat there in the rain and the mud, shaking with tears.

"I'm mad, Justus," he said through his shudders, emotions compounded by recent memories he no longer had.

Justus sat next to him, ignoring the sensation of the spreading sludge and pulling his friend close.

"I know," he said. "You're allowed to be."

· · · · ·

The rain pounded like a heavenly stampede. Gravity around Kim was again tugged in the usual direction. Something bigger than that incendiary storm cloud was berating their surroundings as well—Kim could feel it as strong as her heartbeat.

"Ezekiel, please get up."

She observed her friend lying there in what was quickly becoming mud. His mask was gone and his battle uniform was just as destroyed as she remembered, but, like her, he had no bruises and no lingering injuries, at least that she could tell. If he lay there any longer, however, this torrential rain might do him in.

She reached down to grab his shoulders. "Ezekiel—"

Eyes flipping open, he returned to consciousness as suddenly as he had left it. He briefly choked on the rain as he gasped for breath, before grabbing Kim's shoulders in instant defense, but she was much stronger than he was, simply standing him up and inviting him back to an authenticity of being.

"It's all right," she calmed him. "It's just me. The fight's over."

Ezekiel blinked, water matting his hair to his face in the cutest way. "We won?"

"Kinda." Kim laughed, rain filling her mouth. She sputtered and spit, then continued. "Everything got really spiritual, so I can't say for sure."

Ezekiel moved his hands from her shoulders to her wrists, inspecting her arms and her hands. Once finished with her, he took to examining himself.

"Renata says the police are on the way," Kim said, trying to bring his attention back to the situation at hand, "so I need you to help me get out of here by actually *getting* me out of here. Justus is getting Coda."

He looked up at her, still marveling at their state of health. "The angels…?"

She nodded. "Utterly healed. But seriously, boo, we've gotta go. It's getting real ugly 'round here."

That was no exaggeration. The sky was churning with some seriousness, and the rain was so thick that she had to squint to protect her sight from the barrage of water.

"Tornado weather." He understood. "Sooner we go, the better, huh? I'm not sure how well I can fly in a storm. I never prepared for *this*, if you know what I mean."

The rainfall became rougher, and Kim had to shout for Ezekiel to hear her.

"I know what you mean. On the job training." She resisted the impulse to smile. The downpour was ridiculous.

As she climbed onto his back, he had another concern. "Dare I ask where exactly we're going?" he asked as they lifted into the air.

"Sure, sure," was her response. "Don't worry, 'Zekiel. This part will be quick and fun."

Neither of them realized how wrong she was. The first hint was when the hail began.

• • • • •

The precipitation was bad enough on the ground, but soaring through the sky at forty-something miles an hour was enough to make Kim look at water the way a cat must. The sky was dark the entire way and the team had to map their way to Kim's place by using the lights from the city below.

"Fairgrounds to the right," Rico called out, braving the hailstones. The flying formation shifted to the left.

Renata clung to Rico's back, refusing to even peek, which was probably for the best, because Kim was amazed to see his red wings of fire flapping through her body as if she were just a ghost.

"There's the pulp mill," Coda shouted out. "Straight ahead."

Coda's shoes had gotten caught in the current of Justus's lower torso a few miles back and were lost somewhere on the OCC campus and his socks still bounced sporadically into the water flow. He was handling the flight better than Renata, however, peering over Justus's shoulder. His braids were loosened and soaked to nappy ringlets while still protecting his head from the occasional bullet of ice.

Kim patted Ezekiel on his bare chest, signaling to him to slow his lead. They were nearing the lake.

Kim had decided on her parents' house as the docking point simply because it was closest. Kim had previously made the mistake of attempting to yell out landmarks as Rico or Coda had and the force of air that hit her mouth stuffed the words back down into her diaphragm. It would have been pointless at this particular moment, anyway, because

Ezekiel knew exactly where it was in relation to the lake, and the six of them touched down without ruining any flowerbeds.

As soon as Renata was off of his back, Rico grabbed tight to Coda.

"That's never happening to you again, you understand?" he whispered in Coda's ear.

Kim pulled her house key from a surprising place—"Come one, lots of women keep things in their bras. Get over it."—and unlocked the door.

"Please don't ask any questions," Kim hollered out as the six of them sloshed into her parents' house.

"No one's here," Ezekiel said, listening on the wavelengths only he could perceive.

"Oh, good," Kim said, dropping immediately onto the living room sofa. "I saw dad's truck in the driveway. He wouldn't be happy with this. Especially Rico and Ezekiel looking like they're halfway through their strip show."

"I hope you have twenties," Rico joked easily, heading into the hallway. "Where are your towels?" he asked.

"There's an arsenal of them in the bathroom," she said, and Coda rushed to assist him.

"What time is it?" Ezekiel asked, looking for a clock. How long had they been at Oakwood?

"I think I'm bleeding," Renata moaned, inspecting her elbow. "I would have brought a jacket or something if I had known I'd be soaring through a stratosphere of ice marbles."

"Where are the Hollows?" Justus asked. Thanks to his powers, he was the only one who was dry.

"Where's Solitaire?" Kim asked wearily.

"*Who's* Solitaire," Rico asked pointedly, entering with a stack of towels and his eyes on Ezekiel. "I know you figured that out."

Ezekiel looked to Renata. "What's this that Kim was saying about cops?"

"Wait, wait, wait, wait, wait," Coda interrupted, following with his own towel stack. "Can we go in some type of chronological order? We have time; we're all together and every one of us knows that God is in control—after today, there should never again be any doubt about *that*—"

"Does every inspirational speech of yours have to insinuate righteous judgment?" Kim grumbled. She hated being wet while chilly and it was affecting her personality.

"—so let's talk this out," Coda continued undeterred. "How did you guys find me? You seemed really prepared for the battle with your cool—uh—costumes."

"Kim, can we make some tea?" Justus asked. "Renata's teeth are chattering."

"Sure thing," Kim said, heading into the kitchen. "Relocate the conversation as required," she said over her shoulder.

"Justus had an epic dream," Rico informed Coda, as they shifted into the kitchen. "This buffalicious angel took him caroling through the ages."

"Not following," Coda said, sitting down at the table. "I mean, I get the Dickens reference, but are we talking a metaphorical dream or a giant St. Peter has a Revelation experience?"

Justus explained, sitting as well. "This big, Vin Diesel of an angel was basically sent to show me these moments through the past, mostly the very recent past. I saw Hollow and Solitaire take you…" He trailed off, thinking of the group in white capes. "I saw a lot of things. I'm not sure I understand all of them."

"Tell him about the angel fight," Rico said excitedly, scooting Renata's chair in before taking his place adjacent to her. He draped a towel over his naked shoulders as Justus filled Coda in on all the intricacies of his experience on that nameless world.

"They had a very deliberate way of speaking," Justus said. "I have no idea what language it was, but I understood it, no problem. And I noticed they never called God anything outside of a title. They had no pronouns."

"No pronouns?" Ezekiel asked, leaning against the doorframe.

"For God at least," Justus said. "It struck me as strange, because it would have been way faster to say 'He' than it would to say 'El Roi' and whatever else."

"Maybe they just had no English equivalent for a God-related pronoun," Kim suggested, placing a mug filled with water in the microwave. "Angels certainly wouldn't refer to God as a He or a She seeing how spirit beings have no sex."

"Yeah, and no gender either," Rico cracked.

"Wow," Ezekiel laughed. Things must be getting back to normal. Well, as normal as things could be by this point.

Justus leaned his elbows on the table, folding his arms. "That makes sense," he said to Kim. "Though it's weird that I remember some of it in Hebrew now that it's over. For example, the good angel was named

Baraqiel, which is Hebrew for 'lightning of God' and fits what I saw him —it—do with that sword."

"I thought Barakiel, meant 'blessed of God,'" Coda said, playing with the pepper shaker.

"How do you two know these things?" Kim asked, watching the timer on the microwave.

"I read Dad's schoolbooks," was Coda's response.

"Barak with a 'k' does mean 'blessed,' Coda," Justus said, "but this was Baraq with a 'q,' which means 'lightning.'"

"How could you tell the difference in a dream?" Rico asked.

"I just could," Justus shrugged. "Kinda like when you're having a dream and you just KNOW that there's a big dog waiting behind that one closed door without ever having to verify it personally."

"Huh?" Renata asked, as Ezekiel laughed harder.

Justus continued. "God makes everything pretty plain when you're in His realm. The only things kept from you are the things He wants kept from you."

Rico thought back to the moment he saw Kamiskas strut past Ezekiel, entirely unnoticed buy his overwhelmingly perceptive friend. Justus spoke the truth.

"And Baraqiel kept referring to God as 'El Roi,'" Justus continued, "whereas Kamiskas called God by the name 'El Rapha.'"

"Break that down for me," Renata said, nestling deeper into the beach towel she had draped around her. "All my religious training has been in Spanish."

"'El Roi' means 'God who sees,'" Justus said, "and 'El Rapha'… usually it's heard in conjunction with Jehovah and means 'God of healing.'"

Renata crinkled her nose thoughtfully. "How many branches of God do they have?"

"Huh?" Justus asked.

"You know how humans know of God in His three basic roles?"

Justus nodded. "Elohim, plural Gods as one God."

"*English*, puh-lease!" Renata seemed to be resisting an eye-roll. "I attend public school. But yeah, the Tri-Head God, or whatever. As the Almighty, as the Savior, and as the Comforter. The Thinker, the Speaker, and the Doer. Trinity's the word I was trying to think of. Maybe angels only refer to Him strictly situationally. Baraqiel was telling Kamiskas— at the time, wasn't it Ambriel?—that God had *seen* Ambriel turn away and Ambriel was pleading with God's healing nature. That's possible, right?"

It was hard for Justus to believe that this was sex-obsessed Rico's little sister sounding so naturally versed in the spiritual department. "That makes sense, too," he said.

Ezekiel spoke up. "Didn't you say that Kamiskas seemed like a state that Ambriel was in once it was punished and separated from God; a title more than a name?"

Justus nodded. "Yeah. And when they referred to the Word of God, they didn't say it like it was just written words in the Bible."

"La Palabra Viva," Rico understood.

Renata translated. "The Living Word."

"Exactly," Justus said, bobbleheading. "Because they already knew God the Son outside of time. Because God the Son is part of Elohim and so is El Roi and they knew Him already in those capacities. That's trippy."

Kim had lost track of the conversation. With no idea of what they were talking about now, she went back to something she did understand. "All these angels' names ended in 'el,' right?" She placed the steaming mug and a tea bag in front of Renata. "That must've signified their closeness and deference to God. Maybe by losing that connection, Kamiskas also lost that title."

"Just like—" Justus began.

"Satan," they said in unison. Justus got a chill.

"Hey, mindreader," Rico said after a pause, swiveling to look at his friend.

Ezekiel met his gaze. "'Sabi?"

"What does your name mean?"

"Strength of God."

"Why'd your parents pick that?" Renata asked, soaking the tea bag.

"They didn't," Ezekiel said. "I picked it when we came over from the states. Shen Long Ezekiel Yang. They amended my birth certificate."

"Why 'Ezekiel'?" Rico asked.

Ezekiel began to laugh, moving from the doorway. "You know that song 'Ezekiel Saw the Wheel'? There was this Mormon missionary from Australia who would always sing it to my sister and I whenever she'd come by the house. Well, I thought the song was about some caveman named Ezekiel who had invented the first wheel and he became one of the coolest people to me. Imagine life without wheels, you know?"

Coda burst into laughter. "That's awesome! I'll never think of that song the same way."

"So you named yourself after Ezekiel Cro-Magnon," Kim said. "I can dig it."

Ezekiel smiled. "Ezekiel Cro-Magnon, the wheel inventor."

Now that he was in the room with them, Kim noticed the lightning scar on his back. They were healed, but his Lichtenberg figure remained. Unconsciously, she ran her fingers along his skin. He glanced at her briefly, and silently moved back to the doorway.

"So what's your story?" Coda said suddenly to Renata.

"Hmm?" she asked, looking up from her tea.

"She's not Solitaire," Ezekiel said quickly.

"I don't doubt that," Coda said, "because then she wouldn't be *here* right now and we wouldn't all be acting so cozy with tea and all."

"Who *is* Solitaire?" Rico asked again.

"Eden," Ezekiel and Justus answered in unison.

Rico's jaw dropped and Coda's eyes bugged out of his head as Renata commented, "I knew it," calmly sipping on her tea.

"Stop the press," Kim whispered, taking another glass of hot water from the microwave. "So she knew us inside and out! And she actually was fluent in Spanish, not just reversing Rico's knowledge of the language."

"Now that you say that idea of ours aloud, it sounds completely ridiculous," Rico said. "She reverses, so what would reversed language sound like?" He laughed bitterly.

"That's true," Justus mused.

"How did *you* know?" Ezekiel asked him.

"She couldn't use her powers once Terry attacked her," Justus explained. "She had been using that reversal thing so that no one could see her face and so that her skin was always different, reflecting her adversary. Without her powers, she just looked like herself, just in a white-wigged, hideous Halloween costume."

They looked to Ezekiel for more.

"She became very obvious," he said. "Her thoughts were flying like startled bees once Terry snapped her."

"Like a gingerbread cookie," Coda said.

"Dude!" Justus squealed, disturbed by the memory. Kim noticed then that his bangs were black, while the rest of his hair was yellow. How had she missed that? She wanted to ask him…but later. She giggled in spite of herself.

"What were her thoughts?" Rico asked, looking at Kim strangely.

"She had been deceived from the get go," Ezekiel explained. "The… second Hollow had been kinda stalking her since … the Hollow-fication I guess."

"Hollow-fication?" Kim asked, giving Coda the second steaming mug.

"So many things about them were fuzzy and hard to translate, but both of the Hollows somehow had information about us."

"About us?" Rico slid the sugar in Coda's direction. "What could he have possibly known about us when *we* barely knew about us?"

Ezekiel shook his head. "They were after someone. One of us. A certain power that they needed… Their thoughts conflict on this. But essentially they got wrapped up in the…fun of it all, I guess."

"Reprobate," Kim nodded, back at the microwave. She had cracked open a Twinkle soda for herself. "So originally they were after similarly gifted people."

"Cursed," Ezekiel corrected. "Solitaire… Eden believed they were cursed by God with these abilities."

"Who started this?" Rico asked. "Was it a giant dose of mass crazy?"

"Yeah, mass hysteria?" Kim was asking simultaneously.

"See, that's why it wasn't entirely self-created," Ezekiel said. "The original Hollow was assisted by someone. There was a scientist etched in the thoughts I found."

"A mad scientist type?" Justus asked.

Ezekiel shrugged and continued. "Then Terry visited a fortune teller at the Funfair who did an amazing job at screwing up his brain and leading him to the first Hollow."

"Madame Endora," Coda exhaled. "I saw that tent."

Kim and Justus shared a look. That seemed like a lifetime ago.

"Poor Terry," Coda was saying, and Rico snorted. Coda glared, but didn't speak again.

"Somehow Terry got to whatever was used on the first Hollow," Ezekiel said, "yet I didn't see the scientist in his thoughts along the same…wrinkle, I guess. Like, Terry's method was different, but I don't know how yet. But if we could track them down I could get more. They might even just tell us, 'cause whatever that plan was that they had is pretty much destroyed now."

"You were multitasking out there during that fight, weren't you?" Kim commented, impressed.

"What was Eden's story?" Justus asked.

"Slowly won over by her associates," Ezekiel said. "But, if I'm correct, she had nothing to do with the scientist…though according to Terry's thoughts, the scientist very much wanted Solitaire."

"Does Eden—" Kim began.

"Only guesses," he responded to her unasked question. "But she knew the second one was Terry. He was always bold with her."

"Well we know who the other one is," Coda said.

"We do?" Justus asked.

Rico groaned. "Not with this again."

"Guys, guys, come on, now." Something about that idea didn't sit well with Kim. She picked her words carefully and thoughtfully, desiring to sound neither heartless nor clueless. "I honestly feel that we don't have to…that everything will come clear in due time. And I don't like the distrust we start to form when we're considering our friends."

"Yeah," Renata began, "but if Terry was—"

"He was," Kim interrupted, "but we honestly hadn't even suspected him. We all thought—"

"Not all of us," Rico said quickly, golden flame whipping around his irises.

Touché, Rico. A touchy touché. Kim watched him thoughtfully, before her thoughts moved to Coda. *His* eyes… there was a reason they had each seen their own golden-influence in his eyes. Him and his weird power…

"Peculiar, INC," Ezekiel commented, and his eyes connected with Kim's.

"I don't know, Justus mumbled. "The world seems so different now. Like I think of Eden and I wonder…"

Kim nodded, stirring a teaspoon of honey into her own tea. "I know what you mean, Droxy. I think back on all those times I spoke with Terry and I wonder what was going on in his brain then. What's going on in his brain now."

"You didn't talk to Terry," Coda muttered as quietly as he could, as if he simply *had* to get that thought out into the air.

Rico rubbed his temple. "You know, guys? When I felt those wings sprout out of my back, everything changed. It became a different game. I became this different version of myself. I'm someone else now…for good." He shook his head, as if confounded by his own revelation.

"Can you still do that?" Justus asked. "The purple wing thing?"

Rico nodded. "Not purple, but still all wingy. Is it creepy?"

"Just a bit," Renata said, while Justus shook his head in assurance.

"Wait, wait," Coda said again. "What about these cops?"

"Oh yeah," Kim said, turning to Rico's sister.

"They weren't cops, exactly," Renata said, yet before she could speak any further, the front door opened.

At first they thought the wind, wailing and howling fiercely, had blown it open, but lightning cracked, illuminating the pounding rain and two familiar figures.

"Parents!" Kim squealed, at some crossroad between relief and apprehension.

"Why is the floor wet?" Delia was asking, looking at the puddles in the entryway as she shook out her umbrella over the porch.

Lester stared at the vagabonds in his kitchen, eyes sharpening on half-naked Ezekiel.

"Kim, what are you doing back from Atlanta already? And what's happened to you all?"

Kim hurried over to her parents, yapping a mile a minute, attempting to put them at ease.

Coda, Renata and Justus rose as well, following Kim to assist where needed.

Ezekiel held Rico back, saying under his breath, "You know who the second Hollow is."

He had deduced correctly. Rico blinked stupidly for a moment.

"So do you, don't you?" Rico asked, realizing quickly. "I just saw, underneath all of that...monstrosity, but when Kim was quoting those scriptures you were able to do your head thing, weren't you?"

Ezekiel shook his head. "Trust me, it was a horrible place to be."

Rico cast a furtive glance towards the group barraging the elder Hamiltons with explanations and slick verbal excursions from the situation at hand.

"You found out something that they're not ready for, huh?" he said to his mind-reading friend.

"They're barely ready for who it is," Ezekiel whispered. "On top of that, it's far more complicated than we thought. Both of the Hollows had separate affiliates, and Ter—"

He was interrupted because the next houseguests didn't bother to knock, ring the doorbell, or use keys. They were bursting in through every door, from the backyard and through the garage and right behind Kim's parents.

One cracked a pill beneath Ezekiel's nose, and as the boy helplessly inhaled the contents, he dropped.

"What the—" was all that Justus managed to get out before a shock round rendered him unconscious.

"What's going on?" Lester demanded, as his wife cried out, watching the helmeted crew disable the teenagers almost as one. "*HEY*," he barked as his daughter collapsed into the arms of one of the black-suited intruders

"What is this?" he asked desperately, as a sharply dressed woman entered to observe the handiwork of her team. "SWAT? Military? FBI?"

Her expression was warm. "You have a right to be alarmed, Dr. and Mrs. Hamilton," she said, motioning to another of her agents, "but some *very* important people want to talk to your daughter and her friends about their interesting activities as of late. Namely, me."

A sedative had been administered to Delia without Lester being able to react.

His wife's eyes began to flutter. "My daughter…" was all she could manage.

The woman looked on in what appeared to be pity.

"Your daughter'll be all right, Mrs. Hamilton. She's in the safest hands possible." To her team, she barked, "Bring them. And find out why we lost that trace on the Alexander boy. AND WHY THE HELL ARE THERE ONLY SIX OF THEM?"

The bustle was quick, and the woman told two agents to guide Delia. "She can ride with us. I'm sure Dr. Hamilton would have it no other way." She smiled at Lester and strangely she didn't seem friendly, even after offering her hand.

"Forgive our imposition but respect our mission. I'm Dr. Patricia Preacher and save the jokes—I've heard them all before."

Lester finally found words, but he didn't shake. "It hadn't crossed my mind to joke, Dr. Preacher."

The house was empty, save for the two doctors and one last agent.

"What kind of doctor did you say you were?" Lester asked, desperately trying to produce any grasp on the situation he found himself abandoned in.

"I'm a developmental biologist," Patricia said, steadfastly holding out her hand, her non-smiling eyes sharpening into a glare. Even though she didn't command him with her words, her body language was enough, and he shook.

"Developmental biology is a long way from opticianry practice," Lester commented hazily. "I wouldn't call myself a doctor. Certainly not in the way you are, that is."

"Ah yes, well," she filled the space, not willing to discuss herself or her position any further. "I've dove deep into your medical background and all of your other skills, Lester—excuse the familiarity. I've just been poring over those files and…"

She gestured to the door.

"I *sincerely* hope you don't mind helicopters, Dr. Hamilton," she said, pulling out a pistol. "And I'm *sure* you understand that by flaunting this Browning 9x19 millimeter Hi-Power in such a fashion, I'm enforcing the fact that you don't have a choice one way or the other. Now walk with me or walk with your chosen god—your immediate choice. I *am* on a deadline."

28.

Special

The storm was long gone, and the days had passed with deceptive normalcy.

The Brunswick lights hazed the sky a midnight gold; building lights and highway lights were caught in a combination of the late May humidity and the paper mill smog. Streaming lights on the island causeways disappeared into the silent blackness of the island foliage. Yet if one listened close enough, perhaps while fishing off an abandoned St. Simons pier, there could be heard the royal whisperings of angels above the slapping waves and the distant snore of the causeway bridges.

Somewhere, Shawn Montgomery was throwing a party. Kim was sure of it. It was the only thing she was sure of, because the days and nights had merged together until even her senses seemed confused. Despite this, she was positive that the world outside of her undisclosed confinement facility had continued undeterred. It was too early in the summer for anyone to be missing. Around mid-July, someone would notice. Maybe.

"When will you be done taking blood outta me?" she asked wearily.

Dr. Preacher just smiled. That's all she ever did. Kim had long begun to hate that smile.

"My strength isn't in my blood," Kim said, and the endless needles kept pumping, always more bags to be filled.

Dr. Preacher's smile tightened. "Never you worry about the blood, Kimberly."

"*Kim*," the girl snapped. "And I'll say again that my strength isn't in *my* blood."

The doctor seemed uninterested with Kim's spiritual allusions. "You know, as impressive as your parents have been, I'm surprised the best we're getting from you is this nasty attitude."

"I'll show you a nasty attitude," Kim growled.

Dr. Preacher's smile was real again. "I'm sure you will."

That was another reason they kept drawing her blood. It kept her weak. She could barely string three sentences together before getting lightheaded. She didn't know what would happen if she tried to stand and she wasn't crazy about ripping all those needles out of her body either. For all she knew, they were injecting her with something to incapacitate her while taking out whatever it was they needed.

There was only one day that she had felt the most like herself, and it was the day they had surprised her and wheeled Coda in. Like her, he was strapped to a chair, but his was mobile. His hair was on the extreme side of nappy, but he looked like he had been eating better than he had their entire freshman year of college.

"Kim!" he said, surprised.

"Hey, Coda!" She instantly glared at the nurses, wondering what the game was, but they already had their backs to her, leaving the two in the room.

"Have they put you with anybody yet?" His voice was dry, half whisper, half croak. She wondered what kind of experiments they had been trying on him.

"You're my first," she said, before realizing. "Wait, have they been pairing you with people?"

"At first they roomed me with Ezekiel, and I've had afternoons with Justus and Renata a lot. I seem to give Justus nightmares that he refuses to talk to me about. And they stopped putting me with Rico, after he tried to kill them again."

Kim laughed aloud for the first time in what must have been weeks. "Again?"

Coda nodded sadly. "He almost got one this time. I'm sure they rocked his world for it."

Kim's laughter was gone. "I've missed you guys," she said after a moment.

Coda hadn't heard her. Or he was pretending. "You know, when Rico hugs you, he always hugs you too long," he said, gazing off. "Like he's making up for all the times that if he had been there to hug you, well then he would've. So he doesn't let go. He just presses you closer."

Kim didn't know what to say. It seemed like a random reflection, but she guessed he was allowed it considering the circumstances.

"Terry always hugged too quick, but it was okay because he was always there."

Kim had reflected on this many times while isolated in her room. Coda had basically lost one of his closest friends due to all of this craziness with their powers. It seemed to give him yet another excuse to have a pity party, but this one, Kim felt, was deserved.

"He was always that kind of friend. He'd say hi to my dad and my sister whenever he came over to pick me up. He wouldn't drive off until he saw that I was all the way inside. Don't know what you've got 'til..."

"How are you doing with—"

His gaze was cutting. "You don't get to ask me about him. You don't have that right."

She couldn't believe he had chosen to flip that switch. He's the one who had brought Terry up in the first place! "Lakota, I'm tired of this drama kingdom! Why the hell are you so miserable at the world and so mad at me?"

"Because you came back for me!"

His words were a cannon in the air. Her senses were alien to her, and the only one retained was her hearing.

"You told me that I was part of the reason you came back, and what happened to that? You left. You left and then you let go. So what the hell was I still holding on to you for?"

He was broiling. She was losing her grip on the moment. In reality, and unknowingly for both of them, the power that his presence had restored to her was swiftly receding.

"I was your promise," he said, voice cracking but holding back the tears. "And you broke me. And Terry kept gluing me together and then he broke me, too."

She blinked. Still losing.

"You tell me what the hell good is a broken promise, and then ask me not to feel miserable." Then, quieter, "I came back for you."

He didn't speak to her again, and after some time the nurses reentered to wheel him out.

That was her only afternoon with him, and her only night in tears.

Back in the present, the lights flickered and Kim figured it was her own consciousness, switching off for only a moment. They had her incapacitated to a dangerous level. She had to get out of there. She was as worried about her mental health as she was about her physical health. They hadn't been outright malicious as of yet, but she knew it was just a matter of time.

Dr. Preacher opened the door to the hallway, then paused.

"You know," she said, turning, "you're special, I'll give you that. But I've seen special. I've created special. Sure, some think that special equals freak, but special equals physics, chemistry, biology... Special is science.

A hereditary marriage here, a chemical separation there. Someone born without a finger, or with a dermoid cyst between their shoulder blades that might have once been their twin. Someone with a seemingly imbalanced combination of muscle mass and genetic strength. And eventually you see that special is normal, and special only factors when someone knows how and whether to harness the 'special' for that moment in history." She was still smiling. "You're just special. You're just science. And here, you're just normal."

That's when the lights went out for real. The doc cussed. Kim bet she wasn't smiling now.

A hissing jumped around the dark, like a live wire was in the room, and she heard Dr. Preacher grunt and hit the floor.

A light came on, but it wasn't from the bulbs in the room.

Kim croaked. "Maya?"

"In the flesh," her friend grinned. "Well, sort of."

She was just as modelesque as Kim remembered, titanic and curvy. She was wearing running shoes, tights and gloves, all black, but her upper torso was pure silver-white electricity, with a human neck and head set on top. A mask covered a good part of her head, leaving only her hair, eyes, nostrils and jaw exposed.

"I think you need to explain," Kim said shakily. Maya was doing something to the straps that held her to the chair that had constrained her for the last several days. She was moving so *quickly*.

"When we have the time, Kim, I'll explain happily. That's a promise."

"Ouch!" She was removing the needles.

"Sorry," Maya said, but not bothering to slow down. "You're gonna be bleeding a lot, but once we get out of here, Eden's gonna heal you up real nice."

"Eden," Kim said, running this over in her head. "Maya, wait…"

Maya looked down at her, the last of Kim's needles in her hand. A white crackle of electricity traveled across her left eyeball. "You don't want to wait another minute, trust me. The immediate concern is busting the rest of your folks out of here."

Kim realized she was right. The doctor's people had probably already initiated measures against this breakout. One thing Kim had learned in the past few days (or weeks or however long she had been in there) was how thorough their anticipations were.

She strained against the refusal of her body. "I'll try."

Maya was at the door, glancing out into the pitch-black hallway. When she heard her friend's words, she turned back to her, eyes lighting up like her torso.

"You know, Kim, a great woman once shared these words me. 'Don't try, just do it.' And can't you do all things through Somebody who…?"

Kim felt the strength returning her to form. She looked up in amazement.

A smile stretched across Maya's face, much more welcome than Dr. Preacher's. She could tell what had happened.

"Forgot who and Whose you were, huh?" Maya asked.

Kim stood, and squinted her eyes at the other girl. "Maya," she said again, as if finally believing it.

"That's right," Maya nodded, one hand on the door handle, stepping over the doctor lying on the floor. She held out her other hand to Kim.

"Miracles happen every day, Miss Wilbanks. Let them."

from The Days of Awakening (2ⁿᵈ Edition) *by Dr. Jimmie Stone*

[...] Now that your flesh has allowed the Spirit to take control and you've awakened yourself to the glory within, the Son's rays and ways are beaming through the windows of your seeing eyes. Soak up that strength now. The sky grows dark and the wind is no longer friendly. We know we can walk across waters that are placid and serene, but these are violent, stormy days.

Here is where we walk on tossing waves.

Author's Note

I started writing on the playground.

"The Quest to Save the Forest" was my first, involving elementary-age youth turned into gods and presiding over domains of nature. Like most kids, I had loads of concepts that I never fleshed out, but would scribble down, occasionally illustrating them. I loved adventure stories and heroes.

Best Friends was my first written adventure, about a group of three friends taken to a fantasy land that they had to save from a dark magician. Lots of Little Nemo in there, the cooler aspects of Narnia, and The Brothers Lionheart as well. It became my first franchise. I wrote those stories for years. Forests, sea serpents, uni-horned men, and an evil sorceress named Finallee. The world was endless.

As I got more comfortable with written works, getting good grades on my essays in school and writing full novels of my *Best Friends* series, sixth grade saw me create the story of five classmates who awakened the Greek gods and were gifted super powers. (I was into mythology by that point thanks Edith Hamilton's retellings.) Every couple of years I'd pull out my old notebooks and update the saga, writing characters out and moving new ones in. By my senior year, the Greek god angle seemed played out. Percy Jackson and others existed. What about biblical superheroes? I thought about Moses and David and Solomon and considered the fact that to non-believers, the Hebrew Bible is just another collection of mythological stories. Using these themes and a new set of characters inspired by my high school friends who were reading updates and giving me notes from their college dormitories, I wrote a new version of my middle school fantasy, finishing it early Christmas morning in 2009 while sitting in a hotel lobby in Japan.

I'm rereleasing it today in two formats. I had considered rewriting the whole thing, but I decided to let it stand relatively untouched. I reformatted a few things, amended a few ignorant references and phrases, and augmented the SuperNatural edition with over thirty illustrations commissioned within the first two years after the initial publication. Also gone are two pages of misogynistic lyrics from the sardonic "Women Today (They're Always Pregnant)," a showtune from the fictional ten-time Oliver-nominee *That's How It Goes*.

Additionally, I took liberties with a few dates. Annapolis's Plebe Summer actually takes place from June through August, but in order to root Rico a little more solidly into the Brunswick summer events, I moved it into a late July through September/October timeframe. Finally, to my knowledge there is no town in Georgia called Cedar City.

Kimberly Hamilton, Coda Crenshaw, Ezekiel Yang, and their friends have represented many things to me. They're a time capsule of my initial thrust into adulthood. In some ways they're templates for my more famous characters from my multimedia series *Pretty Dudes* (there's a lot of Shannon Crescitelli in Jericho Kim). But mainly, they're the first characters that gave me the confidence to create and share my art on a large scale, and for that alone, I'm grateful to return them to prominent display in my library of publications.

I'm still indebted to everyone who helped me birth this story—Tony, Jason, Katori, Jasmine, Katrina, Rachel, Leslie, Rocky, Emily, and my best friend Tanner.

This one's for Jesus, the ultimate homie. For deep-thinking Ezekiel, dreaming Justus, and ever-evolving Rico. For Kimberly Hamilton—so patient with me this second go-round—and freckle-faced Lakota, who named me.

C.S.R. Calloway

June 2022

About the Author

CHANCE SION-RAIZE CALLOWAY is the author of several novels and book series including *The Charismatic Chronicles*, *Pretty Dudes*, and *The Gay Man's Guide to Heterosexual Weddings*. Calloway founded CSRC Storytelling for printed media in 2012 with a passion for creating and promoting stories that change how people see themselves and the world around them

In the face of personal, global and systemic challenges, Calloway continues to focus his efforts on advocacy and change through art.

Connect with C.S.R. everywhere.
TWITTER: @ChanceCalloway
INSTAGRAM: @chancescalloway
MEDIUM: @csrcalloway
chancecalloway.com

DISCOVER MORE BOOKS BY C.S.R. CALLOWAY

The Adventures of a Laguna Witch

The Gay Man's Guide to Heterosexual Weddings

Natty Girl Saves the World

Lost: A Never Novella

PRETTY DUDES

Bravo Double Delta

Pretty Dudes: The Novel

Pretty Dudes: The Sequel

Sired

The Ungodly Hours

The Walls of Jericho Kim

MORE FROM CSRC STORYTELLING

Promoting and providing positivity, power and presence in print.

SHADOWS UPLIFTED ANTHOLOGY

Groundbreaking works published by female Black American authors from the nineteenth century.

Volume I: Black Women Authors of Nineteenth Century American Fiction
featuring novels by Julia C. Collins, Frances E. W. Harper, and A. E. Johnson

Volume II: Black Women Authors of Nineteenth Century American Personal Narratives & Autobiographies
featuring novels by Harriet Jacobs, Elizabeth Keckley, and Harriet E. Wilson

Volume III: Black Women Authors of Nineteenth Century American Poetry
featuring collected verse by Mary Weston Fordham, Josephine D. Heard, and Frances Ellen Watkins

MAGNA RELEASES

Newly edited formatted stand-alone classics in print and digital.

Passing
Nella Larsen

The Princess and the Goblin
George MacDonald

EVEN MORE FROM CSRC STORYTELLING

Promoting and providing positivity, power and presence in print.

DOUBLE BOOKED®

Two books bound in one brilliant tête-bêche edition (literally back to back).

Alice's Adventures in Wonderland
Through the Looking Glass

Peter Pan
The Never Boy

Man Cub: The Complete Mowgli Stories
Rikki-Tikki-Tavi and Other Tales from The Jungle Book

A Christmas Carol
Marie and the Nutcracker

Cane
The Conjure Woman: Uncle Julius and His Stories

The Turn of the Screw
Shadows Against the Dark: Collected Tales of Horror

Desiderio
The Veil and the Shade